ALSO BY JENELLE LEANNE SCHMIDT

———

Turrim Archive
The Orb and the Airship
Mantles of Oak and Iron
Hearts of Stone and Steel
The Prisoner and the Pirate
Towers of Might and Memory

———

A Classic Retold
Steal the Morrow

———

The Minstrel's Song
King's Warrior
Second Son
Yorien's Hand
Minstrel's Call

———

The Faelands
An Echo of the Fae

———

HEARTS OF STONE AND STEEL

BOOK 3 OF THE TURRIM ARCHIVE

JENELLE LEANNE SCHMIDT

Hearts of Stone and Steel

Volume 3 of The Turrim Archive

By Jenelle Leanne Schmidt

Copyright 2024 by Jenelle Leanne Schmidt

Published by Stormcave

www.jenelleschmidt.com

Hearts of Stone and Steel

All rights reserved.

No part of this book may be reproduced in any form or by any electronic or mechanical means, including information storage and retrieval systems without written permission from the author, except for uses of brief quotations when due credit is given.

ISBN-13: 978-1-960357-01-4

This is a work of fiction. All of the characters, organizations, and events portrayed in this novel are either products of the author's rather large and vivid imagination, or are used fictitiously. Any resemblance to persons real or historical is purely coincidental.

Cover art by Dragonpen Designs

Book design and maps by Declan Rowe

THE WORLD OF TURRIM

Turrim is a single-continent world with six separate cultures and a calendar that looks slightly different from our own.

Turrim's year is only 336 days long, separated into twelve lunats (what we would call months) and each lunat is exactly 28 days long, separated into 4 sennights (what we would call weeks). Their seasons are much as our own, following the same pattern of fall, winter, spring, and summer.

Their new year begins on what would for us be September 21st, or the Fall Equinox.

The months of the year (starting at the beginning of their calendar year) are named thus:

Chanjar	October
Deepthen	November
Darkthen	December
Edrian	January
Tella	February
Malla	March
Urin	April
Paute	May
Avar	June
Mirad	July
Avest	August
Felling	September

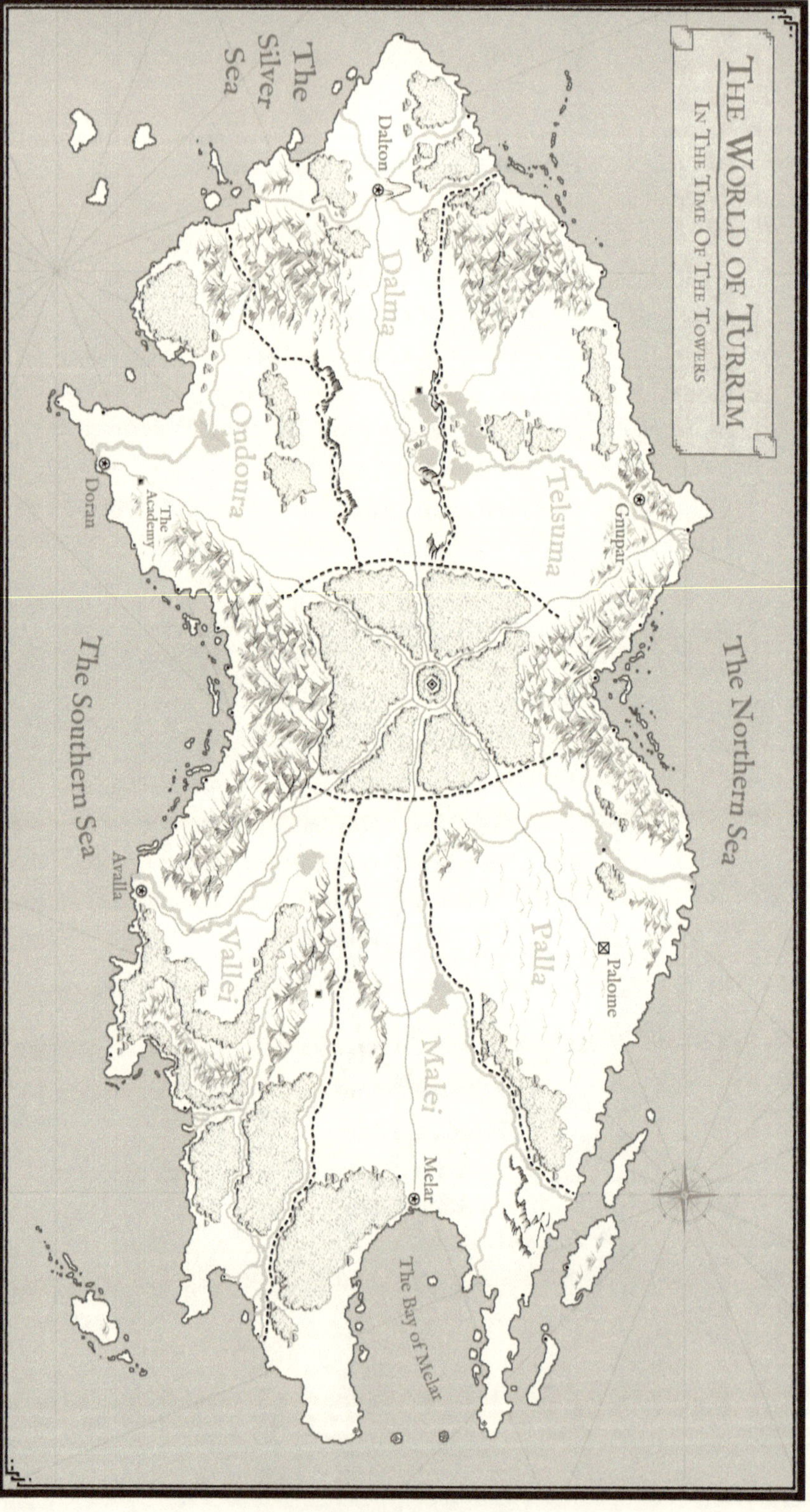

THE WORLD OF TURRIM
In The Time Of The Towers
The Silver Sea
Dalton
Dalma
Telsuma
Gnupar
Ondoura
Doran
The Academy
The Northern Sea
The Southern Sea
Avalla
Vallei
Palla
Palome
Malei
Melar
The Bay of Melar

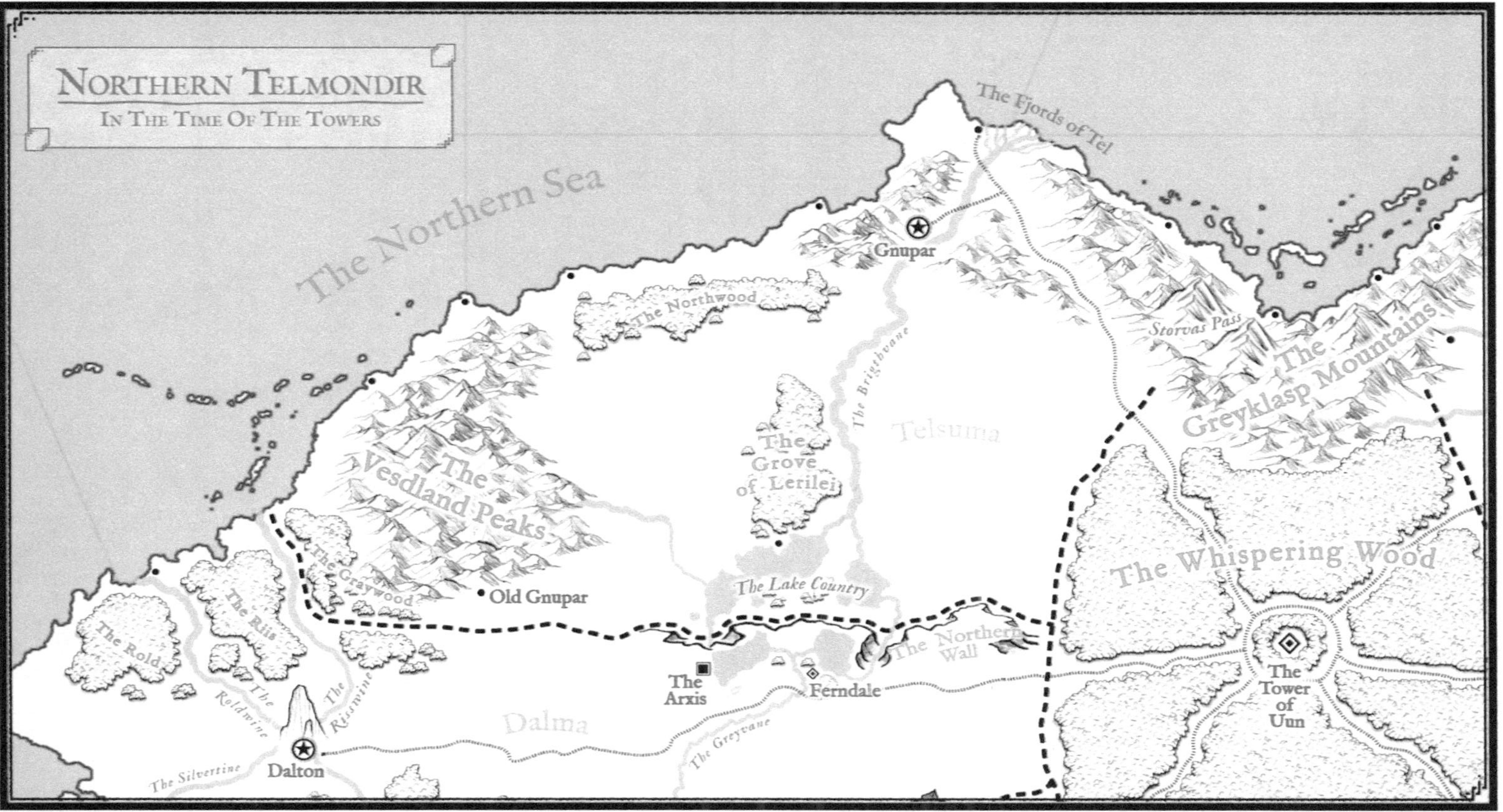

Northern Telmondir
In The Time Of The Towers
The Northern Sea
The Fjords of Tel
Gnupar
The Northwood
Storvas Pass
The Greyklasp Mountains
The Brightvane
Telsuma
The Grove of Lerilei
The Vesdland Peaks
The Graywood
The Whispering Wood
Old Gnupar
The Lake Country
The Riis
The Rold
The Northern Wall
The Arxis
Ferndale
The Tower of Uun
The Roldwine
The Rushwine
Dalma
The Greyvane
The Silvertine
Dalton

THE SOUTHWEST OF TELMONDIR

The Roldmine
The Rilvine
Dalton
The Silvertine
The Emewood
The Greyvane
The Southern Wall
Dalsea
Elricht Harbor
The Emelda
Telseren Grade
The Tyveden
The Obuna
The Living Wood
The Academy
Khosha
Doran

The Lake Country
The Whispering Wood
The Southern Wall
Ondoma
The Ardullam
The Tyveden
Randeau Mountains
The Obuna
The Academy
Doran
THE SOUTHERN DIVIDE

1

Grayden watched in numb disbelief as Lord Adelfried handed each new defender their orders, wondering why he, Wynn, and Beren had been skipped. He tried not to fidget as the others opened their papers and read their assignments. He kept his mouth closed, even though every fiber of his being wanted to step forward and demand answers.

Lord Adelfried gave a solemn nod. "If you have your orders, you are dismissed."

Koen saluted immediately and turned smartly to return to the barracks. Zarek narrowed his eyes and looked as though he wanted to question the order, but he snapped his mouth shut and followed Koen's example.

"I know you are wondering what your assignments will be," Lord Adelfried said to the three remaining men before him. "Before I give them to you, I want to remind you of a few things: first, you need to understand that you are the youngest defenders we have ever had." He raised a hand, forestalling any argument. "But you have excelled in all your assigned work, and you went above and beyond in the Storvas Mission, which means you have earned your place as full-fledged second lieutenants. Second, though you accomplished much over the past year, you lack the tempering I would have preferred you gain through a normal number of years at the Academy. I thought long and hard about your first assignments. They may not be what you were expecting or hoping for, but I believe they are the best fit for each of you."

Grayden resisted the urge to turn worried eyes to his friends. He wondered what this could mean, and what their first assignments would be. Surely Lord Adelfried wouldn't be sending them back to the Academy for more training before he deemed them worthy of the bars they had already earned?

"Wynn Drexel. You will travel with Ioan to Telsuma and begin working with Daegan, our chief artificineer. He is in the midst of various projects to help us in the coming conflict with the Igyeum, though we are doing everything in our power to prevent an all-out war. Based on the ideas you presented in your classes at the Academy, we believe that your unique way of solving problems will be invaluable to him. Daegan himself has already seen a few of your assignments and is eager to collaborate with you."

Grayden turned to grin widely at his friend. There couldn't be a more perfect assignment for Wynn. To his surprise, Wynn's eyes were wide and filled with a strange mixture of reluctance and horror. Grayden felt his own smile falter as Wynn turned his pale face forward and made a noise of acknowledgment in his throat. He wondered what Wynn was thinking. He only made that noise when he didn't want to do something, but surely working with a chief artificineer should be an exciting prospect? Grayden didn't have time to ponder this, however, for Lord Adelfried continued.

"Beren Adelfried and Grayden Ormond. Your assignment is slightly out of the ordinary, and giving it to you is perhaps against my better judgment. However, I believe this task is uniquely suited to you both. As you already know, the Regeont of Ondoura was assassinated recently. Unfortunately, because of my duties, I cannot be there to oversee the investigation. Also, I fear my presence would complicate the investigation, as I am too recognizable. And while my title and position often open doors for me, in this case, they might prove a hindrance. Because of this,

I made an agreement with someone who is helping lead the investigation, but while I know he has the skills and resources to do the job, I do not trust him to be forthcoming with the information he uncovers. I am assigning you to return to Ondoura and work with him to find the assassin responsible and bring him to justice."

Grayden and Beren shared a puzzled look.

Beren straightened. "May I ask who this contact is?"

Adelfried kept his expression neutral. "Ericole Niveya."

Grayden stiffened, his entire body denying that Lord Adelfried had just spoken those words. He resisted the urge to show how much he disapproved of the Councilman's choice, but he could not prevent his shoulders from jerking slightly as he digested the news.

"I realize that this arrangement may seem unwise," Adelfried said, "but Niveya has resources and informants at his disposal that we do not. The trail had gone cold by the time I arrived on the scene. Apparently, Ericole held a certain amount of respect for Roshana, and wishes to see her killer brought to justice as much as I do. I chose the two of you precisely because I know you do not trust Niveya—you will not allow him to get away with keeping secrets. And Beren, given your closeness to Ioan and his grandmother, I trust you will pursue every lead with faithful tenacity."

"Yes, Lord Adelfried." Both young men spoke in chorus.

"Very good. You will travel the first part of the journey with us, and then on to Ondoura. Dismissed."

Head spinning, Grayden followed his friends back to the barracks. Still reeling from Lord Adelfried's announcement, Grayden sat down heavily on his bed. He watched as Beren and Wynn gathered up the last of their things and felt a strange fuzziness in his thoughts as he contemplated the future. Lord Adelfried's assignment had disoriented him, and he was at a loss for how to respond. He wasn't sure how he felt about the idea. Beren's attitude and mien had not changed; his friend seemed as placidly cheerful as always.

"How can you be so calm?" Grayden asked him.

One of Beren's eyebrows arched. "I am not calm," he replied. "The woman I thought of as a beloved grandmother was murdered and her killer walks free. How can you think I am calm?"

Grayden stared at him. "Oh. I just... you seemed... unruffled."

Beren's expression tightened. "It is not the way of my people to let our souls shine through our eyes. Especially in times of great trial, it is the mark of a leader to maintain composure."

"This all seems a bit sudden, doesn't it?" Wynn did not look up from his packing.

"What seems sudden?" Beren asked, turning a quizzical face towards Wynn.

"Just..." Wynn paused, his fingers twitching over the uniform he had been carefully folding. "I figured we would all get assignments somewhere together. Now that I say it out loud, it seems silly. But we've gone through so much together in the past year, it never occurred to me that we wouldn't be..." He hummed slightly to himself. "I guess I thought they'd see what a great team we make, is all."

Grayden nodded. "I thought that, too," he admitted. "I don't know why, but I just assumed that whatever came next, we'd all face it together."

Beren frowned. "Truthfully, these assignments came as a surprise to me, as well. They are not the customary sort. I figured my father would place us in a regiment with a commanding officer barking orders and demanding we do endless drills and learn to work within a unit. To be given such important assignments right after graduating, and after only one year at the Academy, is a great honor. It seems Dalmir was right. The situation between Telmondir and the Igyeum must be more tenuous than I believed."

Grayden scratched the back of his neck. "I'm not so certain I'm thrilled about working with Ericole Niveya. But I am glad we will be doing something important."

"I, for one, am more concerned about making sure that

Ericole Niveya is not comfortable working with me," Beren growled fiercely, but there was a lightness in his eyes. He turned to Wynn and clapped him on the shoulder. "You are going to enjoy your assignment," he promised. "Daegan is a genius. He might even be smarter than you!"

Wynn chuckled. "That would be a nice change," he retorted. The edge to his tone belied his lighthearted expression.

Beren gave a loud, bellowing laugh, but before he could respond, the door to their room swung open and Ioan stood before them.

"Are you three ready? Lord Adelfried wants everyone on the airship now."

The friends sobered at the sight of him. "What's your next assignment, Ioan?" Beren asked.

Ioan stared at them with his unnerving eyes. They had always been green, but now they nearly glowed, and their color was reminiscent of the gold and green of sunlight hitting a forest canopy in summer. Grayden found it hard to meet the defender's gaze now. It was also impossible to ignore how he had suddenly grown several inches, or the strange pattern of dark lines etched in his skin. Ioan kept them covered with long sleeves, but Grayden could still see them on his wrists and above the edges of his high collar.

"I am returning to Gnupar with Uncle Thorben and Dalmir for now. I do not know what my assignment will be."

"Dalmir is returning there as well?" Grayden asked, a pang of disappointment shooting through him. He wished he had more time to converse with the older man and ask him the questions that burned in his mind.

Ioan nodded. "He is. Can I help carry anything? The airship captain does not wish to wait any longer than necessary. He says a storm is heading this way, and he'd like to get out in front of it."

Beren handed him one of his packs, and Ioan walked with them to the airship that waited. It was not as elegant of a vessel as Marik's *Valdeun Hawk*, nor was it the lumbering bulk of the cargo cruisers. It was a medium-sized vessel that bore no exceptional qualities. Dalmir already stood at the rail, and they made their way over to him as the ship lifted off the wooden dock.

"Ioan says you are returning to Telsuma," Grayden said.

Dalmir nodded.

"I was hoping to work with you," Grayden admitted.

"I would have enjoyed that as well. Perhaps we can work together again in the future. I need your help to understand why the orbs are awake. There is much I still do not understand," Dalmir replied. He glanced at Ioan, his gaze intensely curious. "But the assignments Lord Adelfried has for you are equally important. The assassination of the Regeont and the simultaneous attack on the Academy are troubling. Thorben thinks it could be the work of the Igyeum..." Dalmir trailed off.

"You do not?" Beren asked.

Dalmir's hands gripped the rail. "There is more going on there than we can see. What I can tell you is that everything we discovered about the assassination plot was very odd."

"Odd? How?" Beren prompted.

Dalmir stroked his chin. "First, we got word of the ill-prepared attack on the Academy. Later, we discovered the Regeont's murder and the Academy invasion happened at the same time. Though the two incidents were vastly different, I find it difficult to believe they were unrelated."

Beren massaged his knuckles absently. "Do you have a theory?"

Dalmir's eyes squinted. "Nothing clear, but while Ericole focuses on finding the assassin, it would behoove you to keep an eye out for whoever hired him."

Grayden pulled his dagger from its sheath and fiddled with it. "Does Thorben know you suspect a bigger plot?"

"I mentioned it to him. He was at least willing to consider the possibility, but he is also too close to this. Roshana was as dear as family to him, and right now he is angry and grieving, and that is coloring his judgment." He turned to Beren. "Be careful not to let your own grief and anger impede your job."

Beren's fingers tightened on the hilt of his sword, and then his shoulders relaxed. "Words of truth. I will try."

"I'll do what I can," Grayden said. "But I'm still concerned about working with Niveya. I don't understand why Lord Adelfried is trusting him."

"Niveya is an honorable man in his own way. And it seems he had a soft spot for the Regeont. He regarded her as an equal, and from what I can tell of Niveya, few attain that position in his esteem. I believe you can trust him to fulfill his end of the bargain to find her killer and bring that individual to justice. Beyond that, he will act in whatever way he believes will benefit him the most." Dalmir gave a tight smile. "Men like Ericole Niveya cannot be trusted, but once you understand that, you can avoid being surprised by their betrayal." Dalmir glanced sideways at Wynn. "By the way, Wynn, I have met Daegan."

Wynn's eyebrows raised, but then his expression descended into a fierce scowl.

"He's a good man," Dalmir continued. "Brilliant. Focused. The things he is building are... extraordinary."

Wynn's mouth quirked to one side, and he muttered under his breath. Grayden stared at him, concern for his friend rising within him, but he didn't know what to say. Wynn had ever been the builder. Growing up, Grayden had often found his friend reluctant to leave his projects, even for long-awaited celebrations. It had often been his job to pull Wynn away from whatever had captured his attention. It was odd to see him so unwilling to dive into such a project.

"I'd have thought this assignment would thrill you, Wynn," Grayden said at last. "Imagine, you'll have access to all the parts you'll need for whatever you want to build. Those schematics you turned in must have been something special."

Wynn merely stared over the side of the airship, glowering blackly at the ground falling away from them.

Grayden elbowed him playfully. "What's got you so down? I'm not used to you being so quiet."

Wynn huffed out a breath and glared up at him. He spun away. Muttering about getting some rest, he stomped over to the ladder and descended from their view.

Grayden watched him go, mystified and more than a little hurt.

"Let him be," Dalmir said. "It has nothing to do with you."

"What's stinging him?" Grayden asked. He turned to Beren. "Do you know?"

The big Telsuman shook his head. "He has said nothing to me. He's been like this ever since my father gave us our assignments. I figured he was unhappy about his."

"But why?" Grayden asked, posing the question more to himself than to Dalmir or Beren. "This is exactly the sort of thing he's always wanted. You haven't known Wynn very long, but I promise you, this is a dream come true for him."

"Who was it that first wanted to go to the Academy?" Dalmir asked suddenly. "Of the two of you?"

"We've always wanted to go, both of us, for as long as I can remember," Grayden replied.

"But whose dream was it? When you first started talking about it? Do you remember when you first wanted to go?" Dalmir asked.

"Of course," Grayden replied. "I was five. The recruiters came and there was a big tournament; I remember it was all anyone was talking about. It was exciting just being in town, all the tests of arms, and the wondering if anyone was going to be chosen from our village. I remember Wynn's dad telling stories around the fire each night about his time as a defender and all the traveling he'd done before settling down in Dalsea. I knew right then that I would do whatever it took to make sure they chose me someday."

Dalmir nodded. "And when you told Wynn about it?"

"He agreed with me. We always talked about all the adventures we'd go on and how we would defend Telmondir together.

It was what we used to keep ourselves motivated when we didn't want to study or our arms ached from sparring. It was one of the few things that could pull Wynn out of his workshop."

"I see." Dalmir's voice turned soft.

Grayden stared at the man. "You do?"

Dalmir raised an eyebrow.

"What do you see? Do you know why Wynn has been in such a foul mood today?" Grayden asked.

Dalmir stared out at the horizon, his hands gripping the railing. "I used to consider myself an excellent judge of people. Then..." He trailed off. A moment passed, then Dalmir shook himself. "You say you dreamed up adventures and battles. Perhaps Wynn feels those dreams are not coming true for him. Tell me, when you and Wynn were staring at the horizon and working toward it, did you ever contemplate a scenario where the two of you were not together? Where you got to go on an adventure and left Wynn behind in a workshop?"

Grayden gnawed on his thumbnail, considering. "You're right. I don't know why I didn't see it. I never thought he'd see this as a punishment. Working with Niveya isn't what I would have picked, either."

"Wynn knows that," Dalmir assured him. "And I believe he will enjoy working with Daegan very much. But right now, he is probably experiencing keen disappointment."

"What can I do?"

"There is little you can do. The situation is not in your control. But you can let him know you understand. You can listen. Give him the space he needs to work through his disappointment. You have been friends for a long time."

"Like brothers," Grayden said.

"Yes..." Dalmir's expression grew pained. "Like brothers."

"Are you feeling well?" Beren asked.

Dalmir waved a hand. "A touch airsick, is all. I'll be fine."

———

WYNN STAYED HOLED up in his bunk until dinner. When he joined Grayden and Beren in the mess, his countenance was lighter.

"Haven't seen you all day," Beren commented. "Where have you been?"

"Sleeping," Wynn replied. "Or trying to. Finally feeling up to eating." He gave a grin and an exaggerated grimace.

"Ah." Beren nodded sagely.

"Well, I'm glad you're feeling better," Grayden said. He tried to avoid giving Wynn the pointed stare he felt his friend deserved.

Wynn ducked his head and took a bite of his meal.

"So," Grayden said, keeping his tone light, "I've been thinking. You and Beren both spent a lot more time with Ericole Niveya than I did. I was kind of surprised Lord Adelfried didn't assign you to this mission. Seems to me you have more experience and would have made a better choice; you two made a pretty good team when Niveya's men captured you."

Wynn looked up, his eyes startled. "Yeah," he stammered, then caught himself. He waved his fork casually. "I may have had that thought myself."

Grayden grinned. "Guess he has his reasons. Must be they need your ability to take things apart something fierce up there in Telsuma. Maybe I should tell them about the time you took apart your dad's plow and then put it back together."

Wynn uttered a bark of exasperation. "Hey, now!"

"I remember you couldn't quite figure out why you had all those pins left over. Guess you thought they weren't important."

"Come on, Gray!" Wynn's tone hovered between an embarrassed shout and an exasperated wheedle.

"Seemed pretty important the next time he tried to use it to till up that pumpkin patch, though, didn't it?"

Wynn's face reddened, and Grayden worried he had pushed his friend too far. Then Wynn burst out in an explosive laugh and punched him in the arm.

"It kind of disintegrated when old Sally put her head down to pull it along," Wynn guffawed. "Whole thing collapsed. Scared Sally stiff and she stopped so sudden that Da fell right on his seat. When Da found out what I'd done, he tanned my hide so hard..."

Beren roared with laughter. "That is an excellent story, my friends!"

"Best part of the story is what came next, though." Grayden grinned. "Master Drexel took Wynn out to the barn and together they took apart every piece of equipment they owned. Then he taught Wynn how to put it all back together properly."

Beren sat back. "Truly?"

"Took them sennights," Grayden said.

Wynn's eyes glistened at the memory. "He said taking things apart was the play of children. But building things... building things was a man's work, and he thought I was old enough to learn it."

"The next time he went on one of his trade routes was the time he brought home that set of tools for you, remember?" Grayden asked.

Wynn nodded. "After that, we started building a lot of things. Whenever he went to the market in Elricht Harbor, he would always bring back some strange, broken thing for us to fix together. He'd get stuff for a song, or sometimes even for free, we'd fix them up, and then sell them. That's how I made enough money to get the parts to build that small-scale working train set."

Beren whistled. "I would like to see that. My father has talked about the trains, and while the airships are marvels, it has always saddened me that the trains stopped running before I was born. I would have liked to ride on one."

"Same," Wynn said. He swiped the back of his hand across his mouth. "Gray, I'm sorry."

"About what?"

"I've been..." Wynn paused, bobbing his head back and forth. Then he heaved a sigh. "I've been jealous of your assignment."

"Why?" Grayden asked. "Beren and I have to go work with the man who kidnapped the both of you. I'm not so certain we can trust him not to decide to stick a pair of knives in our backs. I know I won't sleep at all until we're done."

"I know that," Wynn agreed. "And I don't envy that part of it, not really. You're right, I'd much rather be in a workshop, building things. I just... I just felt like you were getting to go off on one of those adventures we always talked about. And I'm not."

Grayden took a bite of his dinner and chewed it slowly. "I guess I can understand that."

"Forgive me for being a grump?"

Grayden tossed his friend a quick grin. "Of course."

Beren scraped the last bits of food from his plate into his mouth. "Well, I, for one, almost hope that Niveya tries something. I'd like to introduce him to the sharp side of my sword."

Wynn and Grayden both laughed at that.

2

Wynn managed a genuine smile as he disembarked in Gnupar, leaving his friends behind to travel on to Doran, the capital city of Ondoura. Once on the ground, he waved until the airship was just a speck in the distant sky. Only then did he turn to the others who had been patiently waiting for him. He shouldered his pack, his insides feeling hollow.

"Nadia will be eager to see you again, Ioan," Lord Adelfried said, lifting his own pack. "And you, as well, Dalmir, though I don't think anyone's excitement can rival Hubert's."

Dalmir grinned, his face suddenly beaming with merry youthfulness.

"And everyone will be eager to meet you, Wynn," Adelfried added.

The words took the void inside Wynn and set it spinning. "Can you just take me to where Master Daegan is staying?" he mumbled.

Adelfried turned a strange look at him. "Are you not feeling well? I thought to have you join us for dinner first."

Wynn could sense the concern radiating off of the older man. How would Grayden handle this? He widened his lips into a jaunty, confident grin. "Thank you, Lord Adelfried, but I'd rather get settled in first. I was hoping to sort of get acquainted with Master Daegan and Master Keene, maybe get a feel for where I'll be working."

The smile and the words seemed to do the trick. Lord Adelfried's brow smoothed as he studied Wynn, who kept a bright smile plastered across his face. The expression felt unnatural and obviously fake, but Wynn resisted the urge to let it fall. His fingers itched to tap against his leg, but he balled his hand into a fist. He could do this. The last thing he wanted in this moment was to join a large group of people he didn't know for a meal. Maybe he would be up to that in a few days, but not yet.

"Nadia will be disappointed. She loves entertaining guests. But I can't fault your eagerness to get started." Adelfried hesitated. "If you're sure?"

Wynn nodded vigorously and Lord Adelfried shrugged. "Very well. I'll take you to Daegan's first. Ioan, you and Dalmir go on ahead to the house. Tell Nadia I'll be along shortly."

Up the mountain a ways, where the path split, so did their small company. Lord Adelfried and Wynn took the right-hand path that seemed to lead straight to the base of a cliff rising high above their heads.

"My home is just up the path about a mile," Lord Adelfried said, indicating the way that Dalmir and Ioan had gone. "If you need anything, our door is always open to you. Daegan and Keene don't always join us for meals, but you are more than welcome. There is also a room set aside for you in case you would prefer that. Daegan seemed convinced you'd want to stay in the workshop, but if it's not comfortable enough, you can come stay with us."

Wynn gave a mute nod to show that he understood. His mouth was too dry to speak. He did not enjoy meeting new people. People were difficult. Machines were easier. Panic flooded through him as they approached a door cut into the cliff face. He wanted to back away, turn around and run somewhere far away; he couldn't do this on his own.

Perhaps he could stall.

He remembered how Beren had described his home: a warm, rowdy atmosphere filled with younger children, all clamoring for attention. He could handle that. It sounded like home.

Home.

Wynn suddenly longed for home with a fierceness that was altogether unexpected. He missed the chatter of his sisters, the roughhousing with his brothers, the shouting and wheedling and play, the constant clamor, and the smells of delicious food emanating from his mother's kitchen. He yearned to return to his room and tinker with his models and experiments, to trot out to the shed and watch his father working on a new design or help him fix a neighbor's wagon wheel or harness. In his heart, he knew he would have given anything to hear one of the babies beg him for a horse-a-back ride, or hear his mother's voice asking him to get her more firewood for the stove. He had successfully ignored his homesickness when he was at the Academy. Even though the assignments had been far too easy, they had kept him busy, and the physical contests and trials had been more than enough to keep him focused on improving his own skills. Then, in the mountains, his focus had been solely on survival. Between the need for constant alertness and struggling to solve each problem that presented itself, there had been no time for thoughts of home. Even in the worst moments, he had been far too tired or terrified to even allow the thought of home to cross his mind.

But then the mission ended. Quiet fell. Relief at being alive suffused him, and he had been ready to tackle the next adventure.

Until Adelfried passed out the assignments.

Wynn still stung from the unexpected blow. In all his dreams about the Academy and his future as a defender, he had never once contemplated a scenario where he was alone, where his assignment was separate from that of his friends'. Beren and Grayden were on their way to Ondoura, and Wynn did not know when he would see them again.

He wasn't really upset about the assignment itself. Working

with Daegan, in a real forge, with a real artificineer as his mentor would be a dream come true. He recognized the name and was eager to meet the man behind the legends. He didn't even mind being separated from his friends, not really. He had always been a bit of a loner, a little off the beat from everyone else. What worried him was the idea of being alone with his thoughts. Loneliness, deep and piercing, filled his core with its ache. And the homesickness he had ignored for so long reared up and sank its needle-sharp teeth deep into his heart, penetrating to the very center of his soul.

Lord Adelfried's knuckles rapped sharply on the door.

As they waited for an answer, Wynn studied the door he was about to walk through. It was black and from the sound it made when Adelfried knocked upon it, fashioned out of some sort of metal. The door was not completely rectangular, but arched up to a sharp point at the top. A small grill with a latticework of glass panes that were not completely clear adorned the top half of the door, and he could see a flicker of light through them coming from inside. The black metal lever that served as a doorknob rotated down as he stared at it.

The door opened, swinging smoothly on silent hinges. Wynn could not prevent the corner of his mouth from twitching upward in approval. Before he could even catch a good look at who had opened the door, he found his hand and part of his wrist engulfed, and his arm was being shaken up and down in a warm greeting.

"You must be Wynn," a deep voice boomed. "We did not expect you until morning!"

Wynn stared up into a face darkened by soot and heat and two sparkling brownish-green eyes. Long golden hair was pulled back at the nape of his neck and tucked under a cap. Stubble covered his jaw and chin, and a slightly thicker mustache curved up with his smiling mouth.

"This is Keene," Adelfried was introducing him, "the finest smith this side of the Elspring River."

Keene's bushy brow furrowed. "Every time you introduce me, you give me a smaller area," he complained. "What happened to 'Keene, finest smith in all Telmondir?'"

Adelfried stared at him placidly. "Whenever I reduce your fame, you get all bristly, and then you turn around and craft something exquisite. It's obvious you need the added motivation."

Keene's eyes narrowed, glittering with an expression Wynn did not recognize, and his stomach plummeted. Was the smith a hot-tempered man? He had no wish to get in the middle of an argument, or to be forced to work with someone who was constantly in a rage. But then Keene's face broke into a wide grin and he gave a great, bellowing laugh.

"Fairer words," he roared in a good-natured tone, clasping Adelfried by the arm. "Well, thank you for bringing our new artificer. We have been most eager to meet you, Wynn Drexel."

Keene waved Wynn into the passageway. Lord Adelfried made to follow, but Wynn turned quickly and looked up at him, putting on his most reassuring smile.

"Thank you, Lord Adelfried, for escorting me here. I appreciate everything you've done for me, but I need to forge my own path." He winced internally at the unintentional pun. "And your family is waiting to see you. Please, give Lady Nadia my humblest greetings, and assure her I will be more than happy to accept an invitation to sample the hospitality of your home once I have gotten more settled in." He was quite proud of that speech. He had been crafting it for most of the journey here, and he felt it came out sounding rather nicely.

Lord Adelfried looked a little startled. "As you wish," he replied.

Wynn nodded firmly.

Adelfried gave him a final, searching look. "Ah. Well, then... know that you are welcome anytime, Wynn. You need send no advance notice. Our home is just up the road," he repeated his directions from earlier and pointed at the paved path winding up the hill. With another nod, he turned and strode back out into the evening.

Wynn watched him go, feeling suddenly forlorn.

"Come along, lad," Keene boomed, startling him out of the spiraling emptiness that threatened to consume him once more. Wynn followed him through the entryway and into the main forge.

It was nothing like what he had expected. The entire facility had been built right into the side of the mountain, and great pipes led up into the ceiling of the forge to vent the heat and smoke. The main room of the forge was extremely hot, though not uncomfortably so. Another hall on the other side of the main room led deeper into the mountain, and Keene crossed the forge and strode down it purposefully. Wynn followed, trotting a bit to keep up with the tall man's long strides.

"Daegan wished to see you as soon as you arrived," Keene commented in an offhand sort of way. "The workrooms and living quarters are down this way."

"I expected him to be in the forge." Wynn panted, struggling under the weight of his pack.

Keene grunted. "Daegan is rarely in the forge. He doesn't like the heat and the noise gives him terrible headaches. I'm the smith and the builder. The forge is my domain. Daegan is the one who figures it all out on paper. He refuses to let me build any of his designs until he's certain that they're perfect."

"That seems..." Wynn tried to catch his breath. He struggled for the right word.

"Impossible? Unlikely? Ill-informed?" Keene laughed. "Daegan's a perfectionist. He might take a bit longer with his figuring, but of the schematics he's asked me to build, they've all gone together smoothly and worked the first time as expected. Can't say that of too many designers. Daegan is... one of a kind."

Wynn's interest in this new mentor grew as he listened to Keene talk. His mind whirled, churning over the assignments his teachers had given him at the Academy. What could a man like Daegan do with those ideas? How might they be refined?

Before he could even finish contemplating all the questions he had, Keene stopped before a slightly open door. He knocked lightly and pushed the door open, revealing a cluttered workshop. There were tables along all the walls of the room. Papers and schematics, quills, ink-pots, rulers, and various other devices all tossed together in a haphazard mess littered the tabletops. Wynn stared, overwhelmed by the chaos that greeted him. Nausea suddenly roiled in his brain. How could anyone work like this? His eyes landed on a few of the papers on the table closest to him, and his attention caught on them like a lifeline in a storm. Unlike the papers themselves, which were strewn about in a disorganized jumble, the schematics and drawings upon them were neat and precise. There was an elegance to them that was disturbingly incongruous with the disorder of the room.

"Daegan," Keene's voice boomed in the small space, making Wynn jump a little, "he's here!"

At one table, a tall, thin man sat hunched over a pile of papers, his pen scratching away in a furious rhythm. At Keene's bellow, the man scribbled on the paper in a series of swift strokes, then turned and peered across the room. Grabbing up the lantern, he moved closer. He was taller than Wynn, with thick, unruly white hair that stuck out from his head in an untamed mess. Wynn spotted a dark streak of black on the left side of the man's head and wondered at it. However, a quick glance at his left hand solved the mystery: it was covered in familiar ink stains. Wynn felt a jolt of kinship at the sight.

"Wynn Drexel, isn't it?" Daegan said after a brief study of Wynn's face.

"Yes, sir," Wynn replied politely. "I am pleased to meet you, Master Daegan."

"No need for that." Daegan waved a hand. "We're on equal terms here. Just Daegan will do. Adding the 'Master' takes up time we don't have. Now, I've looked over your ideas, and a few of them seem promising."

"You have? They do?" Wynn asked, suddenly flustered. "I mean, you've seen my ideas?"

Daegan held up a stack of pages. "Freidzen sends me the papers of his most promising students. I pick a few each year to work alongside me."

Wynn stared at the schematics. "I see."

"The design for getting a cart over rough terrain was particularly interesting to me. These continuous treads you designed are, quite honestly, brilliant. You made a lot of assumptions, though."

Wynn sifted through his memories for the assignment in question. "I followed the instructions," he began slowly. "The professor offered limited information on what was available, so I made my best guesses."

"Guesses?" Daegan reared back as though Wynn had splashed water on his face. "Guesses! In our line of work, we do not *guess*." He spat the word.

"Well... no..." Wynn stammered. "But the assignment didn't give specific parameters."

"And you didn't find that odd?" Daegan queried.

"I..." Wynn felt his cheeks heating. This was not going as he had hoped or planned. "I didn't think much about it one way or the other. It was just another assignment."

"Just another..." Daegan sputtered. He glared at Keene. "Why do I even bother putting effort into creating those things?" he demanded. "Did you hear him? He says he 'didn't think.' If the students refuse to think, what good are they?"

"You created the assignment?" Wynn asked, his anger giving way to curiosity. "How did you plan to get around the problem of propulsion?"

"What do you mean?" Daegan turned bright eyes on him, a gleam of excitement sparking to life in his expression.

"Well, the assignment asked us to design a way to move a cart over rough terrain more efficiently. I assumed we should focus on the wheels, but it seemed like a waste of time."

"How so?"

"Because the horses will always limit you. The best wheel-system in the world won't negate the fact that you still need horses to pull the cart. In fact, the system I came up with would hamper the horses and make their job a lot harder. So how did you plan to address the propulsion?"

Daegan stared at him. "Yes, I created the assignment. Did you ask the Master of the class that question?"

"What question?"

"The one about the problem of propulsion."

"No."

"Well, why not?" Daegan sounded exasperated.

"I didn't think he would know the answer," Wynn admitted. "I thought it was just another exercise. Besides, he didn't know the answers to several of my other questions on earlier assignments, so I stopped asking."

"I see." Daegan frowned. "I suppose that's fair. In some ways, it was just an exercise. But it was also a test of your ability to be innovative. And it was designed to make you question whether or not you had all the information you needed. Had you asked, the Master of the class would have given you this." Daegan held out a large piece of paper. "This assignment was not just about solving the problem; it was meant to find minds capable of thinking beyond the information presented, and to find individuals who aren't afraid to ask questions."

Wondering, Wynn took the proffered paper and gazed at it. He studied the diagram, his eyes widening.

"This... is this what I think it is?" he asked, looking up into Daegan's lined face.

"It is," Daegan replied.

"This changes everything," Wynn breathed. Excitement mounted in his chest. "Is this possible?"

Daegan gave a tiny nod. "I believe it is."

"If I had known the cart was to be self-propelled, it would have changed my answer," Wynn admitted.

"As well it should," Daegan replied, snatching the paper back. He scowled at Wynn and Keene for a long moment.

Wynn's heart sank. This was not what he had expected. All the frustration and loneliness he had been struggling against throughout the journey here welled up within him in a rush and threatened to overwhelm him. He had been on the brink of growing excited about this new assignment, working with the genius that Adelfried had promised him he would find within this workshop. But for the first time since he had been quite small, Wynn found himself doubting his own ability. Taking things apart and putting them back together had always been the one place where he excelled. He had breezed through the assignments at the Academy, barely giving them a second thought, never expecting that there was more to them than what was presented on paper. His stomach clenched into a miserable ball of anguish. Why hadn't he studied the assignments more closely? Why hadn't he noticed that there were holes in them? Why hadn't he asked more questions of the teachers, demanded that they explain the parameters that appeared to be missing from so many of the questions they had asked him to solve? But then a new question tickled at the back of his thoughts.

"If you created some of our assignments, why did you design them to have gaps in the information?" He blurted the question before he could even process it.

Daegan's scowl turned into a slow, knowing smile. "Now you are asking the right questions. Very good." He clapped his hands together. "But it is late. You have been traveling all day, and I am sure you are hungry. It is not so late that you stopped for dinner at the Adelfried's..." He peered questioningly and Wynn nodded to let him know he had guessed correctly. "Excellent, I appreciate a man who wants to get right to work. A hunger for knowledge is an admirable trait," Daegan said. "But my assistant keeps reminding me that food is necessary to the process of all other functions a body can perform, so let us put this conversation to rest for the evening. Keene's apprentices don't cook as well as Lady Nadia does, but their creations are edible, at least. Tonight, I want you to bend that excellent, inquisitive mind of yours to your own question. Tomorrow, I will ask you to answer it. For now, come, let us eat."

Daegan exited the room to discuss several ideas with Keene. Wynn followed the two men slowly, his mind churning on Daegan's sudden change of attitude. He had asked a question that pleased the man, but he wasn't sure why. It was a mystery, and one he needed to solve by morning. His thoughts whirled on the problem throughout dinner. Daegan was right. The food was nourishing, but that was all that could be said for it. He almost regretted not taking Lord Adelfried up on his offer, but then he remembered Daegan's complimentary words about a hunger for knowledge and a warmth filled him at the memory. The man was nothing like what he had pictured, but he was intriguing, and there was no denying that he was obviously a genius when it came to designing things. The few schematics he had seen in the workshop, and even the one that Daegan had given him to look at more closely, were proof enough of that.

After supper, Keene led Wynn to the room where he would be staying. It was small and stark. Inside sat a bed, a small desk and chair, and a wardrobe in which he could stash his belongings. The desk had a few drawers and shelves, and they were all well-stocked with paper, pens, and plenty of pencils.

Wynn unpacked his small bag and carefully laid his things inside the wardrobe. Then he turned to the desk and examined each of the items, setting them carefully back in their places when he was done. Using the pitcher and basin next to the bed, he removed his shirt and carefully washed his face, hands, and arms. Then he shimmied into his nightshirt, removed his boots and socks, turned down the lamp, and climbed between the covers. After sleeping in military bunks, on the ground in the mountains, and in the swaying hammocks of the airship, this bed felt like the most luxurious thing he had ever experienced. It was not as comfortable as his bed at home, but it was close. He pulled the covers up to his chin and closed his eyes.

In the darkness, Wynn's mind awoke. Behind his eyelids, he saw again the schematic Daegan had handed to him, and he rolled the artificineer's question over in his mind. Like a ball being tossed from one hand to the other, Wynn contemplated the question, staring at it from all angles, turning it over and over. Long into the night, he pondered.

As his thoughts slowed and exhaustion reached up with gentle hands to claim him and bear him into the realm of dreams, the answer struck. Wynn's lips curled up in a self-satisfied grin.

Despite his success, however, he could not find sleep. His brain continued to tumble through his answer, like waves of the ocean returning over and over to the shore, he pounded at the problem with his mind again and again, worried he would forget the solution he had found. Wynn tossed and turned until finally he gave up on sleep and rose from the bed. He paced about the room, got himself a drink of water, lit the lamp on his desk, and scratched out thoughts and ideas on a piece of paper until he had written down all his ideas and his eyelids were drooping. He neatly stacked up his notes, put away the pencil, turned down the lamp, and crawled back into bed, where he stayed until morning.

3

Nadia welcomed Dalmir and Ioan at the door with a warm smile. They informed her of Thorben's whereabouts and she insisted they come in and make themselves at home.

"It is good to see you again, Dalmir," Nadia said, as Hubert raced down the hall and tackled one of his legs with all the enthusiasm a five-year-old could muster. Dalmir grinned and lifted his leg up and down, raising and lowering Hubert and causing the young boy to squeal and laugh.

Nadia smiled softly at the antics of her son, then turned to Ioan and stared at him for a long moment. He fidgeted under her intense scrutiny, self-consciously tugging the sleeves of his tunic down over his wrists. Nadia's eyes filled with tears and she pulled him into her arms and held him for a long time, swaying back and forth like a mother rocking a small child. Ioan stiffened at first, but after a moment, he melted into the embrace and let the tears pour out.

"I am so sorry, Ioan," she murmured. "So sorry."

Hubert leaped up, switching his hold on Dalmir's leg to one on his arm, as though attempting to pull him over. Dalmir lifted the boy by the wrists and swung him around, giving Nadia and Ioan a moment to grieve together privately.

At length, she released him, and Ioan straightened, wiping his eyes on his sleeve. "Thank you, Aunt Nadia."

"You have always been family," Nadia said firmly, "and now more than ever." She stared into his face, as though registering the differences about him for the first time. "What has happened to you?"

Ioan sighed. "It is a long story."

She gave him a sympathetic smile. Inside the house, a bell clamored.

Though she clearly had questions, Lady Adelfried kept them to herself. "You must be hungry after your travels," she said, her voice soft. "Hubert, let go of Master Dalmir. He might not want you to treat him like a play yard."

"It's fine," Dalmir assured her with a grin.

At that moment, the door swung open and Thorben entered. Nadia embraced him enthusiastically, peering behind him. Thorben took her gently by the arms. "He isn't here," he whispered.

"You didn't bring Beren home to celebrate his graduation?"

"No, there were more pressing matters."

"But I thought..." Nadia trailed off. "All is not well. Something has happened. What is it?" Her eyes darted to Ioan, who ducked his head.

"Inside." Thorben gestured at the door. "I will tell you everything, but not out here. It has been a long day of travel and our guests are weary. Hungry too, and if I am not mistaken, we have arrived just in time for dinner."

Nadia's expression remained guarded, but she gave a nod of assent and ushered them into the house. Thorben gave her a quick peck on the cheek as he passed her.

"You can be proud of our son," he said, a weary smile lighting his features. "He is a true warrior."

Nadia beamed up at him. "This is nothing I did not already know. Food is waiting, and I am curious to hear everything you have to tell me."

They gathered in the dining room and there was a sudden commotion as a boisterous group of children of various ages and heights descended upon the table. The older ones carried platters piled high with steaming food, and the smaller ones dashed about, setting out plates and cups and utensils. It was a picture of organized chaos as the children darted around one another, filling the table and finding their places. A few of the older children seemed to note that they had guests, for they darted away and returned a moment later with a few more place settings. Dalmir watched with bemused nostalgia as a long-forgotten scene from his own youth flashed through his memory with aching poignancy. One brother jostled another, and a mock battle broke out between them before their mother made a gentle warning sound that put an end to their caper. Hubert tugged on his arm, directing Dalmir to a seat next to his own, and Dalmir obliged with a fond smile.

Once they were all seated in their large wooden chairs and consumed with the business of eating, Thorben told Nadia all that had transpired since he left. The politeness of the children impressed Dalmir. They listened quietly as they ate, never interrupting as Thorben spoke in frank, simple words, allowing even the youngest among them to be privy to the entire recounting. Ioan remained silent, only interjecting a few times to fill in details. Nadia listened with little expression, though she made faint sounds of dismay when she heard about the more dangerous things her son and his friends had endured throughout the Storvas Mission.

When Thorben had finished, she turned her gaze to Dalmir. "These changes that the madman caused to Ioan, can they be reversed?"

Dalmir set his fork down. "I do not know. It might be possible, but I would need to better understand what he did and how before I could even attempt to reverse it. This is like nothing I have ever seen, and I have seen quite a bit. Anything I tried now could make it worse. None of what is happening makes sense to me. Things are out of alignment. From what Ioan and the others have said, Ioan's transformation surprised even the madman, almost as though it was an accident. His other creations that they encountered were far more..." Dalmir paused, struggling for the right word. "The changes were far more pronounced. They were more like trees than people."

"I suppose I should be grateful," Ioan spoke up around a bite of food, his face split into a wide grin. "I could have sprouted leaves."

Nadia's face paled. "I do not find this at all amusing. How do you know the changes will not continue?"

"Dear, we are keeping a close eye on him," Thorben reassured her. "His condition progressed rapidly at first, but it appears to have halted and stabilized."

Nadia pressed her lips together, but said no more. Instead, she busied herself with the food on her plate. For a while, there was just the sound of chewing and utensils clattering against plates.

"Master Dalmir," one of Thorben's sons asked when his plate was clean.

"Yes?" Dalmir said.

"Mother said that you are making cynders for our airships."

"That's right," Dalmir replied.

The lad, who looked to be only a few years younger than Beren, frowned. "Daegan's been working on creating cynders for years, but he's never managed it. What's the secret?"

"Drengur..." Nadia's voice sounded like a warning.

"No, it's all right," Dalmir assured her. He turned to the lad. "Well, Daegan is brilliant. But the person who created the cynders is cheating. Fortunately, I know how to cheat, too."

The lad brightened. "Can you show me?"

Dalmir grinned, caught up in the enthusiasm. He pulled the blue orb out and held it up. It gleamed faintly with an inner light. "This is the secret ingredient."

"Is it magic?" Hubert asked, his voice a lilting lisp.

Dalmir frowned. "No, not really. It might seem like magic, but really, it is just knowledge."

"Where did you get it?" Hubert asked.

"I made it."

"How?"

Dalmir stared at the child, and then he glanced up and noticed every set of eyes riveted upon him, awaiting his answer. His throat suddenly closed as memories washed over him. Tears prickled behind his eyes and for a long moment he couldn't speak, couldn't breathe. At last, he managed a few words. "I don't know if I can explain it. The story is a very long one, and much of it is unhappy."

"That's enough bothering Master Dalmir, children," Nadia interjected, seeming to sense his inner turmoil. "You got to stay up late waiting for your father, but now it is time for bed. Everyone except Drengur and Cathrine."

"But I wanted Math-ter Dalmir to tuck me in and tell me a story!" Hubert protested, and the others joined in.

Nadia lifted her voice above the complaints and pleading words. "No, no, I'll not have any arguing. To bed with you all." She looked at Dalmir apologetically. "They've missed you."

"I'll tell you a story tomorrow," Dalmir promised.

Grumbling, but not as loudly now that they had the promise of tomorrow, the younger children filed away. Drengur and Cathrine remained behind, helping to clear the dishes. Once the last of the children had exited the room, Thorben turned to Dalmir.

"What did you mean when you talked about the cynders and cheating?" he asked.

"I have been gone a long time," Dalmir replied. "But the world has sprung ahead much faster than should be possible. The cynders, for example. There are ways to create the same device without my orb, but people will have to discover and build many other things first. Using the orb is cheating. It is... a shortcut, if you will. But I do not understand how it has been done. The cynders bear the mark of my brother, Palte, but he is dead, and it should not be possible for another to use his orb, and yet the cynders exist. I do not know how, or why, but it appears to be possible for some people to awaken the orbs and use their power."

"I think it is time you told us your story," Thorben said, his voice soft.

Dalmir sighed. The man was right. He needed to tell the story. Cathrine and Drengur took their places at the table once more, and Dalmir closed his eyes.

"There were seven of us," he began. "Seven brothers, princes of a small kingdom history has long forgotten; though at the time, we thought protecting it was the most important thing we would ever do. It's funny how time can change one's perspective. Four stronger kings had allied together against us and it felt like we had no chance of surviving. My father sent us to the Library."

"The Library?" Nadia asked.

Dalmir nodded gravely. "The Library held all the knowledge of the world within its walls. It stood on an island south of what is now Ondoura, a place of great learning and peace. Any who wished could travel there and gain the knowledge they sought. We went seeking a way to defend ourselves and save our kingdom.

"Shiori met us when we first stepped out of our little boat onto the shores of the Library's island. She was the Archidian, the caretaker of the Library. She welcomed us and helped us search the archives and scrolls. For days, we combed through the pages. And in the evenings, I walked through the orchards with Shiori and listened to her stories. We grew quite close over the long sennights that we spent there." Dalmir paused, the old guilt surfacing in his thoughts, but he pushed it away, focusing on his tale. "Unfortunately, our friendship distracted her from her primary duty and allowed Uun an opportunity to break the single law she gave us when we first set foot on the Library's shore." He shook his head. "Such a simple rule, really. And yet Uun could not resist. He grew impatient with our search and believed the answers were being withheld from us on purpose. He believed that the rule was a test of our dedication to our people, or our determination to find the answers we sought."

"What was the rule?" Drengur asked, caught up in the story.

"There was a garden behind the Library, a beautiful garden," Dalmir replied. "Flowers of every color ringed a crystal-clear pool, with a single tree growing up from its banks: a golden tree, with fruit that gleamed like the sun. We were not to drink from the pool or eat from that tree. This should have been no hardship. Orchards covered the Library grounds: every fruit tree imaginable, all in perfect season. But Uun could not resist. He plucked from the golden tree and scooped up a goblet of water from the silver pond. All this he did in secret. But that was not enough for him. He mixed the water into all of our wine glasses and made sure a slice of that fruit sat on each of our plates that night. By his hand, we were all complicit, and our disobedience was complete."

"But you didn't do it on purpose!" Drengur shouted.

Dalmir's eyes crinkled at the youth's cry of outrage. "It did not matter. Uun's disobedience would have been enough. That he tainted all of us... well... should we not have been aware of what was in our brother's mind? Should we all not have been far more vigilant than we were?"

"What happened?" Cathrine whispered.

"Our disobedience caused the Library to detach from our world," Dalmir said in a bleak tone. "The island disappeared, and with it, all the knowledge it had once held. But the Builder yet had mercy. He gifted my brothers and myself with the ability to atone for the selfish act that had deprived the rest of Turrim of the Library's knowledge. He gave us the complete knowledge of all that the Library had contained, as well as life long enough to teach that knowledge to the rest of Turrim. In a way, we became the Library we had destroyed."

"Beren said that you held an airship in the sky with no cynders," Nadia said. "That sounds like more than just knowledge and long life."

Dalmir gave her a slight nod. "That is correct. The Builder also gave us powers far beyond the limits of mortal men. And for a time, it was enough. For years, we kept Turrim at peace. But it was not enough for Uun."

The Adelfrieds listened as he related Uun's betrayal, as he had told Marik several lunats before. They remained silent throughout, seemingly not even daring to breathe as he spoke.

When he finished, the room remained silent for a long while.

"When you say 'long life,' just how long are we talking about?" Ioan asked.

Dalmir hesitated, not sure he wanted to say, and yet he also felt that these good people deserved to know the full extent of the truth. He had already told them more than he had told anyone else. "I was born in the days of Dearg Lathair, year three hundred eighty-four."

"The Red Time?" Cathrine gasped. "But that..."

"You're..." Drengur paused, clearly doing calculations in his head. "Five thousand years old?" He stared in unabashed disbelief.

Dalmir gave a weighty sigh. "Give or take a few decades, yes. The Builder granted us immortality when he granted us our power. Not just long life and youth, but we were also invulnerable. Or at least... that is what we thought. Uun found a way to kill us, of course, though I still cannot figure out how he managed it."

"The orb you used to fill the cynder at the Arxis," Nadia said slowly, "there are seven of them?"

"Yes," Dalmir replied.

"And they all have the power to create cynders or"—her eyes flicked over to Ioan—"do *that* to people?"

"The short answer is yes," Dalmir affirmed, "though they need a person to wield them. And each of us had our own strengths and interests. For example, someone using my orb would probably find it more difficult to alter a person the way Lorcan did, I think. But I really don't know. Until recently, I would have said it was impossible to access the power stored within them at all. The orbs were one of the first things we created once we received our powers. We had thought to give the orbs to the people, but it didn't work. In thousands of years, we couldn't even figure out how to use each other's orbs. But Uun appears to have done that, as well."

"Do you know where they all are?" Thorben asked.

"I have two of them," Dalmir replied. "And I have seen signs that Uun has at least two in his possession as well. Lorcan has Avaleun's orb, and someone is using Palte's to create the cynders."

"That leaves three that are potentially still out there?" Nadia asked, her voice trembling.

"Perhaps," Dalmir acknowledged.

"Maybe there's one in the Ember Mine," Drengur burst out. "That's the first place I'd look!"

Dalmir blinked at him. "The Ember Mine?"

"It is possible." Thorben spoke thoughtfully. "It could explain a few things."

"What things?" Dalmir asked.

"There is a mine deep in the heart of our tallest mountain," Thorben replied. "The ore that comes out of it is... unique."

"Unique?" Dalmir queried. "Unique how?"

"It is extremely easy to work with, but when it hardens, it's nearly unbreakable," Drengur said, his voice enthusiastic. "It's difficult to mine, but it has always been worth the extra effort. We've made our best tools and weapons from the ore that comes out of the Ember Mine. It's one of our national treasures."

"It's also supposed to be a secret," Cathrine said, shooting a glare at her younger brother.

Drengur looked abashed.

"We've rarely let outsiders explore the Ember Mine, for obvious reasons. Also, it can be... dangerous," Thorben said. "But if you think another one of these orbs might be down there, I will make an exception."

Dalmir was quiet for a long moment, fingering the spherical jewel he still held in his hand. How had Uun used Palte's and Avaleun's orbs? How were humans wielding them? Was Lorcan driven mad by using the orb, or had he already been mad? Why could some people awaken them and others could not? And swirling through his thoughts like a vein of poison, he could not shake the memory of Uun's betrayal. Marik's comment continued to bother him, gnawing at his thoughts ever since that day at the collapsed mine. He had never understood how it was possible for Uun to carry out his betrayal. He should not have had the ability. Each of them had always been equally matched. But Marik had questioned the wisdom of linking their power through the orbs, of giving Uun that kind of control over them. It was strange, but that thought had never occurred to Dalmir before. And yet the link through their orbs had been Uun's suggestion. Was that the key, then? Had he... the thought struck like a thunderclap, leaving Dalmir reeling. Had Uun used their own power against them? And... his heart quavered at the thought, wanting to shy away from it, but he forced himself to look it square in the face. Could he do it again? Did the orbs, with their remnants of his brothers' power, possess the answer to defeating Uun?

At last, he gave a slow nod. "It might be nothing," Dalmir said, "but it might also be the most important thing..." He looked up. "I do not wish to impose, but I believe it is absolutely necessary that I seek any orbs that might have escaped Uun's control."

"Done." Thorben gestured expansively. "After all you have done for us, this is a small request. Drengur and Ioan will accompany you."

Ioan, who had been silent throughout the meal, looked up swiftly, his face an unreadable mask. He merely nodded and returned to his eating. Drengur, however, fairly bounced up and down in his seat.

"I've been there a few times. I've studied all the maps and I know all the passageways," he boasted.

"Quite true," Thorben said. "The boy has an uncanny knack for holding a detailed map in his head. He won't lead you astray. I will arrange for an airship to take you there in the morning. It is a short flight to Telos."

Dalmir paused. "Telos? The capital city?"

Thorben gave him a quizzical look. "Gnupar is the capital

city." He gestured expansively. "We moved it here because of the train road, which made it easier to collaborate with Dalma and Ondoura after the formation of the Council. But even before that, Telos hasn't been the capital for centuries. In fact, many believe Telos itself is nothing more than a myth."

"Ah," Dalmir replied, "my mistake."

Thorben stared into his mug. Nadia asked Ioan a question, which he answered.

"My thanks for a wonderful meal." Dalmir wiped his mouth on the cloth napkin and pushed away from the table. "However, I am quite tired. If you will excuse me, it has been a long day, and I would like to get an early start in the morning."

Nadia rose, but Dalmir waved a hand at her. "I remember the way," he assured her.

———

THE NEXT MORNING, Dalmir awoke to the smells of frying bacon and eggs wafting through the house. For a moment before full wakefulness sprang upon him, he basked in the amnesia of those moments at the end of sleep: for the first time in centuries, he could almost imagine himself as a child again, could almost hear the sounds of his brothers tussling amongst themselves as they got ready for the day, could almost remember his parents' faces as they smiled at him across the table. Then the moment passed. He opened his eyes, remembering where he was and all that had transpired to that small boy he had once been so long ago. Full wakefulness brought an all-too-familiar darkness with it and Dalmir's body felt heavy. If only he could just stay here in bed; summoning the energy to rise felt close to impossible.

However, voices in the hallway reminded him of all they stood to lose if he failed to stop Uun, and so he rose and dressed, packing what little he had used the night before neatly back into his pack, before descending to the crescendo of breakfast with the Adelfried family. Breakfast was not nearly such a formal affair as dinner, even in the event of a guest. The clamor and conversation were far more lively. Even with everyone finally seated, a level of bustling still occurred as arms reached across the table for another slab of bacon or someone shouted, "Please pass the jam!" It was all a little overwhelming, but not unpleasant. And after a while, Dalmir found himself enjoying the meal more than he had enjoyed anything in quite some time. It felt good to be amid a boisterous family once again. It had been... a stinging sensation rose and threatened to spill out from his eyes. Dalmir shook away the unwanted thoughts. It was his own fault, after all, that he was alone. It was nothing more than what he deserved, he reminded himself sternly.

"Mith-ter Dalmir?" A small voice at his elbow made him look down into the wide eyes of Beren's youngest brother. He was missing a single top tooth, which gave him a funny whistle when he talked. "Are you ready?"

Dalmir straightened and saluted. "Reporting for duty, Building-Master Hubert."

Hubert giggled, saluted back, and then grew serious again. "Can I show you something?"

"What is it?"

"A thu-prise," Hubert lisped, tugging at Dalmir's hand.

Dalmir allowed himself to be led over to a corner of the main room that was little Hubert's haven. The two of them had spent many enjoyable evenings here when Dalmir was helping Daegan with his designs before the attack on the Academy and assassination of Regeont Roshana had called him and Thorben away. Next to a small chair stood a shelf that held a few odds and ends, some pine cones and twigs, the container of wooden blocks, a couple of brightly covered books, and an old-looking, rather ornate box with a large, fancy latch. It was to this box that Hubert went now. With obvious effort, he lifted the box from the shelf and set it down. Curious, Dalmir seated himself on the floor and lifted the box experimentally. It was heavy. He wondered what could be in such a small box to give it such weight.

"This is my 'pecial collection," Hubert confided as he lifted the lid.

Dalmir peered down at the contents, momentarily baffled. An assortment of pebbles, gravel, and stones of various shapes, sizes, and colors filled the box. He raised his gaze to the child, wondering why Hubert had been so eager to show this to him.

"Papa said you're going with Ioan to look for a special rock," Hubert said. "I thought maybe if one of mine was special enough, you wouldn't need to go. I have lots of special rocks. You can have one. Then we can build more towers."

Dalmir smiled gently and sifted his fingers through the collection. "Where did you find this one?" he asked, holding up a perfectly smooth black pebble with a vein of red running through it.

Hubert grinned. "The stable!" He launched into the story, regaling Dalmir with the tale of the first time he had ridden a horse by himself. It had been last summer, and the child was still full of excitement and pride at arriving at such a grown-up moment in his life. Dalmir listened intently, happy to share this memory with his little friend.

When Hubert finished, he reached into the box and picked up another rock. This one was thin, jagged, and gray. "I found this at the docks when Beren left," he said, his enthusiasm dimming.

"Why did you pick that one?" Dalmir asked.

"It looked sad. Like me."

"I bet it's happy now that you brought it home," Dalmir said. "Having a friend like you and a big box of brother and sister rocks probably makes it very happy."

Hubert giggled. "Rocks can't have brothers and sisters!"

Dalmir grinned. "Oh, they can't? Are you sure?"

"Yes!"

"Well, but have you ever heard the story about the rock family?"

Hubert squinted one eye. "No," he said, his voice quiet. "Tell me!"

Dalmir grinned as he set a handful of rocks on the ground, naming them as he did so. "There once was a rock family, and there was a Mama Rock, and a Papa Rock, and lots of rock brothers and sisters. Then, one day, the oldest rock brother had to go on a quest." He lifted one of the larger rocks.

"Why?"

"Because the rock family needed to find a new place to live."

"What was wrong with the old place?"

"It was too small," Dalmir said, making up answers on the spot.

"Oh." Hubert seemed content.

"So, he had to leave. And the littlest rock brother was very sad. 'Please stay,' he begged, but the biggest rock brother reminded him he would be back soon. 'And when I come back,' he said, 'I will take you with me to our new home.' And he left. He rolled over the mountains..." Dalmir made a swooping motion with the hand holding the rock.

"Why didn't he walk?" Hubert interrupted.

"Because rocks don't have legs."

"Oh, right!"

"And he rolled along riverbanks. And he rolled through forests. It was hard work, all that rolling. But every place he found had something wrong with it. The riverbanks were steep, and he worried that the littlest rock brother would fall into the river. The forest was dark, and he worried that the littlest rock brother would be afraid. The mountains were too tall, and he worried that the littlest rock brother would get too tired trying to roll uphill. So on and on he searched."

"I'll bet the littlest rock brother missed him a lot," Hubert whispered.

"Oh, he did. The littlest rock brother waited and waited. Every day, he would get up and stare out the window. He would watch the road. He would wait. And he would remember."

"What would he remember?"

"He remembered how the biggest rock brother made him feel

safe when he was afraid. And how he told him stories when he was sick. And how he told jokes to make him laugh. But most of all, he remembered how proud he was of the biggest rock brother. And then one day..."

Hubert leaned forward, his eyes wide, his complete attention fixated on the story.

"The biggest rock brother came rolling home. And the littlest rock brother was so excited. But as he rolled out to greet him, he noticed that his biggest rock brother was different."

"Different?" Hubert tilted his head to the side, his little brow wrinkling. "How was he different?"

"He was smaller than the littlest rock brother remembered. And his edges had all worn off and were smooth. And he looked tired, oh, so very tired. But he was smiling, and he looked down at the littlest rock brother and said, 'I found it. I found the perfect home for our family.' And the littlest rock brother was glad." Dalmir stopped, feeling that the story had come to a happy ending.

"Well?" Hubert bounced up and down. "Where was the home?"

"Oh!" Dalmir fumbled for a moment. "Well, it was in a beautiful, grassy valley covered in bright flowers. It was just outside the entrance to a rabbit warren, and each spring, the baby bunnies would come out and play with the rock family. A shallow stream, too shallow to fall into, trickled along nearby. It was the perfect home for the rock family."

"And the biggest rock brother? Did he stay home?"

"He stayed for a while," Dalmir said. "But he had grown to love the road, and he had met friends along the way. So every now and then he would leave again to go visit them, or to discover unknown places."

Hubert's face fell. "He left again?"

Dalmir nodded, but then he craned his neck to peer into Hubert's face. "But he always came home again. And when the littlest rock brother had grown up enough that his mother didn't worry about him so much, the biggest rock brother invited him to go on one of his adventures."

Hubert beamed. "He did?"

"Of course he did! And they had so many wonderful adventures together on the wide, open roads. The end."

Hubert sat for a moment, staring down at his thin, jagged rock. "I like that story," he said quietly. Then he held the stone out to Dalmir. "This one is my specialest," he whispered. "So it might be the one you're looking for."

Dalmir's heart swelled, and he felt like it might break if he moved too fast or spoke too loudly. He reached out and folded his hand over Hubert's little one, enclosing the rock in the child's fist. "No, Hubert. This rock is not the one I'm looking for. This one is too special for me."

Hubert looked up, his expression puzzled. "What do you mean?"

"I can tell, just by looking at it, that this rock needs someone to take very good care of it, and give it a lot of attention. I can't do that," Dalmir said.

"You can't?"

"No."

"Why?"

"Well, because I have a few other important things to do."

"Like the oldest rock brother?"

Dalmir nodded. "Yes. Like the oldest rock brother. So I need you to look after this rock for me."

Hubert looked down at his rock. "I wanted to build towers again."

"So did I."

Hubert looked up. "Really?"

"Really. You keep practicing, because next time I come to visit, we're going to build the tallest tower ever."

"Promise?"

"I promise."

Hubert's face broke into a wide grin. He threw his arms

around Dalmir. "Thanks for the story," he lisped. "Don't worry, I'll take good care of the special rock."

"You do that." Dalmir smiled as the boy jumped up and pattered off, presumably to tell his siblings the story he had just heard. Dalmir rose to his feet with a sigh, regretting all the moments of childhood he had left behind. As he stood, he saw Ioan leaning against one of the large, rough-hewn wood columns, a placid smile on his face.

"How much of that did you hear?" Dalmir asked, feeling a little embarrassed.

"Enough." Ioan grinned. "You're very good with children."

"Children are easy to please," Dalmir replied. "They don't care if a story makes sense."

Ioan laughed. "Uncle Thorben says that if we don't leave now, we'll miss the airship. Are you ready to go?"

Dalmir nodded. "Yes."

"Then let's go find that special rock," Ioan teased. "Come on, Drengur! Let's move!"

4

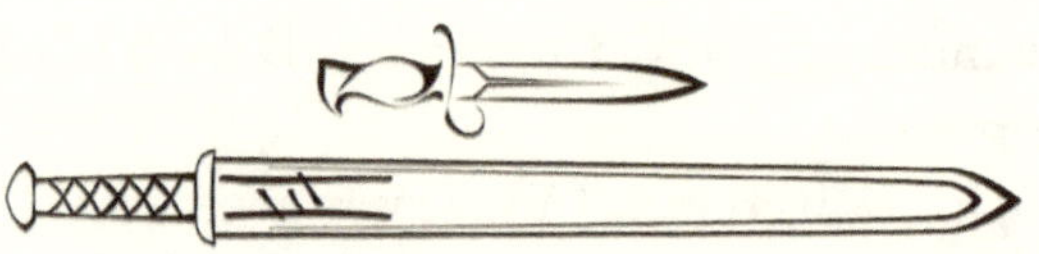

The airship eased into the docks and came to a gentle halt. Beren and Grayden shouldered their luggage and descended the gangplank and down the winding wooden stair to the streets of Doran. The smell of briny sea breeze mixed with cinnamon and nutmeg filled their noses, and Grayden grinned. The warm, damp air enveloped him and the scorching sun embraced him, warming him to the core. After several sennights of struggling through the snowy mountains, accompanied by the fear and uncertainty that had plagued their steps as they made the difficult trek to the Storvas Pass, the humid air of Doran and the friendly bustle of its streets were a welcome trade.

"Where are we supposed to meet Niveya?" Grayden asked.

Beren squinted one eye into the bright, but sinking sun. "My father said he was staying in the Cypress Quarter. But that was over a sennight ago. We may have to do some hunting."

"That should be fun." Grayden's voice was wry.

"Niveya did pledge to my father that he would work with whomever he sent. And he's crafty. He may already know we are on our way."

"How could he possibly know that?" Grayden asked. "There's been no time for messages to travel ahead of us."

"It would surprise you how swiftly an important message can travel." The soft, whispering voice just over their shoulders made both Grayden and Beren whirl around.

A thin, older man stood behind them, a slight smirk on his lips. His hair was white and bushy, and he had a white, pointed beard hanging from his chin. Silver beads entwined in his beard caught the sunlight and glittered like diamonds. He held himself proudly in his tailored suit, but his shoulders hunched slightly. In his right hand, he leaned upon an elegant cane with a golden knob at its top gripped in long, bony fingers.

"Welcome back to Doran," he said in a crackling voice. "My name is Quin. My master sent me to escort you to him. We were not entirely certain which airship you were arriving on. I am quite glad it was the early one. I was not looking forward to waiting in the dark."

Grayden shared a wary glance with Beren as he lifted his pack off the ground and slung it over his shoulder.

"And your master would be...?" Beren asked, folding his arms and leaning back as though he had every intention of remaining where he stood forever if need be.

The man's eyes darted between the young men. "I cannot say his name here," he whispered. "But he told me that if there was any trouble convincing you to come with me, that I should tell you he hopes you can move beyond the unpleasantness of your former association, and that there was nothing personal about it. A businessman must always look out for the interests of his business, you know."

Storm clouds thundered in Beren's eyes. Grayden stared at his friend in surprise. He couldn't remember Beren ever looking so wrathful. His friend had been a constant source of enthusiastic, good-natured camaraderie. Even when they had been trapped on an airship with pirates, even in the moments following the avalanche when they were frantically searching for their lost leader, even when facing the madman in the mountains, never once had he seen Beren's easygoing demeanor slip. But now,

Grayden stared as his friend's jaw tightened and his brow furrowed down, his eyes darkening into a simmering glare. Grayden braced himself for the inevitable tirade and edged between Beren and Quin in order to defuse the situation.

However, when Beren spoke, his voice held only pleasant calm. "Then your master is the man we are looking for. Lead on."

The white-haired gentleman eyed Beren with a look that was part relief, part suspicion, but he hiked up one corner of his mouth and swung around, beckoning for them to follow. He led them away from the docks and through the heart of Doran. They passed a marketplace—not the same one they had come to with Lady Adelfried—traveled down several tightly enclosed streets, then came out of the cramped space to an open square. In the middle of the open area sat a large, prominent building that looked awkward sitting all by itself, apart from the rest of the city. A twinge of unease clutched at Grayden's thoughts as they crossed the grassy square. The rest of Doran was so tightly packed together, this open area felt far too exposed. He glanced at the building with suspicion.

"What is that place?" he asked, hoping it was not their intended destination.

Their guide glanced back over his shoulder. "That is the Respite. It is the place where the ill and elderly go for healing and care."

Grayden nodded, his nerves calming a bit at the explanation. They crossed the green and dove back into more long alleyways between towering buildings. After nearly an hour of walking, their guide stopped in front of a ramshackle building with a door swinging aimlessly on broken hinges.

"Here we are," the man said. He rapped smartly on the door and then pushed it open, gesturing for them to enter.

Grayden passed through the doorway cautiously, keeping an eye on the rickety door in case the hinges decided to give way completely. Beren followed close behind, until they stood in a foyer before a much nicer, more elaborate door. The foyer was large enough for several people to stand comfortably, and Grayden noticed with a start that there were several openings in the surrounding walls he had not noticed from the outside, openings that would be perfect for keeping watch with a crossbow. His heart thumped at a more rapid trot for a moment as he contemplated how vulnerable they had been. He was both angry with himself for not seeing the arrow slits, and curious to go back outside and determine if he could spot them now that he knew they were there. However, their guide had come inside and was now unlocking this second door and ushering them into a much grander, more luxurious room than he ever would have guessed could exist in this part of the city.

"Welcome, son of Adelfried!" a voice boomed and Grayden watched in dazed bemusement as Ericole Niveya strode forward, placed his hands on Beren's shoulders, and kissed the air on either side of his face. "And his friend, Master Ormond, if I am not mistaken?" Grayden suddenly found himself being given the same greeting, though Niveya ended by tapping his cheek with his hand in a patronizing manner. "Thank you for bringing them, Quin. You may return to your post." The white-haired man bowed at the waist and disappeared as silently as he had appeared. Niveya turned back to the young men like a host welcoming long-awaited guests. "Welcome to my home away from home. It is not nearly as nice as the one I entertained you in last we met, but it will serve our purposes here in Doran, don't you think?"

"It is located a bit far from the incident we are investigating," Beren said, his voice stiff.

"Yes," Niveya admitted. "But that is for the better, you'll see. We don't know whom we can trust, correct? I thought it best to set up in a place where we would not be as obvious. I am hoping to put our quarry at ease, make him think he has gotten away with his crime. Criminals who think they are untouchable often get cocky, and then they make mistakes, and then they get caught."

"I suppose you would know about criminals and the way they think," Beren rumbled.

Niveya beamed. "But of course! I have seen many criminals brought to justice in just this way."

Beren did not respond. He was looking about the room, studying it as though looking for weaknesses. Niveya's eyes followed him, and then he turned his attention to Grayden.

"Master Ormond," he began, but Grayden interrupted him.

"I can't speak for Beren," he said. "But I want you to know that I do not trust you. I don't know what you said to make Lord Adelfried agree to let you search for the Regeont's murderer, but he did, and it looks like we're stuck working together. Neither one of us likes it, but I suppose we'll have to make the best of it. That said, I'm uncomfortable being called 'Master Ormond.' I would appreciate it if you would just call me by my first name."

Niveya's eyes narrowed into a look of surprise. "Very well, Grayden. Then you may call me Ericole, or just Niveya, whichever you prefer." He turned to Beren, his smirk gone. "I do apologize for the way we first met," he said, his tone low and earnest. "I hope we can put it behind us now that we are on the same team."

"We are not on the same team," Beren muttered.

Niveya gave a slight nod. "As you wish. But before we get started, I want you to know that I was very fond of the Regeont. She was... a worthy opponent, and we were good neighbors, or as good of neighbors as two such as ourselves could be. I was truly distressed by her murder, and it is my fervent desire to see her killer brought to justice."

Beren's expression altered, and his scowl lifted a bit. He studied Niveya silently for a long moment. Then he heaved a sigh. "I believe you are in earnest. Aunt Roshana was important to me. I, too, would like nothing more than to see her murderer punished." He thrust out his hand. "I shall consider this alliance to be in our best interests. At least, until we have accomplished our task."

Niveya took the proffered hand. "An alliance," he agreed.

"What have you learned so far?" Beren asked as Niveya led them farther into the building.

"Not as much as I would like," Niveya replied. "When I last spoke to your father, I had a promising lead, but it is proving... difficult."

"Difficult?" Grayden asked.

Niveya rubbed his hands together as though warming them. "By being observant..."

"Spying," Beren interjected.

Niveya's lips twitched. "By spying," he acknowledged, "I have discovered the name of the last person to see the Regeont alive, other than her nephew, the new Regeont. I went to her home to speak with her, but she was not there. Days passed, but she did not return. I grew concerned, so I..." Niveya cleared his throat, his eyes flicking between Beren and Grayden. He seemed to make a decision in that glance. "I broke in..."

Beren made a disapproving sound in his throat.

"Not the noblest of activities, I grant you. But I chose to tell you the truth about how I acquired the information I am about to share," Niveya said. "The woman, a member of the Regeont's staff, had obviously fled. Her house was in the veritable disarray that is often left behind by someone who needs to pack up and leave in a hurry. She left behind many things, but she appears to have taken everything of value, which leads me to believe she will not be returning."

"You seem proud of this information, but how does it help us?" Beren asked, his voice flat.

"She knows something," Grayden offered.

Niveya eyed him approvingly. "I believe so, yes." He raised an eyebrow. "And?"

"What she knows scares her," Grayden continued, thinking over the information Niveya had just shared. "Scares her enough that she left her home, her job, and whatever she couldn't carry."

Understanding chased the suspicion from Beren's eyes. "She must know something about the Regeont's murder, something she is worried could put her in danger. We need to know whatever it is this woman knows."

Niveya clapped his hands together slowly, a smile spreading across his face. "Excellent. I can see that Lord Adelfried sent me swift thinkers."

"Do you have any idea where she might have gone?" Beren asked.

"Unfortunately, no."

"Well, you figured out where she lives," Grayden mused. "Do you know if she has any family? Friends? Anyone who knew her well enough that they might know where she would go?"

"She has a distressingly small number of relatives," Niveya admitted, "and rather few friends. It seems she was wholly devoted to her work. But I have discovered a cousin who lives outside Doran. We can ask others on the Regeont's staff, but we will have to take care. Most of them are working for the new Regeont, and we don't want him to know we are poking around."

"You suspect Lord Elan had a part in Aunt Roshana's murder?" Beren stared.

"I doubt it." Niveya spoke lightly, but there was a hard glint in his eye. "But Elan benefited most from Roshana's death. And that places him high on my list."

"That's a problem," Beren muttered.

"Why?" Grayden asked.

"Because Elan is the new Regeont." Beren frowned at him like this should be obvious. "We can't move against him without watertight proof. We can't just accuse him on suspicion or whim."

"Of course not," Niveya said, his voice smooth. "That's where we come in. I need your help to gather evidence. And we need to find Ulia and find out what she knows. Without her, we have nothing."

"Let's get started, then." Beren turned to leave the room.

Niveya chuckled. "I admire your enthusiasm, and I appreciate your desire to move swiftly, but the sun is setting. It is a fair drive to our destination and by the time we arrive, dinner will be over.

This is a time in which unwelcome callers are... unwelcome. Nobody will speak to us in the dark."

"Even if it is an emergency?" Grayden asked, puzzled once more by the strangeness of Ondouran customs.

"Is it an emergency?" Niveya asked mildly. "And even if it is, can we prove it? No, we will get much better information and a more welcoming reception if we wait until morning to bother Ulia's cousin." He eyed the two of them. "In fact, I don't believe I trust either of you yet. You both seem the sort to go sneaking out after dark, thinking I won't notice, and then none of us will get a good night's sleep. Therefore, I will keep the cousin's name to myself until morning, as well. Now, come, dinner is being laid out for us, and I can show you to your rooms, unless you wished to seek your own accommodations?"

Beren shot Grayden a strange look. But before Grayden could decipher what it meant, his friend was speaking.

"My father said we should stay where we can keep a close eye on you."

Niveya responded with a surprised laugh. It was the first sound he had made that seemed to betray his genuine emotions. But then the mirth died and Niveya's face returned to its impassive expression. "Very good," he said, leading them up the narrow stairs to a set of luxurious rooms. He paused at the door. "Rest assured that you are more than welcome to come and go as you please. I would only ask that you use the doors, rather than breaking any windows." He gave Beren a meaningful glance before disappearing into the darkened hallway.

Grayden raised an eyebrow. "What was that all about?"

Beren's face went a little red. "Long story."

5

Rhythmic pounding bored into Wynn's brain, pulling him to consciousness. Blinking the sleep from his eyes, he sat up, wondering for a moment where he was until his mind came to full wakefulness. With an eagerness he had not expected, he dressed himself and headed down the hall toward the forge. When he reached it, he stood at the doorway, watching quietly. He knew better than to interrupt a smith at his work. Keene's apprentices stoked the fire and manned the bellows while Keene himself hammered out a long bar of metal, turning it and shaping it with forceful, precise blows. Wynn marveled at the man's skill and strength. Keene did not have the build that Wynn expected from a blacksmith. His arms were not thick like Master Farley, the blacksmith back home in Dalsea. Keene's build was more long and wiry, and yet he wielded his large hammer with a dexterity and precision Master Farley would envy. The piece he was working on took its shape with an obedience that was stunning to watch. At length, Keene laid aside his hammer and thrust the piece into a tall vat. Flames burst up and around the tongs. Wynn frowned. He was used to the hiss and steam of quenching, but this produced neither of these expected side effects. Without meaning to, he moved forward, curious.

As he entered the forge, Keene took notice of him. The smith nodded, welcoming him into the room. The apprentices—their task of keeping the fire hot ended for the moment—eyed Wynn as they wiped their brows and went to a large basin on the far side of the room. The basin sat under the spigot of a pump, and as they worked the pump's handle, water tumbled from it into the copper reservoir.

"You are wondering why there was no steam from the quench," Keene said as Wynn approached.

Wynn nodded, craning his neck to see what the smith was doing. His fingers itched to pick up the tools, to examine every inch of the forge; he tapped them against his leg instead, resisting the urge to handle and touch and know.

"It is not water," Keene explained, carefully bringing the dripping piece out of the liquid with the massive tongs. "It is oil. Water quenching is usually the most efficient, but it can cause cracking and distortion. When I'm working with Daegan, precision is everything. The tiniest blemish in any part of the things we build together could mean the loss of defenders' lives. It is not something your village blacksmith usually has to worry about."

"I see." The yearning to grasp the tools and try out this new technique for himself swelled to a crescendo.

Keene eyed Wynn. "You wish to help here in the forge, not just work with schematics, yes?"

Wynn's mouth went dry. "I just... I..."

Keene nodded at his fingers, which were dancing a frantic rhythm. "I noticed this about you last night when we met. The hunger—it is in your eyes. You are not just a designer, you yearn to build the things you imagine. I have respect for this."

"I would never... not without permission... this is your castle," Wynn blurted, then felt his face flush red. Why had he called the forge a castle?

But Keene grinned and threw out his free hand expansively. "My castle! Yes. I am liking this description. Boys!" he called out to his apprentices. "Who is king under this mountain?"

"Master Keene, you are, sir!" one boy shouted.

"Yes. This is my castle. Here, I am master." He turned back to Wynn. "And you shall be my apprentice, as well as Daegan's. I will teach you. From the spark in your eye, I believe you already have some knowing, yes?"

"Y-yes," Wynn stammered, overwhelmed by the smith's enthusiastic generosity. From where they stood at the water basin, the shorter of the apprentices glared at him.

"But Daegan, he has first dibs. You report to him first," Keene added.

"I understand."

"With him, you will design. And with me, you will build. Your creations will come to life in your own hands. I see the desire for this in you. I, too, have this desire, but I am not so good with the designs." Keene tapped his temple. "It is not so easy for me to see it here. This is why Daegan and I work so well together. But go, he will be wondering where you are."

"Where can I find him?" Wynn asked.

"Daegan is at breakfast. You'll find him in the room where you had supper last night."

"Thank you." He knew the simple words could not convey the true depth of the gratitude he felt. It was rare that someone could look at him and see all the way to his heart of hearts. With most people, a cavern yawned between himself and them. Other people played games and wore masks and changed the rules daily, not saying what they meant, or saying one thing and meaning another with their faces and bodies, speaking a silent language he had never quite grasped. Grayden was one of the few exceptions, always earnest with his words, always honest about what he meant. Even when he teased or played pranks, Grayden was easy to read. But Keene had recognized something inside him and had heard the things Wynn could find no words for. How had he done that?

Pondering, Wynn made his way to the dining area, where he found Daegan already eating. The older man grunted a welcome, and Wynn, who had been on the verge of blurting out all the thoughts swirling in his head, paused. The man's eyes were half-closed, and he was holding a steaming mug reverently, as though contemplating its very existence was the most precious thing in the world. Wynn had seen this sight before. It was how his father sat at the breakfast table, and he had learned it was best to wait until that mug was empty before pestering his father with questions or ideas. He silently slid into his place at the table and piled his own plate high with eggs and fruit and smoked sausage. Then he went to the icebox and filled a glass with cold, foaming milk. He nodded as the two apprentices entered the room, but neither of them joined him at the table. Instead, they piled their plates and leaned against the far wall, eating and conversing in low tones. Wynn studied them. They were as different as night and day. The red-haired boy who had agreed with Keene about being the king under the mountain was lanky and tall, with gray eyes and a healthy helping of freckles trying to take over his face. His arms and legs stuck out of his clothes like fragile twigs, and Wynn wondered at his ability to hold his plate, let alone work in a forge. The other boy had dark hair, bright blue eyes, and the build of a mountain goat, all stocky and broad shouldered.

Keene joined them when Wynn's plate was halfway clean. He glanced at Daegan, then at Wynn, then back, and his face broke into a conspiratorial grin. The master smith winked at Wynn in approval and filled his own plate. A warmth blossomed in Wynn's chest. He knew he had passed a sort of test, and the approval felt good.

Wynn finished his plate of food and looked at Daegan. The man was still sipping from his mug, but now he was flipping through a stack of schematics. With a deep breath in through his nose, Wynn got up and started helping Keene's apprentices clear the table. He followed them into the tiny kitchen behind the dining area and they showed him where the wash-basin was.

"Running water in the kitchen?" Surprise coursed through Wynn when they showed him the spigot sticking out of a permanent wash-basin. Only the wealthiest people usually had running water inside their homes.

"Keene is the greatest smith in the world," the short, dark-haired apprentice said with a smug smirk. "And he's best friends with Daegan, the finest artificineer you'll ever meet. Of course he has running water in his home."

The sneer on his face spoke so loudly that even Wynn caught the disdain that came with the words.

"I meant no disrespect," Wynn said, hurrying to explain his surprise. "It's just that Master Keene seems so..." He fumbled for the right words. "Humble."

The red-haired apprentice gave a chortle. "Poor, you mean."

"No offense meant," Wynn stammered, wondering what he had said wrong. He had truly meant humble, not poor. The two words were very different. The master smith did not seem poor. His clothes were simple, but well-made, and anyone with eyes could see that his well-outfitted forge held only the best tools.

The apprentices shared a knowing look. "Keene more than makes a good living," the shorter one admitted, "enough to live in a palace, most likely."

"But he prefers to stay near his forge," the red-haired boy supplied. "And he's generous, to boot. Gives away anything he thinks he don't need."

"I see," Wynn said, filing away this information. In his head, he was cataloguing the two men he would be working with for the foreseeable future.

"Sure you do," the dark-haired apprentice said, giving a derisive sniff. He grabbed a broom and headed back into the small dining area. "Make sure you scrub those dishes well," he threw over his shoulder as he disappeared.

"Don't mind Gunnar," the other apprentice said as he left. "He's just jealous."

"Oh," Wynn said. He didn't know what else to say, so he stared into the soapy water, wondering where Beren and Grayden were. What were they doing right now? Probably not scrubbing dirty dishes. He sighed.

"Hey, my name is Conrad. You're Wynn, right?"

Wynn smiled and gave a nod, since his hands were covered in soapy dishwater. "Nice to meet you, Conrad."

"Thanks for helping with the dishes and things," Conrad said. "You didn't have to. That's mine and Gunnar's job."

"It didn't look like Master Daegan needed me yet," Wynn said. "I figured I'd best make myself useful until he's done with his coffee."

"It probably is what got under Gunnar's skin, honestly," Conrad said, his voice lowering. "When Master Keene told us you were coming, he got excited about meeting a real live defender and brilliant Academy graduate. Had you all built up in his head as quite the amazing figure. To find out you're just a... well, no offense, but you're young, like us."

Wynn let himself chuckle as understanding dawned. "None taken, Conrad. I never expected to become a defender so young, either."

"Well, I think it was a bit of a let-down, if you take my meaning."

"I can't help it that I'm human," Wynn snorted.

"Don't be too hard on him. Gunnar is just Gunnar. He's just bright enough to realize that he's not dazzlingly intelligent, or extremely talented. He'll never make Master Smith, and he'll never go to the Academy. But he wants to, see?"

"Ah." Wynn thought about his younger brothers and felt like he understood. He'd seen the looks on their faces when he built something that his father had praised. That spark of envy and longing mixed with a hopelessness he would never understand. He chewed on the inside of his cheek. He hadn't known how to soften the blow to his younger brothers, and he had no idea how to ease Gunnar's jealousy, either.

"He'll come around," Conrad assured him.

Wynn didn't reply. Whether Gunnar came around was none

of his concern, after all. He was here to learn as much as he could from Master Daegan, and to do what he could to contribute to the defense of Telmondir should the Igyeum declare war. One smith's apprentice was fairly low on the list of important things in the world. And yet it gnawed at him, the haughty look on Gunnar's face, and the hurt in his eyes. But there was nothing he could do about it at the moment, because Daegan was calling his name. Wynn wiped his hands on a towel and hurried back to the dining room.

"Yes, Master... er, Daegan?" Wynn stammered.

"Have you thought over your question?" Daegan asked without preamble.

"Yes," Wynn replied.

"And? Have you come up with any answers for yourself?"

Wynn paused, trying to collect his flustered thoughts. He had been so focused on his conversation with Conrad that all thoughts of his assignment from Daegan had scattered.

"Well, lad? I haven't got all day," Daegan snapped, rapping his knuckles on the table.

"I... yes, I did," Wynn stammered out. "I... that is to say, I believe you left holes in the assignment on purpose."

"We came to that conclusion last night," Daegan said abruptly, pushing away from the table and standing. "If you can't come up with anything better..."

"I meant..." Wynn began desperately.

"No time for what you meant." Daegan's voice was terse. "When you are presenting your ideas to the Council, you need to be precise, collected, and clear. If you cannot manage that with me, how will you manage before them?"

Wynn stared as the man left the room. His face grew hot, and his temper flooded down his neck and into his shoulders. With purposeful strides, he chased after Daegan.

"Sir, you left holes in the assignments to weed out students with no talent for innovation. You wanted to find the ones who think like you. Even if I didn't ask the right questions before, even though I believed my answer would not work, I still came up with it. I still thought through a solution that was different from anyone else's."

Daegan did not slow. "That is only part of it."

"Yes, sir," Wynn replied, matching the man's long strides. "There is also the matter of security. I imagine you would want to be careful to whom you disseminate information regarding what our capabilities are, particularly with the prospect of increasingly negative relations with our neighbors to the east growing more and more certain. It would never do to allow information on the Trackless to fall into the wrong hands."

Daegan's step faltered. It was brief, almost unnoticeable except that Wynn had been matching his pace exactly. His eyes flicked over to the artificineer's face and he saw a tiny, telltale twitch of the man's lips.

"The Trackless, eh? And who gave you the right to name *my* design?"

Wynn felt his ears grow warm as he realized his misstep. Fantastic. He had only just managed to impress the man, a feeling that was surely fading in light of his seeming arrogance. "It just sort of came to me as I was mulling over the problem last night. I was thinking of the great trains. My Da rode on them before they stopped running. I've always wanted to ride one, always regretted being born in the wrong decade..." He dragged the toes of his boots along the stone floor. "It's your design, of course, yours to name, but I didn't know what you had named it, so that's just what I've been calling it to myself. I wasn't trying to be presumptuous."

"Genius is presumptuous," Daegan snapped. "And it doesn't need to apologize, at least not when it's right. As a point of fact, I hadn't named it. I spent years planning it, but I never gave it a name. I'm no good at names. The Trackless." He nodded. "It has a certain ring to it."

Wynn felt a mystified grin try to spread across his face, but then Daegan turned into the messy workroom he had glimpsed the night before. It was still a shambles, and Wynn's smile changed to a wince. How was he supposed to work in such a room? How could Daegan find anything in such a horribly untidy workspace? The chaos swirled about him, making Wynn feel nauseated and dizzy. He couldn't shut it out. Daegan shoved several papers aside and rolled out the schematic for the Trackless.

"Tell me what you would do differently," he ordered.

Gulping past his discomfort and trying to fix his eyes on just the single large sheet of paper, Wynn approached the table and peered at the schematic, wondering how quickly the man expected an answer. Before he could ask, Daegan waved a hand.

"Take your time. Make notes if you like. I have other things to work on." He turned to another table and shuffled through a stack of papers.

Wynn's eyes flicked over the room, the nausea returning. He wanted to race away or throw up. He wanted to bang his head against the table. How could he impress the artificineer if he were stuck working in this horrible, overwhelming island of disarray? "May I... what I mean is..."

Daegan did not turn to him. "What is it?" he snapped.

Wynn squeezed his eyes tightly shut. The darkness helped a little, though he was still painfully aware of the surrounding disorganization. "I was just wondering if we are to share this workroom?"

"What's that?"

"I..." Wynn peeked out through nearly closed eyelids and gestured helplessly at the small, cluttered space. He could feel the walls closing in on him. Even in his tiny shed, he had always maintained a meticulous level of order. If he had to remain working in this space, he knew it would kill him in a day or two.

Daegan frowned at him over the top of his spectacles. "What?"

"May I take these and study them somewhere else?" Wynn asked, desperation making his voice rise in pitch and volume. "I don't want to be in your way."

"Oh." Daegan blinked. "Of course. Didn't Keene show you your workroom?"

"Uh... I have a workroom?"

Daegan shook his head. "I'll bet he showed you every inch of the forge already, though. Confound the man. Of course I don't want you constantly underfoot in here. Can't have you messing up my work space or rearranging my things. I'm very particular about my organization. Molly is the only one who seems to understand what I mean when I tell her there's a place for everything and everything should remain in its place. Come along, I'll show you."

Daegan darted through the door and down the hall, counting under his breath until he reached "three." He pushed open a door. "Here you go. This is your workroom. If there's anything you need, let Molly know. She'll get it for you. Or if you run out of anything. She should be back... soon? I'm not sure. She'll be back. And now, I'll leave you to it." The older man left, and Wynn stared around the room in a daze.

"Who's Molly?" he whispered, but he couldn't find the energy to be upset by Daegan's abrupt departure, because the room before him had captured his entire attention. What a room it was! He stared in awe. It was fully three times the size of his shed back home. The wall opposite the door held a tall piece of furniture, like a bookshelf, but with its shelves subdivided into small, neatly organized cubbyholes that contained all the tools he would need for his designs. The wall to his left held a long desk with a chair that sat on small wheels to allow him freedom of movement while remaining seated. On his right, the shorter wall held a unique style of desk, one he had never seen before. It had a large surface, but it rested at an angle and his quick eyes immediately identified curious mechanisms for raising, lowering, and changing the angle at which it rested; a tall stool accompanied this desk. In the middle of the room stood an island with long, thin drawers, perfect for storing schematics.

For the first time since Lord Adelfried had given him his

assignment, blissful exhilaration filled Wynn's heart and mind. All thoughts of Grayden and Beren off in Ondoura tracking down a murderer fled from him, along with any envy at the excitement of their assignment or the loneliness that had plagued him in the past few days. This space looked as if it had stepped straight out of his daydreams.

He strode into the room and unrolled the schematic on the island, finding a stack of paper weights on one shelf, exactly where he would have chosen to store them. He spread a few things out on the long table and perused the designs for the Trackless.

Wynn took his time. He studied the drawing, read the notes, jotted down a few of his own, and even grabbed a new sheet of paper and began sketching his own designs. Carefully, he placed a small square of paper under his hand so that his left-handed writing wouldn't smudge his work. The labor consumed him, pulling him in as it always did. It had been the same at home with every project he began—once he got started, he could not stop until he had completed the task. Often, he had heard his mother complaining to his father about it.

"If he doesn't come out of his room soon, he'll starve to death," he had overheard her say once, just after he had finished building the model train he had been working on for five days straight. She had been exaggerating, of course; he had left his room multiple times during that sennight, but hearing her words had alerted him to the truth his stomach had been complaining about: while he had taken short breaks for water, he had eaten nothing in days. This realization had alarmed him. He had not realized just how engrossed he had become in his project.

Another time, he had finished a project he had been working on in the shed and come into the house to find his mother sitting at the kitchen table, head in her hands, sobbing. It had scared him to see that, and he had wondered what horrible thing had happened. His first concern had been that someone had been injured, but she had assured him that everyone was fine. She gave him a hug and then got up and bustled around the kitchen, preparing his favorite meal. When he asked his father about it later that night, he had said it was nothing to worry about, it was just his mother's way of fretting about him.

"It's just you can get so wrapped up in your projects that we don't see you for days, son," his father had said. "Grayden came by a few times, but even he couldn't seem to get through to you. Your mother worries, that's all."

Wynn had nodded and kept to himself that he had no memory of his best friend stopping by even once. After that, he had done his best to be more conscientious, to wrench himself away from his projects and studies more often and be more of a help to his mother, though both his parents had continued to encourage him to study for the Academy entrance exams. If it hadn't been for Grayden, he probably wouldn't have had any friends, or spent any time just having fun. The puzzle of mechanical things fascinated and consumed him, and he always found more questions to ask, more ideas to try. The never-ending aspect of building things inspired his imagination. Machines made sense. They were precise and everything fit together. If something broke, he could fix it. People were harder, and often they did not seem worth the effort, but he had tried, for his mother's sake. And a part of him, a tiny, quiet part, sometimes echoed his mother's fears.

He got so caught up in his thoughts and the work that he lost all track of time. When he felt a gentle touch on his shoulder, he jumped and gave a short cry of surprise.

"Easy there." Daegan held up his hands. The older man's eyes were twinkling. "That must be what it's like for my colleagues to interrupt me. It can take them a few tries to get through, too. Keene just stopped by and said it's time for supper."

Wynn blinked and rubbed at his eyes. "Already?"

Even as the word left his mouth, he suddenly noticed the gnawing ache in the pit of his stomach. He had been ignoring it, so focused on the task before him, but now his stomach rumbled angrily, reminding him that it had needs. His hands trembled with hunger and trepidation. At the Academy, there had been a schedule and plenty of people to keep him from losing himself in his work. And Grayden had been there. Always, Grayden had been able to pull him away from work, had made sure he spent time outside of his workshop, had helped him... function. But here in this place of craft and creation, there was little to anchor him in the same way. His mother's fears reared up inside of him and he wondered what would happen to him if a day came when everyone stopped trying to pull him away from his work. A terrifying image of his own skeleton hunched over a table flashed through his mind and his pen fell from his suddenly nerveless hand and clattered onto the floor.

"Lad?" Daegan peered at him. "Are you well? You just went rather pale."

Wynn shook his head. "I'm fine." He crouched down and searched on the floor for the dropped pen, but Daegan pulled at his arm.

"Plenty of time to find that later. Come on, Keene hates waiting." He nodded at the door. "Time enough to show me what you've come up with after supper."

Dalmir faced the large entrance to the mine and glanced sideways at his companions, trying to gauge their moods. Drengur was an easy read. The boy was eager and alert, viewing this as a grand adventure, and clearly excited to be spending time with Ioan. The defender, by contrast, held himself upright and aloof, his face betraying no emotion. Ioan had spoken little on the short journey to the mine, but Dalmir knew that his heart yearned to be home in Ondoura, helping with the investigation.

"Thorben said the mines can be dangerous," Dalmir said. "Dangerous, how?"

Ioan tugged self-consciously at his sleeves. "In the normal ways. The Ember Mine is unique, but there's nothing inherently dangerous about it that is not true of any mine. Cave-ins and foul air are always possibilities, of course, but the Ember Mine is well-fortified."

"The ore it produces is valuable," Drengur piped up. "So we put more care into maintaining the various shafts. In that way, it is perhaps the most stable and safest mine you could have asked to access. The special qualities of the ore make folks superstitious, but that's all it is."

"The ore itself isn't volatile?" Dalmir asked.

"No," Ioan assured him.

Dalmir allowed himself a tiny smile. "Then why do you seem so apprehensive?"

Ioan gave a low chuckle. "And here I thought I was concealing it so well. Rest easy. It has little to do with the Ember Mine specifically or our purpose here. I have never liked the dark, or enclosed spaces, ever since I was young. Since the madman in the mountains"—Ioan grimaced and scratched irritably at one of his arms—"that dislike has grown more intense. I am uneasy about going down into the darkness. I would prefer to stay aboveground."

Drengur glanced up at Ioan, a pensive line marring the smoothness of his forehead. "What happened in the valley?" Drengur asked. "I mean, I heard the story when you were telling Mother, but... it was like hearing a history lesson. What really happened to you?"

Ioan gave a weary smile. "I will tell you all about it someday, Drengur. But now is not the time."

"Then shall we proceed?" Dalmir asked.

"Yes." With no more hesitation, Ioan strode into the mine, the oil lantern held out in front of him, a tiny glimmer of a beacon against the immense darkness of the cavern. Drengur trotted along next to him, a silent shadow of exuberance.

Dalmir followed, not too close, his eyes taking in every nook and cranny they passed, his senses alert for the slightest sign of the object he sought. He hoped the orb was within these tunnels. When Thorben had told him of the Ember Mine, Dalmir had felt certain that this must be where it rested. But now that he was actually here, doubts crept in. There was no reason the orb should be responsible for the strange ore that came from within this mountain. In fact, if the orb lay dormant, then it should not be doing anything at all, and all his hopes were in vain. The only reason he had suspected its presence was because of how his own orb had reacted to Grayden's presence. He wondered again at the phenomenon and wished he had made more time to experiment, though that was not his strength.

Experimentation had always been the purview of Palte and Avaleun. The answers to his questions seemed to mock him, dancing just outside the range of his vision. He ached to solve this mystery, to come up with a way to defeat Uun, but the solution—if it existed at all—continued to elude him. And now, descending into the darkness of the mine, he wondered if mere foolishness had prompted him to come here. He hated to admit it, but there was a strong chance that this entire endeavor was a waste of precious time.

I could ask... The thought sprang unbidden to his mind, but Dalmir shut it out with an angry shake of his head. *No! That door closed to me hundreds of years ago. She abandoned me along with the Builder.*

Doubts and flurries of emotion he had long pressed down threatened to spill into his thoughts, but he shook them away and hastened his steps to catch up with Ioan, as if he could outrun his own traitorous thoughts. They continued to make their way down the cleared path, deeper, ever deeper into the mountain. They did not talk, each wrapped in his own thoughts, each content to remain silent, each glad for the presence of the other, but needing nothing in the way of conversation. Even Drengur, young as he was, remained silent.

Hours passed. The little flame within the oil lantern held steady, casting its glow faithfully. The shadows within Dalmir's heart grew longer and blacker.

Ask.

The suggestion whispered through Dalmir's thoughts with such clarity that he came to an abrupt halt, looking around for the source of the voice. He took a long moment to turn in a full circle, his eyes peering through the gloom, searching for the speaker. But there was no one. There never had been anyone. A strange, tingling pressure built up behind his eyes and Dalmir squeezed his fingers over the bridge of his nose, desperate to push away the sudden fear that gripped him. With a shudder, he roused himself into a jog to catch up with his guide. However, he did not have far to go, for Ioan had stopped and now held the lantern up to the wall of the tunnel.

"Here. Drengur thought you would like to see it: ember, the ore that braids its way through this mountain. We're still near the surface, so this is a nearly depleted trace, but you can see the thin vein that was left behind."

Interested, Dalmir leaned closer to the wall and gently brushed his finger over the strangely glittering intertwined black and silver lines lacing their way through the rock. He peered at it, and a pulse of energy flooded him, like the memory of a half-forgotten dream rearing its head. It was a sensation akin to the stirring of something long-forgotten, but no awareness or knowledge accompanied the burst. He jerked his hand away as if stung. *Oronite!*

"What is it?" Drengur asked, his voice excited. "Can you feel the orb?"

Dalmir shook his head and he let his hand fall to his side. "No," he replied. "But what you call ember used to be known by a different name. Oronite."

Drengur gave him a lopsided grin. "I know. That's the fancy name for it."

Dalmir eyed the young man with newfound respect. "The orbs are made of oronite," he said. "But they don't cause its occurrence." Now that he knew what the ore was, Dalmir was tempted to turn back, try something else. But something tugged at him, compelling him onward. "Let's keep going. At least, for a while." He ran a hand over the cave wall, feeling dejected. For the first time, the enormity of what he had set out to do overwhelmed him. Finding the orb inside a mountain was a task that could take a lifetime, and even then, it was only possible if the orb actually resided within this particular mountain. Why had the orbs not remained where he had placed them? How had they traveled so far? Even as the questions troubled him, he told himself he knew the answer. Centuries had passed, and he had neglected his post, shirked his duties. It was only fitting that he now reap the punishment he deserved for ignoring his responsibility for so long.

"Do you have any ability to sense this orb we are seeking?" Ioan asked as they continued deeper into the mine. Drengur raised his eyebrows hopefully.

"Unfortunately, no," Dalmir replied.

"Then..." Ioan stopped.

"I don't know." Misery swelled within him. "The orbs are important. I know that now, but I do not understand it. I feel like I am in a race, but I don't even know if I am following the correct course. And yet there is something here, tugging at me. It is worth investigating further, though I fear we are wasting time."

"Well, we can go a little farther before we set up camp for the night," Ioan said.

Dalmir nodded, and they set out again.

———

AFTER A NIGHT SPENT SLEEPING on the hard ground, Dalmir welcomed the chance to get up and move, even if it meant venturing deeper into the oppressive, endless darkness of the mine.

Dalmir trudged along, his steps echoing grim repetitiveness with every footfall. Drengur had opened up a stream of conversation when they awoke, but he had run out of things to say a while ago, and Ioan, grim-faced Ioan, seemed content to march on in utter silence. The tall captain was building a wall around his heart. Dalmir could sense it, but he had no way of reaching out to halt his progress on the construction. He knew in the marrow of his bones that he ought to reach out, say something to bridge the distance Ioan was putting between himself and everyone around him, but he did not know what to say. In truth, Dalmir felt wholly unqualified to reach out to the man. It had been centuries since he had interacted with people, and he felt he had lost the knack for it. Grayden and his friends had piqued his curiosity, restored him to a semblance of a life he had thought lost to him forever, but it was still new, still fresh. He was not sure he was ready to be a balm to someone else's soul. He had spent centuries building his own walls. And yet it was clear that Ioan was in a unique kind of agony. He had brushed off all attempts by Drengur to engage him in conversation, and now the younger boy lagged behind, his face downcast. Dalmir studied Beren's younger brother. The resemblance was undeniable, though Drengur was shorter than his older brother, standing at a normal height for most Telsumans. It was obvious that he looked up to Ioan, and the defender's coldness had cut him deeply. Dalmir sighed.

"Ioan," he began, searching for the words he needed. Then he stopped. "Do you hear that?"

Ioan paused, head tilted to one side. "Hear what?"

"It sounds like water running."

"That's the river," Drengur offered, perking up a little.

"River?" Dalmir asked. "But surely we are far belowground at this point."

Drengur nodded eagerly. "We are. But so is the river. It's an underground river, I mean. We discovered it when we dug the mine. Well, I mean the miners did. I wasn't there, of course. The mine is older than I am." Drengur flushed and turned his face away from the halo of gold cast by the lantern.

"An underground river," Dalmir mused. "Let's head in that direction. I have an idea..."

"What is it?" Ioan asked.

"It may be nothing." Dalmir shook his head. "I have been wondering how the orbs traveled so far from where I placed them in the Whispering Wood. An underground river might answer that question. If an animal knocked an orb loose or carried it away and then dropped it in a river or even a lake that connects to this waterway, then it is conceivable it could have ended up here."

"That would take an incredibly long time." Ioan peered at Dalmir, curiosity chasing the haunted look from his eyes.

"Centuries," Dalmir agreed.

"I know you told my parents you were thousands of years old," Drengur said, his voice small. "But I thought you just meant... I mean..." He paused and then tried again. "Isn't that... kind of impossible?"

Dalmir rubbed his chin. It still felt strange to him to be clean-shaven. The cool air of the mine felt cold to his unprotected face. "Nothing is impossible," he said. "Especially for the Builder."

Drengur frowned, his expression full of disbelief. "Well, but even if you are that old, rivers don't flow uphill. How could a river carry something all the way here from the Whispering Wood?"

Dalmir shrugged. "I don't know. But it's worth investigating, all the same. Lead the way to this underground river. I have a feeling that we will need to follow it in order to find the object I seek."

———

THE MINE DESCENDED into the depths of the mountain, following the sound of the water. Dalmir knew the tunnels could not get darker. His mind knew that there was no such thing beyond "pitch black," but as they continued farther and farther away from the entrance, his mind continued to insist that it was growing darker and darker. They had been traveling for a few days now, though he had no idea how to tell exactly how long they had been underground. They had slept four times, their bodies demanding rest at what Dalmir assumed were regular intervals, but days and nights and time itself were all things that had vanished with the sunlight. Ioan grew grimmer and more silent the farther they went. His posture grew rigid, and his discomfort at being underground radiated from him louder than words.

The mine shaft grew narrower as they progressed. They had reached the end of the large tunnels shortly after hearing the river, and were now venturing into territory that was less-traversed. The sound of running water grew constantly louder, and Ioan believed they would reach the underground river today. He had not asked the question on everyone's minds: what would happen when they made it to the river? Drengur did not know as much about this part of the mine; these tunnels were newer. They had reached the end of what was on the maps he had studied a few hours after waking this morning, if it was morning. What if the tunnel just ended? What would they do then? Perhaps the orb was not even in this mine. Had they come all this way for nothing?

Dalmir kicked a pebble with the toe of his boot and sent it skittering away. It clattered across the ground, rolling down the path and ending in a small splash. The three travelers looked at one another and then raced forward. A moment later, they reached the edge of what they sought, the underground river. The lantern light glinted off the dark water, the liquid rippling slowly and giggling quietly to itself as it wended its way through a minuscule rapid and over a tiny waterfall.

Ioan lifted his lantern, and they peered across the river. The water flowed out of a narrow cleft in the rocks on their left and traveled across their path and on, through a much larger tunnel on their right. Across the river, the tunnel they were following continued to narrow, the chisel marks on the walls growing rougher and more jagged.

Drengur dipped a toe into the stream. "It's not deep, just a few inches," he said. "What should we do?"

"If you believe this stream may have carried the orb here, then perhaps we should follow the water," Ioan suggested. "From the looks of those markings, if we continue forward, we're eventually going to run into a solid wall of stone."

Dalmir stared at the water. He did not like the idea of leaving the known path and burrowing into the mountain like a small rodent, but he knew it to be the most logical course of action. They would not find the orb by sticking to the well-worn tunnels. It was a unique enough gem that if it had been in the path of the miners, they would have taken it. It was far more likely that the orb lay farther down the stream, resting along its banks where the water had flung it, or perhaps even still rolling along the bottom of the streambed.

With a heavy sigh, Dalmir faced the natural tunnel. "I believe we need to follow the stream."

"That makes the most sense," Ioan agreed.

Drengur nodded, eagerness dancing across his features as he sloshed through the water without complaint. Dalmir and Ioan shared a concerned glance.

"Ah, to have the exuberance of youth once again," Dalmir said, his lips twitching slightly. Drengur's enthusiasm was contagious, and he could not help but feel his spirits lift, knowing that at least one of his companions was eager to see this mission through.

"Words of truth," Ioan said drily.

"I know you would rather be stationed at an outpost or instructing at the Academy or seeking your grandmother's murderer," Dalmir said, hesitating another moment before plunging after Drengur, "but I am grateful to have you here."

Ioan's eyes squinted at the corners. "Actually, as much as I dislike being underground, and the darkness, I am happy to be here."

"Oh?"

Ioan fingered the newly pointed tip of one ear, his expression growing awkward. "There are a lot of things I need to adjust to," he said after another pause. "I've always known exactly who I am, what I was going to be, where I fit into the grand scheme of things. But now I find myself suddenly adrift. My grandmother is gone. I have been altered, changed into something I don't recognize. I don't even know if I am truly human anymore. And even in the few interactions I've had since we encountered the madman, I have seen the cautious looks cast my way and the lack of trust in the eyes of men who once would have accepted orders from me without question. No, do not thank me, Master Dalmir. It is I who should thank you. This assignment has given me time to figure out who I am, and if I am still the person I've always been. The time and the space to think, to be away from people, and to come to a better understanding of how everything in my world has changed in the past few sennights... it is more than I expected, and I am grateful. I don't know exactly what Lorcan did to me. I'm a little afraid to explore my new strength and agility, afraid that other changes might suddenly arise. I... I don't want to end up like one of his 'generals.'"

Dalmir nodded. He wanted to speak words of comfort, to tell Ioan that the great trials he had endured were for some greater purpose, but the words turned to ash on his tongue. Though he had once believed such things to be absolute truth, he had long since learned to doubt. How could he offer comfort and hope when he kept none for himself? As a man who had been drowning for far too long, there were no words of comfort that he could offer to another man adrift. Instead, he turned away, wordlessly, and hastened his step to follow the splashing footfalls of Drengur. A moment later, he heard more splashing behind him, and knew that Ioan was following. His conscience pained him, but he ignored it. No, he had no comfort to offer.

7

———

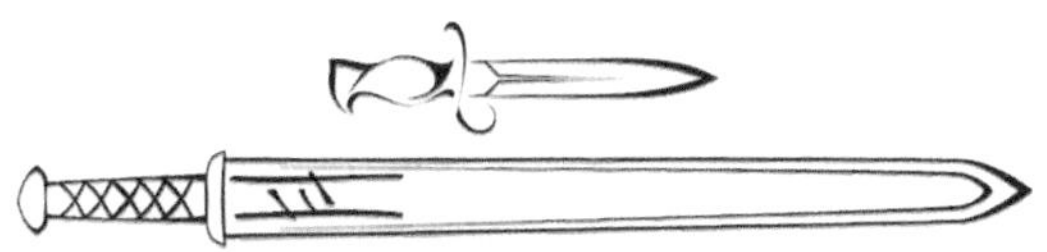

After a night spent tossing and turning and trying to get comfortable in unfamiliar beds, Grayden and Beren descended from their rooms to a lavish breakfast. Beren had spent hours trying to fit his large frame onto the too-small bed in his room before giving up and spending the night on the floor in a nest of blankets. The humid warmth hadn't helped, either. The aromas of breakfast felt like a personal attack meant to appease him for the miserable night. He refused to be soothed. He reminded himself that he was here for a singular purpose: to bring his adopted aunt's murderer to justice.

Niveya already reclined next to the table. Robed in a brightly colorful silk dressing gown, he held a mug of steaming coffee in one hand and a stack of papers in the other. He lifted the mug in a gesture of greeting to the two men as they joined him. Beren found it took effort not to glare at the man who had abducted him nearly a year ago.

"Good morning," Niveya called. "Please, have breakfast while I finish up my business, and then I will tell you what I have learned. I hope we can get information today that will aid in our investigation."

Beren's lip curled in disdain, but then his traitorous

stomach rumbled; with a reluctant sigh, he lowered himself onto a colorful cushion and served himself up a biscuit, spearing a stack of smoked sausage with his fork. Starving himself would gain nothing. Grayden joined him, staring at the table in disbelief: there were breakfast pies filled with meat, biscuits, a thick white gravy heavily laden with crumbled bits of sausage, latticed pastries filled with spinach and a sharp-smelling cheese, along with several platters of fruit. As Beren heaped food on his plate, a woman entered with a platter holding two more steaming mugs of thick, dark coffee, a cup brimming with large cubes of sugar, and a small pitcher of sweet cream. She lowered it to the table, then shot a questioning glance at Niveya. He waved the papers in a gesture of dismissal and the woman curtsied, then backed out of the room. Beren watched her go, wondering why she looked familiar. He thought for a moment, but could not place her, so he turned back to his plate. Grayden had emptied half the sugar bowl into his mug and was now filling it with cream; the liquid rose to the brim, almost overflowing. He took a tentative sip, nose wrinkling slightly.

Beren watched him in amusement. "I take it you don't like coffee much."

Grayden's cheeks reddened. "My Da drinks it, but Ma and I prefer tea or spiced cider."

Niveya turned the page of whatever he was looking at. "I will make a note for Vidia," he said, without glancing up. "Tomorrow, you will have tea. Any particular flavor you prefer?"

Grayden hesitated, glancing at Beren, with an apprehensive gaze. "Oh, anything would be fine," he replied.

Niveya put the papers down and stared across the table at Grayden. "Come, come, lad. Don't be shy," he remonstrated. "We are in Doran, the city of a thousand flavors. Surely you have a preference. It is the simplest thing in the world to accommodate your tastes. Please, let me be an excellent host to you."

Indecision washed across Grayden's features, but then he gave a small shrug. "Anything fruit flavored, citrus would be best, but I don't mind trying new things."

Niveya beamed. "There, that wasn't so hard, was it? I will instruct Vidia to gather a variety of teas from the market for tomorrow."

Beren glanced at the door through which Vidia had exited, a puzzled frown pulling his eyebrows together. Niveya's gaze sharpened on him.

"You may have seen her before," he supplied, "during the brief time you spent as my guest."

Beren nodded, his thoughts distracted. Something about the woman's familiar face bothered him.

Niveya continued to study him. "But you would probably be more familiar with Vidia's daughter. I believe you spent some time in her company aboard the *Valdeun Hawk*."

At his words, Beren felt a shock course through him. Of course! Shaesta. The woman who had betrayed her captain and helped kidnap him and Wynn, delivering them to Niveya. He remembered the brown-skinned woman and her curly brown hair tinged with gold. She whirled through his memories on the deck of the airship amidst the chaos, twin sabers in her hands, long skirts swishing as she fought, her movements more like that of a dancer than a fighter. He remembered sparkling warm brown eyes filled with a teasing light and golden hoops hanging from her ears.

"That's Shaesta's mother?" Grayden asked, pulling Beren from his thoughts. He gave Beren an odd look. "You remember Shaesta, right?"

"Of course." Beren shook his head. "Unpleasant memories."

"Didn't that pirate capture her when we rescued you?" Grayden asked, staring hard at Beren.

Beren frowned, trying to figure out why Grayden was giving him such an intense look. His thoughts felt sluggish. "I think so," he replied slowly. Then he blinked, finally understanding what his friend was trying to do. Shaesta's return to the *Hawk* had been voluntary, but they had hoped to keep Niveya from realizing that.

Well, it was too late to recant his incertitude, which meant he'd have to try a different tack. "You know, that entire couple of days is a bit of a blur, still. I never really got the entire story."

Niveya gave a dismissive snort. "The Torrezi family has served mine well for over five generations, a faithfulness for which I have compensated them richly. I am glad to hear that Shaesta did not leave my service of her own will, though I do hope she is well. I feared she had chosen a new loyalty. It saddens me to think that such a beautiful ray of sunshine might be locked up in a pirate's brig, but you have given me hope she will return to us someday. I know her parents miss her and worry about her terribly."

Beren nodded earnestly, keeping his eyes on the dark liquid in his cup. "Kidnapping is a terrible thing for a parent to endure. There is no worse punishment."

Niveya's expression glinted with a sardonic smirk. "Words of truth." He lifted his cup as though making a toast, then returned to perusing his papers. As Beren finished the last bites of his breakfast, Niveya shuffled his papers together, laid them neatly on the table, and rose. "If you are both ready?"

"Are you going to tell us where we are going?" Beren asked, trying to keep the note of challenge out of his voice. "Or the name of this cousin you discovered?"

"Yes," Niveya replied. "The cousin's name is Matei, and he lives just outside the city in the Khosha district. He owns a sizable farm, and mostly keeps to himself. Supposedly, Ulia's family was not keen on her leaving the farm to work in the city, even in such a prestigious job as the one she secured at the manor. I think it sounds perfect."

"Perfect for what?" Beren grumbled.

"Perfect for hiding out." Niveya took a last sip from his mug.

"But if she's estranged from her family..." Grayden trailed off.

"Then it stands to reason she would feel safe returning to the family farm. It's no secret that she hasn't been welcome there in years, so it's the last place anyone will look for her. Our young maid is intelligent enough to know that she saw something that might put her in danger, therefore I believe she has the wits to come to such a conclusion."

"If you say so," Beren said, standing. "Let's be off."

"And if she isn't there?" Grayden asked.

"Let us hope Matei can give us an idea of where she might have gone," Niveya replied.

"And if he can't?" Grayden asked.

Niveya let out a long-suffering sigh. "We won't know until we talk to him. I suggest you gather what things you wish to take along and meet me out back in a few moments."

"What will we do if this leads nowhere?" Beren asked, narrowing his eyes and staring hard at Niveya. "You are pinning a lot of hopes on this one hunch."

"A lot, perhaps, but not all." Ericole's voice was mild. "I have a few other ideas. And we can always work our way around to questioning the staff and anyone Ulia might have worked with closely. But those conversations are more dangerous and would alert certain authorities to the fact that we are poking around; if we can find out what we need to know by following this thread, then I would prefer to try that first. I am eager to catch Roshana's killer, but I am just as eager to remain in good health myself." His teeth flashed in a brilliant grin, and then he strode through a door, disappearing with a silken swirl of his dressing gown, leaving Beren and Grayden alone.

"Is there anything you need to get from your room?" Beren asked.

Grayden shook his head. "I brought my weapon down with me," he replied, patting his side where Beren knew his friend kept his dagger sheathed.

Not for the first time, Beren wondered why his friend preferred to go about armed only with a dagger. It made him uncomfortable, knowing that the man he may be fighting side by side with did not have a proper weapon. "No sword?" he asked.

Grayden shrugged. "If you think I'll need one, I can go grab it."

Beren frowned at him. He did not want to ask his friend to get his sword. That might convey a lack of trust, or a fear he did not feel. And yet... "I always feel safer with my sword," he hinted.

Grayden gave him a smile and a nod. "It's your best weapon."

Beren tried again. "I would like to know that as many swords as possible are there to defend us, should we need them."

"Do you want me to bring my sword?" Grayden asked.

Beren threw his hands in the air. "What do you have against swords?"

"Nothing." Grayden's expression turned perplexed.

"Then why don't you bring one?" Beren roared, his frustration getting the better of him.

"I will if you want me to," Grayden replied, his tone mild. "I just don't think I'll need it."

"Never mind," Beren muttered. "Come on, let's go find this carriage and wait for Niveya."

"Why're you so mad?" Grayden asked, matching his stride to Beren's.

Beren glanced sideways at him. He had a hard time reading Grayden. His expression seemed honestly confused, but he had also seen Grayden pull several intricate pranks on fellow classmates, and then act completely innocent. Nobody had ever suspected that the quiet, studious Grayden was the mastermind behind so many of the various tricks that had been played in their year at the Academy.

"I'm not mad," Beren sighed, deciding to drop it. Grayden could take care of himself with a dagger better than most men with an arsenal of weapons to choose from.

They reached the back door and found the carriage waiting for them. Niveya was not there yet, so they stood by the doorway and waited. Silence stretched between them. Beren leaned against the side of the building and crossed his arms. The sun's rays shone down on the alley, warming him pleasantly, though the morning air was still cool. He closed his eyes and let his irritation slide away.

"I lost my sword," Grayden said, his voice serious.

Beren cracked an eye open, but said nothing.

"During the battle on the *Valdeun Hawk*," Grayden continued. "I thought I was going to die." He stopped, then crouched down and picked up a small rock. He held it in his hand, studying it as though it were a precious gemstone. "I couldn't defend myself. I had nothing but my hands and my dagger, and I didn't know how to use either properly. The only weapon I had ever trained with was my sword, and it fell over the side of the airship before I had time to use it. I never want to have to depend on any particular weapon again. I never want to be that vulnerable."

Beren mulled over his friend's words. They made many things suddenly click into place that he had not understood before. "That's why you always let your opponent choose the weapon when we sparred at the Academy?"

Grayden nodded.

"Makes sense." The last of his irritation faded and Beren closed his eyes again and leaned his head back against the building.

The silence that fell on them now was calm, companionable. A moment later, Niveya emerged from the building. He now wore a common tunic and trousers, with a long, dark coat over it all. He climbed into the carriage and they followed him. Once the door closed, Niveya called to the driver, "Khosha, please!"

The driver snapped the reins, and the horses set out at a brisk walk, the carriage wheels rumbling over the cobblestones of the streets of Doran. Beren settled back into his seat, relaxing as much as he could. Niveya talked about how they should approach Ulia if they found her, and that they should be careful not to frighten her. He insisted he do most of the talking, having dealt with circumstances like these before.

"I'm sure you have," Beren replied dryly, but Niveya ignored the insult.

However, as they drove down the streets of the city toward the north gate, Niveya fell silent. His forehead creased into a perpetual frown, and his eyes were dark with an emotion Beren could not identify. As Beren watched, the man seemed to age as he turned inward. He realized with a start that Niveya was actually worried, that he really wanted to find Roshana's killer. Whether justice or vengeance was his top priority, Beren could not say; he honestly could not say which was higher on his own list. But he suddenly found that he was glad to have Ericole Niveya working with them on this search. He did not trust the man, not as far as he could swing an axe, but he realized that against his better judgment, he believed Niveya meant what he said when he spoke of his esteem for the former Regeont and his desire to solve her murder. And as long as they were working towards that common goal, they were on the same side, whatever their history held.

8

Wynn soon settled into the steady rhythm of life in the great forge. Although Keene and Daegan were complete opposites in the way they approached their work, Wynn enjoyed his time in the company of both men. Daegan's haphazardly cluttered workroom masked a brilliantly organized mind from which no details escaped unexamined. Although the man often frustrated Wynn, since Daegan constantly jumped ahead in whatever conversation they were having, or often became wholly distracted by any thought that suddenly occurred to him, Wynn was slowly learning that Daegan meant no offense by it. When he jumped away to some new idea that Wynn had sparked with an innocuous word or phrase, the man did not mean to insinuate that what Wynn had to say was unimportant. He just could not quiet his constantly churning brain. Daegan also seemed to have no idea how to handle people in general, unless they simply said exactly what they meant. This suited Wynn just fine, as it meant he did not have to worry about offending the man with a lack of social niceties, which was a relief, as Wynn also often floundered when interacting with people. Grayden had always been there to help him navigate those treacherous waters. Grayden with his inexplicably innate understanding of how hopelessly lost Wynn often was around their friends and teachers and families.

Keene, on the other hand, took everything with a slow and steady approach. He listened intently when others spoke to him, making each person feel as though he were the only important person in the world. He also had Grayden's uncanny knack for discerning things left unsaid. As he had told Wynn earlier on, Keene had a hard time visualizing a finished concept, but as soon as he was handed a schematic, he could bring it into reality, no matter how difficult the process.

The forge room itself overwhelmed Wynn. The constant roar of the furnace, the clinking of Keene's hammer, the whooshing of the bellows were hard to tune out, but every sound had a purpose and a place, which made it easier to live with than the constant shouting and tumult of his younger siblings that had driven him out of the house to his shed. And he enjoyed learning from Keene and seeing their designs become reality.

One morning, Wynn woke to an unfamiliar sound. It was similar in tone to Keene's hammering, but more regular, and with a heavier thump at the end. He lay in bed for a moment, trying to place the sound. When he couldn't, he grew antsy. He squirmed beneath the covers, trying to figure out what to do and wondering how to get away from this strange intruder in his space. Finally, he realized he was still in bed, and that the sound was coming from elsewhere in the forge. He got up, splashed water on his face, and slowly dressed before heading toward the kitchen.

He found Conrad already there, slaving over a frying pan.

"Can I help?" Wynn asked, painting an earnest smile on his face.

"I'm almost done," Conrad replied. "Go ahead and sit down. You're up early."

"The strange pounding woke me."

"Strange pounding?" Conrad frowned. "Ah, the tilt hammer. Don't worry, you'll get used to it in a few days."

"The what?" Wynn asked, trying not to panic at Conrad's

comment about a "few days." He often heard the sounds of the forge from his workroom, but they were soft enough to tune out. This sound, however, was weightier. He had no idea how he could ever ignore it.

"Tilt hammer," Conrad repeated. "It's one of Daegan's gifts to Master Keene. It's this huge hammer powered by a water wheel. There's an underground river running under the mountains, and it comes up near the surface just here. That's why they put the forge here in the first place."

"I didn't hear it before."

"It wasn't running before." Conrad grinned, spooning a ladleful of eggs onto a plate and passing them to Wynn. "It needed oiling, and a few of the pieces needed to be replaced. Got it up and running this morning again, and I know Master Keene and Daegan are pleased about that; it makes a lot of things easier. Ah, good morning, Molly, I didn't know you were back."

Wynn turned to see who Conrad was greeting. It was a young woman, approximately his age, with brownish-red hair that stuck out from her head in tightly wound curls. She had a light sprinkling of freckles over a deeply tanned nose that turned up just slightly.

"Good morning, Conrad," she said, wrinkling her small nose and inhaling deeply. "Is that breakfast I smell?"

"It is," Conrad replied. "How was your trip?"

"Uneventful." Molly settled herself into a chair, leaning it back on two legs and propping her feet on the table. "Who's the recruit?"

Wynn stuck his hand out. "Wynn Drexel."

Molly took his hand and shook it. Her grasp was firm. "Ah, Daegan's new aide. I'm Molly Stromdotter."

"Pleased to meet you." Wynn fell silent, not sure what else to say to this new presence. It seemed it would be a day of the earth moving beneath his feet.

"Ah, Molly, you're back." Daegan's voice rang out from the door. "Were you able to procure the parts I requested?"

Molly nodded, pulling her feet off the table so swiftly that her chair tumbled forward, its front legs colliding with the ground with a loud bang. Wynn shoved a forkful of ham into his mouth to hide his grin.

"I see you've met my new aide," Daegan continued, sitting down at the table. "He has some brilliant ideas."

"Really?" Molly eyed him.

"He's come up with a new sort of wheel for my design, and a name for it, as well."

"What's the name?" Molly asked.

Conrad set a plate in front of Daegan, who nodded at Wynn.

It took him a moment to realize that they meant for him to tell this girl what he had named Daegan's design. Embarrassed, Wynn cleared his throat. "Er... I've been calling it the Trackless."

"The Trackless?" Molly's brown eyes narrowed.

"Well, I was thinking about the trains. I mean, this will be powered like those were, but smaller, and with freedom to go anywhere, not limited to tracks and straight lines. It doesn't have normal wheels, they're kind of like tracks... but it's not bound to a specific set of tracks dictating where it can go..." He wasn't explaining this very well.

"That's funny," Molly said. "The Trackless. I like it."

"And it's a kind of joke, too, since the wheels are kind of like tracks." He kept talking, even though he'd already said that and she'd already figured out the joke. He tapped his fingers against his thigh under the table, using the distraction to help him close his mouth and stop talking.

Molly laughed. "This one has a sense of humor, Daegan. I think he's going to be good for you."

Daegan huffed, but Wynn thought he saw a glimmer of amusement hovering about the man's expression.

When they finished eating, Daegan nodded to Wynn and Molly. "Now that Molly's back, we can get to work. Wynn, your alterations to my design are excellent. And now, I have a confession to make. The schematics I gave you are actually old iterations of the Trackless. I am pleased to report that you figured out many of the solutions that took me lunats to fix. You're a quick study, Master Drexel. I think it's time you saw this beast we're designing. We've nearly completed the exterior, and I believe it is perfect. However, I could use your help on the engine."

"The engine?" Wynn asked. He supposed it should bother him that he had just spent several days doing busywork, but he was too excited and curious to dwell on the past.

"Yes. In order for the Trackless to work, we need to build an engine that will fit inside and give anyone riding in it the ability to move and maneuver."

A fluttering sensation spread up Wynn's arms and down through his chest, where it settled in the pit of his stomach. Here was a challenge unlike anything he had attempted before. He shoveled the last bite of breakfast into his mouth and practically leapt from his chair to scrub off his plate and set it to dry.

Daegan was still speaking. "I have an ancient train engine outside. We couldn't fit it through the door, so Keene had his apprentices put up a sort of tent over it. Of course, it's far too big for the Trackless, but it gives us a starting place."

"What about an airship engine?" Wynn asked.

"They are smaller," Daegan admitted. "But even the smallest one would never fit inside the Trackless. I have one out there with the train engine. I thought comparing the two might give us ideas on how to decrease the size even further."

"Sounds like a good place to start," Wynn said. "Let's go!"

Daegan smiled at Molly. "This one is enthusiastic. I like his energy."

"Energy is good," Molly replied, "so long as he also knows how to focus."

"I do not think a lack of focus is going to be a problem," Daegan said, a hint of laughter in his expression. "Too much focus, perhaps. But you already know how to deal with that, don't you?"

Molly rolled her eyes. "Not another one! I already worry

about you forgetting to do things like eat and sleep." She heaved a sigh and waved her fork mournfully at her half-finished meal. "It's a wonder anyone gets nourishment at all around here. But I am curious to see our new colleague's reaction to your little collection..." She pushed herself back from the table and joined Wynn as he crossed the room.

The train engine was massive. Wynn walked around it, marveling at its sheer size. Then he studied the airship core, shaking his head.

"No wonder they started with enormous trains that could only travel along tracks," Wynn said. "For such a huge device, it's quite simplistic. It couldn't handle anything more complicated than go and stop. I never realized that. I've heard stories of the trains my whole life. My father rode on them a few times before they were left to rust in favor of the airships. Because of his stories, they've always fascinated me, but I would never have guessed the engine could be so... small-minded."

"Every significant achievement has to start somewhere," Daegan barked. "This hulking monstrosity forged the path for the airship."

"But how?" Wynn frowned. "I know they both utilize the power of cynders, but aside from that, these designs are nothing alike. And I don't just mean that different men designed them. It's almost as if the man who designed the airship engine had never seen a train engine."

"Good eye." Daegan nodded to Molly. "Told you this one was sharp. I always believed that the airships were a sort of offspring of the trains, which is why I went to the trouble of digging up an engine from each of them and having them sent here. But when I started examining them more closely, I noticed the exact same thing. It is clear: the Igyeum did not take the train engine and make it smaller. They started with a completely new design. And that is what we must do, as well. But first, there is something else you must see."

Daegan strode off, leaving Wynn little choice but to follow

him back inside the forge. The older man led him to a workroom Wynn had not yet been inside and held the door open.

"This is another part of the hourly duties around here, and now that you are officially part of the team, you will take your shifts along with the rest of us."

Wynn peered into the room. It was mostly empty, but for neat piles of tall, octagonal-shaped stones stacked along one wall. In the center of the room, a strange device stood on a table. From it emanated the single source of light within the room, a pale blue liquid that poured from a spout-like divot in its side, trickling in a steady stream into the top of one of the shaped stones. As it poured, the stone took on a blueish glow at the bottom, which slowly rose up the sides, not unlike a cup being filled with water.

"Are those... Dalmir's cynders?" Wynn asked.

"They are," Daegan replied. "Dalmir's discovery in the abandoned refinery may go a long way to leveling the battlefield before us."

Wynn stepped closer to the device, treading softly, his eyes sweeping up and down as he studied it. "How does it work?"

Daegan shrugged. "I'm not certain. I don't like not understanding things, but whatever Dalmir used is very similar to the power behind the cynders the Igyeum uses. And whatever that power is, it is beyond our understanding. He placed a small orb in the refiner, and that was all it took to get it working. We can get about a thousand cynders out of each charge before we need his orb again."

"Ah." Wynn nodded.

"You are familiar with this orb of his, then?" Daegan gave him a penetrating stare.

"I don't understand it, if that's what you're asking. But I've seen Dalmir do spectacular things with it."

Daegan frowned, making a small harrumphing sound.

"Intriguing." Wynn circled the device, studying it. "The ability to create our own cynders... I know how long we've been trying to replicate them."

"Every hour, a new piece of cut ore needs to be placed under the refiner—it is very simple, I will have Conrad or Gunnar show you how the first time it is your turn—and the full cynder needs to be moved outside to a shed where we are storing the completed ones. We use that cart, there. Molly will work up a new schedule for us now that we're adding you to the rotation. Understand?"

Wynn nodded.

"Excellent. Now, come with me and I'll show you the initial designs I've begun drawing up for our Trackless Engine. I hope your fresh eyes and different perspective will shed some much-needed inspiration on the entire project. I feel like I've been beating my head against my desk on this one."

"Sometimes that's because you actually do," Molly interjected.

Daegan gave her a distracted smile. "Quite right, as usual." He turned to Wynn. "Molly has a unique way of looking at things, as well. I think the two of you will work well together."

9

They sloshed through the water for hours until their boots were soaked through. Dalmir's feet were cold and he could feel the skin on his toes folding in on itself. He ached from the wet and the walking, and he wanted nothing more than to find a dry place to stop and rest, but there was none.

"I'm getting too old for this," Dalmir muttered under his breath, but he did not complain loudly enough for either of his companions to hear. Instead, they persisted doggedly on, the water splashing with every step, the depth of the stream varying from swirling around their ankles to coming almost to their knees. Thankfully, the water was not too frigid, and the cold had more to do with their prolonged exposure to the wetness than to the temperature.

The going was not difficult. The rocky bottom of the stream was not slippery, and the sides of the cavern—though narrower than the tunnels they had followed into the mine—rose tall on either side, keeping the ceiling high enough above them so they could all walk without stooping. Ioan speculated the stream must have once been a much larger, faster river to have carved out such a path.

"Maybe the mining caused a dam somewhere upstream,"

Drengur suggested. The boy's enthusiasm had waned in the darkness and the wet, and now he just sounded exhausted.

Dalmir shuddered at the thought of such a dam snapping and the river sweeping down upon them and burying them beneath its waves. He hastened his steps, and noticed Ioan doing the same, possibly having had the same terrible thought. The sooner they could get out of the water, the better. But after another several hours of splashing through the shallows, the tunnel's ceiling above them sloped down. It was gradual at first, or perhaps they simply did not notice a sudden change in the darkness, lit as their party was by the glow of lantern light and focused as they were on the stream they were following and their aching legs. But eventually, it became impossible to ignore, as first Dalmir, and then Ioan, and finally even Drengur, were each forced to hunch down in order to keep going. Distressingly, the water was also getting deeper, now well above their knees.

"If the ceiling gets any lower, we are going to be forced to turn back," Ioan said, grimly voicing the bitter truth none of them were ready to admit. There had been no other options along the way, no side tunnels to follow, barely any dry ground at all since they had chosen to leave the tunnels and forge into the stream. To turn back would be to resign themselves to the knowledge that they had just wasted many hours, perhaps even an entire day, on this useless journey.

As his head brushed the ceiling, forcing him to hunch even lower, Dalmir was about to reply. Whether he would have advocated for going a bit farther or admitting defeat, even he wasn't quite sure, but either way, Drengur's sudden yelp interrupted him.

Dalmir turned to look in Drengur's direction just in time to see his head disappear underwater. The lantern, which he had been taking his turn holding, also went underwater, thrusting them instantly into complete darkness. "Drengur!" he shouted, thrusting his arms and torso into the river after the lad. But as his hands scrabbled under the water, they found nothing to catch hold of.

At his cry, Ioan leaped forward and dove after Drengur. Dalmir waited, counting heartbeats, debating what to do. If he used his power, it might alert Uun to his location, though the odds were that Uun would neither care nor be able to figure out exactly what Dalmir was doing here. But Dalmir preferred to keep his movements secret unless absolutely necessary. Just as he was deciding to act, a noisy splash and a gasp at his knees made him leap back.

"Dalmir?" Ioan's voice rang out in the narrow space.

"Yes? Did you find Drengur? Do you have him?"

"Drengur is fine. The water gets deep just here and Drengur wasn't expecting it. But it's a good thing, because it's the only way through. Follow me."

"The only way through?" Dalmir echoed.

"This wall isn't thick, and on the other side..." Ioan trailed off. "Come on."

"What's on the other side?" Dalmir found himself loath to continue much farther. He did not relish the idea of a complete dunking, especially if it turned out to be unnecessary.

Ioan remained silent for a moment. "You have to see it," he finally said.

Something in the tone of his voice convinced Dalmir, and he reluctantly followed the younger man. It only took a few steps to discover that the riverbed suddenly dropped away, and he just had time to take a deep breath before he plunged under, swimming forward until he could not hold his breath any longer. He surfaced on the other side, sputtering and treading water, his boots heavy and his cloak swirling about his neck, choking him and dragging him down. Dalmir cursed himself for a fool and wondered why he hadn't had the sense to remove the cloak before going for a swim. He flailed about, gasping for air and wondering what it would feel like to drown. Then, powerful arms wrapped around his stomach and Dalmir felt himself being lifted out of the water and up onto the shore. He crawled up onto the rocky ground that was blessedly dry, and knelt there, wiping the water from his eyes and coughing. He glanced to the side and saw Drengur waiting, as Ioan flopped onto the shore beside him.

"Thank you," Dalmir gasped. "Drengur, I thought we had lost you."

The boy grinned. "Takes more than a little swim to bother me."

Dalmir chuckled, then paused as he realized he could see his companions. "Where is the light coming from?"

"I'm not sure," Ioan replied.

Dalmir frowned and rose to his feet, peering about as he attempted to get his bearings. He could just see over the small incline before him and, as he took in the view, he froze, his blood turning to ice in his veins, his heart missing several crucial cues as it beat out the rhythm of his life.

The stream they had been following had widened into a vast underground lake. The narrow tunnel through which they had traveled was also gone, and the surrounding chamber was so immense that he could not see the limits of it. But it was neither the lake nor the room they had entered that held Dalmir transfixed. It was the tower.

Tel's tower.

It took Dalmir's breath away to see it once more. When it collapsed to the ground at his brother's death, he had believed he would never see it again.

It rose into the air like a shadowy monolith, soaring into the furthest reaches of the cavern, its summit disappearing into the darkness above. In the dim light and at this distance, it was impossible to discern any features of the tower, but Dalmir recognized it instantly.

"Tel's tower," he breathed, awe suffusing him. Tears pricked his eyes. "I thought it had been destroyed."

Ioan and Drengur stood next to him.

"You know what that is?" Ioan asked.

"I had no idea this was down here," Drengur breathed. "It must go up to the very top of the cliffs over Telos."

"That would make sense. It used to stand on top of those cliffs, out in the daylight, a pillar pointing to heaven." Dalmir barked a short laugh. "Tel always was more clever than he let on. Oh, Tel... how did you ever manage it?"

"Who's Tel?" Drengur asked.

"My older brother," Dalmir said. He stared at the massive structure. His chest constricted, making his breaths come in fast, shallow gasps. Sparks clouded his vision as an irresistible beacon flared within his mind. A gentle, yet insistent sensation tugged at him, compelling him to move closer to the tower. "We have to get inside."

"Inside that?" Ioan was aghast. "I don't even want to go near it."

Drengur's head bobbed up and down in furious agreement.

"Don't you see?" Dalmir looked wildly from Ioan to Drengur. "It must be Tel's orb. It came home. I don't know how, or why, but it came home. It's pulling at me. I am certain it is inside that tower." He knew he was babbling, making no sense to his companions, but it did not matter. He could sense in his bones that the orb he sought rested somewhere within the tower before them.

Ioan stared at him, hesitation plainly written across his face. "All right," he said. "But we've been walking for a long time today already, and that thing is so huge it could still be days away. We need to rest and get dry first. How about we make camp here and continue on after we sleep?"

Dalmir opened his mouth to argue, but stopped when Drengur let out a loud sneeze. Reluctantly he nodded. "In the morning, then."

10

Marik stared pensively over the side of the *Hawk*. Below swirled an endless sea of gray; above stretched a matching wash of silver mist. Even at high altitudes, the cloud cover was generally thick over Melar. Marik was thankful for it, as it helped hide his airship from those searching for them. But it also worked against him, muddling his thoughts, making it hard for him to concentrate. The surrounding air was thick with fog, and droplets of water covered everything, making it difficult to stay dry. Marik didn't mind the gloom, but he didn't like the way the clouds obstructed his vision and made it impossible to tell in which direction the horizon lay.

"Captain?" Oleck's gruff voice brought Marik back to the present.

"Yes, Oleck?"

Oleck just stared at him. Marik could read the struggle in the big man's face, the way his eyes were full of pleading and hope, but the set of his jaw trembled in a never-ending battle against despair. These same emotions roiled in Marik's own thoughts, tumbling against each other, desperate for reassurance, some glimmer of hope. A full sennight had passed since Raisa's capture, and it felt as though they had made little progress in even creating a plan to rescue her. The palace was a fortress, the dungeons unassailable. Every avenue they had tried so far had ended in failure. There was no way to bribe a guard or even get information from inside. For all they knew, Raisa had already been executed, and they would never know.

All this, Marik thought, but did not say. While any glimmer of hope remained, he would not give up.

So far, the only thing they had managed to do was maintain their own freedom. It had been several days since they had seen any airships patrolling the skies, searching for them. Marik took this as a good sign, a sign that the Ar'Mol believed them to have left his domain. Meanwhile, they lurked above, held aloft by their enormous supply of cynders, hiding in the mists and biding their time.

"Captain?" Mouse's voice piped through the fog.

"Yes?" he asked, grateful for any reason to delay a response to Oleck's pleading gaze.

"Well..." The boy hesitated. "It's not a very good one, but I might have an idea."

"About what?" Marik asked.

"About someone we could talk to."

Marik stared down at the earnest young face. He waited. Mouse would say his piece when he was ready.

"Someone who might be able to help us get Raisa back."

Marik clasped his hands behind his back. He stayed silent for a long time, letting the misty breeze wash across his face. Now both Oleck and Mouse stared at him, waiting, their gazes boring holes into his face. Marik ignored them. He knew how much it cost Mouse to speak now. "Do you think they would help us?" he asked at last.

Mouse stared at the decking of the ship. He stood steady and still. Most boys his age might scuff the toes of their shoes, or fidget under such intense scrutiny, but Mouse was no ordinary boy.

Mouse nodded slowly, firmly. "I think so, Captain. They

wouldn't like it that I told you about them, but they have no reason to love the Ar'Mol. And... we have nowhere else to go."

Marik gave a sharp nod. "You haven't told me much about the people you lived with before we met."

"No, sir."

"I trusted it was something you wanted to forget."

Mouse looked up swiftly, then looked away. "No, sir."

Surprise tingled in the back of Marik's throat. "No?"

"They were good to me. I didn't mean to lead you to believe they weren't. They just... they trusted me to keep their secret. So I did."

Marik considered. "Then why did you leave them?"

Mouse glanced up shyly. "Well..." Now he did scuff the toe of his boot gently against the decking. "I mean..." He cast his eyes about the ship and then looked up, his expression open.

Marik did not need to hear more. Mouse's face said it all. It was something he could understand only too well. The *Valdeun Hawk* held his heart, too, and the lure of the sky and the freedom of flight was plenty answer for him.

Oleck made a rumbling noise deep in his chest, and Mouse glanced at him.

"If anyone can help us, Oleck, they can. I'm sure they'll help us," the boy said.

"In my experience, people don't help strangers. And nobody helps anyone for nothing," Oleck muttered, his voice thick with despair.

Mouse scrunched his face up and gave Oleck a long, sideways stare. "Crew helps each other," he insisted. "We're crew, ain't we, Oleck?"

The big man scratched the side of his jaw. "I suppose," he admitted. "I've gotten rather fond of you, little rodent."

Mouse grinned. "Well, these people, they used to be my fa..." He glanced at Marik. "They were my crew before I met you. That's why I think they'll help. And maybe we can help them, too."

Marik gave a mirthless chuckle. "I can't argue with that. But I think it's time you tell me about this old crew of yours, Mouse."

———

THE *VALDEUN HAWK* settled down gently onto the glistening ocean like a mother bird returning to her nest to roost. They had chosen a quiet harbor out of sight of any villages. Leaving Oleck to guard the airship and keep her from drifting out to sea, Marik and Shaesta ventured ashore with Mouse, who led them confidently back toward the city of Melar.

"Are you sure this is a good idea?" Shaesta whispered to Marik. "I don't like that we're just walking openly into the city. Even if they believe we've left, this seems overly risky to me."

"Mouse knows what he's doing. He may be young, but he knows what's at stake. I trust him," Marik said.

The road stretched in front of them through brown and dusty land, rippling with small hills and valleys on either side. Melar was not like the desert of Palla, whose borders were north of where they now stood, but neither was it a gleaming emerald beacon of fertility like Vallei in the south. Just like its location, it was somewhere in between. On the horizon, the terraced city rested like a sleeping giant. The sun rose higher in the sky as they traveled until at last they drew near the city gates.

Small houses and farms sprouted up on either side of the road as they neared the entrance to the city, and Marik walked faster. He pulled his scarf up over his face to hide his features, but it did not prevent him from feeling uncomfortable and exposed. There were few people about, but the inevitability of being seen grew more and more certain the farther they traveled. However, just as he was about to say something to their guide about the impossibility of staying inconspicuous if they got any closer to the city, Mouse veered off the road and made his way across the fields to their right. Marik and Shaesta shared a surprised look and then hastened their steps to follow the boy. Mouse led them through the fields into a line of trees that bordered a steep incline with a tiny creek running along its base. With nimble movements, the small boy leaped down the incline, landing precariously on the edge of the stream. He glanced up and gestured at his companions.

"Come on," he shouted up to them. "We're almost there."

Picking their way more carefully, Marik and Shaesta descended, gripping trees as they went to prevent themselves from tumbling down the bank and into the water below. When they reached the bottom, they looked expectantly at Mouse, but he just waved them to follow and trekked along the creek bank toward the city.

Together, they followed the creek as the sun beat down through the trees. They ate the rations they had brought and drank from the crystal-clear water of the stream. Eventually, the bank of the creek grew rocky, and the incline turned cliff-like. Trees sprouted up between boulders, their roots twining down the sides of the cliffs like giant ropes and nets.

"Here it is," Mouse said, pointing to a fissure in the rocks.

Marik eyed it skeptically. "What am I looking at?"

"The entrance," Mouse said. "Well, one of them, anyway. This is the only one on this side of the city outside the gates."

"I see now why you insisted Oleck stay with the *Hawk*," Shaesta said.

Mouse gave her a quick grin. "There are bigger entrances, but I thought this one would be best for us. I figured we didn't want to go back inside the city, and it's a longer hike to go around Melar to find one of the other entrances. Come on!" He darted through the fissure and disappeared.

Marik gestured with a flourish. "After you, my lady."

"Oh no," Shaesta protested. "I'm not going in until I'm certain you and Mouse have cleared away all the spiderwebs."

Marik chuckled, but he ducked down and entered the crevice without arguing the matter further. He found himself in a narrow tunnel, and he could hear Mouse's feet pattering just ahead of him. A rustle of skirts and several sharp intakes of breath let him know Shaesta was following. Something like fine, sticky hair brushed across his face and got in his mouth, and Marik hunched down, spitting and rubbing at his lips with his fingers.

"What's wrong?" Shaesta's whispered voice was tight and clipped.

"Spiderweb"—Marik coughed—"in my mouth." Shaesta giggled, but it sounded more like the beginnings of hysteria than genuine mirth. He spat again and rose. This time, as he started forward, he kept one hand up in front of his face.

Thankfully, the tunnel was not long, though he encountered several more webs before the narrow fissure ended abruptly and opened up into a vast chamber. Mouse rustled around in the dark, and then Marik heard flint strike steel, and a torch flared to life.

In the sudden brilliance of torchlight, it took a bit for him to understand his surroundings, but as his eyes adjusted, Marik could see that they stood in a cave that could only be called enormous. The wall curved up around them, soaring into the ceiling, which disappeared in the darkness above. The tunnel itself was wider than a city street. Torchlight glinted off the nearby walls, and Marik stepped over to investigate the strange glimmerings. His eyes widened as he realized gemstones encrusted the silver-flecked walls. A mere handful of the wall decor could set a man up in princely fashion for a lifetime.

"What is this place?" he asked in a hoarse whisper.

"Nobody knows," Mouse replied. "But as far as we can tell, it runs beneath the entire city of Melar."

Shaesta whistled.

"But where did it come from?" Marik asked. "These tunnels didn't just happen. This clearly isn't a natural mine; it looks constructed."

"You are correct." A hoarse voice sounded from out of the darkness, and Marik's sword sprang to his hand before the newcomer finished speaking. "As far as we can tell, it was a structure of some sort at one time, but for what purpose, we do not know. Lenka, you have returned. Why do you bring these strangers into our home?" The voice was low and harsh, as though the speaker had been speaking for hours without rest.

Mouse walked toward the voice. "Forgive me, Nando. I would not give away our secrets were the need not so urgent. This is my new family." He gestured to Marik and Shaesta. "Or rather, part of it."

Marik gritted his teeth at the word "family," but did not raise his voice to gainsay the youth.

A diminuitive woman in a bulky cloak and hood emerged from the shadows. "You trust them?"

"With my blood."

There was a long pause.

"Very well. Bring them farther in. Papa will hear your urgent need."

Mouse turned and nodded to the others. Marik hesitated, a flutter of unease rippling through him before he sheathed his sword and fell in behind the boy and their mysterious guide.

Their path wound down a side tunnel and then another and another until Marik was hopelessly lost. Even his soldier's training and better-than-average sense of direction were no help to him after the fourth or fifth turn. The unease changed from a flutter to a steady drumbeat. He glowered into the dim light and wondered if they were being taken on a circuitous route on purpose. It mattered little, however, for Marik was certain he was too distracted to keep a map in his head even if they had taken the most direct route. Every tunnel they traversed was breathtaking. Whatever this place had been before, the people who lived here now had worked hard to restore it and make it beautiful. Though Marik knew he was still underground, nothing about the winding corridors or passageways betrayed evidence of that fact. Everything was pristine. The polished floors gleamed; the walls boasted numerous carvings and etched reliefs of intricate detail.

"I have never seen craftsmanship like this," Shaesta said, her hand reaching out to brush a relief featuring a small child picking flowers.

"Did your people find the carvings like this?" Marik asked.

Nando glanced at him over her shoulder. "My people are responsible for their creation."

Marik let out a low whistle. "Impressive."

Without warning, their guide stopped. They had reached the end of another tunnel—this one shorter than the first—and now stood before a wooden door. Without a word, Mouse thrust the torch down into a barrel. It hissed and plunged them into utter darkness. Nando knocked and then pushed the door open.

Marik and Shaesta both had to duck in order to pass through the door. On the other side, the tunnel widened out into a strangely shaped room. Two lanterns hung on either side of the room, but they cast minimal light and Marik had to strain to see anything more than the dim outlines of the seven people seated in a semicircle awaiting them. He noted several more doors leading out of the chamber in various directions.

Mouse crossed the room and knelt before the central chair. "Papa." He rested his head against the shadowy knee.

"Lenka, you have returned to us." The voice rumbled into the room like wind catching in the sails of the *Hawk*. "We have missed you."

"I've missed you, too," Mouse said.

"You have brought strangers among us." The voice grew hard and cold. "You know this is not allowed. Our existence depends upon secrecy. Strangers have never been allowed."

"Yes, Papa. Please forgive me," Mouse replied. "But I didn't know what else to do. These people have become my new family, but the Ar'Mol captured Raisa. We can't rescue her by ourselves."

"What do you expect us to do for them?" The voice was still cold. Marik's eyes had adjusted somewhat, and he could now better make out a few details, though the actual features were still lost to his eyes. "We have not the means to besiege the Ar'Mol's dungeons. We do not have the might necessary for such an onslaught. And I will not put my family at risk for strangers. We do not know these people. We do not trust them. For love of you as part of our family, we have allowed them this far and will hear their request, but be warned, we will not put our own in danger on behalf of these outsiders."

Marik took a step forward. "Will you allow me to speak?"

The central figure held up a hand. "We will hear the request from Lenka. He is one of our own. You will be silent."

Marik growled in his throat but did not attempt to say more.

Mouse rose to his feet. "Papa, I know the codes. I know how important it is for our people to maintain their secrecy. But I also know that you have many windows into the city above. You hear whispers. You know things. Can you find out if my friend is still alive?"

The figure's head nodded once. "We can obtain that information." A pause. "What else?"

"If she is alive, I thought maybe you could tell us if you learn anything else about my friend," Mouse said in a rush. "If they plan to execute her, or if they plan to move her anywhere, or even if you could find out where she is in the dungeons. We don't have any friends in the city. We haven't been able to find out anything useful. All I'm asking for is information. I do not ask for help in retrieving her. I would not put you in danger."

The figure nodded again. "And what would you give us in return?"

Mouse half-turned to Marik, which he took as permission to speak. "What price would you ask? For the life of one of my crew, no price is too high."

The figure made a strange, inhuman noise, a rumbling sound that made Marik's skin crawl. He had the sudden urge to flee back the way they had come. It was the same sensation he had felt once before, as a child in the woods behind his home. Evening had been approaching, and he had heard the eerie barking howl of a wylfen. He would never forget how the sound made his skin prickle with dread. The sound coming from the shadowy man gave him that same sensation: it was the feeling of a predator stalking him, of being considered as prey.

The figure next to Papa leaned over and whispered in his ear. The rumbling noise faded, and Papa stood. It surprised Marik to note that he was short, barely as tall as Mouse. The man paced to the outside of the room and stared at the wall for a long moment. Then, picking up a lantern, he strode to where Marik stood and threw back the hood of his cloak.

"Is that so?" the man asked.

It took Marik a moment to realize that the man was replying to his rash declaration. He was too busy studying the creature before him. The man—for he was a man, though his features were strange—was short, but his shoulders were extremely broad, and his arms rippled with muscles. His stature was not the thing that had taken Marik aback, however, but the sight of his skin: it was covered in what appeared to be large, gray scales. He had a broad nose, and there was something reptilian about his nostrils as they flared in slits. He looked up at Marik with pale yellow eyes that glittered and reflected green in the lantern's light... *Like an animal's eyes*, Marik thought.

The man thrust out his hand. "Hrafn," he said, his voice short, the name sounding more like a cough than anything Marik wished to attempt repeating. "If information is all you seek, then perhaps we can come to an agreement."

Marik hesitated for only a second before he clasped the man's hand and felt another shock go through him. Hrafn's skin was rough. It was more than just the normal calloused leather of hands that had done hard labor for many years. No, this felt more like the skin of a leythan, thick, scaly hide that could turn arrows. He masked his surprise, however, and shook the other's hand without hesitation or flinching.

Hrafn grinned, and pointed teeth glinted in the lantern-light.

"I meant what I said," Marik reiterated. "Name your price."

"Don't worry," Hrafn replied in his gravelly voice, "I will." He barked something at the others standing in the room, the words coming out in a guttural growl that Marik did not understand, but Hrafn's people obviously did, for they immediately scattered, leaving in pairs through each of the three doors.

"Nando will show you to your rooms where you can wait while my people see what information they can gather. You are welcome to stay with us for a few days."

Marik wanted to argue for returning to his ship, or say that he wished to know what price they would demand, but something in Hrafn's tone made him hold his tongue. He had said he would pay anything; to demand to know the price would cheapen his words. And as for returning to his ship, Marik had a feeling that if he left now, he would lose his only chance to barter with these people, and while he was still uncertain whether they could actually help him, Marik was well aware of the fact that he had nobody else to turn to.

They ushered Marik, Shaesta, and Mouse to a set of rooms and told them to wait. At first, Marik prowled like an angry malkyn. But he could not stay idle for long, and so he turned his attention to every facet of his room. A small table and chair sat against one wall. A large oil lamp stood on the table, casting a comforting glow across the tiny space. He tried the door and found it unlocked. This helped ease his nerves. He wanted to exit the room, just to prove that he could, but he reminded himself that he needed to obtain the good graces of his hosts in order to free Raisa, so he forced himself to turn away from the door and focus on other aspects of his surroundings.

It was a small room, furnished with a short pallet made of straw and covered in tattered sheets and a misshapen blanket. Further inspection revealed that the bedding was clean, though worn nearly threadbare. A chest in one corner caught his attention. He opened it and found a tidy array of books. Titles ranged from history to philosophy to texts on architecture and the maintenance of trains to theoretical expositions on the workings of airships and cynders. He had never seen so many books in one place before, except for his single glimpse into the Academy's library. He wondered at the purpose of these books. Did Mouse's former family read these, or had they merely inherited them when they discovered these tunnels?

The same silver of the main tunnel flecked the walls here, though no gemstones glittered at him. It did not appear that any had been pried out of the walls, so Marik assumed that this room had never held any.

He lay down on the pallet, putting his hands behind his head as a pillow, and found that his legs from the knees down stuck off the end. Perhaps this room was meant for a child, then? But he remembered Hrafn and then realized that every person in that strange room had been a similar height. He frowned. Hrafn did not have the appearance or bearing of a child, but he had not gotten a good look at anyone else. Perhaps everyone else was a child, like Mouse? That did not seem to track with what little Mouse had said about his former caregivers. Marik shifted on the uncomfortable pallet. It was a mystery. And one he was unlikely to solve without further investigation, but any queries would have to wait. Raisa was the single most important thing right now. Finding her and rescuing her had to be his sole focus.

He closed his eyes and tried not to think about where Raisa was or what she might be enduring. He tried not to wonder if she was still alive. She had to be alive. Surely there would have been some sort of sign or gossip if there had been an execution? Unless it was not a public affair... his mind clamped down on that thought and he pushed it away angrily. Jumping up from the pallet, he paced the room some more. He lifted the pallet and looked under it, and did the same to the threadbare carpet in the center of the room, but both searches revealed nothing. He eyed the chest, wondering if it was worth the effort of emptying out the books and moving it to see if it concealed anything. Ultimately, he decided against it... for now. Instead, he glanced over the titles again and chose one of the histories. Taking it back to the pallet with him, Marik propped himself against the wall and began to read.

11

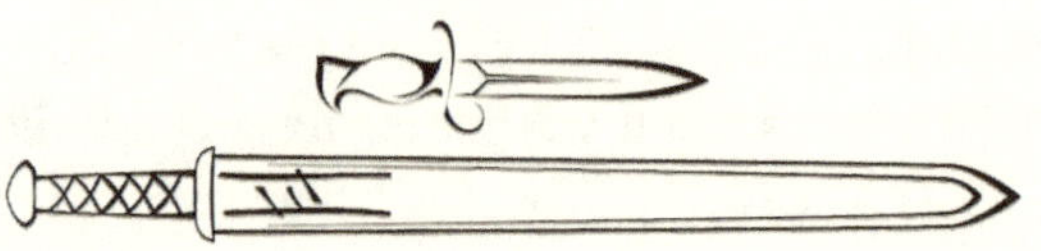

After Niveya's coach passed through the north gate and left Doran behind, the paved streets gave way to rough dirt tracks. Open countryside spread out before them, and Grayden felt more at home. Off to the east, the familiar profile of the Randeau Mountains rose in a hazy blue blur, and Grayden felt a twinge of homesickness for the Academy. He grinned. It was strange; he had spent less than a year in those halls and training rings, but those lunats had shaped him immeasurably. Through his experiences with the other cadets and initiates, through his lessons, and through the ordeal of the Storvas Mission, Grayden knew he had grown. Shared trials had formed the bonds of brotherhood. He had placed his life in the hands of his fellow cadets, and they had placed their lives in his. He had learned to follow orders, and he had learned to lead. He had made decisions in impossible situations, and he had brought his men home. Not all of them had survived, though. His thoughts turned to Enric, and darkness threatened to pull him into its depths. He had not known Enric well, but they had endured much together. They had, at times, been friendly rivals in the sparring ring. They had learned to trust and rely on one another. Enric had not deserved to die in that deadly valley. Not for the first time, Grayden's thoughts whirled into a spiral as he relived the events of that battle, second-guessing every decision he had made, wondering if he could have done anything differently that would have saved Enric's life.

He fell so deeply into his thoughts that he did not notice when the carriage stopped. Beren shook him, and Grayden looked up at his friend dully. Beren's eyes peered worriedly into his own, and Grayden wondered absently why his words seemed to come from so far away.

"We're here."

The words finally penetrated his understanding, and Grayden blinked and glanced out the window.

The house they had stopped in front of was a wide, sprawling thing. It only boasted a single story, but it stretched out to either side and seemed to be vaguely horseshoe-shaped. Grayden climbed out of the carriage and followed Beren and Niveya up a grassy path.

Niveya rapped sharply on the door and a middle-aged man with a receding hairline and a neat, gray goatee answered.

"Can I help you?" the man asked, peering at them with curiosity in his sparkling brown eyes.

"Is Matei at home?" Niveya asked.

The man spread his arms, bronzed by the sun and muscular. "He is indeed. I am Matei. What can I help you gentlemen with? My schedule did not include any private wine-tastings today, but if you are tourists stopping by, it has been a slow morning and I could be persuaded."

"Wonderful!" Niveya replied smoothly. "I would dearly love a private tour of your estate, but first, I am afraid we have come on a different errand; perhaps you can help us. We are looking for a woman named Ulia. She used to work for the Regeont, may her spirit find rest. We were told she is a relative of yours, and so we came to inquire whether you have any information on her whereabouts?"

Matei's smile did not falter, but his eyes narrowed ever so

slightly. "Ulia is indeed my cousin," he admitted. "But I haven't seen or spoken to her in years. We drifted apart when she left for the city, you see." His lips thinned in disapproval. "She opened a rift between herself and the family. She should have stayed here and helped with the family business, but she wanted to strike out on her own, thought the city would be more exciting than the vineyard. It was... messy." His expression smoothed. "But please, what is this all about?"

"Ah." Niveya's face scrunched into a perplexed little frown. "Well, you see, she left without collecting her pay, and we've been trying to locate her in order to give it to her."

Matei's mouth twisted to one side, and Grayden got the feeling that the man did not believe Niveya's words. "I wish I could help you, but Ulia's not here."

"Can you tell us where we might find her?" Niveya asked, giving the man a charming smile.

"Unfortunately, no," Matei replied. "Like I said, I haven't seen or spoken to my cousin in years. She didn't part from the family on good terms. It broke her mother's heart when she left. Family should stick together." He scowled fiercely, as though daring them to disagree.

"Nothing is more important than family," Niveya agreed. "Perhaps Ulia has finally realized that. Is there anyone else in the family she might have gone to?"

Matei rubbed the back of his hand against one eye. "No," he muttered. "There isn't anyone else. If she'd come home, she would have come to me. She knows I can't ever stay mad at her if she turns those brown eyes all watery on me." He scowled.

Niveya heaved a sigh and half-turned away. "Well, if you hear from her, please tell her we stopped by."

Matei nodded. "I will."

He closed the door and Beren and Grayden trailed Niveya back to the coach.

"What do we do now?" Beren asked. "This was your only lead."

But Grayden barely heard him. He was focused on Niveya's expression, which was far too placid in the face of such a setback.

"What are you thinking?" Grayden asked in a low tone.

Niveya eyed him appraisingly. "You caught it, too?"

"Caught what?" Beren asked.

"He was lying," Grayden muttered. "Either Ulia is here, or he knows where she is."

"How could you tell?" Beren asked.

"I'm not sure I can explain it," Grayden said.

Beren's gaze sharpened. "Your sixth sense?"

Grayden shook his head. That particular ability had been distressingly absent since he arrived at the Academy. "No, something about all that just didn't seem right."

"Like what?" Beren pressed.

"He was too chatty; kept giving us more information than we asked for, like he thought if he talked long enough, we might believe he had told us all he knows. He wanted us to leave." Grayden held up his hands helplessly. "I don't know. I just have this feeling."

Beren frowned.

"I agree with Grayden. It felt as though Matei was trying too hard to convince us. And he said that she didn't part from the family on good terms, but then he indicated that there isn't any family left," Niveya added. "But I know Ulia did not start working for the Regeont until three years ago. That's not a lot of time for an entire family to die or move away, particularly if the family had an established place here."

"So either he's lying about there being no one left, or he's lying about knowing where Ulia is," Beren said.

"Or both," Niveya said. "Most likely both."

"And he didn't mention the tour or the tasting again," Grayden said. "We spooked him enough that he didn't care about possible customers or business."

"But if he's lying about knowing where she is, then that means he is protecting her," Beren mused.

"Which would indicate that our theory is correct, and Ulia does indeed possess dangerous information," Niveya replied.

"What do we do next?" Beren asked.

"I have a couple of ideas." Niveya tapped his chin. "But they are all rather unpleasant. Do either of you have any suggestions?"

"Why don't we just tell Matei the truth?" Grayden asked.

"And what is that?" Niveya asked.

"It's when you say something that isn't a lie," Beren replied.

Niveya shot him a glare. "I meant, what version of the truth do you propose we tell him? That we believe his cousin saw the Regeont's murderer and that her life is in danger because of what she knows?"

Grayden raised an eyebrow. "Why not?"

"If that is why she is hiding, then he already knows that. What is to prevent him from concluding that we are the ones who are trying to hurt her?"

"I didn't think of that," Grayden admitted. He pondered the question for a few thoughtful moments. "We could pretend to leave," he said. "Get in the coach, ride out of sight, and then send the driver on without us. We hide in a nearby field until nightfall, and then see what we can discover once Matei believes we are long gone and feels safe."

Niveya tapped the toe of his boot against the ground. "That is a sound plan. You have a good head on your shoulders."

Grayden flushed under the unexpected praise until he noticed Beren scowling at him. He gave his friend a rueful shrug and climbed into the coach. Beren clambered in after him, his lips pressed tightly together.

"What?" Grayden whispered.

Beren narrowed his eyes and opened his mouth, but as Niveya entered the coach right behind him, he snapped his mouth shut once more, crossed his arms, and turned to stare out the window. Grayden's spirits sank. No matter what he did, he could not seem to avoid missteps with his friends of late.

The tower was farther away than it had first appeared. Though they made steady progress, like a mountain that appears closer than it actually is, the tower remained aloof, never allowing them to make progress in reaching it. Though time was difficult to keep track of, Dalmir estimated that they had been trying to cross the enormous cavern for five or six days. He was getting weary of sleeping on such hard ground, and they had burned through the supply of firewood they had brought with them trying to get dry after the river. The strange light continued to fill the enormous space they were crossing, but they still could not discern its source.

Dalmir plodded along, his head down, his spirits low, wondering how much longer they would have to spend in this place, when Drengur gave a sudden exclamation. Dalmir's head jerked up to see that, without warning, as though they had been creeping up on a giant that had been pointedly ignoring them only to suddenly pivot its intent gaze on them, they had reached the base of the tower. Standing in its shadow, the three men stared up, their necks craning back as they peered up at the sheer, flat walls, trying without success to spot its summit. In the dim light, the charcoal walls loomed over them, flecked with bits of crystal that glittered like motes of dust in sunlight, and sky-blue veins laced their way up like captured lightning.

"What is it made of?" Drengur asked, reaching a hand out to touch the smooth wall. "Is that... no, it couldn't be!" He laid his palm against the dark gray stone and stared at Dalmir, his eyes wide with shock.

Dalmir's lips twitched in amusement. "Yes, Tel made his tower completely out of oronite."

Drengur stepped away from the wall, pressing the heels of his hands into his eyes, rubbing them and shaking his head. "I see it, but I don't... I can't believe it," he said. "Oronite is supposed to be rare, and extremely difficult to work with."

"Not for us." Dalmir reached out and laid a hand against the wall. It felt warm to his touch. He leaned his forehead against the wall, closing his eyes. Grief, fresh and raw, poured over him. Tears sprang forth and caught in his eyelashes, held between forming and falling.

"Dalmir?" Ioan's voice was strained.

"We need to go inside," Dalmir mumbled, pulling away from the wall and wiping his eyes on his sleeve.

"How?" Drengur asked.

"Through the door, of course," Dalmir replied.

"What door?" Drengur asked.

"This way," Dalmir said. He strode purposefully along the wall. This was not where he had last seen the tower, but that did not matter. His memory of it was pure. It was a long walk to get to the corner of the tower, and another long walk to get to the door. When they reached it, both Ioan and Drengur were panting with the effort of keeping up with Dalmir, who had been walking vigorously, with more purpose and determination than he had felt in a long time.

"I don't understand," Ioan said. "What is this place? Why is it here? Dalmir, do you know what this place is? You keep talking about someone named Tel. Who was he?"

Dalmir's jaw worked for a long moment as he gazed at the

stairway leading up to the massive double doors. "My brother built this tower," he said at last. "One of my brothers," he amended. "His name was Telsume."

"Telsume?" Drengur's face grew pale in the eerie light. "As in *the* Telsume? The founder of Telsuma, Telsume?"

"You have heard of him?" Dalmir felt pleased.

"Of course I've heard of him!" Drengur exploded. "The stories about him are some of the best we have. But..." His face squished its way into a wary expression of disbelief. "But that's all they are. Stories. Telsume is a legend, but he wasn't a real person. Nobody could have done the things the stories say he did."

Dalmir gestured at the tower. "He built that. Outside of a story, would you have believed it without seeing it?"

Drengur sucked in the corner of his mouth and considered. "No," he admitted.

"Telsume was as real as I am," Dalmir said. "As I said, he was one of my older brothers. And the stories about him... well, they're not just legends."

Drengur's eyes widened, and then narrowed with skepticism, but then he glanced at the tower and pressed his lips tightly together.

"These orbs." Dalmir pulled his gem out and held it up. In the dim light it glittered a pale blue, reflecting off the crystal flecks in the tower wall. "Each of my brothers made one. They are all that remain of the legends, their legacy. They were unique to us, fashioned with the power the Builder gave us. None of us could use any of them except our own." Dalmir shook his head and stared at Ioan. "I do not understand how, but Uun has figured out a way to use the orbs that do not belong to him. I believe it was through Avaleun's orb that the madman altered you, Ioan. It is undeniably Palte's orb that is creating the cynders in the East that make the airships fly. I do not know how many of the orbs he has, but it is becoming clear to me that we must prevent Uun from gaining control of any more of them. I am sure he has his own, and I have mine and Edoran's. That leaves Tel's and Mulemo's yet unaccounted for. I have seen no glimmerings of their power at work in the world, and so I fervently hope that means Uun has not yet found them."

Ioan hefted his pack higher on his shoulder. "I don't claim to understand half of what you just said, and I know you are still keeping secrets," he said. "But if a madman wielding one of these orbs can alter others like he altered me, I say we do everything we can to keep more of them away from him."

"I'm not trying to keep secrets," Dalmir said, his shoulders slumping. Deep inside, however, he knew his words rang false. Of course he was keeping secrets, though not intentionally. But how could he explain thousands of years of history? How could he be certain of imparting the most important details of his past, his brothers, their rise to power, their reign, and Uun's betrayal? And how could he possibly atone for the centuries during which he had neglected the world?

Drengur's brow furrowed. "I still don't understand why we have to go inside." He stared up at the doors, his eyes dark with foreboding.

"Because if Tel's orb is anywhere down here, it will be inside his tower," Dalmir insisted. "I have spent this entire journey wondering why I felt compelled to descend into a mine in order to search for a single stone. Turning back has occurred to me a hundred times, giving up the search and..." He paused, searching for the right words. "I wanted to admit defeat almost before we even began. But something urged me forward. Something would not allow me to turn back."

"The oronite," Drengur guessed.

Dalmir nodded. "That was part of it. Oronite was one of Tel's discoveries, and orthryl was his creation. But even more than that was a feeling, or a hunch, that something rested down here that I needed to see." Dalmir indicated the tower with a tiny jerk of his head. "That has convinced me."

"Why haven't you looked for the orbs before now?" Ioan asked suddenly.

Dalmir's expression fell. "Because I thought I knew where they were," he replied. "I placed them in a wall surrounding Uun's prison. I did not anticipate anyone ever finding them, let alone moving them. They were useless to anyone else, or at least, I believed that to be the case." He sighed. "It was arrogant of me, or perhaps short-sighted. There is much I did not foresee." He straightened. "I need to go inside the tower. I will not ask either of you to come with me."

"I'm coming," Drengur said quickly. "This is a wonder we must explore, and as the son of the Chieftain, I will not cower from the unknown."

"Lord Adelfried charged me with guiding and protecting you," Ioan said. "I will not abandon you now."

Dalmir gazed at them gratefully. "I am not ashamed to admit that I was not keen on entering this fortress alone. Though I have been inside many times, that was when this structure was above ground and my brother was alive. Tel was a brilliant artificineer and had a bit of a suspicious nature. If he had the ability to make his home descend upon his death, there may be other guardians in place within. Though my guess would be that most of his defenses ran out of power years ago."

"Do you think it will be dangerous?" Ioan asked, his eyes darting to Drengur.

"Nothing we cannot handle," Dalmir replied. "I have the means to protect us, though it will alert Uun to my whereabouts."

"We probably want to avoid that," Ioan replied.

"Yes," Dalmir agreed, "but he will not know what I am doing, only where I am. I have been attempting to keep my movements secret from him, but it is not always possible."

"Does it work the other way?" Drengur asked.

"Yes," Dalmir replied. "I can sense it when he uses his power. He has been using the same tactics as I, it seems, in keeping a low profile."

"What about the madman, Lorcan?" Ioan asked. "Can you sense when he is using the orb?"

"No," Dalmir said. "I have been unable to sense it when the orbs are being used."

"That's interesting," Drengur said.

"Yes," Dalmir mused, "quite." He started up the long stair. "But we can ponder these things later. I would like to keep moving for now. If an orb is in the tower, that narrows our search area a little, but there is still a lot of ground to cover."

Together, they climbed the stairs up to the enormous double doors, which were carved from the same ore as the rest of the tower. Dalmir reached out and pulled down on the massive lever-like doorknob. With a rumble like a thousand stampeding leythan, the tumblers moved, and the door swung open on silent hinges.

"Tel never was one for doing anything small," Dalmir muttered. With a wistful smile, he stepped across the threshold. A rustling sound like the whisper of silk rubbing together filled his ears, and his skin prickled as the surrounding air turned icy. Dalmir felt the smile fall from his lips as a warning resounded through him, but then he took another step and the sensation vanished as quickly as it had come. He peered around at the dark interior of the tower. His nerves were taut, ready for whatever might come next. Drengur and Ioan stepped through the doorway to stand behind him.

"Did you feel it?" Dalmir asked, still trying to figure out what had just happened.

"Feel what?" Ioan asked.

Drengur said nothing, but shook his head, looking questioningly at Dalmir.

"What did you do, Tel?" Dalmir muttered. Something was different since the last time he had visited, besides the tower now being underground. It was hard to describe, but he felt... lighter, somehow. And younger. There was a sense of loss, as though something had been stolen from him, but he could not quite point to exactly what it was.

"I see nothing that looks dangerous," Drengur said, his voice in Dalmir's ear making him jump.

"It's hard to see much of anything at all," Ioan said. "Most of the light seems to have stayed outside. Dalmir, do you think we can get the lantern lit?"

"Perhaps. If not, my orb should give us a little light," Dalmir said absently, still distracted by the strange sensation.

Ioan was trying unsuccessfully to light the lantern, so Dalmir reached into his pouch and pulled out his orb, intending to use it to light their way. As he tugged at its power, he fell towards the wall. Ioan and Drengur shouted in surprise as they also fell in opposite directions. Ioan tumbled toward the far wall as Drengur hurtled toward the ceiling.

<h1 style="text-align:center">13</h1>

Wynn swept up the large sheets of paper, wadding them into a giant ball and pushing them to the floor with a groan.

Molly looked up from the other worktable. "What's wrong?"

"It's still too big," Wynn sighed. "I've cut out everything I can think of, but I can't get the physical size of the engine small enough to fit it inside the Trackless." He slumped on his stool, leaning on the table with his elbows, his chin resting despondently in his hands. "I can't figure this one out, Molly. I don't know what else to do."

"Maybe you need to take a break," Molly suggested. She glanced at the small chronometer she wore on a thick leather band around her wrist. She had shown it to Wynn on the first day they had met. Nobody in Dalsea could afford such a luxury, and the tiny gears inside the glass face mesmerized him. His hands itched to take it apart and figure out how it worked. "It's about time for me to go change the cynders. Want to come along? The walk might do you good."

"Sure." Wynn stood up and stretched, arching his back and rolling his shoulders a few times. His body ached with inactivity. He missed the daily sparring sessions that had been part of his routine at the Academy. Even though he had not been at the top of the charts like his friends, he had always held his own respectably in the middle of the boards. Although he would never admit it, he even missed Beren trying to teach him and Grayden the complicated patterns he practiced each day with his blade. Wynn made a mental note to insert some sort of physical activity into his morning routine. It would do him no good to keep his mind active and let his body waste away. He and Molly often took short walks together, but it was not enough to counter the hours he spent hunched over his table.

Molly had taken to sharing his workroom since she had returned, and Wynn had been surprised to discover that he didn't mind her presence. She was one of the few people he'd met who knew how to be truly quiet. Her pencil barely made any scratching noise as she copied schematics for Daegan, and she didn't ask him questions about his own work, or demand that he come look at hers. She interrupted him at mealtimes, but that was more of a relief than a bother. He worried he wouldn't eat at all if nobody came to get him.

"How are your designs coming along?" Wynn asked as they traversed the by-now-familiar path to the workroom, where the refiner was churning away.

"Not bad," Molly replied. "Daegan has already done most of the work. I'm just drawing out the exact patterns so Keene can forge it all out and we can put it together. You have the hard job: getting that engine small enough to fit inside the area Daegan left for it."

"I don't know why he didn't design the engine first," Wynn grumbled. "For everything he wants it to do, he didn't leave much space for it."

"The Trackless has to carry an entire squad and provide cover for them from enemy attacks. If we make it much bigger, it won't be able to move itself."

"I know, I'm just frustrated," Wynn replied. "I feel like there has to be a solution, but I can't see it."

Molly gave him a sympathetic glance as they entered the workroom. Wynn picked up one of the empty rocks and held it ready, waiting for Molly to remove the completed cynder. As she set it in the cart, Wynn finished his task and grabbed the handles for her.

"Thanks," Molly said. "I hate handling these things. They make me nervous."

"Why?" Wynn asked.

Molly shook her head. "I don't know. I just... I mean... I've heard they can be dangerous. Oh, I know they're just tools, like Keen's tilt-hammer. But Keene would never let anyone into his forge who didn't know what they were doing, and we know so little about the cynders. Even though we can make them, we still know nothing about them. We're children playing with a wood stove, with no concept of fire."

"If the cynders were dangerous, I think we would have realized it by now," Wynn said.

"You're probably right. I just don't like things I can't understand, and I don't understand cynders. Why do they have to be that shape or that size? What, exactly, makes them work? Why can this Dalmir person put a jewel in that device and create liquid light, and how does that liquid light turn ordinary rocks into something that can make airships fly? It doesn't make any kind of natural sense."

"You're right about that," Wynn chuckled. "But then, I've seen quite a few things in the past year that make me question whether we really know everything about the laws of nature and science. I'd love to spend more time studying the cynders, though."

"That's right." Molly grew interested. "You know Dalmir personally, don't you? He was the one who helped rescue Lord Adelfried's son from the pirates."

"And me," Wynn grumbled. "Not that anyone ever cares that I was kidnapped, too."

"I'm sorry," Molly said quickly. "I am actually quite pleased that you were rescued. If you hadn't been, we wouldn't be working together now."

Wynn chuckled. "I was just teasing."

"I am glad you're here," Molly repeated. She glanced away, and Wynn wondered at that. It wasn't like Molly to act shy, but then, he had never been good at reading other people. She opened the door, holding it for Wynn as he pushed the cart out into the tunnel. Then she trotted after him to catch up. "Can you tell me what he's like?"

"Dalmir?" Wynn squinted one eye as he trundled the cart along, wondering again why the storage room for the cynders was so far away from the refiner. The shed for storing the cynders wasn't even in the same tunnels as the rest of Keene's labyrinth. He and Molly had to exit the mountain and cross a field to get there. "He's quiet, mostly. Not so quiet that he never tells you anything, but I get the feeling that he knows more than he says. A lot more. Maybe you should ask him about the cynders. I'll bet he knows exactly how they work. Though I don't know if he'll be able to explain it."

"Maybe I will," Molly said. "When he gets back."

"Gets back? Did he go somewhere?"

"Hadn't you heard? Ioan and Drengur led him down into the mines."

"Why?"

"I'm not sure," Molly replied. "Daegan said they were looking for something."

"Huh. I wonder what that could be?"

Molly shrugged and they continued walking.

"You know, you just made me think of something," Wynn said.

"What's that?" Molly asked.

"Just... I was wondering why the cynders have to be the size and shape that they are," Wynn mused. "I need to take a look at those engines Daegan has outside."

"Why?"

"Well, I don't think either of them still has a working cynder inside, but..." Wynn would have continued speculating, but at that moment, the wheel of the cart hit a root sticking up from the ground. The cart tilted to the side, the cynder sliding along the boards and throwing the cart off balance. Wynn struggled to maintain control, but his brief inattention had already cost him his ability to stabilize the cart. It flipped onto its side with a jolt. The cynder flew out of the barrow and across the ground, tumbling and rolling until it collided with the tree from which the offending root had sprung. A ball of thunderous fire blasted the tree into kindling. The ground rumbled and a wave of heat washed over Wynn as he and Molly threw themselves to the ground. Dirt and rocks and other debris rained down on them. Wynn instinctively threw his arm over Molly's head, trying to shield her from the shrapnel hurtling through the air.

The pattering of falling rocks and splinters of wood ceased. Wynn raised his head, cautiously keeping one hand near his face, as though such a poor shield could protect him from any further blasts.

The tree had been obliterated. Broken branches littered the ground and a small, dagger-like point stuck up where the mighty trunk had towered. Molly rose to her knees, her brown face pale beneath a layer of gray dust.

"What just happened?" she whispered.

"I'm not sure," Wynn muttered, his mind racing through the implications.

"Did you know that could happen?" she asked.

"No."

Wynn got to his feet and went over to inspect the remnants of the tree. Molly caught his sleeve, holding him back. "It could still be dangerous," she said.

Wynn scratched the side of his head. "I don't think so, but you can stay back if you like."

Molly hesitated, then fell into step next to him.

The blackened trunk pointed to the sky in jagged spikes, but

Wynn barely noticed it, his full attention drawn to the center of the crater in the ground. Fragments of the cynder lay scattered about; most of them had reverted to lifeless shards of rock.

"What are you looking for?" Molly asked, studying Wynn as he picked up a piece of the broken cynder.

"Hang on," Wynn said. "I had a thought... or the glimmering of a thought... but it was maybe nothing." He sighed, his gaze sweeping the area once more. A soft gleam embedded in the wrecked tree caught his eye and he moved to inspect it. Pulling a folding blade out of his pocket, he dug the tip of the knife into the soft wood. Excitement pounded through his body as he carefully, oh-so-carefully, dug the glinting blue mote out of the bark. He held it in his hand and stared at it, his brain charging into fullspeed.

"What did you find?" Molly asked, coming up and peering over his shoulder at the shard.

Wynn stared at the fragment. Unlike the other pieces scattered about on the ground, this one still held a faint flicker of blue light. "I wonder..." Wynn muttered. With a swift motion of his arm, he flung the shard at a boulder. The resulting blast was nowhere near as big as the initial one had been, but there was a loud boom and dust flew up around them. When the air cleared, the boulder had been split in two. Wynn and Molly shared a wide-eyed stare.

"If you ever do something like that again, you'd better warn me first," Molly said, her eyes flashing.

Wynn barely heard her. "Do you know what this means?"

"You could have killed us both," Molly seethed.

"The cynders don't have to be a certain size!"

"Daegan will not be happy about this. Brilliant or not, he won't tolerate recklessness or danger..." Molly broke off. "What did you say?"

"I said the cynders don't have to be a specific size."

"Why do you say that?"

Wynn gestured at the smaller crater, uncertain how to explain. "Don't you understand?" He racked his brain helplessly. If only he could find the words as easily as he had solved the problem. That had always been one of his difficulties, explaining to others what seemed so obvious to him.

Molly's eyes flicked between Wynn's face and the crater, and he saw her anger fade as light dawned across her features. She grabbed his hand. "Come on!"

"Where are we going?"

"We have to tell Daegan about this."

Wynn pulled back, but Molly gripped his hand in her own. She tugged impatiently.

"Look, I'm sorry I didn't warn you," Wynn said. "I was certain we wouldn't be in any danger, but I should have..."

"Forget about that," Molly snapped, interrupting him. "This is the exact sort of discovery that Daegan is going to want to know about. Come on!"

Realizing that she was no longer angry at him, Wynn allowed himself to be pulled back toward the forge. Before they had reached the door, however, it slammed open, and both Daegan and Keene came pelting out, wild looks on their faces. They slowed when they spotted Wynn and Molly, but their expressions remained filled with alarm.

"Daegan!" Molly shouted breathlessly as they approached. "Come and see... Wynn... the Trackless... solved the problem!"

The alarm on both faces slowly faded to puzzlement and then to inquisitive eagerness. "What have you discovered?" Daegan demanded.

"And what was that horrible sound?" Keene demanded. "It reminded me of the time Gunnar forgot to clean the soot out of the bellows and my forge exploded!"

"It might be best if I just show you," Wynn hedged. He led them to the spot where the cynder had exploded and tried to explain, but he quickly grew flustered and Molly took over.

"We dropped a cynder," she said. "It rolled down the hill, hit the tree, and exploded."

"Exploded?" Keene asked, his eyes widening. He looked at Daegan. "Did you know they could do that?"

"Of course," Daegan replied. "Why do you think I insisted we keep them in the storage shed, away from your forge and the living quarters and workshops?"

Keene blanched. "I had no idea they were so dangerous. What if someone had dropped one inside the mountain? Why didn't you tell me this was a possibility? I don't like the idea of something so volatile inside my home." The man's face darkened with anger.

"I assumed you knew," Daegan replied. "You didn't? How did you think cynders worked?"

"I don't know how they work!" Keene said, his voice growing louder. "You're the inventor. I'm just a blacksmith! I wield a hammer. Why would you think I understood something like the inner workings of a cynder? You should have warned me!"

Daegan gave him a hard look. "You use tools every day. You work with fire. I assumed you would understand the necessity for strength beyond what we can muster in order to power things like the trains and airships."

"It didn't occur to me," Keene muttered.

Daegan eyed his friend in silence, then turned to Wynn. "Is that all?"

"No," Wynn admitted. "I think I might have discovered something."

Daegan stared at him. Waiting.

"A shard of the cynder was still glowing," Wynn continued. "I picked it up, and the thought hit me... well... I wasn't sure if... I mean, I threw it at a rock."

"That was the second explosion," Keene said. "I thought we heard two, but the second one wasn't as loud. We thought it might just be the earth settling."

"Can you show me where?" Daegan asked.

Wynn led him over to the spot and pointed. Daegan ran his

hand along the jagged edge of the split boulder, scrutinizing the area. When he had finished, he glanced at Wynn.

"You understand what you've done?"

"I... I think so," Wynn stammered.

"What has he done?" Keene asked, his voice gruff. "Besides blowing a hole in my mountain?"

Daegan gave the smith a smirk, his eyes gleaming. "Your mountain, eh? Wynn here has discovered that the power the cynders contain is not constrained to a certain size or shape."

"So?" Keene asked.

"Don't you see? We've never had the ability to create cynders," Daegan explained. "And the Igyeum has doled them out to us in such small quantities that we've never had any spares to study. In fact, the cynder shipments always come with people from the Igyeum who install them in our airships for us. Some of us theorized that the power of the cynders could be held in smaller containers, but we never got the chance to experiment. I don't know why it hadn't occurred to me to try now that we have a refiner of our own..." Daegan glanced at Wynn. "Nice work."

Something unclenched in the pit of Wynn's stomach at the words and he realized that he had been tense throughout the entire conversation. Blowing up a tree notwithstanding, he had wasted a precious cynder, and what was worse, he belatedly realized, he had not once expressed remorse over doing so. The sudden release of tension made his head grow swimmy for a moment and he closed his eyes.

"Wynn?" Molly's voice seemed to come from far away. "Wynn? Are you feeling well?"

"Yeah." Wynn opened his eyes. "I'm sorry for wasting a cynder."

Daegan gave him a half smile as if he understood exactly what was going through Wynn's thoughts. "Don't be. You've taught us something important today."

"This could really help us with the engine for the Trackless," Wynn said, his mind churning over the possibilities.

Daegan peered into his eyes. "Go," he said shortly.

"What?" Wynn frowned, puzzled at the man's abrupt dismissal.

"You have an idea. I can tell by the look on your face," Daegan replied. "Go, work it out. Molly, help him."

"Yes, boss." Molly grinned. She looped her arm through Wynn's. "Back to work!" she said, her voice cheerful.

"And make sure he stops to eat!" Keene shouted after them.

14

"Help!" Drengur shouted, clinging to the chandelier, his head whipping back and forth.

"What just happened?" Ioan yelled across the room.

Dalmir struggled to his feet and found himself standing on the wall, staring up at Ioan on the other side of the room. He let out a long, admiring breath and glanced down at his orb.

"Impressive. Tel... now how did you manage that?" he whispered.

"Dalmir!" Drengur's voice held a note of panic. The chandelier clinked as it swung beneath Drengur's weight.

"Just a moment," Dalmir shouted. "I'm thinking!" He took a tentative step toward the wall that had been the floor just a moment earlier. Nothing happened, so he took another step. When he reached the floor, he put his foot on it. Nothing changed. The floor remained oriented as a wall and he could not traverse it any more than he could walk up a normal wall. He looked up at Ioan and over at Drengur; he could just barely make out their shapes in the darkness. "You should be fine," he called out. "But it looks as though this is permanent. Drengur, let yourself up... er... down the chandelier, you'll be able to stand on the ceiling."

Drengur clung to the chandelier and inched his way toward the ceiling.

"Can't you fix it?" Ioan hollered. "Beren told me about the things he saw you do."

"I can try," Dalmir said. "But if I'm right, it won't work. Things could get even more... interesting."

"More interesting?" Ioan called back. "I don't see how that could happen."

"You'd be surprised," Dalmir muttered. This time, he did not use the orb as he concentrated on restoring order to the laws of nature. A yelp from the wall above him alerted Dalmir to the fact that something had happened, though not what he had intended. A moment later, he felt something brush against his ankle. He jumped away as a vine coiled around the place where his foot had just been. "No!" Dalmir growled through gritted teeth. "No, no, no, no! That's not what I meant to do at all! Tel, why'd you have to go and be so forge-fired clever?"

"Dalmir, what's going on?" Ioan called.

"Something about crossing the threshold changed all the rules," Dalmir replied.

"What in the deep world is that supposed to mean?"

"It means that I can't fix this," Dalmir shouted. "At least, not in the usual way. Hold on, let me think. Telsume set a trap. Anyone entering his tower with our kind of power will be confounded. He knew he couldn't take away our powers, but he figured out a way to confuse them."

"These vines are trying to climb up my legs," Drengur hollered, his feet thumping as he threw all caution away, leaped from the chandelier, and ran along the ceiling.

There was a snap-hiss as one of Ioan's matches flared to life. The wick in his lantern caught, and the chamber filled with a gentle glow. The walls of the massive hallway glinted in the light, lined with enormous paintings by various artists. A door stood immediately to the left of where they had entered, and another one waited up ahead on the right. Vines laced their way across the walls and ceiling, but their sudden growth had slowed.

"Perhaps it would be best if we simply proceed," Dalmir suggested. "We are in no immediate danger. Perhaps this will wear off. I recommend walking as close to the actual floor as possible." He glanced at Drengur. "You stay close to a wall, and grab hold of a tapestry or hanging lantern if you feel yourself falling."

His companions nodded and moved to comply as best they could.

"Where do you think we should go?" Drengur asked. "Do we need to check every room?"

Dalmir shook his head. "No, if the orb is here, it will be in the library."

"The library?" Drengur's eyebrows rose in surprise.

"We were each responsible for building a library in our own region," Dalmir replied. "Tel was the only one who kept his within his tower. The rest of us did not want our homes to be so public. But Tel enjoyed being surrounded by people. More than any of the rest of us, he thrived when in a crowd. Mulemo was that way a bit, as well, though not as much. I suppose it makes sense. They were twins, after all."

"Where is this library?" Ioan asked, his face pale in the lamp's glow. "I hope you're right about this wearing off."

Dalmir strode along the hall, outpacing the growing vines. "Upstairs," he called over his shoulder. "Follow me."

The other two followed, their footsteps echoing off the high walls and making far more noise than Dalmir was comfortable with. He made his way to the door leading to the stairs. It took some maneuvering to get it open, but eventually they managed, revealing a long, wide staircase with an elaborate handrail on either side.

"Well, that's a blessing from our predicament." Dalmir's mouth quirked to one side. "No stairs to climb, just a pleasant stroll."

A shout of delighted laughter came from one side, and Dalmir looked over to see Drengur sprinting across the ceiling. When he crossed the top of the stairs, his laughter changed into a cry of surprise as gravity righted itself without warning and he fell. His arms flailed, and he caught hold of a hanging lantern and dangled there for a moment before dropping the rest of the way to the floor. He stared back at his companions, eyes wide.

Ioan and Dalmir proceeded with more caution, but even knowing where the effect dissipated, Dalmir stumbled as the world righted itself once more. Ioan transitioned with enviable grace, stepping down from the wall and onto the floor as though this were something he did every day.

Glancing around, they found themselves in a large, open space. Windows covered one enormous wall, while the other wall curved outward. Couches, chairs, small desks, and long tables dotted the room, a perfect place for quiet contemplation or diligent study, or even just a nice place to come and read for pleasure or to paint. Dalmir spotted an easel covered in dust. He remembered how beautiful the view had been, overlooking the valley far below, the peaks of the other mountains nearby, the green, rolling hills, and the forests far off in the distance. It had been an especially spectacular view when the colder weather approached and the trees had donned their autumn hues. The atrium, Telsume had called it. The room had been a popular destination for many, and yet, though often crowded, it had almost always been a place of serene silence, an interesting dichotomy, Dalmir had always thought. But the people who had used this place had been content to be near others who were studying or creating. They did not need to interact, and they had been conscientious against disturbing each other; it had been a room filled with the quiet buzz of pages turning, quills scratching, and brushes sweeping. Even Dalmir, as much as he disliked being in crowded places, had found this room to be oddly peaceful.

There was only one door, and Drengur had already reached it.

As he turned the knob and the door swung open, something enormous came crashing through, causing Drengur to give a shout of surprise and stumble back. In a flash, Ioan was there, brandishing his sword in defense of his companions.

Dalmir, still standing near the top of the stairs where he had been momentarily lost in his memories, glimpsed the attacking thing. Its massive size nearly filled the doorway. The thing had a wide, rectangular torso balanced upright on four legs. Copper plating, like armor, covered its bulk, and one of its arms held a massive mace. That was all Dalmir had time to notice before the mechanical creature swung the weapon at Ioan's head. The captain danced back, avoiding the blow, but the creature swung again, and this time the end of the mace caught Ioan across the shoulder and knocked him against the wall.

Drengur gave an angry shout and rushed at the contraption, sword drawn. He stabbed with vicious ferocity at the opening in the metal monster's knee joint, but his aim was off, and his sword skidded across the plating with a horrible screeching sound. The creature did not seem to notice the attack. Its square head swiveled to focus on Dalmir, golden pinpoints of light gleaming in its face where eyes would be were it alive. Dalmir stared, petrified. Hoping that the difficulties he had encountered in the entrance were confined to the first level of the tower, he reached for the power that had been a part of him for millennia, but as he attempted to grasp it, all he managed to produce was a sudden whirlwind in the center of the atrium.

"Curse you, Tel!" Dalmir ground out through gritted teeth. The strange effects on his magic clearly stretched throughout the tower. He scowled as the monster approached, his mind running analytically through his options.

Since the day the Builder had given them their power, Dalmir had never struggled to make it do as he wished. He knew it had been the same for his brothers. What would have caused Telsume to create such a defense within his home? And more importantly, how had it been accomplished?

He watched as Drengur attacked again, his thoughts churning with agonizing sluggishness. He was completely defenseless for the first time, and while he knew the contraption couldn't kill him, it could cause him pain, and he was currently incapable of protecting his far more vulnerable companions. The last time he had felt this helpless had been the day of Uun's betrayal, the day he had felt his power slipping away, had somehow sensed Uun's intent before he could complete his foul design. But this time, there was nothing to pull back into his grasp, no way to retrieve what had been lost. The mechanical monster stepped forward, galvanizing Dalmir into action. He drew his sword and ran at the creature, diving beneath the mace as it swung down at him and driving his sword up into the space where the arm connected to the body. A shrieking hiss overwhelmed his ears and a shower of sparks rained down around him, but the creature did not fall.

Dalmir spared a glance at where Ioan had landed and saw to his relief that the man had risen to his feet. Ioan held himself stiffly, but did not seem to be too injured.

"Drengur had the right idea," Dalmir shouted. "Aim for the joints!"

He saw Ioan give a grim nod, and then there was a loud clang as Drengur's sword drove into the creature's knee, connecting this time with another shower of sparks. The monster swung its mace again, slamming it into Drengur and tossing him across the room like a limp doll.

Ioan dashed up behind the creature and drove the point of his blade into the same area where Dalmir had connected, but his sword slid in cleanly, disappearing into the body almost up to the hilt. A forlorn hissing squeal emanated from the gap and the construct slumped, the pinpoints of light in its face blinking out.

"Drengur!" Ioan left his sword and raced over to the young man where he lay on the stone floor. Dalmir followed close behind and together they knelt beside their companion. There was a tense moment of silence as Ioan patted the boy's face, but then Drengur moaned and his eyes fluttered open.

"What was that thing?" Drengur asked.

Ioan rose and walked over to look at the contraption. "Aton-261," he said, studying the plating on the creature's arm. "At least, that's what's stamped on this bracer."

"Ay-ton," Dalmir corrected his pronunciation. "As in: I *ate on* the floor. Aton." He handed Drengur a water skin.

Drengur tipped the skin up gratefully and took a long drink. When he was done, he handed the waterskin back with a painful groan. "What's an aton?"

"It was something Tel and Palte dreamed up together," Dalmir said, glancing over at the now lifeless machine. "Mechanical devices that can be given a set of simple instructions that they will attempt to complete so long as they have power. I've never seen one attack before, though. That is clever, though it feels more like an idea Mulemo would have had." Dalmir pulled at his lower lip in thought.

"How could such a thing still have power after all this time?" Ioan asked. "I don't know a lot about mechanical devices, but I do know that even cynders run out of power eventually, and the way you keep talking, I get the feeling you're referring to extremely long periods of time."

"I am," Dalmir admitted. He rose and walked over to where the aton lay, lifeless, and prodded it with his foot. "I don't think this one has been running this entire time. I think we triggered something when we entered the tower that woke it up. And unless I miss my guess, we will most likely encounter several more of them."

"How many more?" Drengur asked in alarm, scrambling to his feet and joining them.

Dalmir pointed at the plating on which the name and number had been stamped. "If that is any indication..." He trailed off.

"Surely not." Ioan grimaced. "Hundreds?"

"Tel used atons for all kinds of things," Dalmir said, trying his best to sound reassuring. "I'm certain he didn't turn all of them into guardians."

"I hope you're right," Ioan muttered.

Together, they faced the door that led into the library.

"Only one way to find out," Dalmir replied. "Best keep your weapons handy."

15

Raisa held her mouth open beneath the slow drips of water leaking through the roof of her prison. She did not know where the water was coming from, and she did not care. Perhaps it was raining outside and some of it had seeped through the foundation. She fervently hoped that was the case. But it didn't matter, because the terrible ache in her throat consumed her entire being. The rough dryness in her mouth made every breath a torture chamber. The single cup of water and crusts of stale... some-things... were barely enough to keep her alive, let alone strong.

How long had she been down here? Picking up a stone, she counted the scratches she had made on the walls. Forty-four marks. Was that forty-four days? It couldn't be. Somehow, she felt certain it hadn't been more than a couple of sennights, but she had no way to be sure. She could not track the passage of time down here. There were no windows within sight, no change of light. She made the marks whenever they brought her food, if it could be called food, but she had no way of knowing if that was done at any sort of regular interval. Maybe they just sent food down whenever they remembered her. If that were the case, it felt as though they were forgetting her more and more. Her parched tongue—that felt covered in cotton—attested to the fact that the water arrived less and less frequently. Maybe she had been down here for longer than she thought.

The cool drops of water held no taste or lingering flavor. If there was a slight scent of sulfur, Raisa couldn't smell it. Her sense of smell had deserted her long ago, buried beneath the reeking stench of the dungeon that never abated or changed. She held each droplet in her mouth as long as she could before swallowing, but it was not enough. The water dripped so slowly and in such tiny amounts that it only awakened her thirst more. Her cracked lips stung suddenly, and she flinched. It was only then that she realized tears were leaking from her eyes and pouring down across her mouth, their salt stinging her chapped skin. Raisa pressed her filthy palms to her face in a futile effort to stop the tears. They would only dehydrate her more, and they served no useful purpose. Oh, but she couldn't stop them! Her chest heaved with silent sobs as she gave up on the drops of water. Perhaps if she caught them in something, but what? Through her tears, she cast about for anything she might use as a cup or bowl. There was a brick with a hole in it. She didn't know if it would hold water, but it was worth a try for a blissful mouthful of water. What she wouldn't do for a whole mouthful of water!

"What would you do?"

The question came so unexpectedly that Raisa did not realize it had actually come from somewhere outside her own mind. The voice slid over her consciousness like honey and raised a shiver that convulsed her entire being. However, the need for water consumed her, and she ignored the voice and its question, raising the brick beneath the dripping water. Her arms shook with the effort and her vision blurred, but she did not relent. The drops of water splatted into the hole as she counted. Finally, when she had counted a hundred drops and felt that she must rest her arms or drop her precious prize, she slowly lowered the brick and peered inside the hole. The moisture lasted for a tantalizing moment, but before she could lift it to her lips, it spread out and dissipated, leaving only a wet stain behind as the brick absorbed the liquid.

Angrily, Raisa whirled and threw the brick against her cell door with all her remaining strength. It was then that she saw the man standing on the other side of the bars.

"You still have some spirit left, don't you?" The man stared at her with an intensity that terrified her.

"Who... who are you?" Raisa asked.

"You haven't answered my question yet," the man replied. "It's rude, you know. So rude. You don't get a question until you've answered one. That's fair, I think."

Raisa blinked. Her thoughts felt muddled and slow. Had he asked her a question? "What question was that?"

The stranger raised an eyebrow so high, Raisa was surprised it didn't fly off his face. "Another question. Rude."

She stared at him. He stared back. Anger flooded through her, focusing her thoughts, sharpening her mind. She still felt as though she were awakening from a long slumber, but her wits were reviving.

"You're really not going to tell me what question you asked." She did not phrase it as a question.

The man continued to stare at her.

She studied him. He looked to be in his fifties or sixties, but his body was painfully thin, nearly as thin as her own. His clothes hung on him oddly, as though he had lost weight and forgotten to get new attire that fit him properly. White hair stuck up from his head in a wild, thick tangle above piercingly green eyes that did not blink as often as they should. A strange, eager look on his face made him appear slightly crazed. A shudder rippled through her, but Raisa resisted the urge to take a step back. Instead, she focused on the riddle set before her. She liked riddles, had always been good at them. What question had the man asked? She had not heard him until after she saw him... or had she? Was that it? Were the words that she thought to be mere echoes of her own thoughts actually from him? Had she spoken her thoughts aloud without knowing it? How long had she been alone? How long had she been rambling to herself? How long had he stood there in the shadows watching her?

"I don't know, exactly, what I would do for a mouthful of water," Raisa said carefully, scrutinizing the stranger and trying to gauge his reaction. "I know what I would do with a mouthful of water though: I'd savor it as long as possible, perhaps. But then, of course, it might turn warm in my mouth and be less satisfying than if I gulped it down immediately."

He fairly danced a jig in pleasure, his face beaming, and yet that strange expression never left his eyes. "Very good, very good!" he cackled. "I am Lorcan"—he gave a slight bow—"at your service."

Raisa narrowed her own eyes. "Why are you down here? What do you want with me?"

"Just perusing," Lorcan replied. "Just..." His gaze wandered off down the hall and his words trailed to a halt. Raisa heard a swishing sound followed by a sharp slap and then a loud cry; she bit the inside of her cheek to keep from screaming. She knew that sound. It was the sound from her nightmares, the sound she had heard the evening they flogged her father just before they executed him, and the sound that sometimes haunted her still.

Lorcan's eyes snapped back to her face and he grinned. "Such a nasty sound." His tone was smooth, as though he were caressing each word as it passed through his lips. "Could make for some terrible nightmares, should a person have to listen to it for too long."

Raisa gritted her teeth. "What do you want?"

But the man merely smiled at her. "You'll do," he said, almost as if he had forgotten she was capable of hearing or conversing. "Yes, you'll do. But not just yet, I think. No, you aren't ready... yet. But soon. Soon." His eyes went unfocused, and a spasm of fear or anger suddenly flashed across his features. He smoothed out his expression swiftly and turned to one side, bowing low. "My Master."

"Lorcan." Ar'Molon Uun strode into view, his pristine

appearance a stark contrast to the filth and stench that had been Raisa's entire world for the past... however long it had been. The man radiated a simmering rage, and Raisa cringed away from him, as though she might be able to hide in the shadows of her cell and be forgotten. "What are you doing here?" Uun demanded of the white-haired man. "You were to stay in Telsuma to conduct your experiments. Do you remember? You were to build us an army!"

"Couldn't build an army there. Too many prying eyes. Discovered!" Lorcan held up a finger. "They discovered me."

Surely somewhere a storm cloud had been summoned away from a fortunate farmer, for it seemed that one manifested about Uun's head. "You were discovered?" Uun demanded. "How? By whom?"

"Discovered," Lorcan agreed, his voice a wheedling whimper. "They forced me to flee my lord. Forced to leave behind my... your new soldiers. Dead, all dead. But, I was not the only thing that was discovered, no... no... I did some discovering of my own." A laugh bubbled up out of the madman's mouth.

Uun scowled. "What did you discover?"

"The secret! The ultimate secret that I have been searching for, the one that has been years, so many years, in coming to me. It has come to me now. I know the secret now. After over half a century of searching, I have discovered it!"

The storm cloud dissipated, and Raisa saw something eager and hungry in Uun's expression as he leaned forward. "And which secret might that be?"

Lorcan giggled again. "Do you remember Elmrand?"

Uun's breath caught between his teeth. "Truly?"

"I have found the key to creating the army you require." Lorcan bowed with a proud flourish. "I was foolish before, and I was foolish now, for the discovery was quite accidental. But I know how it was done. Oh, yes. And I can do it again. I will do it again."

Uun rubbed his hands together. "Excellent." His lips twitched in a gleeful expression. "Can you do it at the Weald?"

Lorcan nodded, his eyes lighting up. "Yes, yes. I like the Weald."

"What else will you need?"

"Prisoners." The word hissed gleefully from between Lorcan's lips. "Many prisoners."

Uun glanced into Raisa's cage and she pressed her back up against the far stone wall, trying to escape his gaze. His eyes narrowed. "Done. You can have them all if you like."

Lorcan's breath hitched. "When do we leave?"

"It will take at least a pair of sennights before we can depart. I have to gain the Ar'Mol's permission and outfit an airship with enough guards to transport the prisoners."

"Very good, very good, my lord."

Uun gave a sharp nod. "I will begin the preparations at once. If you need anything, make sure you request it before we leave." He spun on his heel and marched out of the prison.

Lorcan turned his gaze back to Raisa, and she shuddered at the light of insanity she saw there. "Did I not tell you? Yes, I shall do much to help you. Give you strength, yes, and long life, yes, and make you very difficult to kill. And we shall teach you obedience and loyalty as well... oh yes." He leered at her through the bars, then turned away and shuffled down the long, dark hallway, his shadow trailing behind in the light of the hanging lanterns.

Raisa wrapped her arms around herself and sank to the floor, trembling. In the other cell, the sound of the lash rising and falling continued. The cries, however, did not.

<h1 style="text-align:center">16</h1>

At some point, Marik fell asleep. He didn't remember drifting off, but the sound of his door swinging open brought him to his feet before he was fully awake. Mouse and a short, hooded figure stood in the doorway, and Marik scowled at them, rubbing the sleep from his eyes.

"Your old family doesn't believe in knocking?" he growled at Mouse.

"We knocked several times," the figure replied in an even tone. Marik recognized the gravelly voice as Nando's. "When you did not answer, I grew worried that you had strayed outside your room."

"Am I a prisoner, then?"

"Of course not." Nando's voice was mild, but Marik thought he detected a note of mocking. "But you are unfamiliar with these passageways. You could easily become lost, and it could take us days to find you. The Deepway is vast, and our numbers are few."

"Ah." Marik crossed his arms. "The Deepway? Is that your name for this place?"

"It is what we call our home, yes."

"We brought you some food," Mouse interjected, holding forth a plate.

Marik took the offering and peered at its contents. The food was mostly root vegetables, though there was also a slightly wizened apple and a large round of bread that radiated warmth and smelled as though it had just finished baking.

"Thank you," he said, sitting down on the pallet and setting to work on the food. As he ate, he realized just how hungry he was. "Any news?" he asked around a mouthful of the bread; it was warm and soft and delicious.

Mouse came over and crouched down, holding out a large earthenware mug. Marik drank thirstily. The water inside was cold and sweeter than any water he had ever tasted. Nando followed Mouse with hesitant footsteps and hovered near Mouse's shoulder.

"Not yet," Mouse said. "But Papa thinks the scouts should return soon. He wanted you to eat and then join him back in the meeting hall to wait for them."

Marik nodded, too busy eating to reply.

"We'll get Shaesta when you're done. She ate already."

"Good," Marik said.

There was silence for a while as he finished the simple meal. When he was done, he glanced up at Nando. "That was exquisite," he said, with more honesty than he meant to express. "I've eaten far worse in far finer establishments."

"I will pass along your compliment," Nando replied.

Marik stared up into the shadows of Nando's hood and felt curiosity stir within him. Seated on the pallet, he was almost at eye-level with the cloaked figure. "Why do your people remain hooded? It is dark, the temperature is even. It seems an unnecessary accoutrement." He glanced at Mouse. "Is everyone here a child? Is that why they all call Hrafn 'Papa'?"

"Marik..." Mouse's tone held a note of warning, but Nando placed a hand on his arm.

"No, Lenka, it is well. If we are to work with this one, perhaps it is better if he knows. You say you trust him. Papa lets him stay and even moves to lend our aid. And you know as well as I that

Papa has a knack for judging character." Nando's ruined voice trailed off to a hoarse whisper. With a deft flick of a hand she threw back her hood.

The flickering light of the lamp illumined little, but it was enough for Marik to see the delicate features of the girl before him. She had a narrow, pixie-like face. Her glossy black hair wound around her head in a braided crown. Her skin held a blueish-gray coloration and was covered in the same scale-shaped markings he had seen on Hrafn's face. The design wound around her neck in a spiraling pattern. Her deep gold eyes glittered in the lamplight. As he stared into them, Marik realized with a start that her pupils were not round, but slitted like a malkyn's.

Marik tilted his head to one side. "Perhaps it is better if I know what?" His gaze flicked between Nando and Mouse.

Nando blinked at him, her expression clouding. "That the people you're dealing with aren't human."

———

"WHAT DO YOU MEAN, you aren't human?" Marik demanded. "Mouse is human." He stared at the boy. "Aren't you? I mean, you don't look like them."

"Mouse is human," Nando rasped. "The only human we've ever allowed into the Deepway. My daughter, Emilee found him, just a baby, abandoned in an alley. He was so weak he could barely cry. She brought him to us and we adopted him, Hrafn and I. The rest of us..." She paused. "The rest of us are like this." She gestured at her face, and Marik saw the same blue-gray scales covering the backs of her hands.

Marik's brows drew together in confusion.

The girl stamped her foot. "How old would you guess I am?"

"Fifteen or sixteen?"

"I am ninety-one," Nando replied. She peered up at him, her strange eyes boring through him. "You do not believe me? I was born human, in the town of Elmrand, ninety-one summers gone."

A surge of horror shot through Marik's body. "Elmrand?"

"Ah, you've heard of it, then?" She nodded sagely. "Lies. What you have heard were lies."

"I don't doubt it," Marik muttered. "Most of what they tell us in the Igyeum is lies. Then it wasn't a plague?"

"Not as such." The woman's voice broke. "Though it might as well have been."

"I'm sorry." Marik reached out and took her hand between his own. "You don't have to tell me any more. Your people deserve to keep what secrets you will. I am not..."

She shook her head. "No, it is time that someone knew the truth."

"I don't know if that someone ought to be me."

Nando's eyes grew brighter, and a tear slipped down her rough cheek. "If not you, then perhaps nobody. Mouse tells me you were a soldier?"

Marik's face grew hot, and he withdrew his hands and stood. "Yes," he said shortly.

"Why did you leave?"

"More reasons than I have time to explain."

"Then you might actually understand."

"What about Hrafn?"

"What about him?" She peered at him quizzically.

"Shouldn't you check with him before you tell your secrets to a stranger?"

Nando's lips thinned into a mirthless smile. "I know you still find my words hard to believe, but I am an elder. Hrafn is Eldest and First, but only by a year. That is why we call him 'Papa.' I am Second. As Second—and as wife of the First—I have the authority to make this decision." She closed her eyes. "It was the Ar'Molon. He brought a young man named Lorcan to our village. He called him a physician. Said that word of a plague outbreak had reached his ears, that he was doing what he could to prevent it from spreading. Lies." She spat. "I was little. Too little to understand. We all went to see this physician. The scare of a plague was more than enough to prompt us to trust him. But then the changes began. It took the oldest of us first. Strange growths appeared on their arms and legs, peculiar patches of color covered their skin. Some lost their minds and acted like animals. It was terrifying. Then the rest of the adults discovered similar changes. Those who still had their senses gathered us children together and hid us in a storm cellar. They gave us food and water enough to survive for lunats and commanded us to stay hidden, charging us older ones to look after the younger." Her voice wavered off to a thin, reedy hiss. "I don't know how long we stayed hidden. We cowered in the darkness until the screaming stopped. Then we heard the tramp of booted feet, and we stayed hidden. We heard sounds we did not understand, and then, finally, all the noises ceased." Nando closed her eyes. "Hrafn and I refused to let anyone leave the hiding place, though. More days passed. I don't know how long. But the silence remained. When we ran out of food and water, we ventured outside. We found only destruction. The town was no more. They had burned much of it to the ground." The woman doubled over, weeping inconsolably.

Marik stood awkwardly, staring down at her hunched form. His eyes met Mouse's, and he lifted his arms in a helpless gesture. But then Nando straightened. She thrust her chin out and wiped the tears from her face. Strength and determination radiated from her tiny figure.

"But we grew strong because of it," she continued. "We lived off the kindness of others for a time until the changes manifested in us. At first we were afraid, believing that what had happened to our parents would happen to us. But time passed, and the alterations remained far less pronounced than what the adults in our village had endured. We stopped gaining height. Our skin and eyes changed. Those who had taken us in grew to fear us, and we fled. We happened across the Deepway by accident and made it our home. We have lived down here ever since."

"How long ago was that?" Marik asked.

Nando gazed up at the ceiling thoughtfully. "Eighty years."

"I would have guessed you to be only a child," Marik marveled.

"Hrafn was twelve years old at the razing of Elmrand," she explained. "I was eleven."

Curiosity filled Marik's mind. A hundred questions swirled in his thoughts, but none of them seemed polite to ask. So he kept his tongue quiet.

"I am sorry for what happened to your village," he said in a soft voice.

"You were not to blame. You were not even born yet," Nando replied, her tone quizzical.

"No," Marik agreed. He hesitated, then plowed on, stammering out the confession. "But I was a part of the Ar'Mol's army for a time, and I did things... followed orders... that I will never be able to forgive myself for."

The woman nodded, her eyes glittering with understanding. She took Marik's hand once more. "Forgiveness is the most difficult virtue to attain," she whispered, "but it is worthwhile to pursue."

Marik swallowed with some effort. "I apologize for my questions; they interrupted your purpose. You came to take me to Hrafn. Shaesta will wonder what has happened to us."

"Yes, of course. Follow me." Nando turned and led the way. Mouse and Marik trailed after her.

"I've never heard anyone in the Deepway speak so openly about what happened to them before," Mouse said in an awed whisper.

"But you knew?" Marik asked under his breath.

Mouse nodded. "Not everything, but enough. Papa told me part of it when he thought I was old enough to understand, and I figured out the rest."

"Are they all from Elmrand, then? Or have they taken in others like you?"

"As far as I know, I'm the only outsider they ever brought in," Mouse replied. "But they're not all from Elmrand." He paused awkwardly. "I mean... well... quite a few of them were born here."

"So there are children."

Mouse nodded.

"And are they... do they...?"

"They inherited their parents' stranger traits," Mouse supplied readily.

"Interesting," Marik muttered.

They stopped at a door; at Nando's knock, the door swung open and Shaesta joined them. She fell in step with Marik, but she remained silent. Marik wondered at this. The Shaesta he had known for so many years was always chattering away, so different from the quieter Raisa. Ever since her betrayal, however, Shaesta had proven far less talkative. He wondered now if her silence was due to some lingering feelings of guilt, or if this was who she had always been, and the constant prattling the mask. His teeth ground together and Marik forced his jaw to relax; he had decided to give her a second chance, but it was difficult when he was constantly questioning whether she had ever been true.

Before he could spiral any further down into his questions about Shaesta, they arrived at the room where they had first met Hrafn. The room was much the same, though this time three times as many people had assembled. Hrafn greeted them curtly.

"We have the information you seek," Hrafn said.

"That was fast," Marik marveled.

"I sent out quite a few scouts," Hrafn replied. "I wish for this alliance to be ended as quickly as possible." The man grimaced, and Marik understood he wanted to be quit of them.

"What have you discovered?"

"Your friend is alive."

A warm flood of relief washed through Marik. He closed his eyes and breathed a silent thanks to any benevolent power that might be listening. He heard Mouse and Shaesta's twin sighs of relief and he realized just how convinced they had all been that Raisa was already dead.

"Thank you. That information is most welcome," Marik said.

"There is more. And it concerns all of us." Hrafn's gaze hardened. He turned and faced his people. "The Madman has returned."

There was a collective intake of breath at this news.

Marik exchanged a querying glance with Mouse, but the boy shook his head. It was Nando who cleared away the confusion.

"Lorcan? Here in Melar?" Her voice rose in disbelief.

An angry muttering swept across the room. Feet stamped. Marik felt the pit of his stomach drop away. Lorcan? The man from Nando's story? How could that be?

"What?" Marik could not hold in the exclamation of surprise. "But that can't be possible!"

Every eye turned toward him.

"What do you know of this, outsider?" Hrafn's tone was frigid.

"Nothing," Marik insisted. "Just what Nando told me a few moments ago. I just meant... just that... it can't be the same man. Even if it is, he'd have to be well over a hundred years old by now."

Hrafn squinted at him. "And?"

Marik paused.

"Look at us, human." Hrafn threw back his hood and spread his arms wide, the sleeves of his cloak falling back and revealing the dark scales along his skin. His strangely colored eyes glittered in the dim light. "If Nando told you about us, then you know some of us are nearing our own century-markers. Do you think the Madman has not tampered with his own body? More carefully, of course. Oh yes, he keeps only the good for himself." Hrafn spat on the floor. "But that is not the worst of my news. Your friend is being kept in the central dungeon on the lower level. We cannot penetrate that level. Our tunnels do not go that deep, nor am I willing to risk any of my people in such a reckless and ill-advised attempt."

"I understand," Marik replied. "You must protect your own. We will figure something out."

"Wait." Hrafn held up a hand. "I am not finished. I have given you the worst of it, but now there is perhaps a glimmer of hope. All prisoners are to be moved to a location in the Plains, along with the Madman."

Another mutter rippled through the room as sudden fear, cold and prickling, crept across Marik's skull. He hardly dared ask, but something deep within him compelled him to utter the words. "What do you think that means?"

Hrafn stared meaningfully up at Marik with eyes that burned with hatred. "I think my people are the only ones who can truly comprehend the terrible fate that awaits your friend should she be relocated to the Plains." He turned to the others gathered before him. "Well, my people? What do you say? I had not thought to help these outsiders, but now they face a fate we know all too well. If we are to carry out a rescue, we have little time to plan, and the odds of failure are high. But we have an opportunity to strike a blow to the heart of the Ar'Mol and those around him. We may even mete out a fragment of justice—and if not that, then at the least vengeance—to the man who murdered our families and friends. Will you march with me into danger for such an opportunity?"

Each voice now rang out strong and proud. They emanated from every throat with a singular cry that struck Marik down to his very bones and made him feel as though he had rooted to the stone.

Hrafn spread his arms and his face lit beatifically. "Are there any reservations?"

Not a sound came from any of the people.

"Then, my brothers and sisters, let us forge a plan of rescue." Hrafn turned to Marik and extended his hand. "Welcome to the Deepway."

17

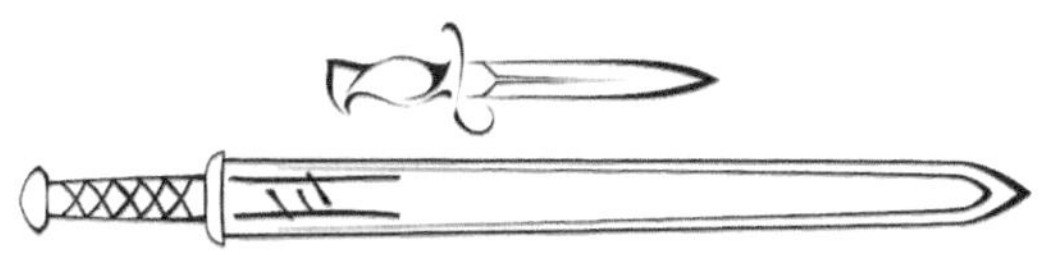

After directing the coachman to ride down the road a short distance and then make camp and await further instructions, the three men made themselves as comfortable as possible. Niveya would not let anyone leave their hiding place until the sun had set and full darkness had spread across the countryside, so they found a clear space in a shallow valley between two fields and settled down to wait. Beren had his knife out and was using it to dig into the dirt, drawing intricate patterns and then erasing them with his boot and starting over. Niveya stretched out on the ground, put his hands behind his head, and closed his eyes. A few minutes later, his breathing slowed and evened until he was snoring lightly.

Beren put his dagger away and paced about restlessly, staring off toward the horizon, hands resting on his hips. Grayden watched his friend unsheathe the enormous broadsword and begin going through his customary series of exercises: not the ones they had learned at the Academy—this was Beren's personal regimen. Grayden had watched him perform this ritual every day since he had known him: at the Academy, in the mountains during their mission, and even when traveling by airship. He marveled at his friend's dedication to his craft. Beren had taught him the exercises, but no matter how he tried, Grayden could not match him for grace.

Beren's silence filled the night until Grayden could not ignore it any longer. He rose and went to stand next to his friend. Beren did not acknowledge his presence. He merely continued weaving his sword through its intricate patterns.

"You've barely spoken a word since we left Matei's," Grayden said, keeping his tone nonchalant.

"There has been nothing to say," Beren muttered. Slice, swing, raise.

"You're angry."

"Not angry." Low sweep, slight twist.

"Uh-huh."

Sweat beaded on Beren's forehead. Raise. Block. Parry. His motions never faltered. Grayden nodded. He suddenly wished he had taken Beren's advice and brought his own sword. He coveted the calming motion of the exercises. A burst of inspiration seized him, and he adjusted his stance, moving his arm along with Beren, following his motions. It was much easier without an actual sword in his hand; the movements came more fluidly, and he experienced a greater amount of control than ever before. Out of the corner of his eye, he saw Beren glance at him, and then a smile curved at the corners of his friend's mouth. Gradually, Beren increased the speed of his motions. Grayden followed his lead. All thoughts fled from his mind. His worries, his questions, his doubts, all fell silent as he focused his entire being on keeping up with Beren.

At last, when they were both panting from the exertion, Beren sheathed his great blade. Grayden doubled over, hands on his knees, gasping for air. Beren passed him a canteen. He took it gratefully, gulping down water.

"You did well," Beren commented as Grayden passed the canteen back.

"I didn't have a sword," Grayden replied modestly.

"That is how I began," Beren admitted. "My father would not

let me do the exercises with a sword in my hand until I had learned the motions by heart."

Grayden grinned. "It was a lot easier to keep up with you without one."

Beren stared out at the surrounding countryside. "This entire venture has me on edge."

Grayden did not reply. He merely stood silent, gazing through the trees as the last rays of golden sunlight clung to the sky.

"I do not trust Niveya," Beren admitted.

"Neither do I."

Beren glanced at him, his gaze searching.

"I don't!" Grayden protested. "But he has been hunting for the Regeont's killer for several sennights, and he has resources and information that we do not. I don't trust him farther than you can reach with a sword, but I do think we need him to trust us."

"Why?"

"Because without us, I'm afraid there will be nothing to temper his actions, and innocent people will get hurt as he searches for the Regeont's murderer. You want to bring the killer to justice, and you loved the Regeont, but with Niveya, I think it's about revenge. He's taking her death personally."

Beren's mouth twisted. "I hadn't thought of that."

"If you're worried that I'm being lulled into a sense of complacency..."

"I am not," Beren said, a little too quickly. "Not anymore," he amended. "I did not understand why you were acting so friendly with him. But now I do." His face turned troubled in the dying light. "Forgive me. I underestimated you."

"I hope Niveya makes the same mistake." Grayden grinned. And that was all. The tension that had been building all day dissipated and together they stood in companionable silence, observing with awe as the setting sun brought the countryside to life.

The horizon glowed in a wash of rosy glory. Across the fields, fireflies sprang to life in an intricate dance. Like a network of tiny golden campfires, they flickered brightly and winked out repeatedly. An owl hooted. A wylfen howled far off in the distance. And with that, the night song of the forest began.

"Enjoying the evening?" Niveya came up behind them with near-silent steps. He grinned, his white teeth shining in the faint light of dusk.

When full-dark had fallen, the three of them moved out from their hiding place and stealthily made their way back to Matei's farm. They spread out and found places where they could watch all angles of the house and the barn beyond, and then settled down to wait.

Grayden perched behind a large haystack at the corner of the barn. From where he sat, he could see both the back door of the house and the front of the barn. He settled himself into a comfortable position and waited.

His eyelids weighed heavily, but he pinched his arms and flicked himself in the face, struggling against the boredom that urged him to rest, just for a moment or two. After a while, a tingling sensation filled his foot, and he adjusted his position, doing what he could to help restart the blood flow to his toes. The ground was cold, for which Grayden was thankful, since the discomfort helped keep him awake. But it wasn't a perfect deterrent. It had been a long day, with much travel, and he wasn't entirely certain that Niveya's hunch would pan out.

Just as he was getting ready to stand up and march in place in order to stave off his drowsiness, he heard a soft thump from the direction of the house. All of his senses came alive. In the dark, he peered around the haystack and watched as a shadow made its way across the backyard with hasty steps. At the barn door, the shadow stopped and swung his head about, listening. Grayden held his breath, his heart hammering in his ears.

The figure—which could only be Matei—made a soft sound that resembled the trilling of a cricket or a frog. He repeated the sound in a steady pattern.

A rustle sounded within the barn, and a short woman peered

out. "Yes?" Her whisper was barely audible, but Grayden could just make out the word.

"You have to leave," Matei hissed at her. "It's not safe here."

The woman's startled gasp made Matei jump, and he waved his hands at her in a shushing motion.

"But why? What has happened?" the woman asked.

"Three men showed up on my doorstep this afternoon asking about you," Matei explained. "They said you were owed wages, but I did not believe them."

"What did you tell them?" Her whisper seemed anxious.

"That we hadn't spoken since you left for the city," Matei said. "They left, but I'm not certain they believed me. I'm worried they will return. They might even be watching the house already. I don't want you to get hurt, cousin. I thought you would be safe here, but now I'm worried I can't protect you."

"What should I do?" the woman asked. There was a trembling quality to her whisper and Grayden felt guilty for being responsible for causing her such fright.

"You must go somewhere we have no connections to, Ulia," Matei murmured. "I can provide you with coin, but I think it would be best if you left immediately, tonight even."

Ulia's breath caught in a half-sob. She wrapped her arms around Matei, clinging to him for a long moment, and then she broke away, wiping her eyes. "If you think it is best. Oh, Matei, I am so frightened. Where will I go?"

Grayden had heard enough. Though he knew startling the two was a bad idea, he had no wish to cause them further panic. Matei's plan to get Ulia to safety was a good one, but not before they discovered what she knew. Clearing his throat softly, Grayden stepped out from behind the haystack, his hands raised in a non-threatening gesture.

Both Ulia and Matei whirled in his direction, their bodies moving into defensive positions. Grayden remained still, letting them study him warily.

"Ulia?" Grayden kept his tone gentle. "I am not here to hurt you."

The woman gave a half-sob and cowered into Matei, who put an arm around her shoulders and glared at Grayden.

"You!" he accused. "You were with the man who came here earlier, asking about my cousin. What do you want? No lies, now. I could tell that other one was lying right off."

"Can we go inside where it is more comfortable?" Grayden asked. "I give you my word that we mean no harm to either of you."

Matei continued to glare, but as it became apparent that Grayden had no intention of making any threatening moves or leaving, he gradually relaxed. "I would feel better if I could look into your eyes and read them for truth or lies," he admitted grudgingly. "Very well. Come along inside. Call your friends in as well."

When Grayden whistled, Niveya and Beren materialized out of the darkness. Together, they entered Matei's home. Ulia sat down on a pillow next to the low dining table, shoulders hunched and head bowed. Grayden saw a tear glistening on her cheek and his heart went out to her. She must be terrified.

"What is this all about, really?" Matei demanded. He shot a glare at Niveya. "I don't want to hear anything from you, truth-twister. I know your kind all too well. I'll hear from this honest lad, and no one else." He gestured at Grayden. "And maybe the young giant... I'll have to hear some of his words to know whether he can be trusted."

Niveya snapped his mouth closed and made an elegant, sweeping gesture with his hands. Seating himself at the table, Ericole tilted his head and eyed Grayden with an amused smirk on his face.

The weight of responsibility settled about Grayden's shoulders. He cautiously approached Ulia and knelt across from her. He wanted to reassure her, to reach out in some way, but she shuddered away from him as he sat down, and so he refrained from addressing her directly. Instead, he looked at Matei.

"As you know, Regeont Roshana was assassinated a few sennights ago."

Ulia uttered a low moan and hid her face in a pillow.

"My cousin had nothing to do with that." Matei's voice was loud in the small room.

"We know," Grayden said, raising his hands. "We know. Did your cousin tell you why she wanted to hide here?"

Matei stood next to Ulia, one hand patting the back of her head.

"I didn't tell him anything." Ulia whimpered. She peeked at Grayden, her face streaked with tears, her dark hair hanging about her face in wild straggles, a frantic light in her eyes. "You have to believe me. I didn't tell him anything!"

"Ulia." Beren leaned forward, his eyes serious. "We are not here to hurt you. We are here to protect you."

Matei crouched down, taking his cousin's face in his hands. "I do not believe these people are a danger to you, cousin. If you were in some kind of trouble, they would not be sitting here with us. They would be dragging you back to Doran. I do not know what haunts you so, I know you are trying to protect me, but perhaps these are the people you must tell. Why did you run away from Doran? You know there is nothing you could do that would make me think less of you. We are family, Ulia."

Beren caught Ulia's gaze and held it. "My name is Beren Adelfried. I am the son of Lord Thorben Adelfried. The Regeont was like a grandmother to me, and I only want to find her killer and bring them to justice. The third assassin is still at large, and we believe you might have seen something nobody else did. Can you not tell us what you know?"

Ulia jumped like a startled sparrow as Beren gave his name. Her eyes fixed on him with rapt attention while he spoke, and when he had finished, she dropped her gaze and nodded slowly.

"I am sorry to put you through so much trouble, cousin." Her face turned pleadingly toward Matei. "But you have to understand. I did not know who I could trust. I've been so scared..."

"What are you afraid of?" Grayden asked.

Ulia gulped. "Matei, perhaps some coffee?"

Matei nodded and busied himself in the kitchen for a moment, setting a kettle on the wood-burning stove. He returned and Ulia nodded as if to herself.

"I will tell you what I know," Ulia whispered. Her words came out halting and slow, as though she were dragging them forth from a deep, dark hole into which she had shoved them. "There was so much confusion that day." Ulia gulped and paused for a long moment. She appeared to be collecting her thoughts. "I was working for the Regeont that day as her personal assistant. That isn't usually my job, but Delia was ill and couldn't get out of bed that morning. It became my job to take her place since I've trained for those duties, and it's easier to find someone to cover my regular assignments than it is to find someone to fill in for Delia."

Grayden nodded. That made sense. A personal assistant to the Regeont was a position of great importance that covered a wide range of skills.

The kettle sang, startling all of them. Matei rose and collected the mugs, filling them with the thick, black liquid. Niveya got up and helped him bring the things back to the table, where they busied themselves with stirring in the desired amounts of cream and sugar. Once she had tended to the coffee, Ulia continued her story.

"I was on my break when the bells started ringing. We found out later about the attack on the Academy. I remember running up to the Regeont's private study. When I got there..." Ulia's eyes widened and she put a hand over her mouth at the memory.

Beren leaned forward, but Grayden caught his eye and gave a warning shake of his head. This was not a moment to pressure the woman. Ulia took a shaky sip from her cup as Beren forced himself back against his chair.

"At first, I thought the Regeont was alone. On the floor..." Ulia shook her head as if trying to dislodge the memory from her brain. "They were dead. Two men. They had attacked when she was alone, but she fought them off."

"But the Regeont was alive?" Niveya's fingers drummed on the table.

Ulia nodded. "Yes. She... she just stood there amid the chaos and death. I remember her sleeve was ripped, hanging off her arm, her hair was disheveled, and there was blood on her face, but she looked so composed." Ulia's voice filled with awed admiration.

"Then..." Beren began, then clamped his mouth shut, his entire attention focused on the woman, not wanting to interrupt the story.

"And then I saw him," Ulia continued, "the third man. He was on the other side of the room holding a dagger, and I just stood there: frozen, terrified. I couldn't think of a thing to do. I couldn't move. I didn't even scream. He attacked her, and she sort of ducked out of the way, and I remember she... she grabbed something out of the fire."

"What was it?" Beren asked.

Ulia closed her eyes. "It..." Her eyes snapped open. "It was her seal. I remember thinking that it seemed so small and frail, like her, and why would she waste time trying to retrieve something like that, and then she buried it in the man's shoulder and he gave a horrible shout and the room filled with a smell..." She shuddered.

"Take your time," Grayden murmured.

"It all happened so fast!" Ulia wailed. "Then Lord Elan came barging in and he started fighting the assassin, and I screamed, and the assassin threw his knife at me, and then Lord Elan ordered me to get out." She was sobbing now, great, gulping gasps of air. "I didn't stop to think, I just obeyed him. I ran and ran and ran, and I couldn't stop."

"Where did you go? Did you alert the guards?" Beren asked.

Ulia shook her head. "I wasn't thinking straight. It never occurred to me that the guards wouldn't hear, wouldn't be there. I ran to my room." Tears trickled down her face. "Later, when I found out that the Regeont was dead... I couldn't help but think that... maybe I could have done something. I just stood there. I should have done something. If only I had... if only... oh, it's all my fault!" A choked cry escaped her lips, and she put her head down on the table and sobbed. Matei patted her back and glared reproachfully at their guests.

"Is that enough?" the farmer demanded. "Have you made her suffer adequately, reliving these terrible memories?"

"Almost." Niveya's voice was calm. "Just a few questions. Ulia, please, it is important."

Ulia stared at him, her eyes red-rimmed and wide with fright. "I've been reliving that horrible day for sennights. Questioning every move I made. Living in fear. I can't bear it any longer!"

"You have a right to be afraid," Niveya assured her. "Think carefully. This is important. The window. Was it broken when you entered the Regeont's study?"

Ulia frowned, a tiny line of concentration marring her otherwise smooth, dark forehead. Then she shook her head. "It was not."

"Did it get broken while you were there?"

Ulia shook her head again.

"How about later?"

Ulia squinted. "Yes. It was broken when I saw the room again." She paused. "That's strange. Everyone was talking about how the assassins must have come in through the window, but that can't be right. They were already inside and the window was whole. I remember that's how I noticed the third assassin. I saw his reflection in it."

"Which shoulder did the Regeont brand with her seal?" Niveya asked.

"His right shoulder. I remember I didn't see it so much as I heard and smelled it." Ulia wrapped her arms around herself.

"When did you find out that the Regeont was dead?" Grayden asked.

"Later that night." Ulia gulped. "I was so shaken, I fell asleep.

When I woke, the manor was in an uproar. I asked what had happened, and they told me... I... I didn't know what to do."

"Why did you flee the city?" Niveya asked.

"I couldn't stay there, not when it was my fault the Regeont was dead. At first I was worried the assassin would come back for me since I had seen him and could describe him, but then I realized he'd have to come back for Lord Elan and Lady Ilya, as well. But I couldn't bear to even walk past that room. I couldn't focus on my duties. Lord Elan must have noticed. He was kind to me; he suggested I take some time off and get some rest."

Niveya stood and paced about the room, a thoughtful expression on his face. He returned to the table, leaning over it and peering intently into Ulia's tear-stained face. "Thank you, my dear. That is very helpful. One final question: you said you saw the third assassin. Could you give a description of him? Would you recognize him if you saw him again?"

"He was short, wiry. He had a narrow face with a sharp chin and a small nose," Ulia said, her eyes closed in concentration. "I couldn't see his hair—he had a cap on—but I caught a good look at his face. I am certain I would recognize him."

"Wonderful," Niveya said. "We will need you to come with us."

"What?" Ulia's voice rose in pitch.

"You got a good look at the assassin. You are the only one who can describe him to the city guard. They have been searching, but without a description, they have little to go on."

"I can't!" Ulia's eyes widened with terror. "Why hasn't Lord Elan told them what the assassin looked like? Or Lady Ilya? She was racing toward the room as I ran out!"

"Both of them claim they did not get a good look at the assassin," Niveya replied.

"How do you know that?" Beren demanded, turning to Niveya.

"I may have peeked at the investigator's notes," Niveya admitted. "Both Ilya and Elan claimed they were so focused on the

Regeont, they did not catch a good look at the killer. Ulia is the only one who can identify him."

"No." Ulia's head shook back and forth in tiny movements of denial. "Lord Elan had to have seen the assassin. He was right next to me. He fought the man. I can't. I just can't!"

"Ulia," Grayden began, trying to keep his voice soothing, "will you please come with us? We must present this evidence to the conscripts. What you saw is the only lead we have to solve the murder of the Regeont. If you don't speak of what you saw, her killer might go free."

Ulia stared at them, emotions warring across her face. "Yes," she groaned into the pillow she clutched like a lifeline. "Yes, I will come with you if you promise to keep Matei safe."

"Ulia," Matei protested, "it is your safety I am worried for."

"We promise," Grayden said without hesitation. "Niveya?"

Niveya did not turn. "My people can keep your cousin safe," he promised shortly, though it was not clear to whom he was speaking.

"Ulia," Matei tried one more time. "I dislike this. Let me come with you. Surely you do not intend to travel alone with these men. What if they are not who they say they are?"

Niveya whirled. Reaching across the table, he gripped Matei by the front of his shirt. "I have been many things in my life," he growled. "And I have borne many insults. Many of them were even deserved. I am a thief, and a liar, and I am loyal to no man but myself. I have always looked out only for my own, knowing that nobody else would do so. I am a law-breaker and some might even call me a criminal. But you mark me: I have never betrayed a friend. And Lady Roshana was one of the few people in this world that I considered not only a friend, but an equal. She was a powerful ruler with a shrewd mind for business. She beat me at our little games of intrigue as often as I beat her. And while we were not always on the same side, I would never have consciously done anything to hurt her. Now, your cousin is the only person who can ensure that the Lady Roshana's murderer is put where he belongs, and that is an event I wish to see with every breath in my lungs. So, when I tell you that you can trust me to take care of your cousin, you can believe that my words are true. Do you understand?"

Matei stared down at Niveya's fist, full of his shirt, and then looked into his eyes—dark with fury—and nodded vigorously.

Niveya released his hold on the man. "Good." He straightened, pulling at his sleeves as though to iron out any unnecessary wrinkles. "Well. Since my two young friends here will most likely endeavor to thwart any scheme I might put into motion involving the most timely death of this assassin once I find him, and since their endeavors in the past have proven to be annoyingly effective, it appears I have no choice but to go along with their current plan." He nodded to Ulia. "My men will be here by morning to protect your cousin. No, do not worry, my good man, they will neither bother you nor disrupt the running of your most impressive farm." He said the word "farm" with a hint of laughter. "You will not even see them if you do not wish to. Once they have arrived and I am assured of your continued safety, we will take your cousin to Telsuma, where she will relay her information to Lord Adelfried himself. And then..." he eyed Beren and Grayden, a wicked gleam in his eye. "And then, my friends, my duty will be fulfilled."

18

Oleck made his opinion clear. He did not enjoy being underground. Despite the adequate headroom, Oleck walked about with a slight stoop to his shoulders, as though constantly worried he might hit his head. Even though Marik and Shaesta tried to convince him it was just like being inside a house with no windows, Oleck insisted he could tell they were underground, and grumbled about it at every opportunity. Marik was simply glad he had agreed to come into the Deepway.

The big man had spent the better part of two sennights taking the *Hawk* to their nearest hideout and returning by boat on the river. And then it had taken an enormous amount of convincing to get his first mate to pass through the riverbank entrance. Only the promise of help in recovering Raisa had lured him inside.

The durven were busy. Everywhere Marik looked, plans were being made and discussed. There was an elegance to how these people considered each plan from every angle, discarding ideas that would not work as easily as casting aside a piece of garbage. They would have made excellent pirates. He and his crew joined these discussions, adding their own ideas into the mix and voicing their concerns about any plans that seemed too fragile or risky.

Hrafn had sent a handful of his people to lurk in the tunnels nearest the Ar'Mol's palace, and ordered them to keep their eyes and ears open for any developments. And though he did not know where they were, Marik knew others were hard at work carving out other tunnels near the palace, trying to find a route that could work for their rescue attempt.

"It will not be easy," Hrafn said. He said much the same every day. Marik wondered if that was Hrafn's optimistic way of saying it was impossible. But he kept his thoughts to himself and lent a hand wherever he could.

The durven had come alive at the possibility of confronting the man who had made them. Marik worried they would get so consumed by their quest for revenge that they would lose sight of the only goal he had any interest in achieving. But Nando set his mind at ease on that score.

"Your Raisa is our priority," she assured him when he voiced his concern. "Lorcan's presence has simply provided my people with the motivation to do the right thing and help you. If it comes down to a choice between rescuing your friend and taking revenge, rest assured that my people will always choose your friend. None of us wishes to see another person suffer as we have."

"Does it hurt? What he did to you?" Marik asked.

Nando shook her head. "No," she replied. "The pain of the experiments faded long ago. It is not physical suffering I speak of, but the deeper hurt of the heart and mind."

Marik winced.

Nando reached her hand up and placed it on his elbow. "Do not despair. We will find Raisa." In spite of her ruined voice, a trait shared by all the durven, Marik found something comforting and oddly melodious about the way Nando spoke, and despite his worries, he felt warmed by her words.

———

It took them three days. Three grueling days filled with arguments and counterpoints, but Hrafn and Marik finally concocted a plan. Marik was not sure how sound of a plan it was, but so far it was the only one they had managed to hold on to.

"I only have one worry," Marik said, placing his hands on the table and leaning forward. "What if our information is wrong?"

"Geira and her scouting party are certain," Hrafn replied. "The Ar'Mol gave orders to move the prisoners to the Weald in two days. In order to do that, they will have to move the prisoners out of the dungeons and onto a transport. It is the only time that they will be vulnerable. We must strike then."

"Captain," Oleck growled, thumping his fist on the table. "I think it would be a much better option to attack the airship once it's left Melar."

Marik sighed.

"Oleck, we've been over this," Shaesta said. "This won't be a lumbering cargo cruiser that's tried to save money by assuming a group of partially trained Academy students can handle an unlikely attack from pirates. They will transport the prisoners on one of their battleships, and you can be sure that it will carry a full complement of soldiers as guards. If we try to attack them in the air, we'll likely all end up dead."

"And what makes this any better?" Oleck argued. "Those soldiers will still be around a docked airship."

"Exactly," Marik replied. "But the airship can't dock at the palace. You saw what it was like when we were flying over. They'll have to march the prisoners out of the city to the royal docks. That's when we'll attack. Yes, there will be some guards, but not as many, because most of them will wait at the airship."

Oleck gave a grudging nod. "I suppose that makes sense. It still feels like there are too many unknowns."

"I wish we knew where or what the Weald is beyond 'somewhere in the Plains,'" Marik agreed. "It could be important."

"We could trail the transport and try to rescue Raisa when it gets there," Mouse piped up. "Then we could get Raisa and information to help Telmondir."

Marik shook his head. "If we do that, we really don't know

what we're getting into. It could be anything from a small bivouac to a fortress. Either way, it might be even more well-defended than the palace."

Mouse's face fell.

"No, this is the best plan we have and the best chance we're likely to get," Marik continued, rubbing a hand across the back of his neck. "Here we have time to plan and a safe place to retreat to."

"Then it's settled," Hrafn said. "We shall begin preparations immediately."

The others dispersed, but Marik remained staring at the table and all their plans, a sense of foreboding welling up within him. Shaesta alone lingered, her movements hesitant and fluttery like an indecisive butterfly.

"We'll get her back," Shaesta said at last, coming to stand next to him. She seemed to hover on the verge of reaching out to comfort him, but then she retreated into herself, pulling away.

"I know."

He could feel her studying him. Her eyes intent and worried, but Marik did not meet her gaze. If he had any hope of rescuing Raisa, he needed to stay focused on the task at hand. Talking about the job ahead would not help, and neither would discussing his feelings on the matter, nor would it assuage his guilt at letting Raisa go into the Ar'Mol's palace alone. She had always reminded him of the little sister he had lost—though no amount of torture would ever have dragged that confession from his lips—but now he had failed them both. He should have been the one to go, he should have been the one captured. But he could not change the past. All he could do was atone for his mistake in the future, and purpose to never make a similar one. So he avoided Shaesta's meaningful look. He didn't want to talk about anything. The time for talking was over.

———

MARIK and his small crew crept through the tunnels, following Nando and the other durven who had agreed to lead them and accompany them in the rescue attempt. As they traversed farther from the main tunnels, evidence of the durven grew scarce. Out here, the tunnels were narrower and full of dust and rubble. There were places where the ceiling had collapsed, and there were no flecks of anything glittering in the walls.

Marik mentioned this in a whisper to Nando. Her eyes lit up, and she craned her neck, peering about the passageway they were traveling through.

"We haven't made it to these far reaches of the tunnels yet. We've been slowly working our way out, restoring passageways as we need to. Our numbers have grown rather a lot in the past eighty-odd years."

"How many of your people live down here?" Marik asked. During his time in the Deepway, he had seen and interacted with perhaps two-score individual faces, but he had not yet seen any of the children Mouse had mentioned.

"All of them," Nando replied.

Marik hid a grin. "I was more curious about the number."

Nando hesitated. "Hrafn wouldn't like me to tell you that, I don't think." Her expression was apologetic. "But I will tell you we have over ten times what we started with."

"Ah." Marik fell silent, pondering the snippets he'd picked up over the past sennight in the Deepway. From what he had gathered, the children who had crept down into these tunnels eighty years ago had numbered somewhere around two hundred. That meant this had become a thriving community of over two thousand by now, right under the nose of the Ar'Mol and the Igyeum, with plenty of space to grow yet. A flicker of admiration lit in his thoughts at what these people had accomplished. It was a quiet achievement, but no less impressive for that.

"Almost there." The whispered words came traveling back to Marik from the durven who had taken it upon themselves to scout ahead and make sure the path was clear.

The muscles in Marik's shoulders tensed as he went over the plan in his mind once more. It was not complicated. Both Marik and Hrafn agreed that simplicity was often the better choice; there were fewer things that could go wrong.

A few moments later, he could see a pinprick of light, and he knew they had reached the promised exit. If they had timed everything right, they should not have to wait long. The durven at the front of the line worked in swift silence, and before Marik could find a comfortable resting position, they had created a doorway through which they could exit the tunnel.

Under the darkening sky, Marik and the others crept outside. The location was perfect. They had emerged from the tunnel near the path along which the soldiers would march the prisoners, but inside a small grove of pine trees and underbrush, so there was plenty of cover to hide them while they waited. Nando was the last one out of the tunnel, and she carefully replaced the sod that her people had cut out. Marik marveled at how cleverly it had been done. Even knowing where the exit was, he could not discern the outline of the door.

The night wore on and the last rays of light eased themselves below the horizon. They waited. Clouds rolled in, obscuring the rising moon and casting the night into a deep darkness that seemed eager to aid their rescue attempt. Anxious energy surrounded them and flooded through the entire company. Then, after more than an hour of waiting, Mouse popped up from where he was lying in the grass.

"I hear something," he hissed.

Instantly the grove fell silent, the few snatches of whispered conversation dying mid-word as everyone froze. Not a pine needle stirred unless the breeze caught it. The soft sound that Mouse had caught grew louder until they could all hear the rumble of wheels and the thumping of feet.

"Oh... no..." Marik breathed as all of his plans crashed to the ground. He shared an anguished look with Oleck and Shaesta and saw that they had heard it, too, and knew what it meant.

Around the bend, the prisoner transport came into view, and Marik saw what his ears had already told him: the Ar'Mol was far shrewder than they had hoped. The prisoners were all held in a cage mounted on a low wagon pulled by a single leythan. At the front of the cage swung lanterns, casting a glow about the transport. Four soldiers marched on each side of the cage, eyes alert and weapons ready.

"I guess they don't feel as confident as we'd hoped," Shaesta murmured in Marik's ear.

"We can still rescue her," Oleck whispered.

Nando looked at Marik, a question in her eyes. "We hadn't planned on dealing with a leythan," she reminded him. "But even so, there are twenty of us. The odds are still good. It's your call, Captain."

Marik's mouth moved as he considered. There were twice as many armed guards as they had guessed, and the leythan could be a problem. Then he saw a familiar face in the lanternlight. Pressed against the bars by the other prisoners, wan and pale from sennights hidden from the sun and lack of food, but still undeniably her.

Raisa.

His decision made, Marik's mouth tightened into a thin line. "We go on my mark, just as we planned. This changes nothing," he muttered. All around him, his crew and the durven tensed, waiting for his signal. The transport lumbered down the path, coming closer to their hidden location. Then it was past.

"Now!" Marik hissed.

They dashed out from the trees, slinking up behind the soldiers in absolute silence, prepared to attack with swift surprise.

However, before they could strike, the leythan gave a loud snort and its lumbering walk turned into a quick trot. The soldiers whirled on their attackers, and the sound of steel striking steel clanged out into the night air.

Marik let out a battle cry and charged at the nearest soldier, shouting for someone to catch the leythan. The rest of the durven closed around the soldiers. From the corner of his eye Marik saw that Oleck had grabbed the leythan's bridle and was hanging from it, forcing the immense creature to turn off the road. The beast's head swung and its body followed, rumbling to a stop.

Marik directed his attention back to the soldiers before him. They had closed ranks and stood in a tight circle, facing the ring of durven.

"There is no need for bloodshed tonight," Marik said. "We merely wish to retrieve something that belongs to us."

A soldier spat on the ground and then grinned.

The air rang with a repetitive clinking, and then the ground trembled as a large hook and chain smashed into the grass next to the road, drawing a deep furrow as the chain tightened until it caught around the trunk of a tree. His eyes traveled up the chain and Marik saw to his horror that an airship had descended from behind the thick layer of clouds. A high-pitched whining sound unlike any he had ever heard before filled the air, and then a beam of light erupted from the deck of the ship. Marik threw himself to the ground, momentarily blinded, then the sound faded, and he sat up, blinking away the spots in his vision. He stared, not comprehending the sight before him. Half of the road and ten of the durven who had stood there but a moment before were gone. All that remained was an ugly ditch of burned earth and the smell of scorched meat.

The soldiers gave a mighty shout and surged forward. What was left of the durven stood there, dumbfounded and confused. They fought mechanically, stunned at the horrifying suddenness of what had just transpired.

"Retreat!" Marik yelled. He fought his way through the chaos, his sword striking out as he carved a path toward the cage. Oleck still clung tenaciously to the leythan's bridle. Marik knew his first mate couldn't hang on for long. The beast wanted to run. Something, perhaps the smell of their ambush or the sound of that weapon, had frightened it badly, and it was trying desperately to get away. If Oleck let go of the halter, the creature would bolt, and they would not be able to open the cage.

Darkened skies! What had that thing been?

Marik raced over to the cage and climbed up to the door.

"Raisa!" he shouted, his hands scrabbling with the lock. He did not have the tools he needed. Maybe he could smash the lock open with something... "Raisa!"

Then she was there, on the other side of the bars, her small hands covering his—her skin felt rough and chapped—her eyes, wide and bright, stared up into his face. In the lantern light, they gleamed with an emerald hue. She gestured frantically to the other side of the cage and he followed her around to a spot where the bars had been wrenched apart, not far enough for anyone to fit through, but if they could pry the bars a bit wider...

"Marik... look out!" Raisa gasped.

He swung out of the way and the sword blow aimed at his back crashed into the bars of the cage. Holding on to the bars, Marik pushed himself straight back, his boots crashing into the chest of his attacker. The man grunted in pain and staggered back as Marik landed on the ground and whirled, sword raised.

"You are going to lose," the soldier sneered. "Scum like you always lose."

Marik did not waste breath on words. He charged. The soldier met his rush with a parry and delivered a well-placed kick to Marik's knee. His leg buckled under the blow, and Marik almost crashed to the ground, but he held himself upright, gritting his teeth against the pain. The soldier attacked again and again, and Marik, his right leg on fire with pain, continued to give ground in hobbling, grudging steps. The soldier was well-trained and powerful. Marik wasn't sure he could have beaten the man even on his best day. But what he could do was keep him occupied as Mouse clambered up onto the transport and worked at the lock. The other soldiers were still focused on their attackers. No one had time to notice a small boy.

That high-pitched whine flooded the air once more. The

soldier facing Marik glanced up at the airship before turning and sprinting back to the prisoners. Marik, knowing that the sound meant death, did the only thing he could think of and chased after the soldier, limping as fast as he could. Another wave of heat and light poured down from above, boring another trench through the road and incinerating a tree. The soldier Marik was chasing bellowed at Mouse, who leapt down and darted off into the woods. The soldier gave chase and Marik checked the door and muttered angrily. Still locked. He turned his attention to the bent bars once more. He gripped them and strained, trying to pry them just a little farther apart. His muscles screamed at him, but he continued to pull.

"Marik. Marik!" Raisa's hand on his arm made him pause. She shook her head at him, a tear sliding down her face. There was a look in her eyes he had never seen before, not ever. He did not recognize it. She leaned her head against the bars for a moment, her hair falling forward over her ears, then she straightened, her shoulders stiffening, her expression filling with determination.

"Here." Raisa and the others shifted as much as they could and a tiny child crept forward. "You can't get us out, but you can save her." There was an urgency in her voice, and her green eyes pleaded with him.

The little girl slipped through the narrow opening, her slight frame just small enough. She landed on the ground next to Marik and stared up at him with wide, frightened eyes in the lanternlight. Fear. That was the expression on Raisa's face. Marik looked at Raisa, his hand gripping hers desperately.

"We are going to rescue you." He forced strength into his voice.

"I know," Raisa replied. "But not right now, not with that thing up there. Go! Get her to safety. Tell Oleck..." Her voice broke.

"I will," Marik promised. He glanced at the man, still struggling to hold the terrified leythan. "But you have to... you have to tell him to let go."

Raisa straightened as much as she could in the cramped cage. Raising her voice, she shouted, her voice a thin waver of ribbon over the tapestry of battle and frightened cries. "Oleck! You need to let go."

"Raisa?" Oleck's answering reply drifted back, sounding strained. "I can't, we have... to get you... out of there!"

"LET GO! Oleck! Let go!" She leaned her face against the bars and her shoulders heaved with sobs. Then the cage jerked sideways and rolled swiftly away as the leythan, rid of the burden on its mouth, plunged on down the road. With cries of alarm, the soldiers broke away from the fight and chased after their cargo. Marik stared across the empty space between himself and Oleck. The big man's expression was unreadable in the darkness, but Marik could still feel the disbelief and anger Oleck was directing at him.

Marik gave a long whistle, picked up the small child at his feet, swung her onto his back, and hobbled painfully toward the hidden door. Oleck was at his side in a few long strides, his shoulder under Marik's arm, lifting him up and propelling him along. The others, hearing Marik's signal for retreat, joined them as they descended back into the Deepway.

They did not stop until they reached the first retreat chamber, several twists and turns down the labyrinth from which they had come. Marik's leg screamed at him, throbbing with every step, every heartbeat, and as they entered the room, he collapsed next to the wall. The little girl slid off his back and scrambled away, tucking herself into a corner and watching them all with wide, frightened eyes. He wanted to go to her, to reassure her that she was safe and that no one was going to hurt her, but bright spots flashed in his vision and he was not certain he could hang on to consciousness long enough to stand.

"Marik? Captain? Are you well?" Oleck's voice seemed to come from a very distant place.

Marik opened his eyes. His head buzzed and breathing through his nose burned as though he had taken a deep breath over a vat of vinegar. He blinked up at Oleck and Shaesta, who now both leaned over him, their faces concerned. He nodded. "What happened?"

"You sort of slumped over there for a moment, gave us a bit of a fright," Oleck said. "Are you certain you're well?"

"My leg." He gestured and earned a sharp intake of breath from Shaesta. Scared to know the answer, he asked, "How bad?"

Shaesta took a moment before she answered, poking and prodding at his leg with gentle fingers. "I don't think anything is broken," she announced.

Marik heaved a sigh of relief.

"But you're not going anywhere for a while," she continued.

Just then, Nando came hurrying over to them. "Have any of you seen Olin?" she asked.

Marik closed his eyes. Before the mission, he had familiarized himself with each of the members who had volunteered to help. He summoned a memory of Olin. He was young, one of the second generation, and somehow related to Nando, her son, maybe? He had been so eager to join them and help rescue someone from the clutches of the Igyeum.

"No, I haven't seen him, but I haven't seen anyone since we came down the tunnels," Marik replied. "I was just trying not to lose consciousness until we got to safety."

"He wasn't..." Oleck's voice was low and gentle. "He wasn't one of those caught in that first blast?"

Nando shook her head emphatically. "No. I saw him fighting after that. He was right behind me when you sounded the order to retreat, Captain. But now that we're down here, I can't find him anywhere." Her voice rose in pitch with every word.

Marik raised a hand to Oleck, who helped him to his feet. "Stay calm, Nando," Marik said. "I'm sure he's down here somewhere. But just in case, perhaps we should send someone back down the tunnel to see if he was injured and fell behind."

Nando nodded, her fingers clasping and unclasping

nervously. "That's a good idea. I'll send Elthen. She's got the best darksight." She hurried off.

Oleck gave Marik a concerned look as he lowered him back to the ground. "What do you think?"

"I think... we should be careful," Marik replied. "Hopefully they'll find him in the tunnel, but..."

"You think he might be dead, don't you?" Shaesta asked.

"Or worse," Marik said, his voice dark. "If he fell behind or got grabbed by a soldier... everyone in the Deepway could be in danger now, because of us."

"The soldiers were far too busy trying to catch their leythan." Shaesta's words were brusque and dismissive, but her expression betrayed her concern.

He felt like his thoughts were trapped in that cage with Raisa, plunging away toward the horizon behind a terrified leythan. Horrible scenarios and possibilities swam before his eyes, and he could not shake them away. Out of the corner of his eye, he caught sight of the small child Raisa had handed him and he went over to where she still sat huddled away from the group. Pressing his back against the wall, he slid down to sit next to her, groaning a little as the pain in his thigh surged once more. Moving it hurt. The child recoiled from him but did not run away.

Marik pulled a piece of dried meat out of the satchel he had slung over his shoulder and held it out, his motions slow and nonchalant. The child grabbed the offered jerky, and she gnawed on it with the ferocity of a ravenous, half-starved wylfen. A pang coursed through him as he watched her. She was just a tiny thing. Surely she had parents? Had they been in that cage as well? What would become of this little waif, tossed about on the winds of the world with no dock to anchor at?

"My name is Marik," he said, keeping his voice quiet. "Captain Marik. I have an airship."

The child glanced up at him, her expression startled at first, but then she seemed to decide that he meant her no harm and she returned to working on the piece of dried meat between her hands.

"That woman who helped you get out of that cage? Her name was Raisa. She's part of my crew. Did you know her?"

The girl gave a small shake of her head.

"She probably saved your life. I was trying to save hers..." Marik trailed off. "You weren't with her in the dungeons?"

Another headshake.

"Do you have any idea where they were planning on taking you?"

"The Weald." The whisper was so soft Marik almost missed it.

"I've heard that term. Do you know what the Weald is?"

"A bad place."

"Bad?"

The girl nodded and finished the last of the meat. She looked up at him, a spark of hope in her eyes. Marik gave her a conspiratorial grin and handed over another piece, as well as his waterskin. The girl drank from it thirstily, spilling quite a lot down her front. When she finished, she looked up, a guilty expression on her face.

"I'm sorry."

"No need to be sorry. I can get more water."

She looked around, her eyes wide. "You can?"

"Yes," he assured her.

"This..." She paused. "This isn't a bad place?"

"Ah." Marik pressed his palms together and rested his chin on his fingertips. "It probably doesn't seem much different from the dungeon, does it? Is that what you think?"

Her expression grew guarded once more.

"We aren't kidnappers. Like I said, we were trying to rescue my friend Raisa. But I am happy to have rescued you. Can you tell me about your parents? They're probably worried about you. We can take you home, if you'd like."

The girl's eyes filled with tears that shimmered as they spilled out over her cheeks. She sniffled, wiping her nose on her sleeve, but the tears continued to flow.

"Hey, now." Marik patted the top of her head. She leaped to her feet at the touch, snarling like an angry malkyn, her fingers curled into claws as though she wanted to scratch his face. Marik raised his hands. "I'm not going to hurt you," he promised. "I just want to help. You don't want to talk about your parents, fine."

Her posture relaxed, and she sank back down to the ground.

"Why don't we start with something simpler? Can you tell me your name?"

She shook her head.

"Come on," he urged, smiling. "I told you my name. And my friend's name. Can't you tell me yours?"

There was a long silence. "Elalli," she finally whispered.

"Elalli. That's pretty."

She hung her head, dirty hair falling forward around her face.

"Is that a smile?" Marik gasped. "No, it can't be. Elalli doesn't smile anymore. And she certainly wouldn't smile for mean Captain Marik, not after eating all his meat and drinking all his water!"

A giggle.

"Nope. Elalli is not smiling," Marik continued. "She is plotting ways to steal Captain Marik's airship and rule the skies with it. All hail Pirate Queen Elalli!"

She giggled again, turning her face up to peek at him. "What airship name?"

"She's called the *Valdeun Hawk*." Marik swung his arms out grandly to either side. "And she's the prettiest airship ever to sail through the clouds."

"The *Balding Hawk*?" Elalli squinted one eye at him, disbelief written across her face. "That a silly name."

"Not the Balding Hawk," Marik protested, "the *Valdeun Hawk*."

The disbelief faded, and she giggled some more. "Val-DAY-uunn." She drew the word out as though tasting it. "What's Val-Valdeun?"

Marik leaned his head back and looked up at the ceiling. "It's a kind of bird that only lives in Vallei. A beautiful bird, graceful and strong, just like the people of my homeland. It's a noble bird. Not at all bald. There aren't many of them left now. It was just a kind of way for me to hang on to a bit of my heritage, naming my airship after..." He trailed off.

"Parents in the cage." Elalli's voice was grave.

Marik looked down at her and was reminded of the tiny valdeun hawk he had once rescued when he was a boy. It had been far too young to fly, too young to be out of its nest. It must have fallen, but try as he might, he could not find the nest anywhere. He had built a small box for it and lined it with soft swatches of fabric his mother didn't need anymore, and then he had stayed outside with it, guarding it day and night for a sennight, hoping that the bird's parents would come find it. They never did, and so he took the fledgling home and raised it as his own pet. It had been a loyal friend and a superb hunter, helping him put food on his family's table. Before the memory could go any farther, Marik shook his head, clearing it.

"I'm sorry," he said.

The little girl's lip quivered. She stared at him bravely for a long moment. Then the dam burst and Elalli threw herself into his lap, sobbing into his shirt.

19

Dalmir led the way through the door and into the enormous room on the other side of the atrium. Ioan and Drengur followed cautiously, weapons drawn and looking a little jumpy after encountering one of Tel's mechanical guardians. The room contained rows upon rows of bookshelves, all of them towering a good ten to twelve feet in the air. Each stack had a rolling ladder attached to it, so that no title remained out of reach. Near the ends of each set of bookshelves rested large desks and couches specifically placed for those who wished to sit and study or read. The shelves stretched across the room in neat rows; it was impossible to see the other end from where they stood at one side of the massive room. Dalmir hunched his shoulders, reaching deep into his memories and drawing out the first time he had been here. Telsume had been so proud of this place, grinning like a child as he showed Dalmir around. The memory came to him, clear as if his brother stood before him once again.

"I SET it up like the first Library," Telsume said, his face alight, he nearly bounced with eagerness to show Dalmir around. "You remember, of course. That place... it still inspires me! Isn't that

amazing? Even though it's gone, it still fills me with a sense of purpose and awe."

Dalmir nodded absently. He did not like to think of the first Library. There was too much guilt down that path. The destruction of the Library had been their fault. Of course, Shiori never brought it up, but he often wondered if she thought of it, if she missed it, if she blamed him for the destruction of her home. It was the one reason he kept her at arm's length, even though his brothers often teased him about her.

As though reading his thoughts, Telsume glanced at Dalmir sidelong. "Shiori seemed to like it when I showed her."

Dalmir's cheeks filled with warmth. "I'm glad," he muttered, trying to hide his jealousy that Tel had showed the library to Shiori first... or was it to hide his jealousy that Shiori had spent time alone with Tel? Then he saw something that made all thought stop. In a small alcove stood a trio of statues. An ache welled up inside him, but his feet insisted upon moving closer. Just as he had suspected, the statues depicted a man and a woman. At their feet, clinging to her mother's skirts, was a tiny girl. His whole body convulsed. This must be what drowning felt like.

"Oh... Tel..." was all he could choke out.

Telsume's eyes crinkled at the corners, and his lips turned up in a sad smile. He did not reply. Instead, he merely stared at the statues for a long moment and then beckoned. "Come on, I have more to show you."

DALMIR NOW STARED at the small alcove once again. It had been centuries since he stood in this spot or had even thought about this trio, this sad reminder of what they had all lost. Of all of them, Tel had lost the most. His eyes traced the familiar faces of the statues, and then he squinted and leaned closer.

"Dalmir?" Ioan asked, impatient to move on.

"There's something different about these statues," Dalmir muttered.

"They're older than the last time you saw them?" Drengur offered. "Dustier?"

"No, it's something about the faces... or just... I'm not sure... give me a minute..."

"We don't have a minute... Dalmir!" Ioan's tone grew urgent, and Dalmir looked up to see three more atons bearing down on them.

He did not mean to do it. Being in this place had rattled him. The memories that this room brought back were so strong they overwhelmed him, driving more recent events out of his thoughts and causing him to act on instinct alone. Without thinking, he held out a hand, intending to use his power to hold the atons at bay. Instead, the room lit up as though nothing stood between them and the sun high above but pure air. In the ensuing effulgence, Dalmir saw more movement in the stacks and knew that there were more atons than he and his friends could fight.

"Follow me!" he shouted, dashing across the room and darting between the shelves. He did not know if the guardians Tel had left would stop at the stairs. He only knew that the devastating effects of his power going wrong had ended when they ascended to the second level. Perhaps these atons were restricted to their own section of the tower, as well.

Ioan and Drengur followed, their boots slapping on the floor behind him. The heavy footfalls of the atons thundered behind. They were almost at the stairs. Dalmir panted from the exertion. How many years had it been since he had run like this? Since he had run at all? A giant sword crashed down toward his head, and he swerved to one side. The sword cleaved through his sleeve, driving into the ground with terrifying force. Behind him, Drengur shouted something incoherent.

"Just run!" Dalmir yelled.

The door leading to the stairs was just ahead. Dalmir raced at it and yanked it open. He stood and turned, waiting as Drengur and Ioan passed him.

"Come on!" Ioan called, taking the steps in bounds.

"Hold on," Dalmir muttered, waiting as the atons drew closer, closer. There were a dozen of them, monstrous, unyielding things. "I hope this works," Dalmir breathed, and then he mustered his power, calling upon it to light up the room as he himself leaped back onto the stairs.

The atons lost their grip on the floor and went hurtling in all directions, crashing into the walls and ceiling with loud metallic clangs and clanks. Dalmir, however, stayed on the ground, and as he looked up the stairs, he could see that his companions also remained unaffected. He allowed himself a tiny chuckle of satisfied delight and mounted the steps behind Ioan and Drengur. For now, they were safe. But the tower stretched above them, and Dalmir feared that the object they were searching for was at the very top.

———

THE STAIR to the next level stretched up into murky darkness with no end in sight. After climbing over two hundred steps, Ioan held his lantern high, trying to light their way or see where the end might be. Dalmir was reluctant to attempt using his power in any way, due to the unpredictable nature of its effects.

"How many steps do you think we have left?" Drengur panted, pausing for breath and peering ahead in a vain attempt to see the top.

"I don't recall exactly how many steps there were," Dalmir replied. "But it was near a thousand."

Drengur wilted visibly at this news, but Ioan did not appear to be affected by the climb or by the daunting number of steps still ahead. He still breathed easily—a beneficial side-effect of the change Lorcan had wrought upon him? Dalmir wondered. Or perhaps just the conditioning of his role as a defender.

They continued to climb.

Four hundred steps.

Five hundred.

Six hundred.

Seven.

By the time they had reached the top of the long stairway, even Ioan seemed winded. They paused for a moment, bent over, their entire focus on taking a well-deserved rest. When they had regained their strength, Dalmir watched as his companions caught their first glimpse of this next level of the tower arrayed before them.

"What is this place?" Ioan asked.

Dalmir gazed about, remembering the first time he had seen Tel's vision made reality. Even more impressive than the library below was the city that lay above it.

They stepped out of the dark stairway and stood on a wide street, complete with cobblestones. Massive trees lined the street, leading to an enormous fountain. Dalmir marveled to see that the trees were still living, and the fountain burbled streams of water just as joyously as ever. Beyond the fountain stretched the city. Massive buildings of stone towered above. They could not see it all in the darkness, but Dalmir knew the walls of the tower were an intricate design of pillars, beams, and buttresses supporting the levels above while allowing the city between to enjoy fresh air and sunlight. It had been a ridiculous design, and so very Tel. He grinned, remembering how the others had all scoffed at him. Even Mulemo, Tel's twin, had laughed at the lack of pragmatism in the idea of an open-air city *inside* a tower. But it had worked. Somehow, Tel had made it work. And it had been beautiful. Ridiculous, but beautiful.

Together, they continued down the empty street. Sorrow welled in Dalmir as they passed the buildings, devoid of life. He remembered clearly the bustling metropolis Telsume had fostered here within his tower, as well as the farms and villages spread out in the surrounding area for miles. It had been a wondrous, genial place. Tel's people were kind and possessed generous natures and hard-working spirits. It saddened him to see it all desolate and barren.

"It's eerie." Drengur shivered, wrapping his arms around himself. "Who would want to live here?"

"It was different, once," Dalmir replied. "Before the tower sank into the ground, it stood on the surface like a mountain... not unlike Dalton, actually. People were happy here." His voice grew wistful. "Some of them may even have been your ancestors, young Drengur."

Drengur's eyes widened.

"Do you think the orb is here in the city?" Ioan asked, his words reminding them all why they had come.

Dalmir considered the city before them for a moment. But he already knew the answer. "No." He shook his head. "I don't believe so. I think we need to continue our journey up."

Drengur groaned. "How many flights of stairs are in this place?"

"Only a few more," Dalmir replied. "Tel's workshop was at the very top. It was his own place, where he would go when he needed to think, or if he wanted to contact one of us, or if he wanted to build something. It's only a few more levels, if I remember correctly. But the next level is like this one, so it's going to be a lot of stairs."

"Let's keep going," Ioan muttered. "I don't relish the idea of spending the night in this place."

Drengur sighed. "Me neither. But I also don't like the sound of 'a lot of stairs.'"

Ioan chuckled softly. "How can you say that? You're mountain-born! I thought climbing was in your blood."

"Climbing is different than walking up stairs," Drengur retorted. "Climbing at least requires skill and strength. Stairs are just monotonous."

"There may be a shortcut we could take," Dalmir said. "I don't know if it will still be functional... but then again, I wouldn't have expected the atons to still be working, either. Or for those trees to be alive. It's strange..." He trailed off, lost in thought.

"Well..." Ioan began, but Dalmir held up a hand, cutting him off.

"Hssst! Did you hear that?" he asked.

Drengur and Ioan immediately fell silent.

"I hear nothing," Ioan whispered.

"I was sure I heard something," Dalmir replied. "We must not let down our guard. I do not believe that we are alone, or that we will be allowed to ascend to Tel's workshop unhindered. I do not yet understand how, but something defends this place in my brother's absence. We should tread carefully."

Almost before he finished speaking, a spidery creature leaped down upon them from above with a metallic shriek and a hiss of steam. It stood before them, its multiple legs glinting in the lanternlight. Sectioned legs, held together with wheels and gears, stuck out from an oblong body.

"Another aton?" Drengur called out.

"It looks different," Ioan shouted.

"Tel made them in various forms," Dalmir muttered. "All with different functions. I never saw him use them for defense. I wonder..." But what he wondered was cut off as the aton attacked.

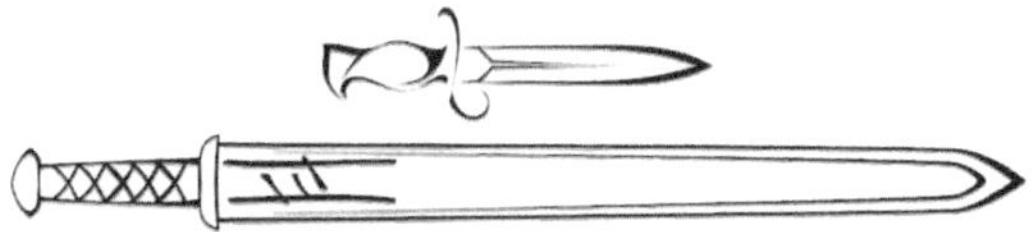

Matei set about helping Ulia gather up the few possessions she had brought with her while Niveya borrowed a horse and went down the road to speak with their waiting coachman. He was gone a long time. Ulia finished her packing and sat down on a worn sofa in the front parlor, her pack on her lap, her fingers idly picking at the loose threads in the cushion. The window looked out to the road, and she would occasionally rise, pace to it, and look out, her feet tapping a nervous rhythm across the floor. Matei busied himself in the kitchen, filling a satchel with loaves of bread, hunks of cheese, and other provisions for their journey. Eventually, Niveya returned with the coach trailing behind him.

"Ready?" he asked as he re-entered the house. His gaze swept over them.

"Just finishing up," Matei replied, stuffing some last-minute sweetbreads into the satchel. He thrust it into Grayden's hands and went to kneel before his cousin where she still sat on the couch, his big hands engulfing hers. "Ulia, if you would rather stay here, just say the word."

Ulia stared at him, a desperate look in her eyes. "I have to see this made right, Matei," she whispered.

Her cousin let out a long, slow breath. "Very well." He stood, then helped Ulia to her feet. She allowed herself to be raised, her form wilting like a sorry apple tree in parched ground.

"We need to get moving," Niveya urged, his tone not unkind. "It is still all too possible that the assassin knows of Ulia. He might even realize that she is the only one who can identify him. If he does, he will most certainly move to eliminate her as a threat."

"Why hasn't he figured it out already?" Beren asked.

"That is what has me worried." Niveya's tone was dark. "Is everyone ready?"

Ulia nodded. There was a sudden clinking sound. The window at the front of the house shattered. And Ulia's hand flew to her neck. Her eyes widened and her lips parted in a tiny gasp.

"Ulia?" Matei was at her side instantly, but it was too late. Ulia was already falling. The pack slipped out of her hands and hit the ground only an eyeblink before Ulia's body.

"Everyone down!" Niveya barked, and they all fell to their stomachs, cowering on the floor.

"Ulia!" Matei'is voice came in hushed, anguished sobs as he rolled her over and patted her face and shook her arm in a desperate attempt to bring her back to consciousness. "Ulia!"

"Hush!" Niveya ordered in a stern whisper. "Can we make our way back to the dining room? There are no windows there."

Working together, the four men slid Ulia's limp form across the floor and into the relative safety of the dining room. Grayden and Beren took up defensive positions at both doorways to the room, their stances low and crouched, their bodies hidden behind the walls so that they had the greatest amount of cover possible.

"Look," Grayden heard Niveya hiss, and he glanced over his shoulder to see the man holding up a tiny dart. "This was in her neck." Niveya sniffed the sharp point of the needle and then touched it gingerly. He licked his finger and spat on the floor. Matei winced. "Poison," Niveya announced.

Ulia moaned. "Matei."

Matei hovered over her, his anxious gaze focused on Niveya. "Can you help her?"

Niveya muttered under his breath. "No." He sighed. "I do not have the antidote, and the poison is already at work. She has minutes, at best."

A strangled sob choked its way out of Matei's throat and he gathered his cousin up in his arms like a small child and rocked her back and forth. "I promised to protect you," he wailed. "Ulia, forgive me!"

"Matei." Ulia reached a hand up to his face and patted his cheek tenderly. "You have been a brother to me. This is not... not your fault. Tell the family... I am sor..." Her eyelids fluttered closed and her breathing stilled. Matei crushed her to his chest, his shoulders heaving with open grief.

Niveya rose without speaking and made his way to Grayden, who was covering the doorway leading into the front parlor. "Did you see anything?"

Grayden shook his head. "I didn't even hear anything until the window broke. The coachman was right outside, and even the horses didn't so much as nicker."

"Whoever it was, he knew his business." Niveya peered around the door-jamb. "That was quite a shot."

"You sound... impressed." Grayden felt disgust boiling up within him. In a flash, he remembered all the reasons he did not like and could not trust this man. A woman lay dead on the floor behind him and Ericole Niveya was expressing admiration for her killer.

"I can appreciate the skill involved," Niveya replied, his voice calm. "But that does not make me mourn our loss any less."

Grayden's brow wrinkled. "Our loss?" he repeated. "We barely knew the woman. Though a senseless death like hers is always a loss, of course."

"I meant in the investigation," Niveya replied. "She was our only lead, after all. To lose her before she could relay to the Council what she told us is hard to accept."

"You are a monster," Grayden hissed, aghast.

Niveya regarded him with cool aloofness. "I am what I have to be." He edged his way around the door and into the parlor, staying low and close to the walls. Creeping across the room, he reached the window and peered out.

There was a moment of stillness, marred only by the stifled sobs of Matei. Sobs that pierced Grayden's heart. He berated himself for not insisting that they stay away from windows, for not suggesting that he and Beren take turns walking a perimeter. If he had followed the protocols he had learned at the Academy, perhaps they could have prevented this tragedy. Not for the first time, he wondered if advancing through the Academy so swiftly had done him more harm than good.

Niveya straightened. "I believe our attacker is gone," he said. "We may have gotten lucky. It appears his only mark was Ulia."

"Lucky?" Beren's voice rumbled through the house. "You promised to keep this woman safe!"

"And I would have, given the opportunity," Niveya replied. "As long as she remained here, she was in danger. I made that quite clear."

"We were making the necessary preparations..." Beren began.

"This area is not secure. They left our coachman and his horses alone, but this location is no longer safe for any of us. We must leave."

"What about them?" Grayden asked, gesturing helplessly at the broken form of Matei.

"What about them?" Niveya asked.

"We cannot just leave them here, not like this..." Grayden trailed off.

"Of course we can, and we must," Niveya snapped. "They will only slow us down."

"No," Beren said, and the word dropped in the center of the room like a stone being set into the foundation hole for a house. It rang with finality. "They come with us, or we all stay here. You made promises to protect both Ulia and her cousin, the least you can do is keep whatever is left of that promise."

Niveya hissed with impatience, but as his eyes flicked from Grayden to Beren and back, his scowl wavered. "Fine." He threw his hand up in defeat. "Into the coach, everyone, now. We will find a proper place to bury the woman when we are away from this place."

Beren gently stooped down and lifted Ulia in his arms. Matei clung to her at first, but Grayden put his hands under the man's arm and lifted him, also, and the man seemed to come back to himself enough to realize that they were attempting to help. Matei let himself be lifted and then led out to the coach, where he climbed inside and sat, his expression blank. When they had all gathered inside, Niveya gave a sharp order and the coachman clucked to the horses, urging them into a swift trot.

"As fast as you can safely go," Niveya called out.

The coachman clucked again, and the horses picked up their pace, the coach bumping along over the uneven patches and holes in the dirt road.

DESPITE THE BUMPS and wobbling motion of the coach, Grayden dozed fitfully during their frantic flight from Matei's farm. Every time he awoke, the awfulness of what had happened sprang at him anew. As dawn broke over the horizon, bathing the trees about them in a friendly glow, he realized that none of their surroundings were familiar. He commented on this to Beren, who was already awake. His friend nodded.

"We aren't going back the way we came," he informed Grayden. "I noticed that earlier when you were sleeping. He"—here he jerked his head toward Niveya, who appeared to be sleeping peacefully—"said we couldn't do anything expected or obvious. So instead of going back to the harbor, we're heading northwest, into Dalma. Then we'll make our way back to Doran."

"That will take sennights!" Grayden exclaimed.

"It could take more than a lunat," Beren replied, his expression grim. "I've been trying to talk him out of it. By the time we return to Doran, every trail will have gone cold."

"Why are we going back to Doran at all?" Grayden asked, trying not to think about the way his heart leapt at the thought of standing on Dalman soil again. He longed for home with an ache that was so fierce it almost frightened him.

"We still need to continue the investigation, don't we?" Beren asked.

"How? With Ulia dead, we don't have any leads!" Grayden exclaimed.

"Weren't you paying any attention at all?" Beren demanded. "Ulia gave us a general description of the assassin. It might be enough to do some of our own investigating. The man bears a brand with the Regeont's mark on him. We know how to identify him."

"But..." Grayden's thoughts moved at a sluggish pace, and he tried to force them into a semblance of intelligence. "But without Ulia..." Grayden paused and peered into Beren's face, and he saw that his friend understood all too well. "I'm sorry. I know how much this investigation matters to you personally."

Beren grimaced and stared out the coach window. The trees slipped past as the coach continued to rumble along. Then, all without warning, they crested a hill and before them spread a valley covered in the brilliant green of summer. A lake sparkled in the valley below. All at once, the carriage jerked to a halt; Niveya and Matei jolted awake. Niveya hopped out of the coach and stood, looking around. Then he climbed back inside and his piercing gaze fell on Matei.

"Come," he said, his voice surprisingly gentle.

Matei cringed away from him, but then his chin dropped to his chest and he exited the coach. Beren and Grayden followed, curious.

Niveya swept a hand at the view. "My friend," he continued in that gentle tone, "do you not think this would be a place where she could rest peacefully?"

Matei jerked and stared at Niveya, his swollen eyes wide with horror. "That is not our way!"

"I know, my friend," Niveya replied.

"I am not your friend." Matei stiffened and drew himself up, glaring at the man. But then, like in the coach, his demeanor slumped, and he gave the valley a single, sweeping glance. "She always did love the water," he mumbled. "She'd be happy to rest here, in the countryside she loved enough to leave."

"Do we have time for this?" Grayden muttered.

Beren gave him an earnest look. "Whether we have time or no, it is the right thing to do."

Grayden met his gaze and held it, then gave a sharp nod.

Their driver unhitched the horses and led them down to the lake to drink, and then allowed them to rest and graze.

The soft earth near the lake shore made their sorrowful task an easier one. As the day wore on, the men continued their sober duty. Nothing disturbed their work, though Grayden kept peering over his shoulder and jumping at the slightest noise. He could not let go of the feeling that they were being watched, and the sensation of eyes on the back of his neck made him uneasy.

"I can't understand it," Grayden muttered under his breath.

"What can you not understand?" Beren asked.

Grayden looked up. "I didn't mean... I was just talking to myself."

"You seem frustrated," Beren said. "If it would help to talk, I am here to listen."

Grayden filled his shovel with earth and tossed it to the side. "I can't understand why I didn't sense the assassin, that's all. I should have. I keep replaying what happened last night over and over in my mind, and I just can't figure it out. Was I not paying attention? Did I sense the danger and ignore it?"

"Surely your instincts are not infallible?" Beren queried.

"They've never let me down before," Grayden replied.

Beren's eyebrows came together in a puzzled line. "Are you certain?"

Grayden took a moment to turn over another shovelful of dirt. "As certain as I can be. I haven't been in many life-threatening situations before going to the Academy, though, so I can't say for certain."

Beren leaned on his shovel. "Maybe it only works if you are the one in danger, then."

Grayden tilted his head to one side. "What do you mean?"

"Well..." Beren drew the word out slowly. "Ulia appears to have been the assassin's sole target. There were no further attacks, even when we went out to the carriage. It appears that no one is following us, and there has been ample opportunity for ambush. So, maybe your instinct or whatever it is only works if you are in danger, too."

Grayden focused his full attention on the hole he was digging. He was silent for a long while as the hole grew deeper and deeper. "It didn't work when we were in the Greyklasp Mountains, either."

"Maybe Lorcan's power countered your sense?" Beren asked.

"Or maybe it was never real to begin with."

"Perhaps," Beren acknowledged. "But I doubt it. There may be some way to test it, when we're not busy trying to catch murderers, that is."

Grayden chuckled, his expression dark. Before he could reply, Niveya called a halt to their work.

"That should be enough," the man said.

There was little ceremony to the occasion. They wrapped Ulia in her shawl and placed her gently in the grave they had dug, then soberly covered her until all that remained as evidence was a small mound of sand. Matei found a large rock down by the lake and they helped him carry it to the mound.

"I'm sorry," Niveya said, staring down at the stone. He seemed on the verge of saying more, but instead he turned and strode back to the carriage without a word.

Grayden and Beren remained for another moment, stealing furtive, awkward glances at each other and Matei. The man's mouth moved, but no sound came out. The silence stretched out for several minutes before Grayden and Beren broke away to follow Niveya. Matei remained by the stone. They watched him drop to his knees and press his forehead to the ground. Then he stood, brushed himself off, and joined them. He did not speak, he merely nodded to Niveya.

Before Ericole could bark a command to the driver, however, Grayden leaned forward.

"I know you are far more versed in this sort of intrigue than we are. But if we continue on this course, it will take us five or six sennights to get back to Doran, and that is only if we stop at the next town and purchase more horses. Perhaps we could get there faster if we each had several mounts, but even then we will waste time we do not have."

Niveya regarded him. "What do you propose?"

"We have spent almost a full day traveling north now. If the assassin saw us leave, he will report that we fled this way," Grayden replied. "I think we should turn and head back to Doran directly. That way, we will only have lost days, not lunats."

Niveya studied him carefully, then gave a reluctant nod. "You are right. I am more familiar with the plots and schemes of deceitful minds than you are. I am used to thinking in terms of safety and survival and making my decisions with those tenets being paramount. However, it appears that we have made a clean getaway; our assassin was only after a single target. It is conceivable that he did not know why he was hired to kill Ulia, nor that he should make certain she had not imparted her knowledge to anyone else. Very well, Master Grayden." Niveya leaned out the window of the carriage. "Enough! We head south for Doran!"

The driver snapped the reins and clicked to the horses, encouraging them forward and then taking them in a wide arc until they were once again facing southward.

———

THEY RETURNED Matei to his home at his insistence. "I will not go into the city," he said. On this point, he remained firm. Nothing they said could persuade him to change his mind. Not even the idea that his life might be in danger could sway him. At last, they agreed and left him behind, dropping him off at his little farmhouse.

By nightfall, they had returned to Niveya's safe house. Grayden was grateful he had persuaded Niveya to turn around, and that they would not have to spend the next six sennights traveling overland, but a part of his heart ached for the missed opportunity to place his feet on Dalman soil once more. It was strange how just heading north had made him feel like he was returning home. He would have sworn on his family's orchards that he could taste a difference in the air the closer they got to Dalma. Every mile they had traveled northward made his spirit sing a song of homecoming. Suddenly he yearned to see his parents, to sit in the orchards, even to throw his strength into the countless chores he had sometimes complained about. An image of Seren dancing barefoot in the tall grasses flitted before his eyes and the sound of her laughter, like a chorus of birdsong, rang in his ears. But then they had turned around—at his own insistence—and home had faded back into a dream behind him. He patted his coat pocket, where the note from his father always traveled still unread.

"What is our next move?" Beren asked as they settled down around the table.

Grayden focused on his friend, pushing thoughts of home into a shadowy corner of his mind.

"I've been thinking about that," Niveya said. "We can ask Matei to relate Ulia's story before the Council. It's not as good as having Ulia herself to tell it, but the four of us together with the same story cannot be ignored. However, we need more evidence."

"What about the dart?" Grayden asked.

The others stared at him in confusion.

"The dart." Grayden's thoughts were moving faster than he could speak. "You know, the dart that killed…"

"Ah!" Niveya's face lit with comprehension and he reached into the pouch at his belt. He held up the tiny weapon that had robbed Ulia of her life. "What do you propose?"

"I'm not sure." Grayden glanced at Beren. "I was just wondering if there might be any way to track down Ulia's murderer through the dart?"

Niveya looked at the dart between his fingers and frowned, his expression pensive. "That is a good thought. The dart is fairly generic, but the poison, well, every poisoner has his own trademark mixtures. If we can track down who created it, we can narrow the list of guilds or crews who use that apothecary and find our assassin."

"Just by knowing the guild?" Beren queried.

"Nobody in a guild takes a job without the permission of his king," Niveya replied.

"King?" Grayden was confused.

"That is what the leaders of the guilds call themselves in Ondoura," Niveya explained.

"But even if we find this assassin, we still can't link him to the Regeont's murder," Beren argued.

"The murderer has done an excellent job covering his tracks," Niveya agreed. "But nobody is perfect. Somewhere he must have slipped up, and that mistake is what we need to find."

"But what if Ulia was his only mistake?" Beren asked. "What if there is no other evidence?"

"The attack on the Academy!" Grayden shouted so loudly that everyone stared at him. He grinned in the firelight. "That's what we've been forgetting."

"What do you mean?" Niveya asked.

Grayden turned to Beren. "When your father was telling us about the Regeont's death, he mentioned the attack on the Academy. We thought little of it, because it didn't seem related. But what if it was?"

"I'm not sure I'm following your logic," Beren replied.

"Consider this: if Ulia's story is accurate, then the attack on the Academy happened at very nearly the same moment as the first assassination attempt. Your father and Dalmir seemed to think that the attack was poorly executed. It was quelled almost instantly, and the mercenaries who were caught confessed almost immediately. But none of them could say who hired them. A few of them insisted your father hired them, but nobody took that information seriously." Grayden sighed. "The siege on the Academy was dismissed as having nothing to do with the Regeont's death because it was so dissimilar in style, and because it would make no sense to use the Academy as a distraction from an assassination attempt. But what if the same person coordinated both, with the attack on the Academy designed solely to distract the investigators after the fact?"

"Why would they want that?" Beren asked.

"I don't know," Grayden admitted. "Unless it was simply a ploy to cover their tracks. But what I want to know, more than who the assassin was, is who hired him."

Niveya's eyes darted to Grayden. "That is the question, isn't it? I've been pondering the same mystery. Assassins rarely work on their own. Somebody wanted Regeont Roshana dead, but who? And why?"

"Lord Elan had the most to gain," Grayden suggested.

"Surely you can't think he would hire someone to murder his own aunt?" Beren exclaimed.

"Think about it," Grayden said. "Who benefited from the Regeont's death? Lord Elan. He won the election easily, in part because the people of Ondoura were desperate to maintain the stability to which they are accustomed, and with the threat of war increasing every day, that stability grows less and less certain. That gives us not only a motive for the murder but also a motive for the attack on the Academy."

"Then what would you suggest we do with this theory?" Niveya asked.

"Find the money," Grayden replied.

Niveya surveyed Grayden through a narrowed gaze. "I like the way you think."

Beren scratched his chin. "Someone paid the mercenaries."

"And obviously, it wasn't your father," Grayden added.

"If Elan set up the attack, he probably didn't pay them directly," Niveya cautioned. "If you're right, then the attack was designed to look clumsy, but I doubt Elan is that much of a fool."

"Of course not. He's too smart for that," Grayden agreed. "But there will be a trail somewhere. If Elan is as careful as he seems, he might even have a ledger with the details."

A cunning light gleamed in Niveya's eyes. "I believe you are onto something, young Grayden." He slapped his knee. "We need to figure out a way to talk to those mercenaries."

Grayden yawned.

"Tomorrow." Niveya grinned. "First thing."

21

Wynn and Molly worked feverishly on the idea that the explosion had triggered. For days, they sequestered themselves in Wynn's workroom, their pens scratching constantly at the large sheets of paper stretched across every available desk and countertop. The calculations were difficult, and Wynn's head spun with numbers. When he wasn't sitting at his desk, he was turning the design over in his head, examining it from all angles. He saw the diagrams even when he closed his eyes for a few hours of sleep each night. His dreams all involved sitting at a desk doing figures. The days and nights blended together, and at times he was not sure if he was awake or dreaming. But he threw all his efforts into the project, certain that he was circling around the answer. The answer that would change everything.

And in the back of his mind, another answer prickled, but he swept it away. The idea persisted, but he buried it under his concentration on the project at hand. He shuddered when it surfaced, an idea so heinous it made him want to hurl himself off a cliff just for thinking of it. How could he even contemplate something so horrific? What kind of person did it make him that he could think of such a thing? He did not want to know the answer, and so he dug a hole in his mind and buried the idea as deep as he could.

Daegan joined them often. Sometimes, he would pick up the latest equation Wynn was working on and read over it with his discerning eye. Once or twice, he caught a mistake or made a suggestion, but mostly he simply observed. He seemed content to let Wynn work out the fury that roiled in his brain, surging to be set free.

It was a challenge unlike any Wynn had ever faced. He bent his entire will and focus upon it, but instead of revealing itself to him, the answer continued to elude him. At least once a day, he found himself staring at a rocky wall, an impenetrable cliffside in his path, barring his way. In frustration, he would crumple up the useless sheet of paper containing his incorrect equations and hurl them to the floor.

At these times, Molly would pick up the crumpled paper, smooth it out, and begin asking questions. Wynn found her questions to be insightful and pointed, getting to the heart of the matter in very few words. She was not afraid to challenge his assumptions. Her mind was curious and inventive, and though she could not do the complicated equations in her head like him, Wynn found Molly to be brilliant at thinking outside the borders. Her ability to ignore the rules of math and science in ways that he could not somehow allowed his own mind to make leaps that he never would have attempted on his own.

Molly also seemed to instinctively know when Wynn most needed a break. Whenever his thoughts ran up against a dead-end tunnel, Molly would inevitably suggest they take a walk. They would head outside and down the little path that led to the river, walking along the shore and talking. Sometimes they would remove their shoes and wade in the shallow waters, startling the minnows and small frogs who lived there. They did not just talk about the work at these times and through these evening conversations, their relationship as colleagues swiftly became friendship.

"I still can't get the engine small enough," Wynn griped one evening during one of their walks. The stars overhead glittered like veins of ore in the mountainside, their light a tapestry of silver in the blue-black sky. The mountains rose around them, shadowy beasts looming protectively, silent sentinels guarding the two friends as they walked along the riverbank. "Even with the smaller cynders, there isn't space for everything the engine needs."

Molly made a small humming noise and Wynn glanced at her sideways. They had worked together for long enough now that he could read her moods. Tonight, she was pensive. He could tell that her mind was hammering at the problem, like Keene's tilt-hammer, powered by the great water wheel that churned up the river.

"What are you thinking?" he asked.

"I'm not sure," she replied, her tone hesitant.

"You sound like you have an idea," he prodded.

"I was just thinking that maybe we're coming at this from the wrong angle."

"What do you mean?"

"We've been using the airship engine as our model."

"Yes."

"But when we started, we all agreed that the train engine and the airship engine are nothing alike."

"Yes."

"Maybe we need to start from the beginning."

"How? We still know so little about the cynders and even the airship engines..." Wynn paused and flung his arms out to either side. "Where would we even begin? It would mean throwing out all the work we've already done."

"I didn't mean to start over completely... not exactly," Molly hastened to say. "I just meant... well, it occurred to me that there are a lot of things an airship does that a Trackless won't have to."

"Like fly," Wynn chuckled.

"Exactly," Molly replied, her voice growing enthusiastic. "So there are controls and functions that we don't need for the Trackless."

"That's true," Wynn conceded. "I've already cut out some of those controls from the Trackless... but maybe I could get rid of even more. If I could eliminate everything but the power that pushes the Trackless forward, then... well, that wouldn't be... actually..." The idea raced through his mind like wildfire sweeping through dead underbrush. Wynn turned to Molly, beaming. "Molly, you're a genius!" He pulled her into a quick embrace, then let her go and grabbed her hand. "Come on!"

"What? Where are we going?"

"To the water wheel!"

"The water wheel?"

"I need to look at something," Wynn hollered, pulling her along behind him.

They reached the small structure with the large wheel attached, and Wynn clambered up the steps and through the door into the little hut.

"What are you doing?" Molly asked.

"Just checking something." Wynn leaned over the railing, peering into the depths of the mill. "Is there a lantern in here?"

A moment later, a small glow filled the room, and Molly was passing a lantern to him. He took it, holding it over the mechanism, studying it, memorizing it for his notes later. He swung himself back up and grinned, feeling lightheaded from being upside down for so long. Molly searched his face, her expression bemused.

"I think I've solved it!" he crowed, triumphant.

"Solved what?"

"How to turn the Trackless without using the cynders. If I can run the gears at different speeds for each set of wheels, the Trackless should turn itself. If the cynder only has to provide thrust, I think I can make the engine small enough. I'll need to discuss it with Daegan, though."

"Well, come on!" Molly cried, tugging at his hand. "He'll want to get started right away!"

Wynn allowed himself to be pulled back to the workrooms,

his thoughts brimming with new ideas, not just for the Trackless, as it had occurred to him that his idea for a smaller engine might have other implementations. He did not speak of these yet, though. It was best to focus on a single project at a time. But as soon as they got back inside, he grabbed his quill and jotted down notes so that he would not forget his ideas.

———

THE NEXT MORNING, Daegan's excitement about Wynn's idea came in a quiet, approving gleam in the older man's eye. Together, they worked day and night on the new design. They barely stopped to eat or sleep, and when they did, it was only because Molly reminded them, insisting that they nourish their bodies and get rest so they could continue their work. Wynn appreciated her logic and stubbornness, which were the only things that could make Daegan pause. The older man would tilt his head and then mutter something incoherent as he stomped off to the kitchen or his bed. At these times, Wynn and Molly would share an amused grin, and Wynn would put his own work down and try to get some rest. He found it difficult to turn his mind off, however, and even exhaustion was not always enough to make him yield to the sweet rest he so badly needed. Often, he sought Molly's company, and together they would walk down to the river and sit on the bank talking about the day's work or all the things they still needed to do. These conversations helped settle and organize his thoughts enough that he could then return to his room and find the sleep he sought.

With the plans finalized, they presented them to Keene, who set to work building the parts they needed to house the engine. In the drafting room, Daegan was master, but the forge was Keene's domain. The fires raged hot as Keene and his apprentices worked tirelessly to create each piece exactly to the specifications in the plans. Even in the brief moments when he left the forge, Wynn could never seem to cool off. His arms ached from working the bellows. No longer did he struggle to find sleep. It often found him before he had made it all the way to his bed. Sometimes he woke in the hall, or curled up next to the forge. Dreams no longer bothered him, as his mind and body were too weary to dream. He could spare no thoughts for his friends, either, and thoughts of Grayden and Beren and their adventures in Ondoura became a distant memory that no longer gave him the slightest twinge of envy. Mornings came early, and the hours stretched out in a monotonous routine of working in the forge, punctuated by breaks in the kitchen, hastily stuffing a pastry or sandwich into his mouth before returning to the back-breaking labor at the bellows. Keene's hammer rang out across the mountains with constant precision as he made every strike look easy.

One day, Keene invited Wynn to try hammering out a piece. Wynn hesitated, unsure he could lift the heavy mallet, but at the derisive glance from Gunnar he mustered up his courage and accepted the challenge. To his surprise, the hammer was not as difficult to wield as he had supposed. Keene pulled the rod out of the fire with a pair of enormous tongs and set it on the anvil, giving Wynn a nod. Wynn raised the hammer as he had seen the smith do over and over again for the past lunat and brought it down on the rod. He did not attempt to shape the rod; he knew that would be fruitless. His task was only to flatten it out. Shaping would come later. With an approving raise of his eyebrows, Keene left Wynn with the rod and tongs. Wynn worked on the piece, heating and hammering it over and over until it was roughly the correct size and shape. He brought it to Keene, who looked it over with an exacting eye while Wynn swiped his sleeve across his forehead.

"It's not pretty," Keene said. "But it's well hammered. You have a good feel for this work. I noticed you did not sacrifice precision for the strength of your strike, a common beginner's mistake."

"It surprised me that I could even lift the hammer as long as I did," Wynn confessed. "I was trying to ration my strength."

Keene grinned. "After all your work with those bellows, I knew you could handle a minor task like this one. What did you think of it?"

"It was..." Wynn stopped. "I'm not sure how to describe it. I've built things before, small things, but nothing that took this kind of effort. The next strike was all I could think of. That kind of focus is... terrifying, but exhilarating... and..." He looked down at the ugly piece of metal he had hammered into a strap that would fasten the engine to the body of the Trackless. "It felt good, putting that kind of effort into this thing we're building. Like a piece of me will forever be a part of it."

"Spoken like a true smith," Keene said. "Even if you do not lift the hammer again, you can take pride in knowing that you helped fashion this tool you've designed. Go get some water, and then I can use you on the bellows."

Wynn smiled and walked out to the water barrel Keene kept just outside the forge. The water inside was cool and refreshing as he ladled it into his mouth. The liquid poured down his throat, and he felt its cool touch as it trickled through his body. Every muscle ached with weariness. The punishing hours he had subjected his body to for so many days and nights in a row all crashed down on him with the force of the tilt-hammer. He closed his eyes and leaned his head on the rim of the barrel, gathering his strength. After a few moments, he raised his head, took one more long sip of water, replaced the ladle, and returned to the forge. The work awaited.

22

A commotion near the entrance to the cave in which they were resting caught Marik's attention. He looked down at the child in his lap. Elalli had cried herself out and then promptly fallen asleep. He shook his head, marveling at how children had an uncanny capability for falling asleep anywhere. Moving as carefully as he could, he extricated himself from being used as a pillow and gently covered her up with his coat. Easing himself to his feet —his leg had stiffened up as he sat on the ground—he hobbled over to find out what was transpiring.

Nando and another female durven were having an argument with Oleck and Shaesta. Marik glanced about, his eyes searching for Mouse until he found him, also curled up on the ground, asleep.

"What's going on?" he asked as he arrived.

"Olin is still missing," Shaesta said. "Elthen combed the tunnels we came down and couldn't find any trace of him."

Oleck crossed his arms. "She wants to go back and see if he got left aboveground, maybe too injured to make his way back here."

Marik gave a slow nod. "I think that would be a good idea. We don't want to leave anyone behind, but we need to be careful about it. Oleck, will you go with Elthen? The rest of us should continue into the Deepway, back to the main tunnels where we can get food and rest and better tend our wounded."

"Yes, Captain," Oleck replied.

"That is a sound plan," Nando agreed. "Elthen, help me put together some bandages in case Olin is hurt. And bring a couple of lanterns."

As the two durven turned away to gather supplies, Marik grabbed Oleck's arm. "Find out what you can, and then make your way back to us as quickly as possible," he said in a low whisper. "Use your best judgment. If there is any sign—any sign at all —that Olin is in the hands of the Ar'Mol, we need to know immediately so that we can get these people to safety."

"Do you think they'll actually agree to leave the Deepway?" Shaesta asked, surprising him with her sudden nearness. "Wouldn't it be better to build up some defenses? Collapse some tunnels and make it impossible for the soldiers to find the durven?"

"That's a possibility," Marik acknowledged. "But we have to be ready for anything. If Olin is in his grasp, the Ar'Mol will undoubtedly get a detailed and very accurate map of the Deepway in short order. Oleck, you and I know better than anyone what the Igyeum is capable of. We can't take the risk. If they find out that these people live down here... you know what they'll do."

Oleck nodded, his expression troubled. "You can count on me, Captain. But I think Shaesta has a good idea. When you get back, talk to Hrafn about what sorts of defenses they can create without too much trouble. Even if we don't end up fighting down here, anything that can slow down the soldiers and give us a few more minutes to get everyone out of here will help."

Elthen returned and handed a pack and a lantern to Oleck and the two of them headed back down the tunnel.

"That's enough resting." Nando's raspy voice rang out. "Time to move out!"

There was no grumbling. Even Mouse, who never woke easily, got up and gathered his things without complaint. Marik shook Elalli awake and invited her to clamber onto his back. She clung there, arms clasped tightly around his neck, and he limped his way forward. Nando came up beside him and shoved something into his hand.

"Take this. It will help you walk," she urged.

It was tall and thin like a quarterstaff, but gnarled and lumpy like a tree-branch. In the spot where his hand naturally grasped it, there were slight grooves that fitted his hand perfectly. It was a perfect walking stick, light to carry, and exactly tailored to his own height, and made completely out of stone.

"Where did you get this?" Marik asked, marveling at its perfection. At first he was afraid to put any weight on it, worried it might crack or shatter—it was so thin—but he soon learned that he could trust it to support him.

"I made it," Nando replied. She made an apologetic clicking sound with her mouth. "I could have done a better job if I'd had more time. It was a little rushed, so it isn't pretty."

"It's wonderful," Marik said honestly.

"Thank you." They walked in silence for a few paces, then she looked up at him. "You think Olin was captured." It was not a question.

Marik sighed. "I hope not."

"If he was, what do you think will happen next?"

"I think they'll take him back to the Ar'Mol's palace, especially when they realize he isn't exactly like anything they've ever seen before. Then I think they'll torture him for information about the rest of you and the Deepway. When they get the information they need, they'll come down here after the rest of you."

"You are so certain he will break?"

"If you think he won't, you're naïve."

She accepted his words without growing defensive. "How long do you think we have before they find us?"

Marik grimaced. "I don't know. Olin was one of the younger generation, right?"

She nodded.

"Then I don't think we have more than a few hours left."

Nando's expression tightened. "When we get back, will you speak with Hrafn? He will know what to do."

"I will," Marik replied. "Do your people have any defenses in place in case of discovery?"

"A few. Not many. We have relied on our secrecy and self-reliance these eighty years. The threat of discovery was never our top concern."

"I understand. But that threat is very real right now. I'm still hoping that Elthen and Oleck return with Olin and this is all just worry over nothing, but in case they do not, we need to be ready to move your people out of the Deepway and get them to safety."

"I understand," Nando replied. "But many of my people will not wish to leave."

"If they don't, they'll be slaughtered."

"Hrafn will convince them, I'm sure." Nando's voice trembled, belying her words. She was not at all sure of anything. Marik knew what that felt like, and he wished he could have spared her this. Nobody should have to experience the terror of their homes being invaded, their families endangered... a wave of nausea shuddered through him and he almost buckled beneath its crushing force. The staff in his hand was the only thing that prevented him from tumbling forward and landing on his face.

"Marik Captain?" Nando's concerned voice floated to his ears, and he pushed the darkness away from his vision, taking deep breaths through his nose.

"I am well," he assured her. "Just tired."

"I can walk, Captain." The tiny voice fluttered in his ear like the whisper of butterfly wings.

He smiled and hiked Elalli further up onto his shoulders. "I had forgotten you were up there, little butterfly." Another musical giggle rewarded his words.

"I love butterflies," Elalli said, a sing-song lilt to her voice.

"What are your favorite colored butterflies?" Nando asked.

"Pink!" Elalli replied. "I love the little pink ones. But I don't see them very often."

"We don't see many butterflies down here at all," Nando replied, a tinge of soft sorrow in her voice. "But I remember I loved watching them flit from flower to flower when I was little."

Elalli made a sound of sympathy, and the two of them continued conversing about butterflies and flowers. Marik was grateful to Nando for her help entertaining the child, as he was having trouble walking, let alone mustering the energy for a conversation. When they finally reached the more lived-in tunnels, he gratefully swung the girl down to the ground and let her walk beside him, cautioning her to stay close until she knew her way around better.

Although he would have liked nothing better than to fall into bed and sleep for days, there was still work to be done. After getting Elalli situated with Shaesta, Marik and Nando went to find Hrafn and report on how their attempt to rescue Raisa had gone so incredibly wrong.

Hrafn was in the room where Marik had first met him. He rose, a troubled wrinkle to his brow.

"Come in," he said, gesturing for Marik to take a chair. "I fear things did not go well?"

"You could say that." Marik sat down, grimacing at the ache in his leg as the muscles stretched. "They were ready for us. And they had a weapon like nothing I've ever seen." He fingered the staff in his hand. "If they have more of those, Telmondir doesn't stand a chance in a war with the Igyeum. Nobody does."

"Tell me." Hrafn stood before him, hands clasped, eyes closed, his mien peaceful. "Tell me what happened."

Nando did most of the talking, though Marik tried to supply any important pieces that he could. He was so tired. His eyelids drooped, and he felt himself drifting somewhere in the strange haze between wakefulness and sleep. Before he knew it, someone was helping him rise and leading him back to his room. Marik had no memory of getting into bed. All too soon, someone was shaking him awake.

"Wazzit?" he slurred, his thoughts slowly emerging through the deep jungle of sleep.

"I'm sorry, Captain." Oleck's voice pulled him toward wakefulness. "I know you're injured and haven't rested enough, but I thought I'd best wake you. You were right. Winds enfold us; you were right."

Marik blinked and sat up, every muscle protesting loudly. He rubbed a hand across his face and stared blearily at Oleck. The man's hair stuck out even more haphazardly than usual, and his eyes drooped with weariness.

"Right about what?" Marik asked.

"Olin," Oleck panted. Marik wondered if his friend had been running; he seemed out of breath. "Olin... they captured him. Near as we can figure, they took him to the dungeons."

Marik sat up, snapping to alertness with a speed that made his head ache. "I was hoping I was wrong," he muttered.

"So was I, Cap'n."

"Very well. Have you told Hrafn?"

Oleck nodded, his face looking old and haggard. "I already talked to him. Told him we'd do whatever we could to help protect his people."

"Good. We need to get moving. That kid won't last more than a couple of hours in the Igyeum's hands. So that's the time we have to prepare."

"What are you thinking, Cap'n?"

Marik rubbed his fingers under his jaw. "I'm thinking we need to move these people to safety."

"If they're not safe down here, where can we take them?"

"Telmondir. I'm sure that the Council will welcome the durven and find a new home for them. Besides, we need to head in that direction and tell them what we've learned about that new weapon the Igyeum has devised. They need to know what they're facing."

Oleck nodded, scratching at his beard. "Did you find out if they have any defenses here?"

"Nando said they have a few. I'm guessing it won't slow the soldiers down much, though. So we need to leave."

"Captain..." Oleck began, and then hesitated.

"Yes?"

"How are you planning on getting them all out of here? We can't fit two thousand durven aboard the *Hawk*, you know that as well as I do."

"You're right," Marik replied. He felt as though he'd swallowed a stone. "But we can fit that many aboard that big sky barge that was sitting at the merchant docks."

Oleck's eyes widened in horror. "That hideous old crate?"

"I don't think the owners would mind lending it to us. For a good cause."

"But... but what about the *Hawk*?" Oleck asked.

Marik shoved down the sudden anguish that ripped through him—anguish that had nothing to do with his leg—at the thought of leaving his beautiful *Hawk* behind. "We won't leave without her," he said, keeping his tone even. "The hideout is on our way out of the Igyeum. We can take a rest there and then fly both ships to Telmondir."

Oleck gnawed on his thumbnail. "We're short-handed as it is, Captain."

"Leaving her behind is not an option," Marik growled. He continued in a low voice that he somehow kept from trembling. "But if it comes down to it... I will sacrifice her. These people need us. Would you rather condemn them to the brutality of the Igyeum?"

Oleck met his gaze. "You're right," he acknowledged gruffly. "We can't abandon these people. I'll go get us a flying crate."

Marik clapped a hand to Oleck's shoulder. "Thank you, my friend."

"Don't thank me yet," Oleck grumbled. "Probably gonna fall outta the sky in that thing... will definitely need to grab some backup cynders from the *Hawk*..." He continued to mutter to himself as he turned and left the room.

Marik splashed some water on his face and went in search of Hrafn.

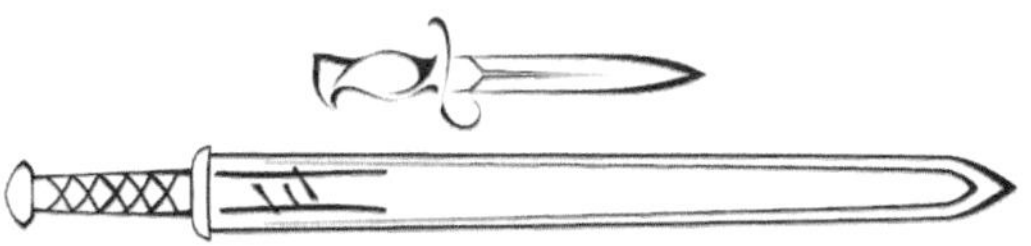

The next morning at breakfast, they made their plans. Niveya laid a piece of paper on the table covered in a short list of names.

"These are all the apothecaries in Doran who sell this particular poison," he informed them.

Grayden picked it up. "It is not as long as I expected."

"It is not altogether legal to sell," Niveya replied. "We will have to be cautious about our movements. We don't know how much our murderer knows, or whether our presence or our intents have been detected. If Lord Elan hired the assassins, then he might also have been responsible for Ulia's murder. My hope is that the news of her death reaches the ears of whoever is behind all of this and causes him to relax his vigil."

"What about the mercenaries who attacked the Academy?" Beren asked.

"The good news is that they are still in custody," Niveya replied. "The bad news is, they are no longer at the Academy."

"Where are they?" Grayden asked. He had wondered where the mercenaries were being kept, since there was no good place to hold them at the Academy.

"In the city prison."

"Then we shall request an audience." Beren stood.

"Not so fast." Ericole waved him down. "We're not in Telsuma, and you have no authority here. Defenders don't go around interrogating captured criminals. Besides that, these mercenaries named your father as the man who hired them, and as ridiculous as that claim is—and the fact that everyone knows it is ridiculous—it is a claim the conscripts cannot ignore. The tirbodh in charge is not going to let you simply waltz in and question his prisoners."

Beren fell back into his chair with a sigh and took a bite of his toast. "What do you propose, then?"

"I'm still working on it," Ericole admitted. "I don't have any associates in the guard. I respected Regeont Roshana too much to infiltrate that deep into her organization; though, in hindsight, that was rather short-sighted and imprudent of me. I shall endeavor not to make the same mistake in the future."

Beren shot a meaningful glance at Grayden and spread a thick layer of marmalade on his toast.

"I believe we should start at the top of this list and work our way down it," Niveya said. He turned to Grayden. "Your question about the dart got me thinking that we should also find out which guild the three assassins belonged to. It would be a marvelous coincidence if they all work for the same king, wouldn't you agree?"

Grayden grinned.

Beren leaned back in his chair. "I expect we should let you do most of the talking as we visit the shops on your list. I have a feeling you will know better than either of us what to say that will not spook them."

"That would be wise. This is my strong suit, after all." Niveya smirked at Beren. "Yes, I can tell what you are thinking. I assure you, you are correct."

A chuckle emanated from deep in Beren's throat. It was so unexpected that even Beren looked surprised by it. But the young giant gave a rueful bob of his head.

"I still do not trust you," Beren said, but there was a flicker of amusement in his eye.

They finished breakfast and set out for the first shop, which was not far. The apothecary, a small, wiry man in his mid-forties with a shock of bright red hair, looked up from the counter as they entered.

"How can I help you today?" he asked, a genial smile on his face.

Niveya sauntered up to the counter. "I was wondering if you had any ithonium on hand?"

The man's expression turned guarded. "That substance is illegal within the city limits."

"Yes," Niveya replied. "But I was told by the Sable Masons that this shop had a bit more... understanding."

"Ah." The man's demeanor brightened. "Well, then. I might be able to help you out. I do have a selection in the back room, if you and your associates would care to join me?"

They followed the red-haired shopkeeper into a small pantry-like room. Shelves brimming with bottles lined the walls. Drying herbs hung from the ceiling in great clumps and bunches; their overpowering scent filled the tiny room, making Grayden's eyes water. His head throbbed, but he lifted his chin and reminded himself sternly that he was a defender, a champion of the realm, and that he had a mission to accomplish.

The man did not go to any of the shelves. Instead, he swept aside a small rug and lifted a hidden latch, revealing a compartment in the floorboards. Reaching inside, he pulled out a glass vial.

"Here you go, this is premium," he announced triumphantly.

Niveya glanced around furtively, making a show of being paranoid. "You are sure we can't be overheard or seen back here?"

"This room is safe," the man assured him. "I've taken several extra precautions."

"Good." Niveya drew out the dart. "I need a mixture that

precisely matches the ithonium on this dart. Can you provide that?"

"Seems a little unnecessary," the apothecary muttered. "Everyone has his own signature, but the poison works the same."

"He's eccentric," Grayden supplied, stepping forward and whispering the words into the man's ear. "Fancies himself a bit of a king, even though our crew is all you see here. Likes to leave a signature, if you know what I mean." He slipped a rune into the man's hand.

"Ah." The apothecary flashed a knowing smile at Grayden. "Well, if you're looking to match a mixture, I'm afraid I can't do that. I might be able to tell you who can, or if there's anyone in the city who sells that particular mix."

"That would be most appreciated," Grayden said.

"May I?" The man reached his hands out for the dart.

Niveya mumbled something under his breath. Grayden didn't catch all of it, but he heard the word "upstart" and he beamed in amusement. He handed the dart to the apothecary. The man accepted it gingerly and pulled out a clean white cloth. He wiped one side of the dart's tip on the cloth, flipping a pair of goggles down over his eyes and peering at it intently.

"Hmm," he murmured. "This is a fairly nasty mixture. Even a pinprick would be enough." His face paled beneath the goggles and he handed the dart back, wiping his hands on his leather apron.

"Well?" Niveya asked.

"Ah. Ah... yes. Well, I recognize the signature. You can get that brand down at Ungaro's. But I'm afraid that doesn't help you much."

"Oh? Why not?" Niveya inquired, raising his eyebrows.

"Because he only does business with the Motley Tailors, that's why." Nervously, the man wiped his sleeve across his forehead.

"I see," Niveya replied. "Well, why don't you tell me where I can find this Ungaro, and I'll ask him myself. It cannot hurt to ask, right?"

"I… I suppose," the man stammered. "But… really… I would advise against it."

"Thank you for the warning, my good man," Niveya said, his voice smooth. "Now, where is Ungaro's?"

The apothecary stammered out a set of directions, informing them what sign to look for above the shop. He was obviously nervous as he did so, and Grayden wondered what about this other apothecary or his regular client could be so terrifying.

Leaving the shop, Niveya put a hand on Grayden's arm. "That was quick thinking back there."

"I'm sorry," Grayden replied. "I know you said to leave the talking to you…"

"Not at all, not at all." Niveya waved a hand. "I appreciate someone who can think on their feet, and it's never a bad thing to know when to break the rules. You saw his reluctance and fabricated a story he would believe, all while acting the correct part. That is impressive. And I am not easily impressed."

Grayden looked down at his feet, feigning the appearance of being flattered. "He just reminded me of someone back home, is all."

"You have crooks like that back home?" Beren asked.

"No, she's not a crook," Grayden protested. "She's a very respected woman in our village. It's just… she sort of sees herself as being above everyone else, too good for our humble little town, if you can understand that. She knows everybody and everything that's happening, and she's suspicious of anything out of the ordinary. If you want to get her to help you out, you have to first sort of wheedle her into realizing that you agree with her opinion of herself and everybody around her. That man needed to believe that Niveya wasn't a threat of any kind, so I figured if I could make him out to be a little eccentric and full of himself, it might reinforce what he wanted to believe about us and he'd be more willing to give us what we needed."

"And it worked." Niveya clapped Grayden on the back. "You have the soul of a spy, my lad."

"I'm not sure that's a compliment," Grayden chuckled, "but since you believe it is, I'll accept it."

Beren snorted a guffaw. "Careful, Niveya, or you might just find that my friend can handle you as well as he handled that apothecary."

Niveya grinned. "Unlikely." But his gaze lingered a moment on Grayden, his expression thoughtful.

Several blocks later, they found the worn sign that told them they had reached their destination. The peeling green paint and flourishing words promised "A Potion for Every Season," but a brief glance through the window revealed a room full of empty shelves. Undeterred, they pushed their way through the door and entered the shop.

"Ungaro?" Niveya called out. A thin film of dust covered the shelves. "Ungaro?"

Hinges creaked, and a door on the other side of the shop opened. A head covered in a shaggy mop of dark hair peeked around the doorframe.

"Who goes there? I'm closed for business for the day!" A creaky voice wavered through the air.

"A bit early in the morning for closing," Niveya replied.

"As you can see, I'm out of wares. I'm expecting a shipment any day. Come back in a sennight. I might have something for you then."

"We cannot wait a sennight, friend."

"I'm not your friend," the man snapped. "I haven't got anything for you. Try another store. Good day!"

The door slammed shut. Niveya strode across the room and yanked on the handle, plunging into the room beyond. Grayden and Beren followed at a cautious distance, on guard in case the man attacked, or the unseen room was full of people the apothecary *did* consider friends. As they passed through the door, however, they saw no other threats. Here was another storage room lined with shelves, but this room was far cleaner, brighter...

and well-stocked. The small man cowered in the corner, staring at Niveya in fear.

"I—I'm sorry," he was stammering. "I didn't know. I didn't expect anyone today. Please don't be angry."

Grayden frowned, confused. Then he saw that Niveya was holding up a slip of paper bearing the design of a needle and thread, and the apothecary's gaze was fixed upon it.

"You have nothing to fear, so long as you cooperate," Niveya said, his voice stern.

The man's demeanor changed. He straightened, smoothing down his hair with one hand. "Of course, of course," he said. "I do apologize for the rude greeting. Like I said, I did not expect any appointments today. You startled me. Had I known you were working with the Motley Tailor, I would have greeted you in a far different fashion."

"Of course," Niveya replied, his tone sounding overly reasonable as he produced the dart from his pocket. "I need to know about the poison on this dart. Did you mix it?"

"Ah." The man leaned forward and stared at the dart, flipping his own set of goggles over his face and adjusting the lenses with long, dexterous fingers. "Ah... this looks familiar..." He glanced up at Niveya. "May I?"

Once again, Niveya handed over the dart.

Ungaro gave it the same treatment the other man had, wiping the dart on a clean cloth and peering at the smudge through his goggles. At last he looked up. "Yes, I believe this is my recipe," he replied. "As I recall, I furnished one of your crew with a set of darts just like this one a few nights past." His eyes rolled up toward the ceiling and he tapped his finger in the air. "Three, I believe. A set of three. He wanted them for a job. Deadly as I could make it."

"And which member of our crew requested this set?" Niveya's voice was grim.

The man pushed his goggles up on his forehead. "Ah... I..." His eyes darted from one face to the other, and his expression changed. "Wait... I do not recognize you... wait... you... you're not part of the Tailor's crew. Who are you?"

"A concerned third party," Niveya replied.

Ungaro's face blanched. He swung his head back and forth. "I can't say any more. I... no. You tricked me!"

"We mean your crew no harm," Niveya assured him. "We just want to ask them a few questions. All we want to know is where to find their king."

"I can't tell you that!" Ungaro's eyes widened. "They would kill me quicker than a wylfen pouncing on a rabbit."

"If you don't tell me, I'll do far worse than simply kill you." Niveya loomed over the man.

"Look... I can... maybe... maybe arrange a meeting. Maybe. But you can't tell them you tricked me, understand? They can't know that I said anything to you."

Niveya tilted his head to one side, observing the man before him. "I think we can strike a deal here."

"Okay. You tell me where to send a messenger, and I'll set up a meeting. If I can."

"That's not good enough," Niveya growled. "I propose a different deal. You take me to this Motley Tailor now."

Ungaro blanched. "I can't do that."

Beren's sword hissed as he drew it out of his scabbard. Shouldering his way past Niveya, he held the enormous blade in front of the man's throat. "You make a deal with my friend, or I'll make your relationship with your head a long-distance one," he thundered.

A squeaking sound like a high-pitched whispering scream escaped Ungaro's lips, and he fell back onto the floor in a dead faint.

24

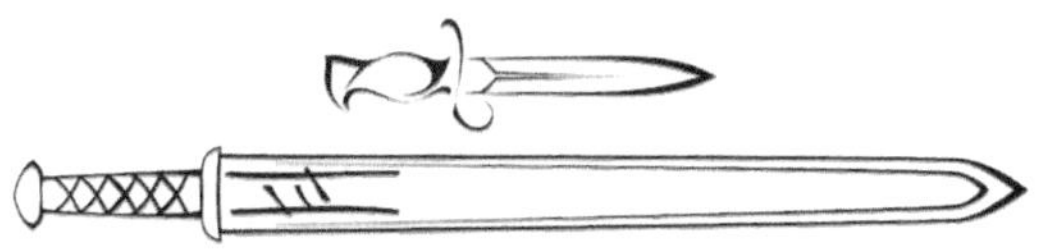

Grayden stared at his friend, wide-eyed. "Really?"

Beren shoved his sword back into its sheath, his face turning bright red. "You're the one who keeps telling me we need to do things his way," he mumbled, jerking his head at Niveya.

Grayden coughed. "Yeah. I... I think you overdid it. Just a bit."

Beren stared down at the crumpled form of Ungaro ruefully, his face flushing even more. He picked the smaller man up off the ground and set him on a chair as Ericole returned with a small bowl of water.

"That was masterful," Niveya commented with a small chuckle, splashing some of the water on Ungaro's face, slapping him to bring him back to consciousness. "Truly. In my vast experience, I have seen few performances of equal effect. I'll have to use that line, myself sometime."

Grayden snickered, earning a baleful glower from Beren. Ungaro's eyes flickered open. Recognition crossed his face, chased by horror, and he closed his eyes again.

"Why can't you just go away and leave me alone?" he moaned.

"Now, now," Niveya soothed. "We just want an introduction. Is that so hard to arrange? Is it so much to ask?"

"You don't get introductions with the Motley Tailors." Ungaro sighed. "They're not real friendly like. There's a reason they've been around for so long. They're cautious. Don't like strangers."

"If you introduce us, we won't be strangers," Niveya countered.

"I'm not their friend," Ungaro spat. "You don't understand. They own me."

"What does that mean?" Beren asked. "How do you own a person?"

"It means exactly what it sounds like. You think I prefer to work for a single client? Think it makes me a good living? But any living is better than none at all, and that's the only choice I have."

"I think I see." Niveya rubbed his chin, a speculative look on his face. "You don't have the clout I expected. Perhaps there is an easier way to do this. We aren't unreasonable."

Ungaro shifted in the chair. "Maybe there is. What if you needed a job done?"

"What sort of job does this crew specialize in?"

"Anything you can think of. They have experts in every field, this crew."

"I see. What about infiltrating the city prison to have a chat with a few of the residents?"

Ungaro's expression grew confused, and he cocked his head slowly to one side. "I think they could arrange that."

"Excellent. How do we contact this crew?"

"If you're a paying customer, I can introduce you."

"Is that all it takes?" Niveya examined the palm of his own hand idly. "Why didn't you just say so?"

Ungaro's eyes darted to Beren. "I was getting around to it when your young giant threatened to decapitate me."

"I remember no such threat," Niveya replied.

"Well, I remember it. Vividly." Ungaro crossed his arms and scowled.

Niveya smiled, showing all his teeth. "My young friends

dislike our kind," he admitted. "But as long as you can get us an introduction with these Motley Tailors, you can consider yourself under my protection from these two."

The wiry little man gave a shaky nod. "I will set it up. Where can I send a messenger to let you know a time and place?"

Niveya gave him the address, and the three men left the shop.

"Do we trust him?" Beren asked.

"Not likely," Grayden muttered. "But now I think he's at least as scared of us as he is of the crew he works for."

"That might be a stretch," Niveya corrected. "But he knows we mean business, and he doesn't believe we're a threat to the crew trusting him, which is about as good as we can hope for. Come on, we probably have time to do a little more investigating before Ungaro sends for us. I'd like to have a look around the prison and see what we're up against."

"We aren't really going to hire this crew of assassins to help us break into the city lockup, are we?" Beren asked.

Niveya gave an eloquent shrug.

Beren glared at his shoulder blades, but made no further protest.

The city prison was not in the center of Doran. It was in the eastern quadrant, a lone, squat building standing by itself away from the other buildings. A patch of grass covered the ground in front, and a few wiry flowers nodded their heads on either side of the door. A guard paced around the prison, his eyes sweeping the surrounding area. Through the front door, they could see another guard sitting on a low bench, leaning against the wall.

"Not the most secure place I've ever infiltrated," Niveya muttered, "but not as easy as it looks, either."

"Why do you say it's not easy?" Grayden asked, honestly curious.

"Two guards are not terribly difficult to get past," Niveya explained. "But there are other considerations: the absence of any nearby cover, which appears to have been purposefully arranged. And two guards means it's twice as hard to bribe one's way past.

Keeps them accountable. Also"—Niveya jerked his head slightly —"that building on the south side? There's another guard up there. I'm guessing he has a crossbow aimed at the prison at all times. Ten sigyls say that entire building is either empty or a barracks for the city guard."

Grayden craned his neck, glancing up at the sky and then pointing at a bird flying overhead, while surreptitiously glancing at the building Niveya had indicated. He could see the faint outline of a man's head poking over the edge of the flat roof.

"So how do we get in to talk with the mercenaries?" Beren asked.

"Like I said, I'm working on it," Niveya replied. "Could be we actually do end up hiring the Motley Tailors, if they're as good as this Ungaro seems to think they are."

"I don't like it," Beren muttered. "Seems like we could start by simply asking."

"And alert Regeont Elan to our presence? Let him know someone outside the guard is investigating? Who do you think the prison guards report to, anyway? You seem to have forgotten that the man we are trying to gather evidence may also be the man in charge of this country."

Beren's lips tightened. "I haven't forgotten."

"Good. Now, you are both quick thinkers and while the idea of working together didn't thrill me at first, I have to admit that you haven't been the burden I feared. I've even been glad to have you both about. However, this is my territory. Assassins and spies and infiltration and dealing with scum like Ungaro and the crew that owns him... this is where I live. I know you dislike it, that you despise me and everything I am. But we have to work together if we are going to prove Elan's guilt, or find the culprit behind Regeont Roshana's murder if he proves to be innocent. And whether or not you like me, you're going to have to trust me. Is that clear?"

Beren and Grayden shared a sideways glance, and then they both nodded.

"I think we'd better head back to my safe house," Niveya said. "We don't want to miss our invitation."

———

THERE WAS no invitation or messenger waiting for them when they returned to Niveya's house, so Grayden went up to his room to lie down. It had been a long couple of days, and he was exhausted. He closed his eyes, but sleep would not come. His mind continued to spin on the evidence they had found, Ulia's story, the mercenaries, the assassins, the crew they were going to meet and, in the center of it all, Regeont Elan. He could not figure out how it all worked together. And more disturbing than that was the fact that his sixth sense had betrayed him. Never before had it failed. Without it, he felt blind. It was an uncomfortable sensation, but even more uncomfortable was the realization of how much he had always relied on it. He had always taken it for granted, but he had not consciously known how much he used it, depended on it. Grayden flipped onto his side, frowning fiercely at the wall. He did not need an additional sense to warn him of danger before it happened. A trained defender should be able to sense danger without aid.

But he wasn't a fully trained defender, a traitorous part of his brain whispered. Could he really consider himself to be ready after a single year at the Academy? No matter how hard they had pushed him, could anyone believe he had experienced the same amount of testing and education that a true graduate had undergone?

Rolling onto his other side, Grayden sighed and got to his feet. This line of thinking was unproductive. There was little he could do to change his circumstances, and the job at hand should hold his entire attention.

His stomach rumbled, and he realized he had eaten nothing since breakfast, and it was well past lunchtime. Perhaps food would help calm his thoughts and help him focus. Or perhaps the messenger would come and they could continue their investigation. Either way, he had to admit the elusiveness of sleep in his current state of mind.

He met Beren in the hall, also heading downstairs. "Couldn't rest?"

Beren grimaced. "No. My mind would not let me sleep, and then my stomach began complaining."

"Same here."

They ventured down to the kitchen, where they found Niveya already standing at the counter eating from a plate filled with cheese and fruit. He raised an eyebrow at them.

"So, we have something in common after all," he commented.

"We feel the need to eat when we are hungry?" Beren asked. "I have the same thing in common with sage-lizards."

Niveya chuckled. "I meant we cannot rest while on the hunt. But hunger is another trait we share, and not an ignoble one. Even sage-lizards have their uses."

Grayden picked up a hunk of yellow cheese and bit into it, grinning at his friend. "He has a point."

Beren gave an unwilling smirk. "I suppose even a broken chronometer can be right twice a day."

Niveya guffawed and popped a strawberry into his mouth. The three of them stood at the counter and ate in silence for a while.

Once they had consumed as much food as they needed, Niveya wiped his mouth on the corner of a handkerchief and glanced sideways at Beren. "I am unused to having my methods questioned. However, in the interest of helping you trust that we are striving for the same goal, I think it would be prudent to let you know that I have sent a few of my associates out to dig up information on these Motley Tailors. I have already learned a few interesting tidbits, and expect to know more tomorrow. When we meet with their king, however, I will endeavor to appear less well-informed than I expect to be. It would be best for you to follow my lead on this."

"That seems easy enough," Beren said, "especially if you do not tell us what you learn."

"I hoped you would see it that way. Now, it is getting late. We should all get some rest."

They retreated to their respective rooms. As Beren pushed the door to his room open, Grayden stopped him. "Beren, do you ever worry that we're not ready?"

Beren frowned. "Ready for what?"

"For any of this, for the duties of a defender. We only had a single year at the Academy... what if it wasn't enough?"

"Our instructors pushed us hard, my friend. They decided we were ready. Who are we to disagree with their assessment?"

"Simple as that?" Grayden shook his head. "I wish I had your confidence."

"What of our time in the Greyklasp Mountains?" Beren asked. "Does it mean so little to you? Not only did we man the outpost we were assigned, but we also trekked across the mountains, survived an avalanche, and defeated an enemy who was attempting to kill us. Had we been unprepared, as you fear, I do not believe we would have survived that ordeal."

"You're probably right. I just... oh, never mind. Good night." Grayden headed off to his own room, pulled off his boots, and threw himself down on the bed. In time, his eyes finally closed, and he drifted off to sleep.

He awoke when the sunlight blazed through his window and he realized he had forgotten to draw the curtains the night before. After washing the grit from his eyes and tugging on his boots, Grayden descended to the dining room. He was the first one up, but even as he sat down, Vidia was at his side with a teapot, which she poured carefully into his teacup. The smell of oranges wafted from the interior of the cup, and Grayden smiled at the familiar scent.

"Thank you for going to the trouble of providing tea," he said. "It smells like home."

"It was no trouble at all, sir." Vidia's words were precise and elegant. "It was my pleasure. Cream or sugar?"

"No, thank you."

"I apologize that breakfast is not quite ready yet. Cook only just fired up the stove a few minutes ago. You just sip that for a bit while I go help him with the preparations."

"Don't rush on my account." Grayden was alarmed. "I forgot to draw the curtains last night, and the sunrise woke me. I'd prefer to wait and eat with the others, anyway."

"Very good, young master." Vidia bobbed. "Master Niveya should be down in a few minutes."

"Thank you, Vidia." Grayden smiled. "Last I saw her, your daughter was well."

A flush spread through her cheeks and her eyes brightened for a moment, then she blinked and the emotion he had seen in her expression was gone. Without another word, she exited the room.

Grayden sat and sipped his tea, relishing the subtle flavor and the warmth that trickled down his throat. In the silence, if he closed his eyes, he could picture his parents' kitchen: the rough wood of the table his father had worked hard to craft for his mother, the bouncing ribbons in Seren's hair, already coming loose and undone. He could smell the gravy simmering on the stovetop, hear his father's steady voice as he outlined the work for the day.

"Good morning." Beren's jovial voice broke through his reminiscing, and Grayden opened his eyes. Thoughts of home and the orchard fled his mind. He missed his family, but he could not deny the thrill of the puzzle before them, nor the way his blood churned to meet the challenge of proving what they knew to be true.

Niveya arrived a moment later and Vidia returned to fill his and Beren's mugs with coffee. Another maid followed with full plates, setting them before each place. When she had finished her task, she drew an envelope from the pocket of her apron and held it out.

"Lord Niveya, this came for you just now."

"Thank you." Niveya took the envelope and opened it with a quick flick of a dagger that materialized from within his sleeve. He scanned it and then handed it over to Beren, who held it up so that Grayden could also read what was written there.

South Avenue. Third shop on the left. 6 bells. Knock twice.

"Well," Niveya said, taking a sip from his goblet. "It looks like we are going to get our introduction, after all. And we have the entire day to spend on other avenues of investigation. Two outstanding pieces of news, and we haven't even finished breakfast."

25

The aton struck with uncanny speed, its legs striking out at all three of them at once. Dalmir fended off the attack with his sword, knocking the leg aside, but he did not have time to feel pride at the accomplishment because at that moment Drengur gave a loud scream. Dalmir turned around just in time to see the boy being lifted into the air, his torso caught between the pincer-like grasp of the spidery metal creature. The aton shook him about and then, with steps that beat a tapping, staccato rhythm, skittered away, straight up the side of the nearest building, Drengur dangling limp in its grasp.

"Drengur!" Ioan shouted. "Dalmir, can you do it again?"

"The ceiling is too high," Dalmir replied. "That fall would kill us, and I can't slow our descent."

Ioan grimaced. The aton had made it to the top of the building and they watched as it squeezed itself through a window.

"Then we go up from the inside," Ioan said.

The two men charged into the building. They could tell it had been an inn, though dust covered everything, and much of the interior had deteriorated. The floorboards groaned under their steps and Dalmir wondered what was holding the place together.

Ahead of him, Ioan raced lightly across the room, his footfalls barely making a sound.

"Is your light-footedness a newfound skill, or have you always trod so lightly?" Dalmir asked as they paused at the bottom of the stairs.

Ioan gave him an odd look. "What?"

Dalmir shook his head. "Nothing. Do you hear anything?"

"No."

Ioan leading the way, they ascended the steps. The building was one of the shorter structures in the city and only had five flights of stairs. When they reached the summit, Ioan gestured for Dalmir to halt. The younger man closed his eyes and tilted his head from one side to the other.

"The last room on the left," Ioan whispered, "and I think there's more than one of them."

"You have good ears," Dalmir commented.

Ioan dropped his gaze, not meeting Dalmir's eyes.

Cautiously, they crept down the hall. It was a narrow passageway, with a long carpet running down its center. Like everything else in the building, the carpet was dusty and tattered. A single, solid strike might cause it to disintegrate completely.

It must be the lack of elements, Dalmir decided. Being kept underground had protected the city from wind and weather that would have leveled it long ago.

They stopped at the last door. Now Dalmir could hear the faint mechanical whirring and a very light tapping. A thud, followed by a muffled groan, came from inside.

Ioan held up a fist. Then he raised one finger, then two. As he raised a third finger, both men kicked at the door with all their strength. They needn't have bothered. The door was no longer a solid barrier: it shattered beneath the force of their combined might, splinters raining down on the herd of atons within the room.

Dalmir's heart sank at the sight. A full score of atons crouched before them, lights blinking along the sides of their oblong bodies, and in the center of the room, surrounded by these creatures, lay Drengur. His eyes were closed, but even from their distance, Dalmir could see his chest rising and falling in the dim light. He turned to Ioan to whisper a warning that they should proceed carefully, but Ioan was no longer there.

With absolute silence, Ioan leaped into the room, his movements so fluid and unexpected that for a moment, Dalmir thought he had vanished. Then his sword came down on the body of the nearest aton with a screeching sound of rending metal and Ioan let out a war-cry that echoed through the building with such ferocity that Dalmir fancied he saw the walls tremble in fear. The atons were swift to converge on Ioan, their legs reaching and slicing through the air with swift precision, but Ioan's body twisted and dodged, always just out of their reach. After the fierce initial attack, Ioan did not seem intent on dealing out damage. Instead, he wove through the milling atons, slicing here, stabbing there, and using the close quarters against the machines. Dalmir stood at the door, watching, and trying to think of something he could do that would not interfere with Ioan's attack. For the moment, the atons appeared to be ignoring him, focused completely on Ioan. Dalmir was not accustomed to feeling useless. But inside this tower, his power had unpredictable consequences. However, as an aton moved away from the entrance, Dalmir then understood what Ioan was doing. Slowly, a path opened between Dalmir and Drengur.

Edging his way into the room, Dalmir made his way toward the young man. He moved slowly, one careful step at a time, so as not to rile the atons into crushing the unconscious boy in their midst. The mechanical creatures continued to ignore Dalmir's advance, their entire focus on Ioan, the only perceptible threat at the moment. Dalmir took a cautious step, then another. An aton swiveled toward him and he froze, holding his breath, gripping the sword hidden beneath his cloak, but ready if he needed it. The aton's legs clicked on the floor as it approached. Dalmir's heart raced, and he cursed his brother's cunning that prevented him from removing the threat these creatures posed to himself and his companions.

There was a scraping, tearing sound and the aton reared up, toppling backward as Ioan pierced the armored underside of the machine with his sword. The aton scrambled to its feet and leaped at Ioan, all eight legs stretching out at him.

Dropping all pretenses, Dalmir dashed to Drengur's side. He slapped the boy's face, shouting at him, willing him to wake.

Drengur groaned and his eyes fluttered open. "Dalmir? What...?" His question turned into an incoherent yell of terror.

Dalmir whirled with precision guiding his sword and the aton fell silent. He helped Drengur to his feet and half-prodded, half-dragged him to the door, shouting for Ioan. The atons, seeing their escape, plunged after them.

"Where's Ioan?" Drengur screamed.

"I'm not sure," Dalmir shouted, holding the boy up and half-pushing, half-dragging him along. "Run!"

Another burst of speed and they were careening down the stairs, the remaining atons right behind them. In desperation, Dalmir used his power, attempting to summon light once more, and hoping that he might reverse gravity again and give themselves a few more minutes of breathing room.

Instead, rain poured down on top of them and Dalmir's feet slid as the smooth wooden stairs grew slippery in the sudden indoor deluge. Drengur gasped.

"Curse you, Tel!" Dalmir hissed under his breath. "I'm the good guy!"

"What is this?" Drengur shouted.

"I'm not sure." Dalmir clung to the railing. "I thought I understood what Tel had done, but I must have been wrong. This chaos reminds me far more of..."

He did not have time to say more, because the atons were upon them. Completely unfazed by the sudden rainstorm that Dalmir had inadvertently caused now occurring inside the building, their feet barely splashed as they crawled down the stairs.

Dalmir shouted and thrust his sword into the nearest one, slowing it down, but not stopping its advance. Drengur, his mind cleared by the cold water, also attacked. He swung his sword about, doing slightly more damage to the railing than to their attackers, but at least he was enthusiastic about his destruction, giving the creatures no easy target to grab hold of. Dalmir backed down the steps, giving ground as two atons advanced on him. With an eye on the railing that Drengur's last swing had damaged, he feinted right. When the first aton followed, Dalmir ducked under its body, whirled, and thrust upward with his sword, intent on pushing rather than skewering. The aton's feet slipped on the smooth, wet wood and with a crash and a metallic clanging sound, it plummeted through the weakened railing and fell to the bottom. Its crash shook the building, but the other atons did not appear to have any ability to feel concern for their fellow and kept advancing.

A shout from above made Dalmir look up in time to see Ioan charging down the stairs after them, his sword slashing.

"The wheels in their legs are weak," Ioan yelled. "Aim for those!"

Drengur, hearing Ioan's voice, straightened. With a mighty bellow, he swung his sword through the mechanism that formed the joint on the leg of the aton nearest him. The blow severed the leg, and the aton lost its balance and crashed to the side, stunned, but not defeated. Before it could rise, Ioan leaped on its back and drove his sword through its body. The lights on the machine flared and then went out, and it slumped to the stairs.

"There are too many of them," Dalmir called. "We need to get out of here!"

"Lead the way!" Ioan shouted, leaping down with a splash to land on the stair next to him.

They raced down the stairs and out the door onto the street. Without pausing, Dalmir let his memories take over as he led his companions through an alleyway and around a corner, then up another street. Left, right, right, left, left, right; he wove them through the streets of the massive city until they reached an impressive set of four pillars. Their surfaces were smooth, except for a single, deep groove on each of them facing the interior of the square they created. The pillars stretched far up into the sky and disappeared into the darkness above. Dalmir bent over, panting at the exertion.

Ioan took him by the arm. "Where to next?"

"One moment," Dalmir said, between great, gulping breaths. "It's been a while since I did much running. My body is a little upset with me."

"We cannot stay here," Ioan insisted, shaking his arm. "They nearly killed Drengur. I can still hear them. We may have lost them for the moment, but they are searching for us and sooner or later, they will find us."

"I have no intention of staying here." Dalmir straightened. "But neither can we reach the next flight of stairs before the atons find us; it is on the far side of the city."

"Then what are we doing?" Drengur asked, his face pale.

"If the atons are still functional after all this time, I thought perhaps more of Tel's inventions might be, as well." Dalmir walked over to one of the massive columns. He ran his fingers over the surface until he found what he was looking for. There was a click and then a faint whirring sound. Dalmir gave a satisfied nod.

"Stand back outside the pillars," Dalmir instructed, backing up as an example.

The others moved back and joined him, looking around in confusion. A minute passed. Then another minute. They could hear the sound of the atons in the distance, the clicking of their feet very distinctive. Ioan fidgeted.

"Dalmir," he began, his tone frustrated.

"Hssst." Dalmir held up a hand. "Patience."

"What are we waiting for?" Drengur asked.

"It is simply easier if you see it," Dalmir replied.

They continued to wait, and then he heard sharp intakes of breath on either side of him as the large platform lowered into view above their heads. It slid down the pillars with no visible mechanism or clue as to how it worked, save for the fact that each corner was affixed in some way to the grooves on the corresponding columns. With a grinding sound, the platform halted approximately half a meter above the ground.

"Climb on," Dalmir instructed.

"No more stairs!" Drengur exclaimed with a sigh of relief, hopping onto the platform without question. It gave a little under his weight, then re-stabilized.

Ioan hesitated. He paced in front of it, leaning down to inspect the underside, tapping it with his sword. "Is it safe?"

"Perfectly," Dalmir assured him.

"Is it magic?"

"Perhaps it might seem that way from your perspective," Dalmir replied. "But no. It is mechanical, though Tel used his power to construct it. I can assure you, it runs more mechanically than the airships I have seen you trust your life to. But I cannot explain how it works; mechanics and building things were never my forte."

The clicking sound was drawing closer. Behind them, in the shadows of the city, Dalmir caught a glimpse of movement.

"Come on!" Drengur urged.

Ioan gave the platform another wary look, but climbed up to stand beside Drengur without any further complaint.

Dalmir flipped the tiny lever once more before stepping up to stand beside his companions, and the platform ascended. Drengur walked to the edge and peered over as the ground fell away below them. Ioan looked as though he wanted to grab the young man by the coat and pull him back, but he did not. Meter by meter, they climbed into the air. Suddenly, Ioan dropped to the surface of the platform and beckoned the others to join him. He pointed down, and Dalmir and Drengur crept to the edge and peered over. The atons had reached the square below and were milling about in circles as though searching. The three men stayed quiet and still, hoping that the machines would not notice the platform rising away into the darkness above. After a few minutes, the atons moved away from the square, spreading out in all four directions like a search party.

Ioan breathed a sigh of relief and raised himself to a sitting position. "Looks like we've evaded them for now."

"Let's hope they don't decide to try the stairs." Drengur's tone was light, but his voice trembled.

"The ones in the library didn't," Dalmir reminded him.

"That's encouraging," Ioan replied. "But if the lower levels are any sign, there's probably something waiting for us up there." He nodded in the direction they were ascending. "We need to be ready for it."

"Dalmir..." Drengur's voice was quiet. "Why did it rain inside that inn back there?"

Dalmir sighed. "I have no idea. Obviously there is no consistency to whatever protections Tel constructed around his tower. I still don't know how he did it. I would not have thought it possible..." He trailed off. "I had not thought a good many things possible until recently."

"No, I meant... did you make it rain?" Drengur asked.

"Unintentionally, I assure you."

Drengur stared at him. "What else can you do?"

"Many things," Dalmir said. "None of them enough, it seems."

26

H rafn was not pleased at the idea of abandoning their home. None of the durven were.

"The Deepway is our home!" several hundred different voices shouted at Marik.

"And it's about to be invaded by the Ar'Mol's finest," Marik reminded them again.

"We have defenses," Hrafn argued. "We can collapse tunnels, spring traps, hide in the areas we haven't finished clearing yet. They will never find us in the maze."

"They have a map." Marik was getting tired of repeating himself. "They have young Olin. You can slow them down, but I guarantee you cannot stop them. And you cannot hide forever. They will find you, and they will kill you... or worse, force you to work for them."

"This is exactly why we never allow outsiders into the Deepway," one of the older durven growled. "All this suffering for a single human. One!"

A chorus of angry shouts joined their agreement with the one who had spoken.

"How many of us will die?"

"They have killed so many of us already!"

"Get them out of here! Let the durven look to the durven as we have done for eighty years!"

The shouts grew louder and angrier.

"Hrafn, I'm sorry," Mouse whispered. His shoulders slumped. "I never meant..."

"You're not the only one who broke the rules," Nando said, putting a hand on Mouse's shoulder. She eyed her fellow durven with a steady gaze. The shouting diminished, lowering to a soft rumble. "This is not helpful, my people. Yes, mistakes have been made, but we made them together. Please, turn your attention to our leader."

"The Deepway is no longer safe for us," Hrafn intoned, his voice resounding in the darkness. He raised a hand, forestalling the clamor of voices. "We knew what consequences we might bring upon our heads when we voted to help the outsiders. We knew full well what any action on the surface might yield. And yet we offered our aid. There is no way to take it back now. We must move forward. And if that means we move out of our beloved Deepway so that we may continue to safeguard our people and our children, then so be it."

"Where will we go?" someone asked.

"Telmondir," Marik said, raising his voice to be heard. "I will fly you to Telmondir. Your people will be safe there."

"We know nothing of the lands to the west!" someone cried.

"Why should we trust the ones who brought this trouble upon us?" another voice shouted angrily.

"Turn them over to the Ar'Mol!" someone yelled. "Perhaps he will leave us alone as payment."

Hrafn's eyes burned like deep, angry coals at this last suggestion. "Don't be a fool, Clargh. Or have you forgotten why we have kept our very existence hidden for all these years?"

Clargh recoiled as if slapped, but he continued to mutter angrily under his breath. The rest of the durven stomped their feet and hissed in anger and fear.

"My people." Nando's voice rose again. "I have seen the might of the Igyeum. Those who went with us to rescue Raisa have seen it, too. They will blast their way into our home and snatch us from our tunnels if we stay. And Hrafn is right: with young Olin in their clutches, they will not rest until they find us all to give as a gift to Lorcan. Captain Marik and his crew brought this danger down upon us, that is true, but it was not intentional. Let them atone for it by carrying our people to safety."

Her words seemed to apply a healing salve to the raw emotions running rampant through the crowd. In the end, the durven reluctantly agreed to be transported by airship to the safety of Telmondir. Hrafn ordered his people to go to their chambers and pack only what they could carry. He sent his scouts to set the traps and collapse what tunnels lay between them and the entrances within Melar, and Marik breathed a sigh of relief that the discussion was finally over.

Mouse went with the scouts while Shaesta and Elalli stayed near Marik throughout the entire event; Elalli's eyes were wide with fear at all the commotion. As the durven scattered to gather their belongings, she tugged at Marik's coat.

"The bad people? Are they coming here?" she asked.

Marik picked her up, trying not to wince. "Yes," he said, truthfully. "But we are going to be gone long before they get here."

At that moment, Mouse came dashing back down the corridor. "Captain! We have to get moving! The soldiers have found the city entrances. They're coming! Oleck is at the river exit. They don't seem to know about that one, but we have to go now!"

Marik spun around and handed the child to Shaesta. "Get her onto the airship and tell Oleck to take off as soon as he sees any soldiers. If I'm not there yet, don't wait for me."

"Marik!" Shaesta's protest sounded frightened.

"Don't worry about me," Marik said. "I'm not planning on getting left behind. Now go!"

She gave him one last unreadable look, some mixture of pleading and terror, before she whirled and ran off toward the tunnels leading to the exit with Elalli clinging to her. The little girl's frightened sobs echoed down the tunnel.

Marik found Nando and Hrafn and set to work helping the rest of the durven hurry in their last-minute preparations. All too soon, he heard the familiar sound of booted feet echoing throughout the tunnels.

"We have to go," he urged.

Everyone ran, but there was an orderliness to their movements. Nobody got trampled or knocked over. Even amid panic and their reluctance to leave, Marik was gratified to see that Hrafn and the other elders must have prepared their people well for this eventuality. He scooped up a small durven child who was lagging and trotted along with the mass of bodies filing their way to the river exit.

A shout resounded behind them. Arrows zinged through the air with deadly effect. Several durven fell without a sound. The orderly exodus turned instantly into panicked chaos. Marik was jostled and shoved. At one point, his leg buckled, and he fell to his knees, nearly dropping the child he carried. Then Nando was at his side, helping him up. The air grew warm, and Marik's heart thudded with dread. He barely had the courage to look back, and when he did, he wished he hadn't. The soldiers had built fires to set the tunnels ablaze. Though there was little that would burn, the smoke would soon become an issue. Already it was a choking, thick cloud. Marik pulled his shirt up over his mouth and nose, but it did not help much. The next volley of arrows sent into the ranks of fleeing bodies were flaming darts, and more people fell. Those left continued to stampede toward the river, but Marik despaired of reaching it in time. There was just too much distance to cover, too many people to get safely on board. Perhaps Oleck had already left. Perhaps this was where they would all die. He coughed as smoke went into his nose and came out through his eyes. Or at least that was how it felt. His eyes stung and watered and he choked and coughed, stumbling forward blindly in the darkness and trying to keep himself upright and moving along with the mass of fleeing bodies.

Then there was a new mighty shout, and two hundred fully armed durven came hurtling out of a hidden side tunnel. Armed with battle-axes, maces, and great hammers, they charged the line of soldiers and swung their weapons with mighty yells. Crashing and clanging and screams resounded off the walls of the tunnels. He could not see what was happening, even had he been able to stop and turn to watch the chaos behind him, and so he continued on, helping anyone he could. Someone collided into his side, nearly knocking him over. He was being jostled from all sides and he had lost all sense of direction. Those battling behind them could not stand for long against the ranks of Igyeum soldiers, but they were providing a few precious moments for those fleeing to escape to the safety of the airship. Every swing of hammer or axe meant one more person safely on board whatever Oleck had commandeered for their flight. Where was the exit? Had he missed it in his disorientation? Had he... there it was!

Then he was in the narrow tunnel, edging his way through. Those who had gone before him had cleared away most of the spiderwebs. With a final shove and a lunge, he made it through the final crevice and out into the open air. Gasping and gulping, Marik pulled the clear, cool air into his lungs. It was dark outside, still predawn, and at first Marik did not realize he had reached the riverbank. He stumbled out of the entrance and his boots sloshed into the water, the icy chill of the liquid rousing his senses and bringing him out of the stupor brought on by the smoke he had been breathing. The small child, still in his arms, whimpered.

"Captain! Up here!" Oleck's voice pierced even further through his haze and he looked up to see the large, unwieldy air barge that Oleck had somehow brought to their rescue. It was a misshapen, bulging, hideous vessel, with no grace or elegant lines. Even her sails were worn, tired-looking things that had been repaired so often that there were patches on top of patches. Paint hung from her hull in great, peeling strips, and her wing-sails were mismatched. But at that moment, Marik had never seen anything more beautiful in all his life. A grin spread across his face and he leapt up the bank in great strides, jumping to grab hold of one of the rope ladders hanging from the side of the airship. The child tightened his arms around Marik's neck, letting out a small squeal of terror. Marik swung himself one-handed over the railing and onto the already crowded deck. A woman reached out and took the child from his arms with a glad cry. Shaesta and Mouse ushered people down the large stairway to the decks below, and more durven clambered up the rope ladders and crossed the planks they had set between the airship and the cliff-side to make it easier to board dozens of people all at the same time.

Marik wanted nothing more than to slump to the deck and sleep, but he knew they were not yet safe. Mustering up the last dregs of energy he had, he pulled himself across the deck to the wheel where Oleck stood, holding the barge steady.

"Hold the wheel, Captain?" Oleck asked. "I need to go down to the engine room and adjust a few things or we'll never get out of here."

A loud noise made them both whirl about. The durven who had just boarded the ship were knocking the planks away from the airship and using hand axes and daggers to hammer through the rope ladders.

"What are you doing?" Marik shouted at them.

"We have to take off, Captain!" one of the durven shouted back. "We are the last of those who escaped. The rest are lost!"

"But..." Marik looked around. "But the others..." He stared into Oleck's grim face.

"Captain, I promised Hrafn that if such a choice was required..." Oleck hesitated. "That we would save some, if we could not save all."

"When was that?" Marik demanded. "I didn't agree to that!"

"Begging your pardon, Captain, but it was before I woke you. I figured you'd try to get as many out as possible."

"No!" Marik shouted, reaching for a rope that still tethered them to the ground. "We have to wait for the others!"

"There's no time!" The durven who had shouted at them came over and shouted some more. "We have to leave. The soldiers are right behind us. They cut us off. There are no more coming. We are the last." He swung a hand-axe, severing the rope with a single stroke.

Marik looked again at Oleck, shaking his head in denial. Oleck's mouth tightened as he pulled the lift-lever forward.

"No!" Marik leaped toward the railing, peering over. Below, he could see a few durven straggling out of the cavern. They looked up and saw the airship ascend. A wail of alarm rose, echoing across the river, the water amplifying the sound. Marik clenched his fists and squeezed his eyes shut.

"Look! There are more of them right there! Oleck, I'm ordering you to go back down!" Marik bellowed.

"I'm sorry, Captain." Oleck's voice sounded strained. "I'm sorry."

Marik pounded on the railing and opened his eyes. Below, he could see the taller figures of soldiers quickly overwhelming and surrounding those left behind. The airship continued to ascend. The people on the ground grew smaller. Soldiers herded the durven away and Marik knew all too well what their fate would be: the very fate they attempted to save Raisa from had now become their own. Marik raged in his heart, his fists smashing down on the railing once more.

This cannot be. I cannot let this stand. I cannot let this happen again! The words echoed in his mind like the screams of a tortured man, bouncing within his skull, throbbing with the horror of what he had brought on these people who had tried to help him. He sank to the deck, breathing quick, shallow breaths as his chest constricted in on him. He could not get enough air. Fire flowed through his lungs. There was no air! The darkness of the night grew suddenly even darker, and Marik fell to the deck, unconscious.

27

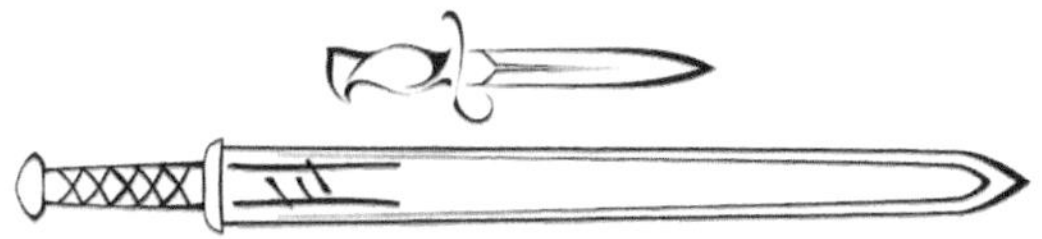

At precisely the last stroke of the sixth bell, Niveya raised his hand and rapped twice on the wooden door. Above them swung an ornate sign depicting a needle and thread, with the words "Motley Tailors" inscribed in large block letters. The window out front boasted a fine cloak on display, as well as a partition that blocked any further view into the store. The street was silent and abandoned, but Grayden knew they were being watched. Even though he could not sense it he was certain that any crew worth its salt would have sentries posted to survey these unknown clients as they approached.

The door swung open, and the interior of the shop yawned before them. Niveya entered without hesitating, and Beren and Grayden followed his lead. The door slammed shut behind them.

Along one wall of the modest tailor's shop stood racks of capes, stockings, hats, and tunics. From where they stood, the items looked well made, but simple. Mirrors lined the walls. Raised platforms stood in an even row, where customers could stand and be measured. A man being fitted for a coat currently occupied one of these. Tools of the trade lay scattered about on long counters.

"Surely it's not an actual tailor's shop," Grayden muttered to Beren, who shook his head in agreement.

Along the back wall of the shop stood a long counter, behind which a woman eyed them suspiciously. Niveya walked directly to the counter and leaned his elbows on it. Two burly men stepped out from the shadows at either end of the counter, hands on their swords. Grayden resisted the urge to grip the hilt of his own sword, which he had buckled to his waist before leaving Niveya's safe house.

"Welcome," the woman at the counter said, looking Niveya straight in the eye. She was of medium height, not more than one and a half meters tall. Tightly wound burnt-brown curls that she had pulled back from her face in a series of barrettes adorned her head. Her eyes were a warm shade of green in her darkly tanned face. She wore a long, sleeveless waistcoat over a long-sleeved tunic and close-fitting breeches. But the strangest thing about her apparel were the seven buttons sewn prominently on her left sleeve.

Niveya bowed. "Am I to understand that I have an audience with the queen of the Motley Tailors?"

The woman's lips, a vibrant shade of red, curved upward. However, she did not answer his question. "Our friend, Ungaro, gave me reason to believe that you were a prospective client. It is plain to me that he is an idiot, if not a liar, and will be punished for not recognizing the head of the Niveyan Syndicate." She gestured gracefully with her hand. "It is my honor to meet you, Lord Niveya, though I would have preferred an introduction that was not shrouded in deception."

"It was not my idea, I assure you," Niveya said. "I asked your associate for an introduction outright, but he seemed to think you would not meet with me unless I needed your services."

The woman's expression twitched. "I see. And do you require the services of my Tailors?" She surveyed the three of them with a critical eye, as though silently measuring them.

For grave clothes. The thought sent a chill creeping down Grayden's spine.

"Perhaps," Niveya replied evenly. "We have some business here in Doran and might require assistance."

The woman tilted her head to one side. "Very well. If you will consent to leave your weapons under the watchful care of Heath" —she gestured at the burly man looming on her left—"I would be pleased to invite you and your associates to join me in more comfortable surroundings, perhaps share a drink, and discuss exactly why you so urgently wished for an introduction with a small-time crew leader like myself."

Niveya spread his arms. "Gladly." He began laying weapons on the counter. The man had a surprising number of weapons stashed about his person, and it was all Grayden could do to refrain from gawking like the country-boy he was at the accumulating pile. Niveya glanced over his shoulder at Grayden and Beren and indicated that they should follow his lead.

Beren tensed, and for a moment Grayden worried his friend would object. Violently. Then the Telsuman relaxed and unbuckled his great sword, laying it down with a heavy thump. He glared at Heath.

"It had better be in the exact same spot when I return," he growled.

"On my honor," Heath said calmly, arms crossed.

Beren glared at the man but did not reply. Grayden joined him and laid his sword down as well. Behind the counter, the woman thumped her boot on the floor and a hidden hatch lifted from the floorboards, revealing a stair leading down into the darkness. With a sideways glance at her guests, she descended, giving them no choice but to follow. The other guard came behind them. Grayden heard the door clap shut, plunging them into complete darkness.

A moment later there was a scraping, clicking sound and then a sudden hiss followed by a flare of light and Grayden realized that the woman had struck a match. She lit a lantern hanging on a hook protruding from the wall at the base of the stairs, then plucked it from its spot and held it up, illuminating the narrow staircase.

"Come," she said, proceeding down.

Grayden wrinkled his nose as the stench of sewer overwhelmed him. The woman did not hesitate as she reached the bottom of the stairs, and so they followed her purposeful strides, their feet making small splashes and squelching sounds that made Grayden's skin crawl as he tried to ignore the reality of where they were. They traveled for a while, following a route that took them past several places where they had a choice of which branch of the sewer to follow.

After five or six such decisions, they came to an unobtrusive door in the wall, which the woman led them through. It was immediately apparent that this new tunnel was not part of the sewer network. The walls were closer, the ceiling lower, and planks instead of bricks lined the walls. It felt a little like a mineshaft, but Grayden could tell that description did not quite fit, though he could not put his finger on why. He crossed his arms and his fingers found their grip on the reassuring hilt of his long knife in its hidden sheath under his left arm. Its presence reassured him, then flooded him with caution. He had completely forgotten about it when the woman asked them to leave their weapons behind. For a moment, he worried that its discovery could jeopardize their undertaking, and then it occurred to him that nobody had searched them. Either this woman trusted the honor of their guests, or she expected a few things to be held back and had enough muscle wherever she was taking them that a dagger or two was not a concern. Grayden suspected it was the latter.

Proceeding down the tunnel, they came to a few places where the hall split off in multiple directions. Grayden tried to keep track of which tunnels they chose, but after several turnings, he was hopelessly lost. They were in a maze beneath the city of

Doran. Finding their way out on their own would be next to impossible.

After a few more twists and turns, they emerged into a comfortable chamber. This room boasted a much higher ceiling than the tunnels, and, except for the lack of windows, Grayden could have imagined himself aboveground.

The woman sat down in a fancy, high-backed chair that gave the impression of a throne, crossed one knee over the other, and tilted her head to one side.

"Now," she said. "Why don't you tell me what this is all about?"

"First, I must confess you have me at a disadvantage," Niveya said smoothly. "You know who I am, but have yet to give me your name. How can we conduct business under such a lack of trust?"

The woman narrowed her eyes. "You may call me Lady J."

"Very well, Lady J." Niveya stepped forward, holding out the dart in his open palm. "A woman we were acquainted with was murdered with this dart a few nights ago. We are trying to find her killer, and our investigation has led us here."

The woman glanced at the dart impassively. "Is that supposed to mean something to me?"

"The dart was poisoned with ithonium. Ungaro admitted that the mixture is his signature blend. We already know he only works for your crew." Niveya closed his fingers over the dart. "Why not make this easy on yourselves?"

"You are a stranger in my home," the woman replied, her manner unruffled. "Yet you abuse my hospitality by accusing my crew of... what... exactly? Murder? Why? You wish me to confess? To what end?"

"I have no desire to bring down you or your crew," Niveya said. "I am merely trying to solve a murder."

The woman stared at him through slitted lids. Abruptly, she spread her hands. "I see no harm in admitting it. Someone hired a member of my crew to hunt down and assassinate a young woman, one Ulia Embirs, if I remember correctly. It was difficult to track her down. She had gone into hiding."

"Was he given a reason for her murder?" Niveya pressed.

"We don't usually ask. But apparently she had stolen something valuable from her employer and run off with it," the woman said.

"I see." Ericole narrowed his eyes. "I don't suppose you would tell me who hired your crew for this task?"

"No." The word was abrupt and final. The woman arched an eyebrow at him, disbelief written plainly across her face. "I am aghast to even hear you ask it. Surely the lord of the Niveyan empire knows how important the code of silence is to people in our particular line of work."

"Forgive me, I had to ask. The answer is of some curiosity to me as this murder I am investigating is in relation to the death of a close friend, but I understand your need to protect yourselves and your clients," Niveya replied, his voice smooth and unconcerned.

Grayden marveled at his composure. Next to him, Beren stiffened, clearly growing impatient and angry at the lack of information being given.

Ericole looked around at the well-furnished room. "You seem to have done well for yourselves. I have not heard the name of your crew before, not something many on this side of Doran can boast."

"We like to keep a low profile," Lady J replied.

"Are you a newer crew?" Niveya pressed.

The woman laughed, an amused, breathy laugh that made Grayden's skin crawl. "No. We have been around for nearly a hundred years."

Niveya's eyes widened, and this time Grayden could tell the man was not putting on an act. He was honestly surprised.

Lady J's lips curved upward in a smug smile, and she rose from her chair. She sauntered forward and held out her hand to Niveya, fingers down as though she were a true queen of old, reaching out to accept a kiss from a serf. Niveya took her fingers and lowered his lips to her knuckles.

"I am Lady Jynna Arval, leader of the Motley Tailors. Though perhaps you are more familiar with our previous name: Tanners Emporium."

"Ah." The word escaped Niveya's lips, ending in a long, drawn-out whisper. "I thought that crew had disappeared. There was some speculation about a new entity that brought them down, but nobody could identify them."

"We started those rumors ourselves. You see, every dozen years or so we take on a new name and new recruits, change out our members—there are always a few interested in retiring—we scatter a bit to the winds, and continue our business with a new identity," Lady Jynna explained.

"Intriguing idea," Niveya said. "What have some of your other names been?"

"Oh..." She tossed her head. "The Embroidered Scarf, the Flowering Wreath, the Gray Spider, the Worn Tome... any of those sound familiar?"

"I have heard most of those names," Niveya admitted. "I had no idea they were all the same crew, though. Impressive. These names are associated with some"—he hesitated—"delicate work."

Pride shone in Lady Jynna's eyes. "It is refreshing to meet someone who appreciates our skill. Changing our identity so frequently affords us many advantages, but fame is not one of them."

"My lady, if fame is what you desire, I believe you could easily rise through the ranks and rule this side of the city."

"Flatterer." Jynna lowered her lashes. "But even you must understand that not everyone desires to be king."

"I recognize that as truth, though it is not a sentiment I can comprehend." Niveya flashed a grin.

A low chuckle purred from her lips. "In our line of work..." She paused, her tongue flicking out to caress her upper lip. "There are limited options for people like us. We either spend our lives building a mountain that everyone around us wishes to tear down, or we die in prison, alone and unmourned. My great-grandfather had a unique vision for a man of our particular breed. Because of his foresight and cunning, most of our previous members have retired to lovely homes in the countryside with respectable positions in their communities. None of them feels the need to peer into the shadows, or worries that one day a dagger will find its way into their backs. On our side of the law, anonymity has its... advantages."

"I can appreciate that," Niveya replied. "Who doesn't dream of a comfortable retirement without fear of retribution? Of course, like most advantages, it presents a certain... weakness."

"Weakness?"

"The anonymity you cling to, the treasure that protects your dream... like all treasures, can be stolen. Can be used against you."

Jynna's gaze sharpened, though the smile did not leave her face. "Surely you are not threatening me, Lord Niveya?" She spread her arms with a gentle laugh. "Here in my own domain, weaponless, without your vast resources or associates? I have heard rumors of your cunning, but at the moment, you appear to be toying with foolishness."

"Am I?" Niveya asked. "What if I told you that I know this room has four exits, two of them cleverly hidden? And that we are currently just below the cellar of Bida's Patisserie—I'm sure you know it well; after all, Bida makes the best borek in the city."

For the first time in the conversation, Lady Jynna's expression betrayed a minute amount of dismay. Her ruby-red lips parted slightly and her gaze darted to the side, as though looking for an escape. Then she tossed her head, resuming her regal air of confidence.

"You have impressive powers of deduction."

"Not really." Niveya inspected the nail on his forefinger, as though he had found an irritating bit of dirt there. "You gave me nearly an entire day, after all. It was my associates who discovered where your hideout was located. They merely reported it back to me. Even now, some of them stand behind each of the doors into this room. So you see, my dear lady, you do not have the upper hand here. Killing me to maintain my silence would be an imprudent action, and ultimately, quite disastrous to the tiny empire you have built for yourself." He gave her a sympathetic wince. "And I am afraid it would ruin those beautiful retirement plans you just told me about."

Lady Jynna let out a long, hissing breath through her teeth. Slowly, she walked backward, never taking her eyes off of Niveya, and sat down in her chair once more. She held him with a steely gaze and in a clipped, icy tone, she said, "I could kill you before your men could get inside."

"If you could see your way to helping us, I would, of course, make it worth your while." Niveya grinned disarmingly. Then his expression hardened, and he took a slow step forward. "However, if you would prefer me as an enemy, know this: it does not matter where you move or what you change your names to. Even if you kill me, my empire will remain stable. Consider how many of your secrets I have been able to discover with a mere twenty-four hours worth of effort. Cross me, and there will be no safe haven for you anywhere on Turrim. I will bend my entire will to finding and destroying you, your crew, and everyone who has ever been a part of this crew under any name. I will take away everything you have gained and leave you with nothing, not even the ability to start over. That lovely dream will become your unattainable nightmare for the rest of your days."

"On second thought, you make a rather convincing argument," Lady Jynna said, her lips tight and her voice small.

"Very good," Niveya replied, the menace falling from his features like a bit of dandelion fluff being carried off in a summer breeze. "Now, who hired your man to kill Ulia?"

Jynna cleared her throat nervously. "Honestly, I am uncertain. All I can tell you is that the money came from within the Manor itself."

"Who brought the payment?" Niveya pressed.

"A servant, a nobody," Jynna said.

"And what about the Regeont?"

"Lord Elan?" Jynna's brow furrowed. "I have had no dealings with him... not yet, anyway."

"No, I mean the former Regeont," Niveya barked. "Was your crew hired for that job?"

Jynna's lips parted in surprise. Her expression grew wary. "Why do you want to know?"

"She was a close friend of mine," Niveya gritted out between his teeth.

"Ah." The woman licked her lips. "In that case, yes. We were hired for that job. I lost two good men, too. Thankfully, the third made it back with only minor injuries."

"Who hired you?"

"I do not know." Lady Jynna held up a hand. "Honestly, I do not."

"I need to speak with the man who made it back." Niveya's voice was a low growl.

"I can arrange that," Jynna replied.

Grayden observed the woman. Though her tone and body language were indicating subservience, her eyes told a different story. Rage simmered there.

"And you said the reason given for the hit on Ulia was that she had stolen something from the manor?" Niveya asked.

"Yes," Jynna muttered.

Her attack came without warning. In a silent, fluid motion, Lady Jynna threw herself at Niveya, a small blade glinting in her hand. Grayden acted without thought, pulling his dagger from its hidden sheath and tossing it with all the precision of long hours of practice. The dagger sliced across the woman's outstretched hand, causing her to utter a startled shriek of pain and falter just long enough for Niveya to side-step the attack. Ericole wrapped one arm around her throat, using her own momentum to propel her to the floor, where he pressed his knee into her back, holding her arm back at a painful angle. Grayden rushed across the room to retrieve his dagger, standing nearby in case further aid was necessary. Niveya glanced up at him and gave a grateful nod, then turned his attention to the woman on the floor.

"That was not at all hospitable," he reprimanded. "I thought we had an understanding."

"You know I had to try," Jynna muttered.

"I warned you what would happen if you crossed me," Niveya replied.

"You may be powerful, but the people we work for are also powerful. Do you have any idea what would happen to my crew should it be discovered that we did not keep our clients confidential?"

"You would go underground, move to a different city, carry on," Niveya growled. "I will give you no such recourse. Think carefully now, because I'm only giving you this one chance to decide: who would you rather have as an enemy?"

Her body went limp as she stopped struggling. "Now we have an understanding," she muttered bitterly.

"How can you possibly expect me to trust you after that?" Niveya asked.

"Because now I am beaten. Tell me true, if I hadn't attacked, could you have trusted me?"

Niveya loosened his grip and took a wary step back, eyeing her. "I need more assurance than your word."

"Of course." Jynna rose, tossing her hair. "Mirianne," she called, "come here."

A young girl, perhaps fifteen or sixteen years of age, glided from the shadows. She crossed the room and came to stand next to the head of the Motley Tailors. The resemblance was instantly obvious.

"Lord Niveya, this is my daughter, Miri. I give her to you as collateral, your assurance of my cooperation."

Next to him, Beren stiffened with an outraged intake of breath. Grayden tensed. He did not know how Beren would react, and he was not at all certain that they could get out of this hideout alive if it came to blows, despite Niveya's confident words. However, Beren merely cracked his neck a few times and remained where he was. Grayden breathed a sigh of relief. From long hours sparring at the Academy, Grayden knew his friend was settling into a ready stance, but that he would not act first.

Mirianne tucked a dagger into her belt, glanced at her mother briefly, and then glided forward to stand before Ericole. She spread her arms, showing that her hands were free of weapons.

"That will suffice," Niveya said smoothly. "Mirianne, is it?"

The girl's cheek dimpled. "Most people just call me Miri."

"Very well, Miri," Niveya replied. "Why don't you go get acquainted with my two partners while your mother and I press out the details of our new arrangement?"

Miri tipped her head to one side and tripped lightly over to stand with Grayden and Beren. Her hair was as curly as her mother's, but a more pronounced red in hue, and her eyes were a mesmerizing shade of gray. Her slightly upturned nose gave her an incongruous air of both innocence and mischief at once. She grinned conspiratorially at the two young men and twirled her dagger back and forth across brown knuckles. Grayden's fingers itched to try the trick, but he opted to keep his dagger sheathed.

Jynna leaned back in her chair, her expression wary. She reminded Grayden of a cornered fox he had once seen. The result had not been pretty. Once more, he resisted the urge to reach for his dagger.

"I am at your command, Lord Niveya," Jynna said. "What aid would you have from me?"

"I am going to need to speak with the assassin who was part of the crew you sent to kill the Regeont," Niveya replied. "As well as the man who killed Ulia. And I wouldn't mind a peek at your ledgers."

"You don't ask for much, do you?" Jynna's lips twisted in a wry sneer. "Very well. I can arrange both requests. Anything else?"

Niveya scratched his neck thoughtfully. Grayden wondered if

it was all an act, if he were drawing out the moment on purpose, or if he was really trying to think of anything else they needed.

"We need to get into the prison to speak with the mercenaries who attacked the Academy," Niveya said at last. "Is there any way you can help us with that? Without harming any of the guards." He shot a look at Beren.

A genuine smile replaced the cornered look. "Done." Jynna waved a hand.

Now it was Niveya's turn to look startled. "That easily?"

"It won't be a problem," Jynna replied. "We own a guard. He will happily look the other way for me."

"Excellent." Niveya rubbed his hands together.

"It will take me an hour or so to pull together all the information you asked for. Miri can escort you back to your lodgings."

"I am most grateful for your assistance." Niveya bobbed his head.

"You did not leave me much choice." Jynna's eyes narrowed. "Miri, show our guests the way out. Take them through the patisserie. I will have one of our crew bring them their weapons, as I am certain they will not wish to leave them behind or wait for us to deliver them. Do you understand your role?"

"Yes, my lady." Miri bobbed a curtsy, then spun in a circle and beckoned for the men to follow. She led them, not the way they had come, but through one of the hidden doors Ericole had mentioned and up a flight of stairs. They emerged a moment later into the coolness of a root cellar. They climbed the steps leading out of the cellar and into a hallway across from a bustling kitchen. Scents of warm borek wafted through the air. Grayden's stomach rumbled, reminding him that it had been hours since breakfast.

Niveya grinned at them. "I think we should get some pastries for the road," he announced. "Bida does indeed make the best borek in town."

28

The platform ascended in a smooth, gliding silence until it reached the ceiling. It rose through a square hole, precisely formed to let it through, and came to a gentle stop. Dalmir, Drengur, and Ioan stepped off and looked about. From here, they could see the tops of the columns they had used to ride the lift, and Drengur exclaimed over the fact that they were hollow. He peered down into one.

"I understand it now! There are pulleys and counter-weights like the ones we use in the mines, and I've even seen a few in Keene's forge. But these are lots more intricate," he added. "I can't imagine how they could have run so much cable inside such a narrow space."

Dalmir barely heard him. He was staring at the door off to one side. A prickling sensation crawled over his arms at the familiar sight.

"Dalmir? Are you well?" Ioan came to stand next to him.

"Tel's workshop." Dalmir gestured at the door. "Whatever has been calling to me is inside that room."

Ioan's eyes narrowed. "And whatever is guarding it?"

Dalmir nodded. "That is my concern." He looked Ioan in the

eye. "I'd like you and Drengur to stay out here. I can't protect you in there."

"We've come this far," Ioan said. "We could have turned back at any moment."

"You have done enough."

"This object you're looking for, it is crucial to the safety of Telmondir?" Ioan asked.

"I believe it is, yes. If only to keep it out of Uun's hands."

"Then it is my duty to accompany you," Ioan said. "I am a defender, whatever else I may also be, now."

"I need you to protect the lad." Dalmir kept his voice quiet.

"I don't need protecting," Drengur insisted, coming up behind them.

Ioan and Dalmir shared a glance, and then Dalmir lifted his hands in surrender. "Very well. If I can't keep you from coming in with me, then so be it. But I dislike this, and I wish you would let me go on alone. There is a strange presence here, something I cannot quite identify, and I am worried about what it means. My own powers are not working properly, and I cannot guarantee my ability to protect either of you. Just promise me you will do nothing foolish."

Ioan and Drengur nodded, expressions serious. Dalmir reached out to the door and tried the knob. It turned easily. Dalmir marveled at this a bit. Now that he had a moment to think, he could not account for how well everything still worked within Tel's tower. Why were the atons still active? What kept the city from falling to ruin and decay? That the lift-platform still worked—and so beautifully—after all these centuries was incredible. The orb was the only thing that could account for these wonders, and yet, what had activated it? How had it kept working throughout all these years? It was a mystery.

His heart sped up. Could Tel...? No. If his brother had somehow survived Uun's treachery, he would surely have contacted Dalmir before now. Besides, he had seen the bodies of his brothers. Had buried them. And yet his heartbeat pattered away with a thrill of hope despite his stern conviction that hope was for the foolish.

The door swung open. A gentle hiss like the sound of cold water falling on a hot stone was the only warning. Dalmir missed it, but Ioan gave a shout and pushed him and Drengur to the ground as a line of darts flew out of the darkness behind them.

"That was quick thinking," Dalmir said. He lay on the floor, panting a bit and trying to calm his racing heart. "Is everyone well?"

Ioan groaned and toppled to the ground next to them. Three darts protruded from his shoulder.

"No! Ioan!" Drengur shouted, shaking him. "Dalmir, Ioan is hurt!"

"I can see that, lad." Dalmir frowned, studying the darts. "Hold that lantern up and let me examine him. It doesn't look like they hit anything vital." The darts were small, and barbed, as Dalmir discovered when he tried to remove them. He worked them out of Ioan's skin with care. Ioan's face was pale and his eyes rolled back and his body went limp when Dalmir pulled the first dart out.

"Are they poisoned?" Drengur asked, a hint of panic in his tone.

Dalmir delicately pressed the end of a dart to his tongue and shook his head. "Not poison," he announced. "But they are coated in something... amarylth, if I'm not mistaken."

"Amarylth?"

"Physicians use it to help patients sleep or to dull the pain of more serious wounds," Dalmir explained. "Unfortunately, I do not know how long it will take for the effects to wear off."

"But it will wear off." Drengur's eyes were wide with fear.

"Yes, it's not dangerous. Just... inconvenient."

"Is there anything we can do to wake him?"

"I don't think so." Dalmir sat back and stared into the workshop. "Though I guess it can't hurt to look around Tel's workshop. There may be something that could counteract the effects.

It appears to be empty of any atons, at least. But watch your step. I don't know if there are more traps waiting. Tel never had traps in his workshop before." Of course, that had been before Uun's betrayal.

Drengur nodded and cautiously picked his way around the perimeter of the room. Dalmir rose and went the other direction, inspecting the shelves along the wall and wishing he could produce more light than the lantern afforded.

"Tel, I don't know why you set up these traps," he muttered, "but they are effective. I feel blind, deaf, and dumb. It's been so long... how did we ever function without Emri's gift? This would drive Uun mad." He couldn't help but chuckle a bit at the idea of Uun's reaction to this place. "Perhaps I should lure him here." But no. Uun would never allow Dalmir to choose the battleground. Uun was too smart to fall for a trap.

"I don't know what I'm looking for," Drengur called across the room. "I found some vials, and they're labeled, but I don't recognize any of the names."

"You'd be looking for something called drynalene," Dalmir replied distractedly. He closed his eyes for a moment, concentrating on the subtle tug he had been sensing since they found the tower. Why Tel's orb might be calling to him was a mystery, but then little about this expedition had made any sense to him so far.

The sensation was still there, stronger than it had been earlier. He could sense the glimmerings of a direction. Above. The call was coming from above.

"I thought this was the highest room in your tower," Dalmir muttered to himself. "Though last time I was here, your tower was aboveground, so I can concede that things have altered in the past several hundred years."

"What?" Drengur asked, his voice a hoarse whisper.

"I was just talking to myself," Dalmir replied, keeping his voice at a normal volume. "Have you found it?"

"Not yet."

"Well, keep looking. We have to go higher still, and I don't think we'll be able to move very fast if we have to carry Ioan between us. I don't like the idea of leaving him here; he's too vulnerable." Dalmir perused the shelf in front of him. The vials and equipment were free of the dust he would have expected to find after all this time. He shook his head, frustrated that he could penetrate none of the mysteries surrounding him. As he glanced about, his eyes caught a label and he pounced on it. "I have it!" he exclaimed, holding up a vial.

Drengur hurried to join him. "How does it work? What do we need to do to give it to him?"

"Injecting him with it would be best." Dalmir looked around. "I thought I saw... ah, there! Grab me that cylinder on the table by you."

Drengur picked up the object and stared at it, his expression puzzled. "What is this?"

"It's a needle," Dalmir replied. "It will carry the drynalene straight into his bloodstream and work more swiftly than if we tried to get him to swallow it."

Drengur's eyes widened. "That's barbaric!"

"No, actually, it's rather advanced," Dalmir said as he calmly poured the correct dose of drynalene into the syringe. "It was something my brothers were working on before Uun's betrayal. They never got a chance to introduce it to their people, and I..." Dalmir's hand trembled a bit. It was as though the entire weight of the mountain above them was resting upon his shoulders as the memories coursed through his mind. Tired, he was so tired. Too long he had carried the suffocating pressure of Uun's betrayal, too long he had hidden, withdrawn from the world that needed him. Once again, he had failed to act, and others had paid the price for it. Regret and shame crashed through him over and over, relentless waves rolling against the cliffside, wearing him away, breaking him to pieces. It was not enough. He could not crumble, but he could be eaten away a fragment at a time until nothing remained but the raw, gaping wound... he squeezed his eyes shut, clamping his thoughts down, filling them with silence. He could not change the past, only the future.

Opening his eyes, Dalmir pressed the needle into Ioan's skin —it was more difficult than he had expected, as though the man's skin had grown thicker and harder—and pushed the plunger to deliver the drynalene into his body, then he withdrew the needle.

"How long until we know if it worked?" Drengur asked.

Ioan's eyes flew open, and he sat upright. Then he moaned and put his head in his hands.

"Not long," Dalmir replied.

"What happened?" Ioan asked.

They filled him in on the details and where they were heading next. Ioan heaved a sigh and rose to his feet.

"I am starting to question whether or not continuing on this venture is wise, but I do not relish the thought of fighting our way back down just yet, either. Lead the way, Master Dalmir," he said.

"That's the thing," Dalmir replied. "I'm not sure how to get there. When the tower stood aboveground, this was the highest chamber. If there is a room above, or any space over what used to be the roof of this place, I do not know how to access it."

"Maybe there's a hidden doorway somewhere." Drengur's voice held a note of excitement. "I didn't think to look for anything like that before, I was so worried about Ioan. But I'll bet there's some sort of secret door or passageway in here. There wasn't anything else outside the room, just the platform, and that can't go any higher."

Dalmir and Ioan shared a glance.

"That actually makes sense," Dalmir said.

"Let's look for a secret door, then." Ioan turned and examined the shelves. He lifted vials and set them down, careful not to break or jostle anything, setting each item back in its place. Drengur bounded across the room and searched the walls themselves, peering at the seams in the wood and even examining the cracks in the floor. Dalmir stood in the center of the room, lost in thought as the others worked around him.

Where would his brother have hidden a secret passageway? Would he even have known that he needed one? Tel could have had no way of knowing that his orb would make its way back here to the tower after his death. Seeing into the future had not been a part of the gifts the Builder had given them. That his brother had possessed the foresight necessary to hide his tower and set up traps for unwelcome visitors was beyond Dalmir's understanding. How could Telsume have suspected that any of this would ever be necessary? And yet here was the evidence before his eyes. The atons defended the tower ardently, and he could not deny the pull of his brother's orb. But something niggled at the back of his mind, worming its way into his thoughts and pestering him quietly. This was not like Tel. It lacked something of his nature, or perhaps had something added to it he could not quite identify.

"There's nothing here," Ioan said, coming up beside Dalmir. "If there is a secret door, Tel hid it beyond our ability to discover."

Drengur sank to the floor, dejected.

Dalmir glanced up at the ceiling. "I've been thinking about my brother. If Tel was anything, he was straightforward. His twin, Mulemo, was the more volatile one, always experimenting and leaping before he looked. Tel worked a problem from every angle until he believed he had found the most efficient solution possible."

"What are you saying?" Ioan asked.

"I am saying"—Dalmir glanced up—"that if Telsume needed a secret door that led to the roof... he would have hidden it in the ceiling."

They all looked in the direction that Dalmir indicated. Drengur clambered onto the table in the middle of the room and lifted his lantern into the air. There, in the center of the ceiling, they could just make out a shallow handle. Drengur reached up and tugged on it, causing part of the ceiling to swing down. A ladder slowly unfolded.

Dalmir grinned. "That's more like the Tel I knew." He took

the lantern from Drengur and ascended the ladder. The others followed close behind.

29

When Marik revived, he was not where he had fallen. Everything swayed around him, and for a moment he felt the awful blackness surging back up around his vision. He closed his eyes, and the sensation faded, though the world continued to sway. It took him another few minutes to realize he was lying in a hammock, swinging with the rhythm of the airship. The airship which appeared to be flying like a drunken bat. He sat up and examined his leg. The area above his knee was swollen and painful to touch, but it did not appear to have grown any worse while he slept.

With an effort, he swung himself down from the hammock and rummaged around for his boots. Finding them, he pulled them on and made his way through the maze that was the crew quarters of the barge. He finally made it to the wide stair and heaved himself up one step at a time. Somewhere in the race to leave the Deepway, he had lost the staff Nando had carved for him. He missed it. A pang of regret coursed through him, the sudden surge of sentimentality surprising him.

As he emerged onto the deck of the vessel, he understood the violent rocking. A massive storm had caught them in its grip. The wind buffeted their rickety sails and rain lashed at them from above. Oleck clung to the rigging, furling every sail he could. Mouse scurried about coiling up ropes and checking knots, tying down anything that flapped in the wind. Shaesta stood at the wheel, her knuckles white as they gripped the handles, her eyes darting about. Sympathy shot through him; Shaesta hated steering, even on the balmiest of days. He made his painful way over to her, sloshing through the puddles forming on the deck.

"Mind if I take a turn?" he asked, giving her a grin. "I appear to have taken a nap."

She gave him a tight nod, so he stepped up and took the wheel. Shaesta released it with a grateful sigh and stepped back, but her posture did not relax.

"Bring me up to altitude," Marik said, noting her tension. "How long was I out? How are the durven? Where are we?"

"You were out for a couple of hours. We got away without much incident. They weren't expecting us to have an airship capable of carrying so many," Shaesta replied. "But they mustered up one of their own quickly enough, for all the good our surprise did us." She jerked her head to the stern. "We have a tail."

Marik glanced over his shoulder and through the driving rain caught sight of the sleek silhouette behind them. Its tall sails sliced through the clouds as it matched their speed with ease.

"What's keeping them from overtaking us?" Marik asked.

"The storm," Shaesta replied. "And... believe it or not, this bucket actually has a surprising amount of speed. She's nothing to look at, but I'm starting to wonder if the merchants who owned her were completely on the level with all their dealings. This little gal appears to be able to outrun an Igyeum battlecruiser."

Marik felt his estimation of the run-down airship rise, but only slightly. He longed for the sleek elegance of his *Hawk*, the swiftness and agility of her flight, the ease of her handling. He hated leaving her behind.

"We got nine hundred eighty-four of the durven aboard before we had to flee," Shaesta said. "Hrafn said we saved roughly half of his people."

Marik winced. That meant that the soldiers had captured or killed at least that many. He had lost half of the durven people.

"Mostly the women and children made it aboard. Hrafn organized them so that they were the ones to get out first," she continued. "Though I don't think anyone has had time to do a thorough check of who got left behind." She hesitated. "So where does that leave us, Captain?"

Marik strained against a sudden gust of wind, his mind racing as he considered his options. They had to outrun the Igyeum ship. The storm provided cover for now, but how long could it last? He doubted they could outrun the other ship in fair weather. He glanced up. Rain splattered in his eyes, and he blinked the water away, trying to shake the crazy idea that had just occurred to him. Could the ship handle it? He wasn't sure. The *Hawk* could, but he had done things to ensure that capability when he was working on her.

Lightning arced across the sky, and the storm intensified. Wind roared into the sails of the barge, tearing it off course. Marik strained at the wheel, but it was as though a giant had his hand against the hull of the ship and was pushing it with steady, unyielding force. Glancing back, he saw their pursuer was still behind them, just off their starboard side. He shouted his frustration into the wind, wiping an arm across his face. It did little good in the deluge assaulting them from above.

He made a decision. "Shaesta!" he called out over the sudden roar of the storm. "Go below and tell everyone to strap themselves in."

She peered at him, rain plastering her hair to her head and dripping from her nose. "Captain? Why?"

"We're going to climb above these clouds."

"But... Captain... this isn't the *Hawk*. Do you think this ship can handle it?"

"I don't know," Marik replied grimly. "But I don't believe she'll hold together much longer in this storm. If it keeps getting worse, the wind and lightning will soon tear us to pieces. And if it doesn't, the Igyeum soldiers will. I'm just glad they haven't used that weapon of theirs yet." Vaguely, he wondered why. "Tell Oleck and Mouse to get up here, too. I'll need all three of you helping if this is going to work."

Shaesta ran below to carry his orders to the rest of their passengers. While he waited for her to return, Marik stared out into the darkness. He supposed it might be morning by now, though the storm made it impossible to tell. Well, they would find out soon enough. A moment later, Shaesta returned with Oleck and Mouse in tow.

"Are you sure we should try this, Captain?" Oleck shouted as he climbed onto the deck, his expression dark. "Most ships can't reach the same altitudes that the *Hawk* can."

Marik considered. A sudden heavy gust of wind roared into the patched sails of the barge, tearing the ship off course again.

"Perhaps we should try to find a place to land." Shaesta's voice sounded frail and thin through the buffeting rain.

"There's no way we can do that without those soldiers spotting us. They're too close!" Marik bellowed back, the wind tearing his words from his lips and flinging them into the clouds.

He stared ahead, his thoughts grim. He knew what his crew was thinking. They had no good options. Their pursuers weren't gaining, but they weren't losing ground, either. Landing an airship was no simple task under the best of circumstances, but in an unknown vessel, in the middle of a storm of this magnitude, with no known lake or dock nearby, it could be catastrophic. And he had more than just his own crew to worry about right now; there were the durven down below, counting on his ability to fly them to safety, away from the Igyeum ship chasing them. Worse than all of that, was the sense of failure filling his spirit whenever he thought of those he'd abandoned, or Raisa. Her frightened eyes floated across his vision as he had last seen them, shining in the darkness while the Igyeum rained terror down upon their heads. She was still out there, and while there was even a flicker of breath in his lungs, he would not give up on attempting to rescue her. Frowning into the storm and wiping water out of his eyes, Marik made a decision.

"Everyone strap in!" he bellowed into the tempest. "We're going above the storm."

"Are you insane?" Oleck shouted into his ear. "You have no idea how high this storm goes. In these conditions, I'd question even the *Hawk's* abilities!"

Marik set his jaw and reached down for the lift-lever. "Strap in," he barked.

"Are you trying to get us all killed?" Oleck glared down at him, his looming form silhouetted in a flash of lightning.

Marik ignored him, hand still poised above the lever.

"Captain!"

"Strap in," Marik growled.

Oleck's jaw worked as though he were having a silent debate with himself. He held Marik's gaze unflinchingly for a long moment. Marik felt someone clip a safety line to his own belt and saw Oleck's expression waver.

"It's our only chance," Shaesta said, her tone even.

Oleck growled something unintelligible and stomped across the deck to grab a safety line, his feet sending up sprays of water. Angrily, he fastened the line to the belt-harness every member of the crew wore whenever they were flying. Marik waited until the others had secured themselves, his hand hovering over the lever the entire time. A gust of wind slapped at his face.

As soon as he had confirmation that his crew was ready, he gripped the lift control and pulled, aiming the bow of the barge at the sky. Laboriously, the airship climbed. The clouds pressed in around them, thick and wet and seemingly endless. Oleck stood at the mizzenmast, his feet planted solidly on the deck, his entire being straining to see what was ahead, his hands holding the sail lines. He never so much as glanced over his shoulder, but Marik knew what he was thinking. This would test Oleck's loyalty. If they did not come through the storm, he might not retain Oleck's faith in his leadership. Of course, if this didn't work, Marik reflected ruefully, it was likely they would all be dead long before Oleck could say, "I told you so."

They continued to climb. The air grew thin, and Marik forced himself to take long, slow breaths, trying to get the most out of every inhalation. His chest heaved, his lungs burning with the effort. Weakness flooded through him. He forced himself to keep his fingers wrapped around the controls, but he could feel his grip loosening with every passing second. His vision grew hazy. The dark clouds roiled and rain pelted his head, and he knew with a sinking feeling of frustration that he had failed. If they could only get a little bit higher...

"Captain!"

"Captain! Captain!"

"Cap'n!"

The voices sounded like they were coming from a long way off. Marik blinked. The world was a dark, rolling blur. Where was he? What had he been doing? Confused thoughts buffeted against each other in his mind, and he could not focus on any of them for long.

"Captain! Marik!"

Who was calling to him? Marik's head throbbed. He desperately wanted to close his eyes and succumb to a long, peaceful slumber. But something was preventing him from getting comfortable. What was it? If only he could figure it out, he could get some much-needed rest. He was cold, so very cold, he imagined his joints freezing solid; himself turning into a statue. But it was important that he keep going. Everything was fine. He had everything under control. If they would just trust him for a little while longer, he would bring them through this. And then they would see. Raisa. They had to rescue Raisa.

"Marik!"

His face flared with a painful stinging sensation. Marik shook his head, trying to clear it, and found all three of his crew members clustered around him. They had their hands on his arms and were pulling at his fingers, their expressions desperate.

Shaesta pulled her arm back and slapped him across the face again.

Anger surged through him, clearing away some of the fog.

"What?" He could not form any more of a sentence than that, for the rest of the words escaped him, flitting away from his thoughts like glittering specks of dust in a ray of sunshine.

"Let go, Captain!" Oleck hollered in his face, tugging at his arm as if trying to pull it from its socket. "Let go! We've done it, you've done it, but you need to let go!"

"I... what?" He blinked at Oleck stupidly, trying to comprehend what the man meant by the multitude of incoherent sounds pouring from his mouth. He felt he ought to understand them, but he was too tired to sift through the syllables to make sense of them.

Intense pain lanced through his hand. He shouted, letting go of the lift control and shaking his hand wildly as he stared in horror at Mouse. Mouse, who had just bitten him! Ungrateful whelp! Shaesta wrapped her own hand around the control and eased it forward, sending the airship into a gentle dive.

"No," Marik objected. "We have to get above the storm. Have to lose the other ship."

"We are above the storm, Captain," Shaesta replied, her words coming slowly, as though she were pushing them out with great effort. "You've done it. The other ship couldn't follow us. We're safe."

Marik stared at her, startled out of the fog around his thoughts enough to glance about and see that she was right. The storm clouds formed a thick blanket far below while above glittered stars, brighter than he had ever seen before and more beautiful than anything he could remember. His chest felt compressed, like someone had tied ropes around him and was slowly tightening them. The air about him was cold, what little breath he had steamed in front of his face, and ice crystals were already forming along the rigging.

"Too high," Oleck wheezed, and then slumped to the deck.

Marik stared at him, not comprehending at first what had happened.

"Down," he ordered Shaesta, trying to control his sudden panic. "Not too fast." The words took all his energy.

She nodded tightly and continued to push the lift control forward. Marik scanned the storm below them and kept both hands on the wheel, aiming at an area in the clouds that seemed thinner and less turbulent. The vessel descended with aching slowness, but Marik knew they needed to be careful how quickly they changed altitude. His hands trembled where they gripped the wheel, but not from the cold. As it grew easier to breathe, he tried not to think about what had nearly just happened. He had heard stories of captains who took their airships too high. Those who had survived claimed that their captains had remained reasonable and calm, certain that everything was going well until they lost consciousness.

Finally, they reached the clouds, their hull just brushing across the wispy surfaces. Marik shuddered, thinking how high above the storm they had actually gone. Oleck stirred and groaned, pushing himself up to a sitting position; he put his hands to his head and groaned some more. The barge skimmed lightly in the clear air above the storm and Shaesta eased her hand off the lift control and sank to her knees next to Oleck. Marik gazed up at the stars, studying their positions. He adjusted their course slightly, then set the wheel down into its stabilizers. Slowly, he sank to the deck with the rest of his crew. His body shook as the weight of what they had just narrowly avoided crashed over him. Covering his face with his hands, Marik took several slow, steadying breaths.

Mouse recovered first, climbing to his feet and peering about. "We've lost the other ship for certain sure," he announced. "They couldn't keep up."

"Captain?" Oleck muttered.

Marik's head throbbed. "Oleck... I..." His throat was tight and the words would not come.

Oleck pushed himself to his feet. He held a hand out to

Marik. After a long moment, Marik grasped it and allowed Oleck to pull him to his feet. The taller man gave him a hard look, and then the corner of his mouth twitched up into a rueful grimace.

"Looks like you've brought us through another one of your crazy schemes," he said.

"Thanks to the three of you," Marik replied. "A captain is nothing without his crew." He looked at each of them as he said the words, his gaze lingering a little on Shaesta. Her eyes widened, and he gave a small nod. In the moonlight, he could not read her expression well, but she dropped her face and her shoulders trembled ever so slightly, though when she looked up again there was no trace of emotion to be seen.

"Where are we?" Marik asked. "Oleck? Do you mind getting the sextant out and charting our position? I'd like to head straight for Telsuma and Lord Adelfried's home. After we stop at the hideout and retrieve the *Hawk,* of course."

"Right away, Cap'n," Oleck said.

"Shaesta, will you go check on our guests and make sure nobody was injured in our flight? And do what you can to reassure them they are safe now."

"Yes, Captain." Shaesta nodded sharply and turned on her heel.

"Mouse..."

"Yes, sir?"

"You bit me."

Even in the dim glow of the moonlight, Marik could see the distress in his face.

"Yes, sir." Mouse's voice grew tiny.

A long silence stretched between them in the frosty night air beneath the distant, glittering stars.

"Good job," Marik said.

Mouse looked up. "Cap'n?"

"It was exactly what I needed. Good job. That was quick thinking in a dangerous situation. I'm glad to know that I can count on you to do what needs to be done, even if it's an action most would counsel against in calmer times."

"I..." Mouse stammered a little and then stopped, his mouth hanging open.

"Thank you, lad."

"Thank me? For biting you? I mean, for biting you, sir?"

"Yes, lad." Marik looked at him gravely. "But I do not recommend doing such a thing again. Let's reserve that particular course of action for only the most dire of circumstances, understood?"

"Yes, sir." Mouse straightened. "Of course, sir."

"Very good. Now, would you like to take the wheel for a bit?"

"Me?"

"You've flown the *Hawk*. We're above the storm. There's no danger."

"Yes, but..." Mouse gestured about.

"It's no different. She lists a bit to port, but she's got more heart than you'd think, just looking at her," Marik encouraged. "Besides, I need a breather."

"Yes, sir, Captain, sir."

Mouse came forward and grasped the wheel. Marik kept a hold on it until he was certain Mouse had a secure grip. Then he backed away and slumped against the railing. His teeth chattered uncontrollably. It was not the cold, he knew, but rather the realization of what had nearly happened. Drawing deep breaths in through his nose, he forced his muscles to relax, and by the time Shaesta and Oleck returned, the shaking had stopped.

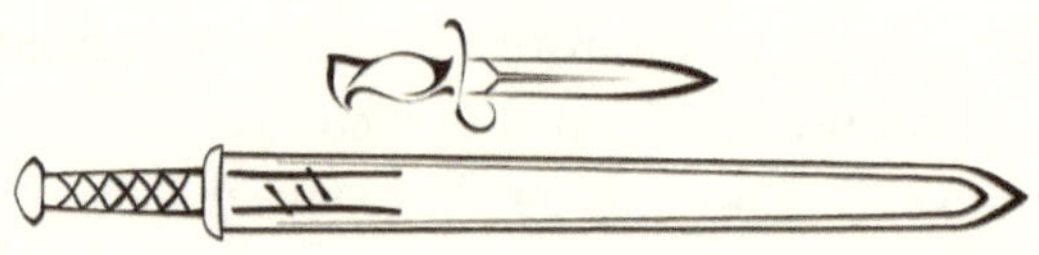

30

Dalsea did not have borek, but it should, Grayden thought as he bit into the pastry. The outer layer flaked off between his teeth and practically melted on his tongue. But the creamed cheese and spinach filling lasted longer, with a hearty, savory flavor that filled him with warmth. He munched happily, chewing slowly to ensure that he did not miss any of the flavor and being careful not to drop any crumbs. The pastry was simultaneously light and filling. From the intricate way the crust was woven in and out of the center, keeping the filling in little pockets, he could tell this was not a simple thing to construct. It was exactly the sort of challenge his mother would love. She enjoyed baking, and the more difficult the dish, the more she seemed to relish tackling it.

The pastry was gone by the time they reached Niveya's apartments. Miri had been silent throughout their walk, munching on her own treat. Grayden wondered at this. Niveya had not included her in his purchase, and he had not seen the girl make a transaction of her own with Bida. He could only assume she had stolen the food. Beren had also been silent, though that was not an unusual occurrence.

"Miri." Niveya stopped at the door. "I hope you do not take offense, but will agree that it is only fair for me to ask this of you.

We left our weapons behind when we entered your mother's domain. I need to ask that you leave yours behind here. I will keep them safe, and return them to you when we part ways, that I promise you."

Miri's lips twitched into a smirk. "Prudent." First she unbuckled her rapier, then she pulled daggers from holsters she apparently had around her wrists and upper arms. An evil-looking dirk came out from a hidden pocket beneath her long duster. She had more daggers in her tall boots, and then she clicked the heel of her left boot and pulled out a stack of shurikens. Niveya gave her a sidelong glance.

"All of it," he insisted.

Miri grimaced. "That one didn't leave all his weapons on the table." She gestured with her elbow at Grayden, then sighed and pulled a cord from where it hung around her neck and handed Niveya the cord. It had a small vial attached to it.

"What's that?" Grayden asked.

"Poison." Miri smirked. "It's not the most elegant of weapons, but it has its uses. Mostly for last resort type situations. But I trust this isn't one of those."

Niveya rapped on the door, and a servant opened it. "Keep these safe," Niveya instructed. The servant nodded and gathered the weapons before retreating inside. "You may come in now." Niveya pushed the door open and held it, gesturing for Miri to proceed.

Once inside, Niveya sent for Vidia and told her to prepare a room for their new guest. Then he informed them that he had some other business to attend to, ordered Grayden and Beren to "keep an eye on our guest until her room is ready," and disappeared.

Beren crossed his arms, frowning down at Miri, who suddenly looked small and out of her element. Grayden wondered if she was doing it on purpose: staring about with wide eyes, swinging her arms awkwardly as if unsure of exactly what to do with them, shifting her weight from one foot to the other, and darting glances toward the door. She perfectly embodied the look of someone who yearned to escape, but considering who her mother was, Grayden didn't feel like buying her act.

"So, how young does a person start learning the assassin's trade?" Grayden asked, tossing himself into a chair and pulling out his dagger.

Miri jumped at the sound of his voice and edged her way to a chair across the room from him. "I'm not an assassin," she replied in an injured tone. She sat tentatively on the edge of the seat, as though worried it might not bear her weight.

"No?" Beren rumbled. "Too young to start?"

Miri tossed her head, a spark igniting in her eyes. "Not everyone in my mother's crew is an assassin," she informed them hotly, her tentative mien dissolving. "It takes a variety of skills to run a successful crew. We have thieves, pickpockets, spies, and forgers, in addition to assassins. Plus Ungaro, the apothecary."

"Ah." Grayden spun his dagger across his knuckles, as he had seen her do. He started slow. He had no desire to lose a finger. "A unique blend of honorable talents."

"Honor is overrated," she retorted. "All it generally gets you is your pockets emptied by someone cleverer than you."

"What about honor among thieves?" Beren asked.

Miri snorted. "A myth created by bards and writers and dreamers. There is no honor among thieves. Even for those at the top, like your friend"—she jerked her head in the direction Niveya had disappeared—"he's powerful enough to wear an illusion of honor, but I guarantee you that's all it is."

"You might be right," Beren replied distractedly, his gaze focused on the doorway.

Grayden continued to spin his dagger. He was getting better at it, and the blade flashed through his fingers.

"You picked that up quick."

Startled by the voice suddenly in his ear, Grayden lost his concentration and nicked his finger. He sat up with a frustrated growl and stuck his knuckle in his mouth, sheathing the dagger and glaring up at the girl suddenly standing over him. Her gaze was intent, and he thought perhaps he saw a glimmer of admiration in them, but then she tossed her head haughtily, curls bouncing on her shoulders.

"Not quick enough, though." She smirked and flounced back to her chair.

"Which one are you?" Grayden asked sourly, pressing his thumb and forefinger around the cut to stanch the flow of blood.

That seemed to catch her off-guard. "What?"

"Thief, pickpocket, spy, forger... you said you weren't an assassin. What, exactly, is your role in the Motley Tailors?" Grayden expounded.

Miri settled back into her seat. "A bit of everything, actually," she admitted. "Lady Jynna disapproves of a limited skill-set, at least, in her daughter."

"Then you are an assassin," Beren accused.

"I could be," Miri shot back. "I have the training." Her chin dropped, and she stared at them suspiciously, peering at them through narrowed eyes. "I suppose I should have said I'm not an assassin... yet." She crossed her arms and glared, daring them to reply.

"Who is this guard your mother said the crew owns?" Grayden changed the subject, hoping to get something useful out of her. "How did that happen?"

Miri tossed her head. "Simple, really. He's a good guard, but has a nasty gambling habit. Unfortunately"—she gave an insincere smile—"his ability doesn't quite match his appetite."

"He owed you money." Beren's voice was blunt and bored.

"More than he could repay on a script's salary," Miri retorted. "We bought his debt and forgave it. In return, he belongs to us."

"That doesn't sound like an accurate definition of forgiveness," Beren muttered.

"We paid a large sum of money to prevent this poor man from being killed," Miri said. She stared at him with honest astonishment. "Why shouldn't he belong to us? He gets to keep his money, and I can assure you, he no longer gambles it away when he's off-duty—from the job he gets to keep, by the way. Instead, he goes home, takes his entire paycheck to his wife and children. We not only saved his life, we saved his reputation, his marriage, his family... all we ask are a few small favors in return."

"That's all?" Beren replied. "In return for your so-called forgiveness, he breaks the law every time you ask him to. Do you have any idea what kind of hole you're forcing him to dig within his own soul?"

Miri's chin tilted up. "Would you rather we have let him die, then? It certainly would have been less convenient for you now if we had. I'm sure his children prefer having him come home at night. I've heard he's become a very attentive and devoted father and husband since our... arrangement."

Beren heaved a disgusted sigh. However, before he could respond, Vidia entered the room with a gentle tapping of her shoes to alert them of her approach.

"Lady Miri, if you will follow me, your room is ready," Vidia said demurely.

Miri leaped from her chair in a fluid motion. "Is there a bath?" she asked, following Vidia to the stairs. The servant's answer was lost in the echo of their footsteps.

When they were gone, Beren shot a look at Grayden. "What do you think of all this?"

"Honestly, I don't know," Grayden replied. "I don't like any of it. But if we're going to find out who killed the Regeont, we may need to work with these people a little while longer."

"What about her?" Beren jerked his head in the direction Miri had disappeared.

"She's a bit of a puzzle, actually. I can't quite figure her out, but the one thing I'm positive about is that we can't trust her. She's her mother's daughter, that much is clear."

Beren's face wrinkled in a pensive frown.

"Beren..." Grayden peered at his friend.

Beren heaved a sigh, his eyes still locked on the stairs.

"She might remind you of one of your little sisters, but she's not," Grayden reminded him.

Beren glared at him but did not argue. After a while, he got up and left the room. Grayden did not follow. He understood his friend needed space. And Grayden wanted to do a little exploring.

He discovered a few interesting nooks and crannies in Niveya's building, and a spot where he thought there might be a secret room or perhaps it was just a secret exit out onto the street, but he could not find a way to open the door. He was still working on it when a servant found him and informed him that Lord Niveya wanted them all to join him in the den.

Grayden made his way to the small, dimly lit room and found that he was the last one to join the group. Niveya acknowledged his arrival with a nod and then turned to Mirianne.

"Miri, your mother said there is a guard who can help us get into the jail to talk to some prisoners being held there. Does he know you? Can we get in tonight, or do we need to give more notice?"

Miri stretched her arms above her head. "I can get you in tonight, but we'll have to wait until dusk; that's when our guard will be on duty."

Niveya considered this. "It's not ideal, but I suppose it's better to do our work in the dark. There should be fewer prying eyes to wonder what we're up to. Very well. We leave at dusk. You all might as well get some rest; it may be a late night."

———

THE SKY WAS a deep shade of purple, and they could see few stars in the patches of sky above the narrow alleyways. Grayden longed for the open air of the wilderness, the wide swath of night above him, room to breathe. Doran had much to offer, but nothing compared to the openness and big sky of the countryside. He yearned to lie out in the familiar orchards, where he would hear nothing more than frogs, crickets, and the night breezes rustling through the leaves.

They made their way to the center of the city, not making any attempt to sneak about. Every instinct Grayden had screamed that they should slip from shadow to shadow, but Niveya and Miri were in agreement about this idea, reminding them that sneaking around would look far more suspicious than simply going for an evening stroll. So they sauntered the several blocks to where the jail stood in the square. Niveya and Miri even managed to have a lively conversation about various restaurants they had visited in the city and which were the best. Around the jail, the sky opened up and Grayden glanced up, pulling in a deep breath, like a man who has been underwater for too long. They walked up to the jail-house door and Miri tapped upon it.

A guard, dressed in a crisp, pristine uniform, answered the knock. Lantern light spilled out around him, framing him in its halo as he peered out into the darkness. His eyes searched their faces, his expression blank until he came to Miri. Recognition sparked.

"Ah, it's you," he said in a weary voice, stepping inside and inviting them to follow. He closed the door and sat down at a small table. Now that they were inside, Grayden could see the man better. He had close-cropped dark hair, heavily streaked with silver. His mustache and goatee were mostly white, peppered with black. His face was thin and lined. He was not at all what Grayden had been expecting.

"What do you want, Miri?" the man asked in a defeated tone.

"You have in your charge a group of mercenaries who attacked the Academy a few sennights ago," Miri replied.

"Yes."

"We need to speak with them." Her tone brooked no argument.

"Miri... there is an official investigation..." The man sighed and his shoulders slumped. "Very well, follow me." He rose to his feet. Retrieving the lantern from the table, he walked over to open a door, revealing a dark stair leading down.

"The long-term cells are below," Miri explained.

The guard hesitated for the briefest instant, then plunged down into the darkness. Grayden stared at the guard's retreating back.

"What's wrong?" Beren asked.

"Nothing, I just... based on Miri's story, I kind of expected him to be younger," Grayden replied. "How long has he been working for your crew?" he asked Miri.

The young woman grinned in the dim light of the jail. "He's been our man for nearly twenty years, I think. He was one of Lady Jynna's first rescues, back before she had me."

"Twenty years?" Grayden squinted at her. "And he's still a common guardsman?"

"Didn't I mention that?" Miri's eyes widened innocently. "We like him where he is. I can't even count the number of promotions he's turned down. It was part of the deal." She made her way down the hall, her feet making no sound at all.

Grayden grimaced at Beren.

"I tried to warn you what it would be like, working with Niveya and people like him," Beren said.

"Yes, you did." Grayden wet his lips. "Come on, let's get this over with."

They followed the guard down the stairs into the depths of the city prison. The lantern barely made a dent in the darkness around them as they emerged into a hallway lined with bars.

"The mercenaries are in the last cell on the left," the guard said tonelessly, handing the lantern to Grayden. "I assume you prefer to speak to them privately?"

Miri nodded.

"I will wait here, then. Just... don't take too long. I'm here by myself only until the next bell."

"Thank you for your help, Captain." Miri smiled.

The man gazed at her mournfully. "My rank is no more than a bond servant to your mother, which you well know."

"You're a captain in my book." Miri grinned, her dimple showing as she went up on tiptoe and kissed the man's cheek. The guard's eyes hardened, and he stood as immobile and silent as the bars on the surrounding cells.

With a merry giggle, Miri turned to the others. "Well, you heard the man. We don't have much time."

They found the correct cell without difficulty. Within, six men lounged about, looking grimy and uncomfortable.

"You there," Niveya called out, gesturing to Grayden to hold up the lantern so they could see the occupants better. "Which of you is the leader?"

The men inside shifted a bit until, finally, one of them rose to his feet and crossed over to the bars. "That'd be me," the man said, looming in the darkness. He wrapped thick fingers around the bars and glared at them. His face was wide and brutish, with a nose that looked as though it had been broken multiple times and never set properly. His dark eyes were dull as he scanned their faces. "Who're you?"

"That's none of your concern," Niveya replied. "But we have some questions for you, and if you want to live to see your trial, you'll answer them truthfully."

Laughter rumbled from the men behind the leader.

"You might hafta unlock this door and make me," the man snarled.

"Who hired you to attack the Academy?" Niveya asked.

"We already been over this," the man yawned. "Thorben Adelfried." He turned his back as if to walk away. He never made it more than two steps, for with swift silence Niveya slipped his arm through the bars, grabbing the man around the throat, the edge of his dagger pressed against the man's neck.

"That's a lie," Niveya said. His tone remained calm, but it held a hard edge. "Now, you are going to tell me who really hired you or the executioner is going to be missing part of his pay."

"Threaten me all you like," the man gurgled, choking against the pressure around his throat. "It's the only answer you'll get."

Niveya's arm tightened. The man on the other side of the bars writhed with discomfort as Niveya continued to squeeze.

Grayden watched. He felt he should stop this, but the information the man had was important. There had been some training at the Academy about extracting information, and so far, Niveya appeared to be following the rules they had learned. Still, a voice within argued that there ought to be a better way. Perhaps there was. But they did not have time to befriend this man or make him trust them. They only had these few moments, stolen moments, to discover the truth. If they did not discover who was behind Regeont Roshana's murder and the attack on the Academy, the real killer might go free.

The man's feet scuffled and danced across the dirt floor. His friends, realizing that Niveya was apparently in earnest about his threat, rushed to their feet, preparing to help their leader. They froze as Miri moved up to the bars with a slight cough, training a tiny crossbow at them.

"The best assassins in the country have trained me," Miri said, her voice cool. "I can shoot and reload faster than you can blink, and if you are gambling men, I promise you can bet on my aim every time. Before you reach your friend, I'll drop every one of you. I dipped these bolts in ithonium. You'll all be dead before my friend here finishes strangling your leader."

The leader of the mercenaries let out a gurgling scream and frantically beat his palm against Niveya's arm. Ericole loosened his grip slightly.

"Yes?" he asked.

"I'll... tell you... what you... want to know," the man gasped.

"Good." Niveya released him and the man fell to his knees, panting and sputtering. "Whenever you're ready," Niveya murmured, as if they were simply having a pleasant tea and the minutes were not ticking away. He pulled a handkerchief from his pocket and wiped the edge of his dagger on it, his gaze intent on the task.

The man turned, his fingers gripping the bars so hard his knuckles showed white. "Thorben Adelfried didn't hire us. We were just paid to say that and stick to it."

"I figured as much." Niveya's voice was dry. "It's not like anyone believed your wild claims. But I appreciate hearing you admit it. Who did hire you, then?"

The man shook his head. "Dunno. I only interacted with the messenger, never saw his face."

"That's not good enough," Niveya said, his tone sympathetic. He reached down, pulled Miri's crossbow from her hands, and leveled it at the man.

"I swear, that's all I know!"

Grayden darted forward and grabbed the crossbow from Niveya's hand. "Nobody is going to get shot," he announced. "Think hard. What did the messenger sound like? What was he wearing? Can you remember anything about him that might give us a clue about who he worked for?"

The mercenary shut his eyes, his brow wrinkled in concentration. "He wore a fancy coat," he said at last. "Blue, with a gold braid. Spoke real smart and used some big words I didn't recognize. Offered us a heap o' money. Never made that much on a single job before."

"Educated and wealthy," Niveya mused. "Anything else?"

"Our payment came in an envelope with a wax seal," one of the other mercenaries piped up.

"Do you remember the seal?" Niveya demanded.

"Yeah," the man replied. "Course I do. It was the seal of the Regeont."

"Are you sure?" Niveya asked, his gaze intense.

"Yup," the leader confirmed. "A dove flying over the mast of a ship. Thought it was strange, us being hired by the Regeont to attack the Academy, but the pay was too good to pass up. Besides, orders was to make sure we didn't hurt nobody. Figured it was some kind of test for the students."

"You were ordered not to hurt anyone?" Beren asked, leaning forward with interest.

"Wouldn't a-taken the job otherwise." The man drew himself up. "I may be a sell-sword, but I ain't an assassin. I'll knock a few heads together if I have to, but I avoid killing; it's not my line o' work. 'Sides, them students is what protects us from the Igyeum, eventually. Want me kids to grow up without fearin' the Ar'Mol and his ilk, don't I?"

Grayden stared at the man, perplexity mounting in his thoughts.

The man behind him spoke up. "'Ere, he's tellin' you the truth. You can ask at the Academy, they'll tell you, we didn't hurt nobody, neither. Took a few lumps ourselves, though. Pay still would'a been worth it if we hadn't ended up in jail."

Beren scratched his chin thoughtfully.

"Who has been questioning you?" Niveya asked.

"The headmaster of the Academy, and the head of Doran's guard force," the leader replied.

"You will give this same information you just gave us to the headmaster the next time he comes to speak with you," Niveya ordered. "If you do, I believe your jailers might release you. It may mean a bit more time in prison, but I doubt you'll be executed."

"Really?" The man looked up, a shimmer of hope gleaming in his unintelligent eyes.

"Really," Niveya replied firmly. "Whoever hired you wanted to get you killed. That money's no good to you if you're in prison or dead."

The man nodded slowly. "Right. You make a... solid point."

A low whistle came from the other end of the hall.

"Time's up," Miri announced. "Did you get what you needed?"

"I think so," Niveya replied thoughtfully.

"Either way, we have to get out of here," Miri said. She held out her hand. "My weapon?"

Niveya gave her an amused grin. "I think not, my dear." He tucked the crossbow away and spun on his heel, heading to the stairs. The others followed him. Grayden frowned, puzzled. Every time he thought he had Ericole Niveya figured out, the man did something completely unexpected.

"Why did you do that?" he asked, trotting up to walk beside Niveya.

"Why did I do what?" Niveya asked, his tone weary. "If you're going to take issue with the way I threatened the man, let me be clear: I don't have to explain myself to you or anyone else. I have only one goal: to find out who killed Roshana. You should know this right now—nothing is going to stand in the way of that task. Not you, not some mercenary, not even a crew of assassins."

"That's not what I meant. I just wondered why you showed him mercy. Why did you tell him that the truth would save his life? He's a sell-sword. What does his life matter to you?"

"He might be a sell-sword, and not a very bright one," Niveya muttered, staring straight ahead, "but he's not a killer. Whoever hired him planned to discard him like so much mud scraped off one's boot. If our guess is correct, then that same person is also responsible for the Regeont's death. I will do everything in my power to make sure none of that person's future plans succeed, not even the casting away of people he considers to be rubbish." Niveya bit out the words with cold precision. Then he glanced at Grayden and smirked. "Besides, I might need a group of mercenaries in the future to knock a few heads together. Can't let talent like that go to waste."

Grayden fell silent, pondering Niveya's words. They were incongruous with everything he knew of the man, but he couldn't deny the way the sentiment resonated deeply within him. They passed the guard, who gave them a nod and took the lantern, following them up the stairs and locking the door behind them.

"Give my regards to Lady Jynna," he growled.

Miri's eyes twinkled. "I will."

They plunged out of the jailhouse and into the street, where Beren boomed out a question about a sailing race he had heard was being held later in the sennight. Miri replied, betting on the name of a schooner she said was the fastest ship in the harbor, and Niveya countered with another ship, saying that her captain had more tricks up his sleeve than a swindler in debt. Behind them, Grayden heard booted footfalls in the street. He knelt down as though he had dropped something and glanced back. The second guard had arrived for his watch. He walked straight up to the jailhouse and entered, never giving their loud group a second glance.

31

Nothing could have prepared Dalmir for the sight that greeted him at the top of the ladder. The moment his head poked through the hatch he stopped so abruptly that Ioan and Drengur almost climbed right over him.

"Dalmir?" Ioan whispered. "Is everything well?"

Dalmir stared about, his eyes wide, his throat too dry to give a response. He nodded dumbly, then realized neither of his companions could see him and he managed to clear his throat enough to whisper back that nothing was wrong. Slowly, he pulled himself the rest of the way up the ladder and stepped aside so Ioan and Drengur could join him. When they did, they were as dumbstruck as he. For several long moments, the three of them simply stood, gazing about in awe.

"Did you have any idea this was up here?" Ioan finally asked.

"No," Dalmir replied. "And even now, I can barely believe it."

"How did all of this get here?" Drengur breathed. "How is it even possible? It... it shouldn't be possible, right? I mean, we're still underground. This shouldn't..." He swept a hand before him. "Without sunlight? How?"

The landscape before them was a stark contrast to the darkness they had come through. A gentle glow filled the space above the tower, like the pale light of dawn or those last moments before the sun disappears completely from view at the end of a long summer's day. At their feet, soft green grass rippled, stretching off into the distance as far as they could see. Garden plots dotted the landscape, punctuated by small homes that were little more than a twisting of roots formed into dome-like shapes.

"This is impossible," Ioan muttered. "Where is the light coming from? How are plants able to grow here? This shouldn't... this shouldn't be."

"I think we need to take a closer look," Dalmir replied. "Those houses must mean someone lives here, though I don't see anyone at the moment. Perhaps if we can find the inhabitants, they can explain."

He stepped out onto the grass, and instantly the air filled with a sound like the screeching of metal and grinding of gears. Ioan and Drengur clapped their hands over their ears, wincing at the sudden, painful cacophony. Dalmir endured it, his eyes scanning the area. From one of the huts, a figure emerged. It came closer, and Dalmir stared in fascination. This was no mere aton, but neither was it human, though it had a human face and wore human clothing: a loose robe-like dress covered its frame. As it approached, Dalmir gaped.

"Lerilei?"

The creature paused, its metal head twisting to one side in a stuttered motion, as if mimicking a human's movements. Its face remained a smooth, metal façade that bore no range of expressions, but looked as though Lerilei's likeness had been stamped there upon its bronze features. "That is part of the password." The aton's voice had a hollow, echoing quality to it. "Do you know the rest of it?"

Dalmir stood still, wracking his brain. What password would Tel have created that used his dead wife's name and face? He studied the strange aton before him for more clues, but found himself at a loss for ideas.

"Thera?" he suggested at last. If Tel had used his wife's face and name, perhaps the rest of the puzzle was simple, perhaps it was the name of his daughter.

The aton's head swiveled. There was a whirring sound all around them as more atons—a full score similar to the ones they had fought in the levels below—rose out of the ground, surrounding them.

"I think that may have been incorrect," Ioan commented.

"Mulemo!" Dalmir shouted the name of his brother's twin. The atons advanced.

"Nope," Ioan muttered.

"Let me think." Dalmir's eyes darted about, thinking frantically. What would Telsume have used? What could the answer to the riddle be? What else had been precious to him? "Library?" he asked, his voice wavering with uncertainty.

The atons around them converged, closing in on the small group of travelers. The nearest one struck out at Drengur, who gave a yell and fell back into Dalmir's side, nearly knocking him over. In the same instant, Ioan blocked with his sword, protecting them both from the attack.

"Dalmir!" Ioan shouted.

"I'm trying, I'm trying!" Panic gripped Dalmir in its talons. Had he brought them here to die? Then he had a sudden thought: perhaps he did not need to find the answer. They had left the tower; perhaps the effects of Tel's dampening field were not present up here on the roof of the tower. He reached for his power, intending to push the atons away. Instead, flowers sprouted all around them. "Flowers!" Dalmir yelled in frustration.

At his shout, the atons surged forward, weapons striking at him and his companions, and Dalmir was forced to focus his energy on using his sword. As he blocked and parried, whirling about to defend his companions, he desperately flew through a dozen more attempts to speak the correct password, but none of them worked. His mind churned sluggishly. Tel had been a private person, with few consuming passions. His family and the library had been his greatest treasures. Dalmir had no idea what else his brother would have deemed an acceptable password. Then, as he intercepted a blow aimed at Drengur's unprotected side, an idea sparked. For whom had Tel left this riddle? Of all their brothers, Tel had been closest to Mulemo and Dalmir himself. If he was correct in believing that Mulemo had helped construct some of these obstacles, then that meant they must have left the message for Dalmir specifically. Could Telsume have wanted him to be the one to find this place? Would the word be something that held meaning for Dalmir, rather than for Tel? But what would that be? He dodged a blow and drove his sword through an aton, wincing as he destroyed yet another of his brother's creations. What would the word be? What... and then he knew. Without knowing how he knew, it simply clicked. Emotions he could hardly name filled his entire being. Falling to his knees, he cried out in a loud voice.

"Shiori!"

The atons paused.

Panting, Drengur and Ioan held their weapons in defensive postures, eyes darting about. But when the atons moved again, it was only to sink back into the ground from whence they had sprung. The aton who bore Lerilei's beautiful face gazed at him impassively.

"That is correct," she intoned. "I grant you safe passage through Chasm." She turned away from them and raised an arm, indicating the small village.

"May I ask questions?" Dalmir queried.

"Of course."

"Are you the guardian of this place?"

"I am many things in this place. Guardian..." She paused, her head tilting to one side. "Yes. That term could apply to the roles I fulfill."

"Are there people living here?"

"You will see in a moment. They were afraid you might be the one we have been waiting for."

"What does that mean?" Ioan asked. "Afraid?"

"Two were... told of," the guardian replied, her voice halting and mechanical. "Both spell doom. But one... would only bring destruction. While... the other... hope. Leader can explain better. Come."

The guardian led them across the grassy plain to the largest hut in the center of the village. As they followed, Dalmir glimpsed faces peeking out from the dark interiors of the homes. None of the houses had doors, and the structures themselves would not do much against any kind of weather, though he supposed that would not be a problem underground. When they reached the hut, a man stepped out to greet them.

"Welcome to Chasm," he said. But though his words were welcoming, his expression and tone were dark. He made a strange gesture, clasping one hand over his fist in front of his chest, the muscles in his arms bulging. His posture was guarded, as though he felt the need to be ready to defend himself.

Dalmir studied the man for a moment. He did not look much like a Telsuman, though he was broad in the shoulders. But his face was rounder, his nose did not have that hawkish arch that most Telsumans possessed. The man had dark hair, worn close-cropped, unlike the longer style the Telsumans had adopted. He wore a simple tunic and breeches, and he was barefoot.

"I greet you in friendship," Dalmir said. "And I have many questions, so many that I am unsure of where to begin."

"You wish to know how all this came to be." The man gestured about.

"Yes, I am quite curious about that," Dalmir replied.

"Walk with me," the man said. "The others will be less fearful if they can see us out in the open."

They followed him, Drengur craning his head this way and that in curiosity. Dalmir's gaze darted about as well, but he tried to have a bit more decorum.

"May I ask your name?" Dalmir asked of the man.

"Forgive me, I should have told you that right away, but I have never met a stranger before," the man said. "I am called Jorgen."

"That sounds Maleian," Ioan commented, turning sharply. "Your accent is Maleian as well."

"It is," Jorgen agreed. "My ancestors were from Malei. We are all descended from Maleian heritage." He spread his arms to the village.

"How many are you?" Ioan asked.

Jorgen gazed up thoughtfully. "There are perhaps five hundred of us here."

"How long have you been here?" Dalmir inquired.

"Many years," Jorgen replied. "My great-great-great-grandfather was among the first. I never met him, as he died before I was born, but I have heard his stories passed down through my grandparents and parents about the journey that led him and the others here."

"That is a story I would very much like to hear," Dalmir said.

"And it is the story you will hear," Jorgen replied. "But first, may I ask your name? I already know your purpose. Frieda would not have let you pass had you not known the password, thus you must be one of the two foretold, the one who will bring both destruction and hope. I am afraid that you will not get a warm welcome, but the people will stand by Frieda's decision."

"Frieda?" Dalmir asked.

"Our guardian," Jorgen explained. "The one you spoke with when you arrived."

"Ah." Dalmir nodded. "I'm afraid none of this makes any sense."

"Forgive me," Jorgen said. "We have known of you our whole lives, but of course you did not have the same luxury. I will start at the beginning just as soon as we... ah, here we are."

Dalmir looked up and saw that they had arrived at a raised, circular platform that held rows of benches.

"Please, sit here." Jorgen indicated a spot. "This is our meeting circle, where the elders of the village gather when there are important issues to discuss. Here, where the entire village can see and hear, I will explain, and then you will tell us what we are to do next."

Dalmir shot a helpless glance at Ioan and Drengur, then scowled and seated himself. The others joined him. Jorgen settled himself on a bench facing them and gave them a weak smile.

"I am not the storyteller my grandmother was, but I will do my best," he said. He paused for a long moment, then he raised his voice and began, "Generations ago, a village sat on the western border of Malei by the Whispering Wood, which was said to be haunted by ghosts. Warlords vied amongst themselves for supremacy, and the commoners lived in fear and poverty, not knowing where their next meal would come from, nor whether their sons and fathers would be forced to serve in their armies.

"One day, the villagers awoke to the sounds of fighting in the fields nearby. They knew their fears were about to be realized, and so the men swiftly led their families into the depths of the Whispering Wood. Their fear of the soldiers was that much greater than their fear of ghosts, you see.

"They intended only to go deep enough into the forest to avoid being found, but the commanders of the army, finding only empty homes, flew into a rage and ordered their men to search the forest. The soldiers trembled, but obeyed; their fear of their leaders was greater than their fear of the forest. The families hiding in the trees were forced to flee deeper and deeper into the wood until, frustrated with their failure and filled with superstitious terror, the warriors abandoned their search. However, the stories about that forest were not completely without roots, for the families soon discovered that, try as they may, they could not find their way out again. Their steps always led them back to a dark and forbidding tower that terrified them. But no matter how often they tried to flee, they always found themselves drawn back to its gates."

Drengur leaned forward, elbows on his knees, his face alight with the draw of youth to a good story. "What happened next?" he asked.

Jorgen gave him a small smile. "It was then that the silver lady appeared."

Dalmir's blood turned suddenly to ice at these words. He was momentarily caught in an instant, frozen in time. It couldn't be true, it couldn't be her, and yet his heart recognized her hand in this. How could he not? Now that the words had been spoken, he could allow himself to see the truth his heart had been trying to impart to him since they first reached the tower.

"The silver lady?" Drengur's voice sounded enraptured.

"Yes," Jorgen replied solemnly. "She stretched out her hand and drew a glittering gemstone out of the wall. She offered it to the leader of the group and told them that if they were willing to follow her on a long and perilous journey, she would lead them to a place where they would be safe. But she warned them it would not be their original home, and that sorrow would eventually befall them once again, many years in the future.

"Well, the leader knew that sorrow befalls everyone, eventually, and though they loved their homeland, they also had no desire to continue an existence cowering in fear. He accepted the lady's gift. They followed her through the forest, across great rivers, and far into the mountains. She brought them to a cave deep underground and told them it was their new home."

"Here?" Drengur breathed.

Jorgen nodded. "Here. But the people were frightened of the dark, and they cried out against the Silver Lady and their leader, wailing that this would be their grave. The leader was angry with the people and reminded them of all the perils they had come safely through on their long journey, but the Silver Lady understood their fright. She brought them the Guardian and placed the glittering jewel into its heart, bringing it to life. Then, the Silver Lady informed them all that so long as they or their descendants lived within the cave, Frieda and the jewel in her heart would give them light and life, causing plants to grow and flourish underground. And, as you can see, she spoke truly, and here we have lived for nearly two hundred years."

"What about the foretelling?" Dalmir asked.

Jorgen's face turned grave. "I was just coming to that. Before the Silver Lady left, she issued a warning. She said that the jewel in the guardian's heart was precious, and that there were two who would come seeking after it. When that happened, the land of Chasm would cease to thrive, and all would return to the way it had once been, and it would be time for our people to come out of hiding. She told us that one of those who desired the jewel would come only for destruction and death, but the other would bring hope. She could not see who would arrive first, and so she gave Frieda a riddle that only the one who brought hope could solve so that we would know you by Frieda's response."

"What would Frieda have done had I not known the answer to the riddle?" Dalmir asked.

"She would have summoned all her warriors to fight against you," Jorgen replied. "She would have done her best to give us time to flee."

"I see." Dalmir was silent for a long moment. "Then... what happens now?"

"You will remove the jewel from Frieda's heart and lead our people out of this place," Jorgen said.

Dalmir stared. Unbidden, his gaze searched the surrounding area, taking in the tranquility and otherworldly beauty of Chasm. The light did not have the same beauty as that of the sun, but there was a lovely serenity to the way it bathed the land in a dusky purple glimmer. It was inconceivable that these people had lived underground for so many years, thriving and flourishing in a place where such things should not be possible, and yet here they were, and it was his destiny to destroy what they had built. A rift opened within his soul.

"Oh, Shiori," he whispered, "is this my only option?" He straightened and held Jorgen's gaze. "What if I do not take the jewel? What if I leave here without it?"

Jorgen's expression turned sorrowful. "Then the Betrayer will come, and he will destroy us all… not just Chasm, but all the world, as well."

Dalmir's heart pounded in his temples, beating out a rhythm of anguish at the terrible choice before him. He bowed his head. "Very well. Inform your people that the time has come for them to leave. Pack what you can carry."

"No!" A cry rang up from one side, and Dalmir turned, startled at the sudden shout, to see a group of young men assembled there.

One of the young men stepped forward. "Jorgen, this is not a decision you can make for all," the youth said, fists clenched. "This is our home. It is all we have ever known. This stranger may be the one we were told would come, but he has indicated a willingness to leave without taking Frieda's heart. Why should we not let him?"

"You know why," Jorgen said. "If he does not take it, the other one will, and he will take everything and bury us here in the mountain. Is that what you truly want, young Kaj?"

The youth scowled. "I think we should at least put the matter to a vote. The village has a right to decide their own fate. Convene the elders."

"And should the elders vote to leave, will you abide by their decision?"

Kaj thrust his chin forward. "I will."

Jorgen gave Dalmir an apologetic glance. "It will not take long to assemble the elders."

"There is no urgency," Dalmir replied. "Am I to assume that Frieda controls the atons below?"

Jorgen gave him a puzzled look.

"Atons," Dalmir explained. "Like the creatures who threatened us earlier—what did you call them—warriors?"

"The Silver Lady also called them atons," Jorgen replied. "But what did you mean by 'below'?"

"The tower," Dalmir said. "The one we came through?"

Jorgen shook his head. "You speak of strange things," he

mused. "How can a tower be below us? We are underground. I do not know this place of which you speak. You say there are more atons there?"

"Yes," Dalmir replied. "Don't worry about it. If your people decide to come with us, you will see it soon enough."

Jorgen gave him another strange look and then rose. "I must assemble the elders. You may stay here or venture through the village. None will hinder you." He hurried away, shaking his head and muttering to himself about "towers below!"

Dalmir turned to his companions. "I would like to see more of this village," he said. "But I don't know if that would be wise."

"Young Kaj had murder in his eyes," Ioan said, keeping his voice low. "Jorgen may believe in the words of the Silver Lady, but those youths were not so trusting."

"Do you believe they would try to do us harm?" Dalmir asked.

"I'm not sure. I think remaining here would be best," Ioan said. "Though it is uncomfortable."

"The benches aren't that bad," Drengur protested.

"That is not what I meant," Ioan growled, but his lips curved up in a fond smile. "I meant that I find it uncomfortable being watched so closely."

Dalmir had already noticed that quite a few villagers had come out of their homes and stood about, their gazes constantly darting to the strangers in the meeting circle. They were being studied with suspicion and curiosity, and he agreed with Ioan that it was an uncomfortable experience. Drengur, however, seemed unperturbed by it. He sprawled on the ground, plucking a longer piece of grass and sticking it between his teeth, then he flipped over onto his back, put his hands behind his head, and closed his eyes. He looked peaceful and unconcerned, lying there. Dalmir envied his ability to be so at ease, and he hated himself for being destined to steal that same peace from these people.

"You'd think I would be more used to having people stare at me," he muttered. "Ah, for the resilience of youth."

"You are not old," Ioan said, "despite your white hair."

Dalmir barked a short laugh. "You know that is not true."

"I did not mean that you have not seen many years," Ioan said. "If you are as old as you say, then you are the oldest being in the world, except for Uun. I meant you have not quite lost all the wonder of youth, nor its innocence. You try to pretend that you have, but I don't think you're quite as curmudgeonly as you'd have everyone around you believe."

Dalmir eyed the young man before him. A weight pressed on his chest, like stones being piled on top of him one at a time. "You have no idea what horrors I have witnessed," he said, his voice hoarse.

"No," Ioan replied. "But it hasn't wrung you out completely. I saw you with little Hubert. If you had lost all faith, you wouldn't care about the treasures of a five-year-old. If you had no more hope, you wouldn't struggle so hard against the schemes of the Ar'Mol."

"Perhaps I have lost all my faith, all my hope. Perhaps I only struggle because I have nothing else to do."

"Perhaps," Ioan acknowledged, "but I don't think so."

Dalmir's vision tunneled, growing fuzzy around the edges. The young man before him, so earnest, so trusting, even after all that had been done to him, bothered his conscience more than he cared to admit. He *had* lost hope, had given in to despair. It was only rage that prompted him to act once more, rage... and... curiosity. He had to admit that Grayden's entrance into his tower of solitude had piqued his interest even more than his rage at discovering that Uun had somehow slipped his bonds.

"Perhaps you are right," Dalmir allowed. "But hope won't get us very far if the villagers vote to keep their jewel and remain here."

"I disagree. I think hope is the only thing you can offer that will sway their decision. You know as well as I do that if their guardian has one of your orbs inside her, you can't just leave it here, much as you might like to."

"I know," Dalmir whispered. "But I wish there was another way. Removing the orb will..."

"Will destroy this place. But they can build a new life up aboveground in Telsuma, in the real sunlight."

"It won't just destroy this place. It will destroy Frieda, as well."

"So?"

"There is no way you could understand."

Ioan peered at him. "Frieda resembles that statue you stopped to look at in the library. Who was that woman?"

Dalmir sighed. "Lerilei. She was Telsume's wife. From before..."

Ioan nodded. "I am guessing she died?"

"Thousands of years ago," Dalmir said. "It broke Tel's heart. I don't think he ever truly recovered. She was everything to him. When she died... well, we all feared that he would follow. But he couldn't, and that was perhaps the cruelest stroke of all." Dalmir shook his head. "We had already suspected that the change had altered our lifespans, but we did not quite understand fully what that meant until Lerilei died. It was then that we realized just how different we had become."

"He had a daughter, as well, didn't he?" Ioan asked, his voice gentle. "What happened to her?"

"She grew up," Dalmir replied, his tone emotionless. "She married, had children. Her children had children. Eventually, they all died. We didn't. After Thera's children grew old, Tel distanced himself from his family. It was too painful for him to grow close to them, only to watch them die."

"Did you have a family?"

Dalmir shook his head. "No. I was the youngest. Tel was the only one of us who was married before the change. Edoran was promised to the daughter of a neighboring king, but he never did end up marrying her. The rest of us... we were too caught up in our own projects and interests to have time for love. Tel was the only one who suffered that scourge."

"That seems like a bitter way to view it."

"It's a realistic way to view it," Dalmir snapped. "Love is not a luxury I could afford. None of us could. We had other responsibilities."

Ioan opened his mouth to reply, then snapped it shut. He kicked Drengur, who scrambled to his feet. Jorgen had returned, and trailing behind him were ten men, the elders of Chasm. Behind them, more people assembled, filling the area around the circle of meeting until it was clear that the entire village had come to hear the verdict.

32

Marik flew the barge in a circuitous route as he made his way to their hideout. Although they had sighted no more pursuers, he still felt anxious. With a wary eye scanning the surrounding skies, he eased the barge, which the durven had dubbed *Oddhaven*, down onto the river. Her planks groaned as the airship settled into the water, but despite her ramshackle construction, no leaks made an appearance. He knew that he could have landed on the ground—the barge boasted a flat bottom to her hull so that she had greater flexibility in her landing options—but he still preferred to land on water. It was easier, and water was a more forgiving surface. As they settled into the river, he was well aware that this was not the *Oddhaven's* favorite terrain; the barge listed to one side and bobbed at a precarious angle, but it floated, and that was all Marik cared about. Mouse slithered down the rigging and landed on the deck.

"I'll be glad to see the *Hawk* again." Mouse grinned. "Though the *Oddhaven* hasn't been as bad as I thought she would."

"Well, this old lady is going to be with us for a mite longer," Marik reminded him. "We can't possibly fit all the durven on our ship. So we'll be flying both of them out of here."

Mouse nodded. "I know. Oleck said he's going to captain

Oddhaven, and that you were going to fly the *Hawk.* Can I be your first mate?"

Marik reached down and tousled Mouse's hair. "Sure," he promised.

Hrafn and Nando poked their heads up above the stairway, and Marik walked over to the opening without needing assistance. His leg felt better, despite standing on it for three days. "Mouse and I are heading to our hideout to get some provisions," he informed them. "If your people want to stretch their legs and refill water skins, let them know they should do so now." He glanced up at the cloudless sky. "For the moment, I believe we are safe. Nothing could sneak up on us from that sky. But I don't want to linger here, so make sure nobody wanders too far."

Hrafn nodded.

Marik glanced away, unable to meet the other man's eyes. His chest tightened. The durven wouldn't have been in danger in the first place if it hadn't been for him. The sounds of falling rocks and the screams of frightened people haunted him, preventing him from finding sleep. He had not gotten a full night of rest since leaving Melar, and he did not know how many more days it would be before he could sleep again. That Hrafn only treated him with kindness and that there was no reprimand in the eyes of the durven only made it worse.

"Hopefully we can get airborne again in a couple of hours," Marik mumbled, crossing the deck and lowering himself over the side. He cursed himself for a coward, but he could not stay and face any more gratitude.

Mouse followed, trotting to keep up with Marik's long strides.

"They don't blame you," Mouse said.

"I know," Marik replied tersely. "That just makes it worse."

"They've wanted to strike a blow at the Ar'Mol for decades. You merely provided them with the chance."

"A lot of good we did." Marik bit out the words. "We barely even annoyed the Ar'Mol. We didn't save Raisa, we didn't gather any intelligence. All we did was cause a lot of good people to lose their safety, their home, their lives, their freedom..." Marik clutched his head between his hands. "How can they not hold me responsible? How can they ever forgive me? I will certainly never forgive myself."

"We learned about that weapon," Mouse reminded him, his voice sober. "The Council will want to know about that."

"And the Ar'Mol is going to do everything in his power to make sure we don't take that information out of the Igyeum."

Mouse glanced up at the sky. "How can they stop us?"

Marik also turned his gaze upwards. "I won't breathe easy until we're across the border," he said darkly. "Come on. The sooner we can get out of here, the happier I'll be."

They quickly dismantled the bits of disguise still clinging to the *Hawk* from their first foray into Melar. Then Mouse helped Marik sort through their provisions and make the trips back and forth with crate after crate of supplies.

"You're packing all that?" Mouse's eyes widened as Marik brought out the last crate of cynders from the back of the cave. "How come?"

"We don't know how long we'll be gone." Marik set the crates down and took a swig of water.

"I thought you didn't like putting all your bets on one throw. Isn't that what you always say? Wouldn't it be better not to have everything on one ship?"

"Sometimes that's better," Marik allowed. "But other times you have to know when to give up on the game and walk away. We'll put most of these on the *Oddhaven,* though."

"But..." Mouse eyed the stack. "You're not leaving anything behind."

"Of course we're leaving things behind." Marik gestured at the bits of furniture and scraps that were still sitting on the other side of the cave. "I'm not taking any of that."

"I mean..." Mouse trailed off. "We're packing everything important. You don't think we're coming back, do you?"

Marik leaned on the stack of crates and stared away toward

the entrance of the cave. "I hope we come back someday," he said, his voice soft. "But this hideout may already be compromised. Or they could find it while we're gone. I'm not taking any chances, Mouse. I've already lost Raisa. I can't leave anything here that could endanger the rest of the crew."

Mouse's eyes filled with tears. "I see."

"Hey." Marik put his hand on the boy's shoulder. "This cave isn't home, remember? It's not even our most-used hideout." He pointed at the *Hawk*. "That's home. And we're taking her with us."

Mouse sniffled a little and then looked up with the glimmerings of a smile. "And I get to be first mate for a while."

"That you do." Marik grinned. "That you do. Here, help me haul this crate to the *Oddhaven*. She'll need the extra cynders before the *Hawk* does, that's for sure." He glanced up at the sky as they left the cave.

"You've been a bit jumpy today, Cap'n," Mouse observed.

Marik nodded absently. "I just have a feeling..." He trailed off.

"A feeling?"

"The ship that was tailing us," Marik said as they reached the barge and set the crate into the netting. He rapped on the hull of the ship, which took up most of the narrow river in which he had settled it. "Oleck! Last load!"

The ropes attached to the net went taut and the durven above began hauling it up. They could hear Oleck shouting for everyone to get back to the airship and take their positions.

"We'd better go get..."

A shadow swept over them. Marik shouted and shoved Mouse to the ground, throwing his own body over the boy. There was an intense heat, a brilliance of light that rivaled the sun, and then a strange whining sound as the ground in front of the hideout exploded in a shower of rocks and dust. Marik jumped to his feet.

"Mouse?" He pulled Mouse from the ground and peered at him.

Mouse gagged and coughed.

"Mouse?" Fear lanced through Marik as he searched the boy for visible injuries.

"I'm... I'm..." Mouse coughed and waved a hand. "Just inhaled dust. I'll be all right."

"Good," Marik replied, relief coursing through him. "Come on, we have to get the *Hawk* out of there."

"What?" Mouse's voice was horrified. "We can't go in there!"

"Their weapon is devastating, but they can't fire it quickly. We have a bit of time before they can use it again. And they didn't drop their anchor this time..."

"What anchor?" Mouse panted, tripping over rocks and his own feet, trying to keep up with Marik.

"They dropped an anchor last time," Marik explained. "I think the weapon creates a backlash that throws the airship off course." He risked a glance up. "See? They're circling around to get back into position. Come on!"

They dashed into the cave and scurried up the ladder of the dock, throwing themselves onto the deck of the *Valdeun Hawk*. Mouse immediately started unfurling the sails while Marik raced up to the wheel and threw the lever that activated the cynders below. The airship hummed with the sudden rush of power and Mouse climbed into a harness and clipped one of the safety lines to it. With a gentle vibration, the vessel lifted away from the dock and floated toward the exit. Just outside, Marik could see that Oleck had already lifted off in the *Oddhaven*. The barge lumbered its way into the sky as the *Hawk* slipped out of the cave.

That strange whining sound filled the air once more. A blazing blast of light hit the cave's entrance just behind them, throwing more rocks and debris into the air. The airship shook and a few boulders hit the *Hawk's* stern as the entrance to the hideout collapsed.

"Hang on!" Marik shouted.

Mouse's face was pale, but Marik had no more time to focus on him. He was too busy swinging his airship sideways as they ascended, trying desperately to evade their pursuer as a volley of arrows hissed through the air in their direction. Ahead of them, he could see the *Oddhaven*. Quicker than thought, a realization flooded through him. Though he could not see them, there were nine hundred eighty-four durven on that barge, and they were depending on him to protect them. They were, perhaps, the only survivors of their race, and he had promised them safety. Lowering his head with steely determination, Marik gripped the wheel and steered his beloved *Hawk* after the barge, keeping himself between the *Oddhaven* and their pursuers.

"Captain!"

He heard Mouse's cry of alarm, but dismissed it without answering. There was no time to explain himself.

"Don't worry," he muttered, knowing Mouse couldn't hear him. "I fully intend to make it through this alive."

The three airships raced through the sky over the western half of Malei. The *Hawk* danced under Marik's precise adjustments. Sweat beaded on his brow and dripped down his face. If they could just reach the border, he was certain their pursuers would cease and fall back. It required every bit of skill he had to weave this intricate pattern, using the *Hawk* to draw the fire and protect the *Oddhaven*, but also keeping just out of range so that he didn't get blasted out of the sky. The Igyeum battleship was powerful, but Marik noticed a sluggishness to her movements that grew more pronounced the higher they went. He wanted to use that tidbit of information to every advantage possible, but the *Oddhaven*'s lack of agility limited his options. Marik ground his teeth and yanked the lift-lever as another blast came from the Igyeum ship. If he were piloting the barge, he could have lost their pursuers by now, but Oleck was clearly not as willing to take risks, and perhaps had not noticed how much the Igyeum battleship struggled with the higher altitudes.

Mouse had caught on to Marik's strategy and scurried about in the rigging, adjusting the sails when necessary. Gratitude coursed through Marik as Mouse reefed a sail at exactly the right moment, giving them a boost of speed as another volley of arrows fell through the air behind them. The lad had become rather handy in the past couple of years, Marik had to admit.

Weariness suffused him as he glanced down, trying to get his bearings. How much farther to the border?

As if reading his mind, Mouse's voice drifted down. "Forest off starboard, Captain!"

They had reached the edge of Malei. Marik did not allow himself a sigh of relief. This was the most dangerous place they could be. The forest did not signal safety, far from it. If his suspicions were correct, this was the point where the Igyeum commander would do everything in his power to crush both of the airships he was pursuing.

The telltale whine sounded behind them and Marik pushed the lift-lever, forcing the *Hawk* into a steep dive. Oleck, commanding the barge, veered to port, causing the sudden roar of energy to blast harmlessly through the open air between both ships. Marik grinned. He rarely got to fly in concert with another pilot, and despite the danger, the experience was exhilarating.

A new sound reached his ears, and the grin fell from Marik's face as the battleship accelerated. The commander was pushing his vessel to the limits, but to what end, Marik was not certain. And then the battleship swept past him. Marik felt as though the deck of his ship had just fallen out from under him as he realized the commander's strategy.

Tired of trying to pinpoint the nimble *Hawk*, the commander had decided to ignore him and go after the much more cumbersome and clumsy *Oddhaven*. A numbness crept over Marik, like an icy breeze tickling the back of his neck and creeping over his skull in a soft caress. He had no weapons to fire at the battleship, and no crew to fire them even if he had. But there was one option left to him, if he could stomach it. Marik closed his eyes and pictured the durven. Nando's eyes stared at him in his memory as she offered him the staff, as she calmly explained her people's devastating history, as she realized she was about to lose the only home she'd ever really known, and the grim resolve she had shown as she helped her people escape. He had come to respect the durven. They were a stoic group of people, but not without kindness; they had helped him, and in return he had put them all in danger.

Gritting his teeth, Marik called out to Mouse, "Get down and brace yourself!"

Mouse stared down at him from his perch in the rigging, his white face looking even paler than usual. But he did not utter a word as he scrambled to the deck and caught hold of the mast. He was a tough kid. Marik appreciated that about him. If they made it through this, he would have to make a point to tell the boy.

Spinning the wheel, Marik sent the *Hawk* into a steep climb, sailing away from the battleship. Counting under his breath, Marik knew that precision was key. If he miscalculated, he would ruin his only chance to protect the *Oddhaven*. Without his crew, the maneuver might be impossible, since he would have to rely on instinct alone.

"I'm sorry," he whispered.

They had reached the pinnacle of their ascent. Marik yanked the wheel, spinning the *Hawk* into a hairpin turn while simultaneously pushing the lift-lever and sending the airship into an almost free-falling dive. Looking ahead, a grim smile hovered around his lips. His timing had been perfect. They were aimed directly at the port-stern of the battleship.

"They'll never see us coming," he muttered.

For a moment that seemed to stretch into eternity, the *Hawk* fell. Then, with a jarring suddenness, the prow of the *Valdeun Hawk* cleaved into the side of the Igyeum battleship. There was a wrenching and a tearing as boards popped and shattered. The battleship lolled to the side like a wounded whale. Distantly, Marik could hear the shouts of the crew on the other ship. Swiftly, he spun the wheel, tearing apart more of the battleship as he moved the *Hawk* away, trying to get to a safe distance. A quick glance showed that the *Oddhaven* had reached the edge of the forest. Apparently, with safety so near, Oleck had finally decided to risk higher altitudes and greater speed in order to escape their pursuers.

His airship limping slightly, and now with a definite preference for veering to port and fighting his hands at the wheel, Marik tried to follow Oleck's lead. Glancing down, he saw nothing but green trees beneath him. They had done it. They had crossed the border!

Far off in the distance, poking up from the center of the forest, stood the tower where he and Dalmir had rescued the young prisoner. Its ugly black heights soared above the trees like a menacing mountain. He shuddered at the sight as unwanted, vivid memories of that journey flooded his thoughts. So focused on the tower and his flight was Marik that he did not register the sudden whine that pierced the air behind him.

A blast of heat washed over him and flung Marik over the wheel like a rag-doll being savaged by a large dog. The *Valdeun Hawk* screamed in agony as her planks splintered. Fire surged across the deck, lapping hungrily at the sails and then careening past the prow. With a jolt and a shudder, the *Hawk* died.

Desperately, Marik pulled himself upright. He fought with the controls, using every trick he knew to pull them out of their uncontrolled dive. No response came from the airship. The *Hawk* plummeted lifelessly, her trim sails fluttering wildly and tearing to shreds as the air sliced through the canvas like knives. Wind shrieked past his ears as the ground sped towards him. His last thought before they crashed into the forest was that he hoped he had bought Oleck enough time.

33

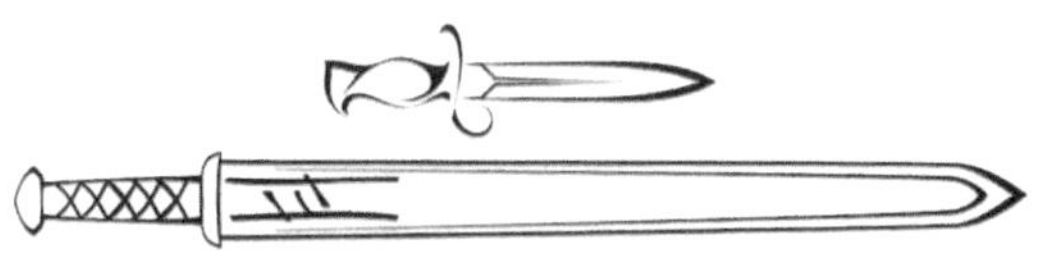

The next morning, Lady Jynna herself arrived on Niveya's doorstep. A short, wiry man stood beside her. Grayden and the others had convened in the small sitting room, discussing what their next move should be, when Vidia ushered in the guests and announced their arrival. Niveya looked up from a note he had been perusing and invited them to sit and have coffee.

Lady Jynna's eyes swept the room, lingering ever so subtly on her daughter. Grayden caught Miri's slight nod to her mother and vowed to keep an even more attentive eye on the young criminal. Jynna glided across the room and settled herself into a chair next to Niveya. With a grudging sigh, she handed him a small, leather-bound tome.

"I am going to need that back," she said.

"I give you my word, just as soon as I have given it a thorough examination to see if it holds any answers to our mystery." Niveya tucked the book into the folds of his robe.

"I trust you had a profitable evening last night?" She leaned forward and put a hand over his.

Niveya folded the paper he had been reading and slipped it under his saucer with a wry grin. "Quite profitable, my thanks."

He glanced at the man still standing stiffly in the doorway. "Why don't you introduce your friend? He is also welcome to sit with us."

"This is Paulo, and he is the reason I have come, as per our agreement," Jynna said. "He was the third man I assigned to the job of assassinating the Regeont."

Niveya's eyelids drooped, making him appear bored and sleepy. Beren, however, exploded from his chair, sending it toppling backward. The veins in his neck stood out and his face turned red as he caught the hilt of his great sword, which had been leaning against his chair. Grayden eased himself forward in his own chair, tensing, his eyes sweeping the room for possible weapons.

"Come, come," Niveya intoned, his voice cool. "Young Adelfried, we must keep our heads."

"That man murdered my Aunt Roshana." Beren growled. "Give me one good reason why I shouldn't execute justice this moment."

Paulo stumbled into the doorframe, away from Beren's rage, hanging on to the wood trim as though it might somehow protect him from the young giant.

"One reason?" Jynna's voice rang calmly through the air. "Well, to start, he did not murder the Regeont. Is that a good enough reason for you to listen to what he has to say before you attempt to execute him?"

Beren froze. Lowering his sword, he stared at Jynna. "What?"

Jynna gestured with a graceful wave of her hand. "Why don't you ask Paulo? That is why I brought him. Oh, sit down, Paulo, and stop shaking. I won't let our hosts murder you." She rolled her eyes at Niveya. "Used to be one of my best, but ever since he took that last job, he hasn't been the same. Jumpy."

Niveya gave her a sympathetic look, then slapped her wrist, pulling the paper out from under her hand. He folded it up even more and tucked it away into a pocket. She batted her eyelids at him with a sweet smile. Niveya ignored her.

"Please, sit, Paulo." Niveya made a slight gesture with his hand and a servant entered the room with a silver tray filled with small cakes and cookies, as well as two more cups and a teapot filled with the strong coffee Doran was so famous for.

Paulo edged his way into the room and took a seat, settling himself tentatively on the edge of the only remaining chair, which he scootched back until it stood a reasonable distance from Beren. He accepted the cup and saucer, and they clattered together in his trembling hands until he set them on a nearby end table and pressed his hands together between his knees.

Niveya took a long, slow sip of his coffee. With great deliberation, he pressed the elegant handkerchief to his lips a few times. Then he leaned forward. "Why don't you tell us what happened, Paulo?"

The man took a shaky breath. "We were hired to assassinate the Regeont," he began. "The job came through Lady Jynna as it always does. No identifiers, just instructions and payment. The instructions explicitly asked for a group of three assassins. Nothing was to be left to chance. We were given a date and the exact schedule of the Manor guards and their rounds, we were even provided with a detailed map of the Manor and the Regeont's daily itinerary so that we would know which room to enter. There would be a ruckus up Academy way to draw attention away from our activities. We were supposed to get in and get out. No collateral was acceptable. It..." He shook his head. "It was the perfect scenario."

"But something went wrong," Niveya pressed.

"We managed to get into the Regeont's library. I was hiding behind the curtains. When she entered the room, the other two attacked. It..." Paulo swallowed with obvious difficulty. "That woman... I've never seen anything like it; she was so calm, so composed. She fought off their attacks with obvious skill. When it was over... she just stood there, cleaning her rapier. I couldn't move. I could hardly believe what I had just seen."

"What happened next?" Niveya prodded.

"I didn't have a choice, did I? I attacked her," the man admitted. "It was what I was paid for. I pulled my dagger and jumped out. Must have surprised her, because I knocked her sword out of her hand, but she kicked my wrist, and I lost hold of my dagger. She leaped toward the fireplace and I ran after her. Dunno what happened next, exactly. I caught hold of her, and she whirled around and pressed something against my arm. There was a hiss, and then this terrible pain raced up my arm. I couldn't bear it. I let go of her." He rolled up his sleeve and turned his arm so they could see it. An angry red welt stood out on his skin, its swirling pattern easily recognizable as the symbol of the Regeont. It was not a perfect image; the dove's wings were flared, but the ship's mast was marred and the ship itself was little more than lightly raised red lines.

Grayden rose and moved closer, examining the burn. "How were you marked?"

Paulo shrugged. "Like I said, it's a little blurry in my memory. My best guess is that her seal fell in the fire in her fight with my comrades, and she saw it and used it as a weapon against me. Must have burned her hand, too, but she never even whimpered." There was obvious admiration in his voice.

"Then what?" Niveya asked.

"I got my knife back, but just there was this scream from the hallway and this servant girl was standing there in the doorway. She looked like she might fall over, but Lord Elan came running in and shouted at her to run, and she did. I knew I couldn't take on both the Regeont and Lord Elan, so I took the only way out available—I threw myself through the window and fled as fast as I could."

Beren's eyes widened. "Wait... you mean... what? Then..." He stared at Grayden, the blood draining from his face. He picked up his chair and sat in it with a dazed thump. "Then... but that means..."

"Elan killed Roshana himself." Niveya finished Beren's thought.

"And hired the mercenaries," Grayden added.

"To draw attention away from himself and weave webs of confusion around the entire plot," Niveya said.

"Amateur," Miri scoffed. "The best plan is always the simplest one. That's what my mother always says."

Jynna's lips twitched.

"What do we do now?" Beren asked, looking at Niveya. "We can't prove this, not on the word of an assassin."

"Now, young Adelfried"—Niveya rubbed his hands together—"now we must think like criminals." He rose and bowed to Lady Jynna. "You have been most helpful. You may go, but I will need to keep your employee here for a little while. We will need his testimony. And I would appreciate the loan of Miri for a few more days as well."

Grayden expected the woman to protest, but she merely stood, gave a small nod to Paulo, extended her hand to Niveya for a kiss, and swept away without so much as glancing at her daughter again.

When she had left and Paulo had been escorted to a room of his own, Niveya paced across the room. "In order to prove Elan's guilt, we are going to need a paper trail," he began. "Paulo's story, along with Ulia's testimony, will not be enough, though the brand on Paulo's arm will help. But we need positive proof that Elan hired the assassins."

"But everything we know only connects him to the assassins by tenuous threads," Beren objected. "How do we prove he was the actual killer?"

"That may be a bit trickier," Niveya conceded, "but I have a few ideas."

"What kind of proof are we looking for, and how do we get it?" Grayden asked.

"Someone hired assassins and mercenaries," Niveya replied. "That means large amounts of money; sizable sums like that always leave a trail. Even Lady Jynna keeps a ledger with all the transactions her crew receives. Quite a few of the inhabitants of this city would rest far less easily if they knew how much information she has stashed in this little book." He tapped the leather journal.

"You think Lord Elan kept track of his transactions?" Grayden scoffed. "You really think you'll find some little book where he's written: 'four hundred stin to assassins to murder the Regeont, two hundred stin to mercenaries to attack Academy and frame Lord Adelfried'?"

Niveya shot him an amused glare. "Of course not. But he will have written the amounts down. If we can show that the numbers in his ledger line up with the number in this one"—he held up the leather-bound book Jynna had given him—"then we can show a direct line from his pocketbook to hers, and prove that he was behind the assassination attempt."

"It still doesn't prove that he committed the crime," Grayden pointed out.

"No," Niveya agreed. "But he also did not act alone. We can use that against him."

"Then what is our next move?" Grayden asked. "How do we get into the Manor? How do we find this supposed ledger?"

Beren tugged at his upper lip. "I can get into the Manor."

"How?" Grayden asked.

"I didn't know Ilya or Elan well, but I've interacted with them before at various events. I always got along better with Ioan, because he was closer to my age, but our families have been friends our entire lives. It would not be suspicious for me to call on them to offer my condolences over Roshana's death and my congratulations to Elan on being elected as the new Regeont."

Grayden studied his friend. "It's a good plan," he began, "but could you do it?"

"What do you mean?" Beren asked.

"I mean—" Grayden cleared his throat, not wanting to offend his friend. "I just mean that you tend to wear your emotions as openly as that sword of yours. Knowing Elan killed the woman you thought of as a grandmother, do you really think you can shake his hand and congratulate him on usurping her position? Can you embrace him as he pretends to cry on your shoulder over the murder he committed? Can you do that without giving away everything we hope to achieve?"

Beren stiffened, a muscle twitching in his jaw. "If you go with me, I can."

"Me?" Grayden asked. "How will that help?"

"We're about to have a falling out, you and I. And I'm going to be extremely upset that I'm stuck on an assignment with you here in Doran," Beren replied.

"What are we having a falling out over?" Grayden asked, at once intrigued and skeptical.

"Easy, you're going to believe my father really hired the mercenaries, and maybe even that he's trying to take over the Council and turn himself into Telmondir's equivalent of an Ar'Mol." Beren smirked.

"That's ridiculous," Grayden protested.

"That could work," Niveya mused. "Put Elan off his guard by having someone actually believing his wild rumor. But that is only part of a plan. We need to find the ledger and get a good look at it."

"That's where I come in." Miri raised a hand from where she was lounging on the couch.

"Is it?" Niveya asked.

"Yep." She sat up and swung her legs over the side of the couch, her booted feet hitting the tiled floor softly. "Entering and procuring are my strongest skills. As long as those two"—she pointed at Grayden and Beren—"can keep the Regeont and his sister busy, I can get you what you need."

"Excellent," Niveya said, rubbing his hands together. "According to my associates, the Regeont is planning a small dinner party two days from now to celebrate his new position. If you call on him tomorrow evening, he is sure to extend an invitation. To not do so for such an old family friend would be the height of a social misstep and it would look strange... and strange things can quickly become viewed with suspicion. Elan cannot afford something like that at this early, fragile stage in his new role of authority."

34

"I have brought the elders," Jorgen announced, gesturing to the small crowd that now followed him. More and more people emerged from their houses until it seemed the entire village stood before Dalmir. Kaj and a group of younger men and women stood in a restless bunch on the outskirts of the crowd, their faces grim and angry.

"My friends, my family," Jorgen shouted, his voice rising above the murmuring commotion and calling for silence. "These three travelers have come from above, as was foretold at the beginning of our time here." He pointed to Dalmir. "This man knew the correct response to the Guardian. You all know what that means. However, he has offered to allow us to keep the jewel in Frieda's heart and says he will leave in peace. Thus, the decision has reverted to our hands. What say you?"

The people muttered and shifted, turning to each other with questioning sounds. The oldest of the elders, a man with a gleaming bald pate above bushy white eyebrows, squinted at Dalmir.

"What is the meaning of this?" he demanded in a gruff voice.

Taken aback, Dalmir frowned. "I am loath to destroy this beautiful place," he replied. "If I can avoid it, I will."

"But it is your duty to destroy it," the man retorted, scowling fiercely. "You are a destroyer."

"I do not wish to be a destroyer," Dalmir replied.

"Why?"

"Because I prefer to be a builder."

"But isn't it true that sometimes destruction must precede creation?" the man asked. "For a house to be built, mustn't trees be chopped down? For a sword to be created, mustn't ore be melted in a forge and hammered into shape? You cannot be a builder without also being a destroyer."

Dalmir stared at the old man, at a loss for words. "There is one who builds without need for destruction." A tenderness filled his heart, a tenderness he had not experienced in centuries; words flowed from his mouth unchecked. "But I am not Him."

"We know not of this Builder," the man replied. "Though I would be interested to hear more along our journey."

"We do not wish to go!" Kaj's angry voice rang out across the crowd. "You cannot make us go!"

The old man whirled. "You swore to abide by the decision of the elders, young Kaj. But nobody will force you to accept hope. For many years, we have waited, wondering which of the two destroyers would find us first. You all know what will happen if we take this man's offer and keep the jewel: the other destroyer will come, and he will not be so kind. There is nothing more to discuss. This man offers us a choice between leaving here with him in order to grasp hold of hope or waiting for our utter destruction. The elders have chosen hope, the hope that was promised to our fathers by the Silver Lady. We will leave Chasm and rebuild."

Kaj strode forward, his face red. "How dare you decide our fates without a thought? Without allowing other voices to be heard?"

"Young Kaj, would you grieve your mother in this way? She has no desire to see you left behind. There is nothing left for us here, son of my daughter. The elders are as one on this matter; we always have been. There is no need to discuss it further. Every person in our village knew this day was coming. That it has come in our time is a bittersweet thing. But we will be like our forebears: their courage brought us here, now let it be our courage that takes us away. We shall prove our mettle equal to theirs, and there is much honor to be had in such a sacred opportunity. Be at peace, grandson, the journey before us may yet hold dangers; we will need your strength to face them. Would you stay behind? That is your choice. But know this: when the jewel leaves, so does the light. Nothing will grow here, nothing will thrive here. How long will your pride and stubbornness succor you?"

The redness slowly receded from Kaj's face and his shoulders slumped. "Forgive me, grandfather," the youth muttered. "I..." His face twisted as though he had bitten into something bitter. "I was wrong." With those words, the rest of the fight drained from him, and he looked up at the old man, his eyes bright. The elderly man held out his arms, and Kaj flung himself into the embrace.

"You are young," the man said. "Youth has many advantages. But age comes with tempering and wisdom you have yet to acquire." He pushed the boy away and held him by the shoulders and Dalmir saw just how young the boy actually was. Then the elder looked about at the people and raised an arm. "Go home. Pack your things. The man who brings us hope has arrived and he will lead us to our new home."

There was a rumble like thunder as the crowd dispersed, all talking at once. Dalmir glimpsed a variety of emotions on each face: excitement, sorrow, scowls, and even a few who were laughing with delight at the idea of an adventure. He hoped he could keep them safe.

"You will be my guests," the older man said, authority in his voice that could not be denied. "It will take our people some days to gather their things and say goodbye to our home."

Dalmir nodded. "My thanks."

"You... will take... the orb." The halting, mechanical voice suddenly at his side made Dalmir jump in surprise. He stared at the strange, lifeless image of his sister-in-law's face. Nodding slowly, he let out a long sigh.

"Yes. But first I will give these people a chance to pack their belongings and say goodbye to the only home they have ever known. May I ask you a few questions?"

"You... may."

"Do you know why Telsume gave you Lerilei's face?"

"I was... his greatest achievement." Her head tilted mechanically as she spoke. "He wished to... honor... his wife's memory... through me. He said it was... a way for her... to live on."

"And what will happen to you when I remove the orb?"

"I will... sleep."

"What if you came with us instead?"

"What do... you mean?"

"What if I don't remove the orb from within your frame? What if you continue to guard it and simply come with us when we leave this place?"

A whirring sound emanated from within the aton. "It... is not practical. You may not... understand... but I am... losing functionality. Tel never meant me for such... long-term function."

"How can you be losing power? The orb cannot be losing efficiency."

"It is not the orb... it is myself."

"I see." Dalmir grimaced. "I am sorry."

"It has been... a privilege... to serve this community. I believe... Telsume... would have been proud."

"I believe you are right." Dalmir sighed. "I wish he could have seen this." His gaze swept across the village, taking in the peaceful scene. Even as they hurried to pack and uproot their lives, the people of the village did so in an orderly fashion. There was no chaos, no panic. This was a moment they had been aware was coming. Perhaps some had hoped it would not come during their lifetime, but they had known of its approach. They were a remarkable group... Dalmir's brow furrowed.

"Guardian—"

"Yes?"

"Do you know of the atons in the tower below us?"

"I am... their leader. As I guard... above, so they function... below. They are... my arms."

"Then, when I remove the orb, those atons will cease to function as well?"

"Correct."

Dalmir nodded, but something still bothered him. "The orb... the original leader of these people activated it?"

"Yes. Though he was... helped by the Silver Lady. She... taught him."

"But, these people... their story..." Dalmir frowned. "They are Maleian."

"That is correct."

"Then how have they been able to activate the orb and keep it running for all these years? Is there Telsuman blood in their veins, somehow?"

The Guardian gazed at him with her impassive, unmoving face. "Your assumption is... in error."

"What?"

"The orb that powers... myself... is not Telsume's. It is... Mulemo's."

Though externally he did not move, inside his mind Dalmir staggered back, the world falling away from him, spinning off its axis and hurtling through space in an entirely new direction. "Mulemo's?" he gasped, his mind reeling. "But why...?" He did not finish the question. He already knew the answer. Shiori had understood Uun better than all of them. And why wouldn't she? It had been on her watch that all this had begun. Had she been watching and waiting all this time? Had she known from the beginning that more treachery would follow? He shook his head, pressing the palm of his hand to the bridge of his nose. No. She could not have known, or she would have warned them. Though she might have suspected. Perhaps she had even tried to tell them. "Perhaps she tried to tell me... but I wouldn't listen," Dalmir whispered. A burning sensation tingled in his throat and he experienced the powerful urge to flee, to run, and never stop. But he could not do that, and so he remained, standing on the hill overlooking the village he was doomed to destroy.

Drengur and Ioan returned from their exploration of the surrounding area.

"Some of these people are not happy about leaving," Ioan announced in a low voice. "We may have more trouble coming. Kaj seems to have settled down, but many of the people in his age group are still muttering amongst themselves. I am not sure what it will lead to."

Dalmir grimaced. "I'm not sure there is anything we can do. Even if I left the orb here, the Guardian says she is already failing. The orb might remain active, but I believe it is the Guardian who focuses its power, allowing it to serve a useful purpose. These people don't know how to use that power. Without Frieda, all they will have is light while their world dies around them."

"Then there is no choice, after all. Somehow, that is comforting, though not all will see it that way, and some may even choose to disbelieve it," Jorgen said, joining them. A woman clung to his arm and three small children peeked out at Dalmir from behind her skirt, wide-eyed and bashful. "My family," Jorgen introduced them. "I heard Elder Baehr issue you an invitation to stay with him until our people are ready, but my wife and I would be honored if you would dine in our home tonight."

"How many days do you think it will take?" Ioan asked.

"Perhaps two or three," Jorgen replied. "We have spent our lives awaiting this day. Even though it held much apprehension for us, we preferred to be prepared. Our possessions are few. We travel light."

"Good," Dalmir said. He was ready to leave this place. The task that lay before him was a burden he could hardly stand. Having accepted it, now he simply wanted it to be over.

———

JORGEN'S ESTIMATE had been a touch generous. Three days passed, but many of the villagers were now having to be pushed and prodded by those who were ready. It was no easy thing, packing up their lives into satchels and packs, choosing what to bring and what to abandon. However, by the fourth morning, the elders' patience ran out, and they issued a statement that anyone not ready to leave by lunch would be left behind.

When the villagers had all finally assembled, Dalmir called Frieda over. She moved to stand before him with jerky, mechanical strides. Dalmir hesitated, uncertain how to proceed. Frieda made it easy for him. With a deft motion of her jointed fingers, she flipped open a metal hatch in her upper torso, revealing the flickering gray light of Mulemo's orb. Dalmir marveled at the construction of the compartment and the cleverness of Shiori's plan. Even activated, he would never have been able to tell the difference between Tel's and Mulemo's orbs. Finding this one here in Telsume's realm, he would have assumed its owner had been Tel. Uun would have assumed the same. Perhaps even now Uun had Tel's orb in his possession. If he did, how frustrated he must be in his attempts to activate it!

"When I remove this, the tower below us isn't going to collapse or anything, is it?" Dalmir asked in a low voice.

"It will not," Frieda assured him. "I only control... the atons. The rest is Tel's doing. It will remain."

"Good." Dalmir sucked his cheek in, chewing on it nervously. Then he reached out a hand toward the orb.

"Stop!" a voice rang out, startling Dalmir. He looked toward the source of the shout and found himself staring down the shaft of an arrow aimed at his chest. The young man holding the bow raised his chin defiantly. "If you so much as twitch a finger toward the jewel, I will shoot you where you stand."

Everything went still. Slowly, Dalmir withdrew his hand and held it up above his head. "You don't want to do this," he said, his voice quiet.

"Yes, I do," the young man retorted.

"Aron," Kaj said, stepping out of the crowd, "put the bow down. The village elders have spoken. We all decided together. The time for this has passed."

"No." Aron's voice trembled, though his hands remained steady. "This is our home, Kaj. We can't just abandon it. Why should we? Maybe you lack a spine, but I don't. I'm willing to fight for my home; I won't just let this stranger take it away from us."

"Aron," Dalmir said, internally cursing the fact that he could not use his own power to disarm the boy, "listen to me, Frieda is dying. She told me her functionality has diminished significantly. Even if I don't take the orb, she has little time left. When she fails, everything in this village will cease to flourish. The plants will die. What will your people do for food when that happens?"

Aron's face reddened. "You think I am a fool? Of course you want me to believe these lies! You want the orb for yourself." His head swung back and forth wildly. "Why can't anyone else see the truth? This stranger wants the power of the orb. He doesn't care about us. How do we even know he will lead us out of here? Once he has the orb, he will abandon us and we will perish here in the wasteland he has described so vividly. I will not let that happen!" His voice rose to a scream of rage and before anyone could move or speak, he released the arrow.

"Marik!" Shaesta's scream was all but lost in the wind as Oleck pushed the *Oddhaven* to even greater speeds and altitude. "Oleck! We have to go back! We have to..." She was at his side in an instant, tugging desperately at his arms, trying to wrench the wheel from his hands.

"We have to use the time he gave us," Oleck growled, fending her off.

"But..." Her desperate reply rose into an incoherent wail.

"Shaesta, we're not leaving him behind," Oleck shouted, pushing her away with his elbow. "But we have to hide and wait for the Igyeum captain to turn back. I doubt he'll risk a trip down to the forest floor to search for a broken airship inside the Whispering Wood. We can go back for Marik once the sky is clear."

Shaesta gave a shaking, shuddering sob, but she nodded and stopped trying to grab the wheel. She stayed at his side, her eyes fixed on the edge of the forest behind, where they had seen the *Hawk* fall.

In a detached sort of way, Oleck was aware of everything around him. He heard the whine heralding the Igyeum weapon at their stern. Time seemed to slow. His body reacted of its own accord, straining at the wheel and sending the airship into a spiraling dive as a brilliant beam of whitish-yellow light launched from an opening in the battleship's side, fiery tendrils and curls dancing along the edges. A sound that was a mixture of sizzling bacon in a frying pan and a rock slide thundered over their heads. Part of the beam caught the top of the mizzenmast and smoke drifted up from the rigging, but nothing ignited. The distance between them and the battleship widened, and Oleck noticed that firing the weapon had forced the other vessel backward through the air, which explained the anchor they had dropped the night of the failed rescue attempt: every discharge of the weapon in the air caused the battleship to lose ground. Not a very efficient or effective tool against another airship, Oleck thought idly.

"They're turning back!" a durven cried.

It was true. The battleship, thrown backward nearly to the border once more, did not surge forward after them or resume its chase. Oleck grinned. They were outside of Igyeum territory, and as expected the captain did not wish to pursue them further. He glimpsed the commander of the battleship standing at the wheel and imagined the powerless rage the other man must be experiencing.

Oleck pushed the vessel on, not varying his course, except that he slowed their pace and adjusted the lift-lever, sending them into a slight descent that would gradually take them to the ground. It would appear to their enemy that the *Oddhaven* was continuing its flight, obscuring them from view below the tree line, while they actually stayed near the crash site and could effect a search for Marik and Mouse and the remains of the *Hawk* without losing as much time.

Even after the battleship had finally disappeared beyond the horizon, heading east and presumably back home, Oleck continued to wait. He ached to return to the crash site, but he had little hope for what they would find there.

"We have to go find them," Shaesta urged. "They could be..." She did not finish the thought. Oleck knew what she was thinking: Marik and Mouse might already be dead, or they could be suffering from severe injuries, mere minutes from death.

The durven were restless. Some of them had seen Marik's maneuver into the path of the sun-bolt and word had spread among the survivors. They also knew that Mouse was on board, and even though he was not technically durven, they still considered him family. Many were in favor of risking everything to attempt a rescue, but Oleck reasoned with them, pointing out that if they moved out before their enemies had truly departed, Marik's sacrifice would be in vain. That bit of logic quieted them, though none of them liked it.

So they waited.

Finally, as the sun sank and altered into an incandescent red ball, Oleck raised the *Oddhaven* above the forest and began the tedious search for the wreckage of the *Hawk,* hoping to find it before the light died. Skimming the tree-tops, they started in the area where they had last seen the smaller airship, though it was hard to tell exactly where the vessel had gone down.

Shaesta maintained she had seen the airship go down just just inside the border of the forest, so that was where they began, going in low, sweeping half-circles that grew gradually larger and larger with every pass.

The sun continued to set, and the world grew dim and shadowed, and then true darkness set in.

"We have to stop for the night," Oleck said, his voice quiet.

"We can't," Shaesta argued. "He saved us. We can't just give up on him."

"We're not giving up," Oleck replied. "But we can't go on. In the dark, we might miss the signs and never know it."

"We can see in the dark," Nando reminded him. "Can we help?"

Oleck considered this, then shook his head. "From this height, it's still better to wait until morning."

Reluctantly, the others agreed with this assessment. Setting watches, in case Marik and Mouse were somehow well enough to light a fire, the inhabitants of the barge spent a fitful and worried night.

As soon as dawn broke the next morning, they resumed the search. By midday, they had increased their radius several miles inside the wood. Oleck maintained his heading with relentless determination, but doubt crept into his thoughts. He had seen the *Hawk* as she fell, her entire stern and most of her starboard hull blasted into fragments, her prow splintered from the collision moments before. Oleck still could hardly believe Marik had done that, even though Shaesta and several of the durven had seen it happen.

"What if we can't find them?" he asked Shaesta when she came to take a turn at the wheel.

The young woman stared at him, her gaze empty of emotion. Dark circles stood out like purple stains beneath her eyes, and her dark skin looked stretched and tight across her face.

"I don't know," she whispered. "I can't... I..." Anguish laced her tone as she fumbled for words. Oleck had never seen her so shaken. It unnerved him. Shaesta, normally so confident and composed, even when she had betrayed them, even when she feared for the lives of her family, now trembled before him like a lost child. He wanted to comfort her, assure her they would find Marik alive and well, but he could not speak the words, too afraid they were a lie.

"I'm sorry," he muttered, his mind desperately grasping for words that would not be full of awkward emptiness. "I did not know... I did not realize you felt..." He stopped, embarrassed, and turned away, running his hands through his hair as though trying to comb it.

There was only silence behind him. He wondered if she meant to confirm his suspicions by not speaking. Something in his chest constricted painfully but he ignored it.

"I see something!" A cry sounded from the prow of the ship. The durven had lined the rail and joined their efforts in the search by scanning the forest below with their much sharper vision.

Oleck, intensely grateful to have a reason to discontinue the uncomfortable conversation with Shaesta, raced to the rail and peered over. Directly below them, he saw a gap in the dense canopy, as though something had crashed through it. Broken trees and limbs lay scattered everywhere. Oleck dashed back to the helm.

"I'll take us down," he offered. Shaesta did not argue, but relinquished the wheel, relief apparent in her eyes.

They descended into the opening in the forest, and Oleck settled the barge onto the ground, grateful for the flat bottom and the relatively level terrain. As soon as they touched down, the durven swarmed off the ship and fanned out into the trees. He could hear them shouting for Marik and Mouse at varying intervals, and he powered down the cynder with swift efficiency. Shaesta waited for him, her gaze questioning. Glancing at the trees and noting the direction they had been bowed and splintered, Oleck pointed and they joined the group of durven traveling that way.

The trees were tall and thick-trunked. Their branches created a heavy canopy overhead, allowing only faint dapples of light to filter down. There was no path, and the underbrush was dense in places, slowing their progress. Occasionally, they came upon a splintered plank or a shred of canvas, which led them deeper into the wood. The farther they went, the more scraps they found. It amazed Oleck how far the *Hawk* had flown after crashing into the treetops. They had been traveling for nearly two hours and still hadn't found more than discouraging fragments.

As they continued their trek, Oleck was glad they were not traversing the area by night; the wood was dark enough by daylight.

"Do you think the rumors about this place are true?" he whispered to Shaesta.

She stared at him, then, slowly, her eyes widened. "I hadn't thought about where we were landing," she admitted.

"Me neither," Oleck replied. "Not until just now."

Shaesta played with the numerous bangles around her wrist, her gaze darting about, her steps slowing and growing hesitant. Then she shook her head, her dangling earrings swaying. "I haven't seen anything unnatural so far."

"That's true," Oleck acknowledged. Her words cheered him enough to chase the shivery sensation away from his spine. With a renewed spring in his step, Oleck hacked through a particularly stubborn patch of thorn bushes and shrubs that bordered the edge of a little stream. On the other side of the water, the ground sloped up dramatically. They sloshed across the shallow brook and scaled the other bank. It wasn't a sheer cliff, but the steep incline made the climb difficult. They had to pull themselves up using tree trunks and roots, and they stopped for frequent rests.

When they finally crested the hill, they found the *Hawk*. All thoughts of exhaustion fled from Oleck's mind as he surveyed the disaster spread out before him. Immense trees lay strewn about like so many arrows recklessly scattered across the ground. A huge furrow marred the forest floor, displacing small bushes and plants. The *Valdeun Hawk* itself lay at the end of the ruptured earth, tilted completely onto its port side. The stern of the ship was even worse than Oleck had feared. In fact, there wasn't any stern. The back section of the ship was, quite simply, gone. Warped and splintered planks stuck out at odd angles from what had been the hull. Oleck raced to the ship, circling it to assess the rest of the damage. Branches had ripped the port trim sail completely off the airship and the crash had snapped the mainmast in half. The proud sails now dangled in tattered fragments that flapped sadly in the light breeze. Amazingly, the mizzenmast still stood tall, but the foremast no longer existed.

"Marik?" Oleck wanted to shout, but the word stuck in his throat and came out as the barest breath of a whisper. No one could have survived such a landing. His head whirled and his vision darkened. Voices around him called out to Marik and Mouse, but dizzy despair threatened to engulf him. After a minute or two, his vision cleared and Oleck ground his teeth, frustrated with himself. Standing around fearing the worst would accomplish nothing. Pushing himself forward, he joined the others, calling to Marik and Mouse.

There was no answer. Oleck caught sight of Shaesta, climbing into the wreckage of the ship, and they shared an anguished glance before she disappeared into the remains of the *Valdeun Hawk*. Her voice drifted to his ears in a sudden cry of alarm, and he raced through the rubble to get to her. He found her in what remained of Marik's quarters. She was on her knees, bending over two bodies.

Oleck froze. A thundering sounded in his ears. He did not want to move forward; he did not want to know. But he had to. His feet moved him forward of their own accord. He stumbled over a chair and almost fell.

Shaesta looked up at his approach. Her face was wet with tears.

"They're alive," she said in a choked gasp. "They need help, but they're both alive!"

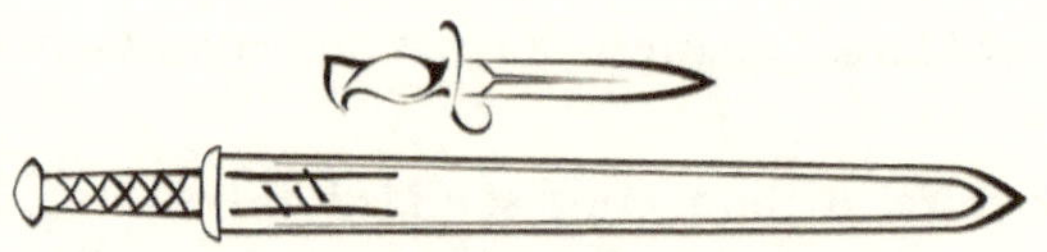

Grayden stood on the large front porch of the Manor next to Beren, feeling strangely disconnected. The last time he had been in this building, it had been as a guest of Beren's mother. Grayden had never actually met the former Regeont. She had been away at the Arxis for a Council Meeting at the time, and Lady Nadia had been watching the house and entertaining the Regeont's guests while she was away. He had not given it much thought then, their brief visit to the Manor, the seat of power in Ondoura, but now he wished he'd had a chance to meet the woman who had so graciously opened her home to him and his friends. It seemed wrong, never having met her.

The great door swung inward, and a servant appeared. He peered down his long nose at both of them with an imperious look. "Welcome to the Regeont's Manor. Do you have an appointment?"

"We do not," Beren replied. "But I am an old family friend. I have been stationed here in Doran since graduating from the Academy, and I wished to pay my respects to Lord Elan and Lady Ilya. However, I realize I should have arranged an appointment beforehand and I find myself embarrassed that I did not think of it." Beren bowed his head and took a step back. "I do not wish to impose on the new Regeont's busy schedule. If you would just tell him that Beren Adelfried stopped by…"

"Adelfried?" The servant's nose lowered and his head darted forward on his neck to peer more closely at Beren. "Adelfried, you say? Not the son of Lord Thorben Adelfried?"

Beren bobbed his head. "Yes."

"Come in, come in, young sir." The servant's demeanor altered completely now that he understood the importance of this visitor, and he stood back, beckoning for them to enter. "There are very few names on the Regeont's list that he wishes to be disturbed over… and yours is one of them." He gave Grayden a long glance, as though holding an internal debate. "Your colleague is also welcome, of course."

Grayden bit back a smirk at the veiled dig.

The servant ushered them into the room where Lady Nadia had received them nearly a year ago, and Grayden found it impossible to sit. He paced to the window and stood staring outside, paying little attention to the servant as he prattled on about something and then excused himself to go inform the Regeont of his guests. As soon as the servant had exited the large open parlor, Grayden recognized his cue.

"I can't imagine why the Regeont would put your name in such a place of honor after what your father did," he remarked, still staring out the window.

Beren, who had been settling himself onto a bench, paused and stared up at Grayden. "What do you mean by that?" he asked in a dangerous tone.

"I mean that the son of the man who hired mercenaries to attack such a prestigious institution as our nation's Academy must warrant some level of suspicion. You don't really think your former friendship with this Lord Elan will erase your father's guilt, do you?" Grayden put as much snide contempt into his tone as he could muster.

Beren rose slowly and paced across the room where he loomed

over Grayden. Grayden stared up at his friend and was grateful that this was not a real argument.

"You will not say such words about my father. Is that clear?" Beren growled, his tone taking on a menacing edge that made Grayden want to take a step back.

Instead, he stood his ground and rolled his eyes. "Oh, are you threatening me now? That must be what Adelfrieds do when they come across something they don't like. Must be a hereditary trait."

"That's enough!" Beren shouted.

The sound of a throat being cleared reached their ears just as Beren raised his fist. They both turned. Elan stood at the room's entrance dressed in traditional Ondouran garb: his shirt a dark blue, high-collared jacket-style tunic that fell to mid-thigh; all up the front and along the collar, an intricate pattern of embroidery in gold and silver threads traced its way, with just a touch of bead-work trailing down the long sleeves. Draped around his neck and falling down to wrap over his arm flowed a gold scarf, the symbol of the office. Under the tunic, he wore dark gray trousers and tall black boots. A small, questioning smile hovered about his lips.

"Forgive me, am I interrupting something?" he asked.

Beren snapped to attention. "Not at all, dear cousin. We were merely having a bit of a disagreement." He tossed a dark glower at Grayden before striding across the room, his hand outstretched. "My deepest condolences on your loss, my friend," he said.

Lord Elan clasped Beren's arm with both hands. "My thanks. My aunt was an exceptional woman, and she will be missed."

"Indeed, she will," Beren agreed, with a stunning lack of irony in his tone. "But I was glad to hear that Ondoura will continue to be safe and in capable hands. May I also extend my most sincere congratulations on your recent appointment?"

Elan looked at the ground modestly. "I'm still not sure I am up to the task," he admitted. "It all still feels very surreal. But Ondoura deserves my best, and that is what I shall endeavor to give."

Beren's brow lowered and he gave a firm nod. Grayden marveled at his friend's ability to restrain himself from grabbing Elan's throat with both hands and wringing the truth out of him.

Elan glanced at Grayden. "I remember you," he said, "you were here with Beren before, right? Visiting his mother? Forgive me, I do not recall your name."

"Grayden Ormond, your lordship." Grayden bowed his head. "I'm stationed here in Doran with Beren."

"That's right." Elan raised an eyebrow. "Congratulations are due to you as well, if I am not mistaken? Are you not recently graduated?"

"That is correct," Beren replied. "Probably why they stationed us here."

"Oh?" Elan asked.

Beren met his gaze with a mildly annoyed one of his own. "Doran is one of the safest and most crime-free cities in Telmondir, isn't it? It's a good place to put young graduates where they can continue learning without finding themselves in situations that might be overly dangerous."

"Beren means it's boring here," Grayden supplied with a grin, marveling at his friend's acting ability.

"That is true." Elan frowned. "Though the recent attack on the Academy and the assassination of Aunt Roshana might alter the perception of our fair city. I hope to do everything in my power to reassure our citizens that they are safe."

"How is the investigation into the murder going?" Beren asked.

"Sadly, it has all but come to a standstill," Elan replied. "With no witnesses to the murder and the mercenaries insisting that your father hired them, the city guards have little in the way of leads to follow."

Grayden feigned a coughing fit, shooting a meaningful smirk Beren's way. His friend scowled at him, and Elan's gaze darted back and forth between them.

"Is something wrong?" Elan asked.

"My so-called friend here believes that my father actually hired the mercenaries," Beren gritted out.

Elan's eyes widened. "Surely you cannot believe such a thing," he said. "Anyone who has met Lord Adelfried knows that such ridiculous charges must be a lie."

"But you just said you couldn't prove anything," Grayden pointed out, putting on his most supercilious air. "With the evidence against him, I don't understand why he's not at least in custody."

"What evidence? Just the word of cutthroats and murderers?" Beren scoffed. "What is that worth?"

"A man's past and character ought to count for something," Elan replied in a placating tone. "The word of a few mercenaries means nothing when weighed against a man of Lord Adelfried's stature."

"But if no further evidence comes to light? And if the mercenaries stick to their story? What then?" Grayden asked.

Elan's expression grew troubled. "Then..." He hesitated, giving Beren an apologetic glance. "Then the investigation would have to turn and give a more thorough look at Lord Adelfried's activities and contacts. But hopefully it won't come to that."

"Hopefully." Beren's voice was flat.

Elan gave a forced smile and took Beren by the shoulders. "Beren, I am so sorry that this is happening. You know I would never suspect your father of such treason. It is my great hope the Conscripts can clear this up soon. My best investigators are working tirelessly, of that I can assure you."

"My thanks," Beren said in a hoarse voice. "And thank you for taking the time to see us. I know you must be busy. I do not wish to impose on you any longer."

"It has been good to see you," Elan replied. "I wish we could spend more time catching up..." He paused. "Well, in fact... there is a small gathering planned here tomorrow night. Just a little thing, really, a dinner some friends are putting on to celebrate my appointment. I wish they wouldn't, really, but Ilya insisted. I know she would love to see you; she'll be sorry she missed your visit. Why don't you come? Can you?" He glanced at them both. "You're both invited. It would honor me to have some of our nation's newest defenders at my table."

Beren squinted as though considering. "We'll have to clear it with our supervisor," he said.

"Just a moment." Elan snapped his fingers. A servant appeared.

"Yes, my lord?"

"Get these two an invitation to tomorrow night's dinner party," Elan said. "Make sure my seal is on it." The servant nodded and scurried away, and Elan glanced at Beren, a question in his eyes. "Surely that will be convincing enough for your commander?"

"That should do it," Beren said.

"Excellent! I must go now. I have a meeting shortly, but I will see you both tomorrow evening. Ilya will be so pleased to see you, Beren! Thank you for stopping by." Elan shook Beren's hand once more and exited the room. A few minutes later, the servant reappeared and handed Beren a large, cream-colored card with silver lettering. Beren bowed his thanks, and the servant showed them out.

They walked in silence down the street until they had gone several blocks toward the defenders' barracks before darting down an alley and winding their way back to Niveya's safe house via a twisting route complete with false stops and doubling back a few times. Once they were certain nobody was following them, Grayden nudged Beren with his elbow.

"You know I didn't mean any of those things I said."

Beren frowned, his expression confused. "What?"

"About your father. That was just for Elan's sake."

"Of course. That was the plan, after all," Beren replied.

"Yes. But I want you to know I have nothing but the highest regard for your father and your family and you."

"I know that." Beren frowned as though puzzled. "Why..."

Then he grinned, suddenly seeming to understand Grayden's distress. "But I appreciate you saying it. You need not worry that your words wounded me, friend. We fight on the same side."

"Glad to hear it." Grayden grinned back. "I would not want you as an enemy. I almost feel a little sorry for Elan."

"Never," Beren growled.

"I said *almost*," Grayden chuckled. "By the way, I can't believe how convincing you were."

"My thanks. It was not easy. And the hardest part is yet to come."

Dalmir had never spent much time contemplating death. Before the change, he had been a young man, and youth does not concern itself overmuch with the concept of mortality. After the change, he had been immortal, with unparalleled power at his fingertips, and death had ceased to be a concern. Certainly, there had been times since the change when he longed for it, but then it had been denied him.

As the arrow sped toward him, the stark reality of death gripped him in its clutches for the first time since Emri had bestowed his gift. For thousands of years, Dalmir had been untouchable. Even time had no hold on him that he did not allow. His white hair was merely an affectation, brought about by his own will. But now, here in this strange place, where his brother had reached out from beyond the grave to weave an intricate barrier that prevented him from touching his power or using it correctly, Dalmir found himself helpless for the first time in millennia.

Time slowed. The world around him froze and stood still. Clarity filled his mind, even as panic rushed through his veins causing his heart to speed up, racing full-tilt in a surge of adrenaline. There was little he could do. He had already found his power to be useless in this place, anything he attempted could backfire terribly, making the situation even more deadly. Or worse, it could put everyone around him in peril. That was not a risk he was willing to take.

There was no time to duck or dodge out of the way. No time for anyone to push him to safety or leap to his defense—and even if there had been, Dalmir was not certain he had earned that kind of loyalty from either of his companions, and definitely not from any of the watching villagers.

Perhaps this was Emri's plan all along. Perhaps this moment was Dalmir's last—the final punishment for all his failures, with no chance to put anything to rights. Well, if that were the case, he would accept it. Here, at the very end, he was Emri's man through and through. No amount of wandering could remove him from the Builder's hand. Sorrow and regret at all the time he had wasted flashed through his thoughts, suffused by a radiating repentance and a humble acceptance.

Time resumed, speeding up in a blur around him. He felt the arrow pierce his skin. Oddly, there was no pain. It happened so fast that at first he wasn't sure it had actually happened at all. Then he felt a warmth spreading down his torso and he glanced down at the arrow protruding from his chest. Blood seeped from the wound, a blossoming stain growing across his tunic. In a numb daze, he pressed his hand to the wound, his finger and thumb spreading to either side of the arrow in a futile attempt to stop the bleeding.

Then the pain struck him like a tidal wave crashing against a cliff face. Waves of pain, an ocean of pain, a world of pain consumed him. His body seemed to pulse about the arrow shaft, convulsing in an effort to reject it from himself, but unable to do so. A deafening wail filled the cavern; in a dazed sort of way, he was aware that the wail emanated from his own mouth as the hoarse, raw scream scraped its way up and out of his throat in a painful gurgle.

Dully, he heard voices around him, voices raised in shouts and cries of alarm and accusation, but he could not focus on them; pain filled his entire existence.

Darkness flickered around the edges of his vision, just shadows at first, but they quickly grew longer and darker and deeper, filling his entire vision and blotting out the world. Before he lost consciousness and crumpled to the ground, he felt arms reach out and grip him, holding him, lifting him up. His last thought before the darkness overwhelmed him was to wonder if the pain would ever end.

38

Carefully, with deft fingers, Shaesta examined Marik and Mouse to assess the extent of their injuries. Astonishingly, they were both alive, though Marik's left leg was bent at an unnatural angle. He groaned a little under her gentle ministrations—which she took as a good sign—though he did not awaken. He had numerous contusions and cuts on his face and arms, as well as a large gash across his thigh. A bloody shirt lay on the floorboards next to him and it appeared that he had been trying to use it to stop the bleeding before he lost consciousness.

Mouse lay still, his skin paler than usual. She examined him as thoroughly as she could, worried that he might be bleeding internally, but she could find no obvious signs of anything wrong with him other than a nasty lump on the back of his head. At length, she agreed to let the durven carry both of the injured men out of the wreckage, admonishing them to be careful and not jostle them overmuch. She wished they had some sort of bed on which they could carry them, but realized that it would be impossible to keep them stable on such a device down the steep embankment.

It was a tedious journey back to the *Oddhaven*, but they eventually made it there. Shaesta kept glancing up at the sky, fearful that their pursuers would return to finish what they had started.

She knew in her head that they would not come back, but every rustle of leaves or trill of birdsong set her heart to racing and made her glance up nervously. Back at the air-barge they laid Mouse and Marik on pallets made up of blankets and Shaesta set about tending their injuries. She cleaned out the cuts with water and bound up the gash on Marik's leg. As she wiped a cool cloth across his face, his eyes flickered open.

"Raisa?" he asked.

She smiled at him, fighting down the tiny fluttering of tears that threatened to spill out of her heart. He was alive! "No, it's Shaesta, Captain. You've been through an ordeal, but you're safe now."

Marik's jaw worked. "Thirsty."

She tipped his head up and brought a cup of water to his lips. He drank a few sips and then closed his eyes again.

As much as she fretted over the captain, Mouse was the patient that worried her most. He was breathing well, but he had not yet woken, which was not a good sign. Other than the bump on his head, there were no obvious wounds, like the ones covering Marik's body. Even when she splashed his face with water, the boy did not react. She did what she could for him and then went out to give Oleck and the durven an update.

"Marik woke up for a moment," she informed them. "He even spoke."

"That's good," Oleck said, pinching his beard between his fingers. "What did he say?"

"Just that he was thirsty," she replied. "I gave him some water, and he fell back asleep. I think he'll be fine, though I'd like a physician to look at him. Mouse is the one I'm concerned about. He hasn't stirred at all. I'm afraid he has injuries in places I can't see, but I've done all I can for him." She gave Oleck a meaningful glance and lifted an eyebrow before leaving the room. Thankfully, he picked up on her cue and followed her into the galley.

"What are you thinking?" he asked.

"Mouse needs help," she replied. "From an actual physician."

"Dalmir could cure him," Oleck said. "Or we could take him to Ferndale."

"That might be best. We don't know exactly where Dalmir is. It could take us sennights to find him, and I don't think Mouse has that kind of time."

"Then we should go now," Oleck urged.

"I agree..." She hesitated.

Oleck gave her an odd look. "What?"

"What about..." She grabbed a handful of her long, full skirts and fiddled with the fabric nervously. "What about the *Hawk*?"

"What about it?"

"We can't just leave it here."

"We can't take it with us." Oleck stared at her, his expression inscrutable behind his beard.

"Oleck." Shaesta hated how pitiful her voice sounded, how helpless and pleading. "She's the *Hawk*. She's our home. Don't you understand what she means to all of us, to Marik? It will kill the captain if we leave her behind. How can you even think about leaving her here in the forest to rot? Don't you even care? We can't just... we can't just leave her."

Oleck's face darkened. "That ship is my home." His voice was low and tight. "That ship and her captain saved my life. And you betrayed her. You betrayed us. So you don't get to stand there and lecture me about what the *Hawk* means. I know it better than you. Marik may have forgiven you, but that doesn't mean you're one of us. It doesn't mean you'll ever be one of us again." He rose and stormed out of the galley.

Shaesta stood under the angry barrage of words, her back mast-straight and her face expressionless. But as soon as Oleck had disappeared from view, something within her shattered. She sank to the floor with a little gasp. Curling in on herself, Shaesta wrapped her arms around her knees and sobbed like a child.

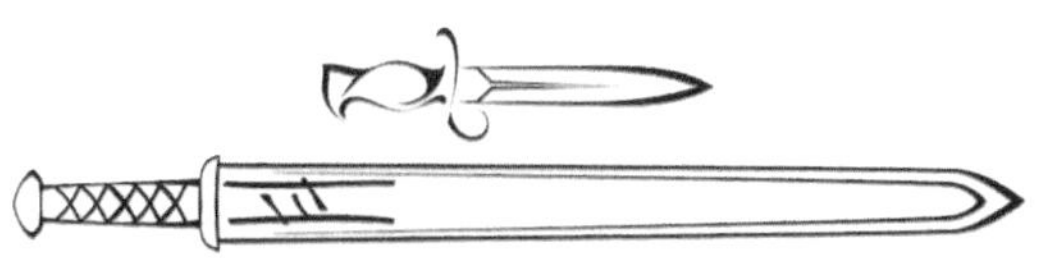

39

The more preparations they made for the party, the more Grayden's unease grew. Getting in to talk to Elan for a few minutes and convince him of their sincerity was one thing. Spending an entire evening with him and his friends celebrating his promotion to Regeont while attempting to ensure that nobody noticed Miri breaking in and rifling through his study was a completely different and altogether more difficult proposition. Far too many things could go wrong. They had already lost Ulia; Grayden feared that this was their last chance to both clear Lord Adelfried's name and implicate Elan in the murder of the Regeont. If they failed at this task, they would not get another chance.

At five bells, Grayden and Beren stood nervously outside the Manor once more. They were splendid in their dress uniforms, which Niveya's servants had pressed and starched until the fabric was so stiff that Grayden was certain he would not be able to move. But Miri had given them an eyebrow raise of approval, which was rather a high compliment, so Grayden knew they looked the part.

It was not a servant, but Lady Ilya herself, who opened the

door. She beamed at them and threw her arms around Beren in a joyous embrace.

"Berenger Adelfried! I am so glad you could tear yourself away from your duties to join us at this little gathering," she enthused. "When my brother told me I had missed you yesterday, I could hardly bear it. Please, please, come in. A few of the others have already arrived, and we are just waiting for a few more of our friends before we get started with the celebration. You cannot know how good it is to see you." She grabbed them each by the arm and propelled them into the Manor. "And you are Grayden. I remember we met last year," she added. "Please, set yourself at ease; any friend of Berenger's is a friend of ours."

She ushered them into the large dining hall. The main low table had been removed, and narrow tables now lined the walls at serving height. Guests mingled about the room, conversing and laughing. A small band of musicians stood in one corner, warming up and tuning their instruments. Grayden's stomach did a complete flip. There had to be at least a hundred people already in the room. He threw a panicked look at Beren, who caught his eye and held it, his expression calm. Grayden took a deep breath. Beren was right. There was nothing they could do but continue with the plan and hope that the larger-than-expected crowd would provide a greater distraction for Elan and the guards.

A servant brought them wine goblets on an elaborately decorated silver tray.

"Elan will join us shortly," Ilya said, taking a goblet.

"Where is he?" Beren asked.

"He was called away." Ilya fluttered a hand. "Nothing urgent, I'm sure."

Grayden's stomach froze and clenched. "Called away?" He tried to keep his tone bored and neutral.

Ilya nodded.

"So soon before his celebration dinner?" Beren sounded aggrieved as he plucked a goblet from the tray. "Where was he called off to?"

"The city prison." Ilya waved a hand. "Apparently Headmaster Freidzen was there speaking with the mercenaries this morning, and he sent Elan an urgent summons. Who knows what they're saying now?" She put a hand on Beren's arm. "Don't you worry, dear. Elan is doing everything in his power to clear your father's name."

"I'll bet," Beren muttered.

Alarmed at his friend's careless comment and tone, Grayden pretended to lose his balance, knocking into Beren and sending his glass crashing to the floor. Lady Ilya gave a little shriek, stepping away from the spatter of liquid, but as Grayden had no wish for her to exit the room and change, the wine missed her by a generous margin, spilling harmlessly on the tiles.

"Oh!" he exclaimed. "I'm so sorry! So clumsy of me... I must be nervous. This is such a gallant occasion... and I'm just... used to the farm." He focused on his feelings of embarrassment and unease until he could feel his ears burning. "I confess I am out of my element."

Lady Ilya examined her dress, but upon finding no stains, she gave a little laugh and turned to Beren. "Your friend is quite the country boy, isn't he?" she said archly. "This event is a tad above his station."

"Quite," Beren agreed, giving Grayden a glare as servants rushed over to clean up the mess he had made. "Won't you excuse us for just a moment? I think my friend needs me to help him calm down a bit."

"Of course." Ilya's smile was gracious. "I mustn't neglect my other guests, just because one of my favorite people is here."

Beren beamed at her as he and Grayden exited the dining room.

"Thanks," Beren muttered as they stood in the hall. "That just slipped out. I was so rattled by her news about where Elan is right now. If the mercenaries took Niveya's advice, this timing could ruin everything."

"I know." Grayden rubbed his hands down his face. "But we

need to continue with the plan. There's no way to alert Niveya or Miri to this development, and even if the mercenaries did tell Headmaster Freidzen what they told us, that doesn't mean he knows Elan was involved. And it doesn't mean Elan will have any inkling that we are investigating him."

"But it could spook Elan," Beren whispered. "He'll have his guard up, be jumping at shadows and suspicious of everything. We can't say a single wrong word."

"Well, thankfully, our job is simply to be guests at a celebration. Just remember, if Elan says anything about your father's name being cleared, act surprised and grateful or relieved."

"Right," Beren agreed.

Footsteps echoed from down the hall. Grayden felt his body tense and forced himself to relax as Lord Elan appeared. The new Regeont caught sight of them and beamed.

"I am so glad you could make it," Elan said, approaching them with his arms outspread. He glanced between them. "Is something wrong?"

"No," Beren hastily replied. "My friend nearly spilled his drink all over your sister... this sort of grand occasion is overwhelming for him. I thought maybe stepping out of the crowd for a moment would help calm him down."

Elan put a sympathetic hand on Grayden's shoulder. "It is a hard thing, being out of one's element," he said. "But we are all friends here. Please, come in and enjoy yourself."

Elan reached for the door, then paused. "Oh, Beren, I have just come from the city jailhouse."

Beren shot Grayden a nervous glance. "Yes?"

Elan stared at him for a moment. "Right. You are probably too new to your posting to know this, but that is where the mercenaries who attacked the Academy are being held."

"I see," Beren replied, his voice even. "Are there any fresh developments in the investigation?"

Elan lowered his eyes. "Sadly, no."

There was a long pause.

"Beren," Elan said, "you do not need to worry. I am officially dropping the investigation here in Doran. Duke Langston has already voiced his reluctance to take this matter any further, and as nobody at the Academy was hurt, I have no wish to see any more harm come to your father's good name. Nobody believes these wild and ridiculous claims, and no good can come of allowing them any further credence."

"You're dropping the investigation?" Grayden asked. "What does that mean?"

"It means that we are going to move beyond this unpleasant business and focus on the future. As a defender, surely you are aware of the tensions rising between Telmondir and the Igyeum. We need to spend our energy there, and not on these petty squabbles at home."

"I'm not sure I understand," Beren said. "What of the mercenaries? Shouldn't we continue to investigate who hired them and why?"

"They will serve their time, but with no further leads, there is little we can do." Elan spread his arms in a helpless gesture. "I thought you would be happy about this news."

"Happy?" Beren sounded mystified.

Grayden tried to catch his friend's eye to issue him a warning, but Beren was fixated on Elan.

"What, exactly, is there to be happy about in this news?" Beren demanded.

"Why, that your father is no longer under investigation, of course." Elan's smile faltered.

Beren's face reddened. "That is not the same as having his name cleared. As a son of such a prestigious family, you cannot make me believe you do not understand the shame and embarrassment this has brought upon my father and my family. To have the investigation dropped is nothing like the same as being proven innocent, of having one's honor restored. My father will never be able to hold his head up in Ondoura again. Surely you do not expect me to tolerate such incompetence."

Elan narrowed his eyes. "Whom are you accusing of incompetence? Choose your words carefully, cousin."

Beren gritted his teeth. "Whomever is heading up this investigation."

The door to the dining room swung open and Ilya peeked out. "Oh, there you are, brother!" she gushed, wrapping a hand around his arm and pulling him toward the doorway. "I'm so glad you've joined us. Your guests are getting impatient to celebrate."

As she propelled him into the dining room, Elan met Beren's gaze. "The head of the investigation is your Uncle Freidzen. I suggest you take up this argument with him if you have further complaints." His face smoothed into a smiling mask. "But for now, no more talk of business, please. Eat, drink, and enjoy yourselves."

Beren and Grayden followed Elan through the doorway, staying a few paces behind. The crowd in the hall cheered at his arrival. Elan raised his arms and gave a rousing speech that Grayden paid little attention to. The musicians played a lighthearted tune, and a few couples made their way into the middle of the room and began dancing.

"If you had gotten us kicked out, everything would have been over," he hissed at Beren from behind his glass.

Beren glared at him.

"Look, I know it wasn't what you expected to hear, but we know the truth. It's up to us to prove it." Grayden tried to console his friend.

"He knows me too well to believe I would take his news with a sigh of relief," Beren whispered calmly. "I had to show him Telsuman pride or he would have been suspicious."

Grayden chewed on this for a minute, then glanced Elan's way. The man had moved on and was laughing with another guest, seemingly unconcerned by Beren's outburst of a few moments ago.

"Why didn't the mercenaries take Niveya's advice?" Beren muttered.

Grayden's brow creased. "They had little enough reason to trust him." A thought struck him. "Maybe they did."

"What do you mean?"

"We don't actually know what they told Headmaster Freidzen. All we know is what Freidzen told Lord Elan. Think about it. If you were investigating this strange set of occurrences, and the mercenaries suddenly changed their story and told you that their orders came from within the Manor and that the money was under the seal of the Regeont, would you trust anyone from the Manor? Or would you tell Elan that the investigation was stalled and couldn't go any further?"

"You make a good point," Beren admitted. "But what if you're wrong?"

"At the moment, we don't know what the situation is," Grayden said. "We have to focus on our current mission. Tomorrow, we can go to the Academy and talk with the headmaster, especially if we have any further evidence to present. But we need to stay focused here, for now."

Beren nodded. "Have you seen any sign of Miri?"

"No. And if she's as good at her job as we hope she is, then we won't." Grayden let his eyes wander over the guests, scanning the room for any signs of disturbance.

"Are you looking for someone in particular?" Ilya's voice from behind them nearly made Grayden spill his drink for real.

"No," he assured her. "The chances of me knowing anyone in this crowd are quite small."

She smiled at him, then turned her attention to Beren. "Cousin, be a dear and go give a toast. You've known Elan longer than anyone else here. All the other stories are turning out stuffy and boring, and I was so hoping this party would be more entertaining."

"I'm not comfortable speaking in front of such large crowds," Beren said.

"Oh, please, I insist," Ilya urged. "As the eldest son of the

Lord Adelfried, you're going to have to get used to it. Besides, it will give me some time to get acquainted with your friend."

Beren shot Grayden an apologetic grimace and wove his way through the crowd toward the front of the room.

Ilya turned to Grayden with a coy smile. "He probably doesn't have any stories, either," she whispered in a conspiratorial tone. "Our families have known each other for ages, but Beren was always better friends with Ioan; they were closer in age. Cathrine and I got on rather well." She shook her head and smiled impishly at Grayden. "You don't look like you're having any fun. Or is it just that you defenders all learn to practice that aloof stare? What *have* you and my cousin been discussing over here? You both looked rather pensive."

"Your brother gave Beren some disturbing news about a turn the investigation into his father has taken," Grayden said. "I'm afraid I had begun to believe the rumors about Lord Adelfried. Beren took some offense. But I am having a lovely time, Lady Ilya. I apologize if I have been a bit too preoccupied consoling a friend to spend time laughing at jokes."

"Ooh," Ilya cooed. "A sharp tongue resides in that gentle, country face. I like it." She leaned closer to him. "But I couldn't help but overhear Beren asking if you had seen someone named Miri. Who is Miri? I don't believe I remember putting her name on any guest list."

Grayden hesitated, his mind racing through his options. Then he forced a laugh. "You misunderstood, my lady." He stared down at his boots, shifting a bit and doing his best to look embarrassed. "Beren didn't mean here at the party. He meant..."

"Yes?" Ilya's gaze was intense.

"Well... there's... this girl," Grayden admitted, his mind whirling to make up a convincing story. "She works at a patisserie on one of the streets on our rounds. I've... I've been making excuses to stop in every day, just hoping to catch a glimpse of her. I don't think she knows I exist... but Beren's taken to teasing me."

"How cruel of him." Ilya fanned herself with a hand. "To mock love in such a way."

"I don't know if I'd call it..."

"Don't lie to me. I can see clearly that you love this girl. You must tell her," Ilya urged. "If you don't, another may sweep her up and you would regret your silence for the rest of your life."

"Well..." Grayden gave a sheepish grin. "Maybe you're right." He straightened. "Maybe I will tell her tomorrow. But perhaps..." He paused, giving Ilya an impish smile. "Perhaps it would give my courage a boost if I could have a dance with such a beautiful woman as yourself?" He gave a bow and stretched out his hand.

Ilya's cheeks reddened, and her lips curved up in a delighted grin. "I cannot deny such a charming offer." She took his hand and they whirled out onto the dance floor.

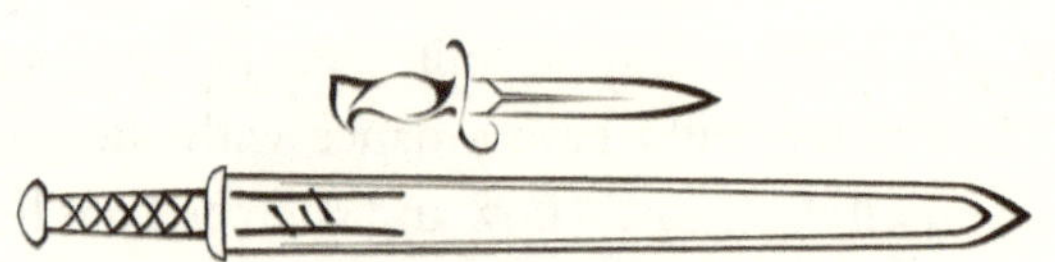

40

Grayden danced six more numbers with Lady Ilya before another man drew up the nerve to cut in and claim her as his partner. Laughing, Ilya whirled away without a backward glance. Grayden drew a long sigh of relief as he backed his way off the dance floor, avoiding eye-contact with any of the women sashaying about or waiting with anxious expressions for someone to ask them. At any other party, he would have been pleased to beg any of them for a dance. One pretty young woman had caught his eye; one nobody had yet asked to dance. He could not fathom why this might be, but it was not an injustice he could solve at the moment. Grabbing another glass of wine, he made a surreptitious sweeping glance of the room and let himself out of the party and into the hallway.

Standing in the silence was both disorienting and liberating. He could still hear the laughter and revelry on the other side of the door, but in a muffled, disconnected sort of way. Glancing up and down the hall, he made his way to the study. Despite what he had told Beren, he was anxious to make sure the plan experienced no snags.

He found the study door and pushed it open. The interior of the room was dark, lit only by a little moonlight trickling in through the window. Grayden stood still, listening. No sound reached his ears. He frowned. Miri should be here by now. But no shadowy figure lurked in the corners, no papers rustled, nothing appeared disturbed. Had she finished already? He strode over to the window and peered out. No movement or sound interrupted the peaceful night.

A light tap on the glass made him look down. A dark face stared up at him, shrouded in shadows, her back to the moon, but her curly halo of hair let him know instantly that it was Miri. She waved a hand with an impatient gesture. Setting his glass on the desk, Grayden quickly opened the window and Miri slipped inside.

"I'd almost given up," she whispered. "This place is locked up tighter than a prison. A lot tighter." She twirled her dagger.

"I thought entering was your area of expertise," Grayden said. "What's the problem?"

"You try breaking into a house where half the windows don't actually open." Miri scowled.

"The night is wearing thin. We don't have much time."

Miri waved a hand. "You've obviously never been to a party like this one before. Believe me, they're just getting started." She stepped over to the large desk, opening drawers and shuffling through papers. He noted with some relief that she appeared to be taking care to put everything back exactly as it had been before she picked it up. She came to a drawer that did not open. She pulled on it, rattling it a bit. The noise grated against Grayden's ears, and he flinched.

"This one's locked," she said, pulling out a dagger. "I wonder what's hiding inside." She fiddled with it for a moment, sat back, stared at it, then fiddled with it again.

A suspicion grew in Grayden's mind. "Just how many places have you broken into before tonight?" he asked.

"I lost count a long time ago," Miri said, working the dagger against the lock.

"How many places were like this one?"

"No places in Doran are like this one."

"I mean, how many were well-guarded and had locks?" Grayden pressed.

"The Regeont's Manor is unique." Miri continued to work.

"Look, I know you probably have a reputation to maintain, being Lady Jynna's daughter and everything, but I need to know... how good at this are you, really?"

The lock clicked and Miri slid the drawer out. Grayden could not see her expression in the dim light.

"I am a capable member of my mother's crew. That's all you need to know." Miri held up a large, leather-bound book. "I think this is what we're looking for."

Footsteps sounded in the hall outside the door. Grayden's heart thundered in his ears. He whirled, searching frantically for a place to hide. His eyes lit on the curtains, but he dismissed them as an obvious choice—there was little else in the room other than the desk and a few chairs; nothing presented itself as a good place to hide. He stared at Miri with wide eyes. In a flash, she picked up the goblet he had set on the desk and threw its contents at his face. Before he could react, she dove under the desk. Sputtering and wiping the liquid off with a handkerchief, he scanned the room again.

The doorknob clicked. Understanding Miri's intent, Grayden grabbed a decorative pillow from the nearest chair and threw himself on the floor on top of it. As the door swung open, he closed his eyes and forced himself to take long, slow breaths.

"You there!" the voice rang out. Grayden resisted the urge to leap to his feet and dash out of the room. Instead, he drew a long, noisy breath.

"What's the trouble?" another voice asked.

"Thought I heard a noise in the Regeont's study," the first voice said. "Came down to check in and look what I found!"

The voices stopped and footsteps sounded, approaching Grayden's position. A light fell on his face, but he did not flinch.

"Looks like this one got a little lost and maybe had a little too much to drink." The second voice sounded amused.

"What should we do with him? We can't leave him like this. He shouldn't be in the study. Regeont Elan made it clear that we should keep this room secure; it's off-limits to the guests."

"You think he's a thief?" the second guard guffawed. "Sure, because thieves who think they're about to get caught pretend to be sleeping on the hard floor in plain sight. It's brilliant! You've solved the case! Why didn't I think of that?"

"There's no cause for you to be mocking me." The first guard's voice lowered to a mutter. "I'm just trying to follow orders."

"Look, we'll try to wake him up, and either take him back to the party or go put him in one of the guest rooms until he sleeps it off."

"Do you think that's wise? What if he's not a party guest but a thief?"

"Don't be ridiculous. If he were a thief, why would he be in this room? Lord Elan doesn't keep valuables in here."

"That's a good point."

"And look at what he's wearing, dressed up in his finest, he is. Does that look like anything a thief might wear?"

"I don't know."

"Of course you don't know. You're new here. And that's the point. I'm going to wake him up."

A large hand patted at Grayden's face. He snorted, but kept his eyes shut.

"Smells like wine," the second guard commented, crouching over him. "Come on, then, wake up, good sir."

"Another dance, my lady?" Grayden mumbled, rolling over and curling his knees up to his chest.

The guards chuckled.

"Looks like you're right," the first guard admitted.

"I usually am. The sooner you learn that, the farther you'll go. Come on, help me carry him to a guest room."

Grayden allowed himself to go limp as the two guards carried him out of the study and down the hall; they laid him on a bed and left him there. He waited, counting in his head until a reasonable amount of time had passed before he opened his eyes and sat up. He wondered where Miri had disappeared to when the guards entered the room. Presumably, she had simply ducked behind the desk and allowed Grayden to occupy their attention. He hoped she could get out of the study by herself. He certainly couldn't go back there. Neither could Beren; if the guards discovered two party guests in the study, it would seem far too much like an actual plot, and uncomfortable questions might get asked. No, Miri was on her own now.

He waited a few minutes more, giving the guards time to make their way farther on their rounds and giving his nerves a chance to calm down. Then he got up, buttoned up his jacket to cover the spatter of wine spots on his shirt, and headed back to the dining hall and the party.

"Where have you been?" Beren muttered at Grayden as he wandered over to stand next to him. "Ilya seems to have taken a shine to you, and I had to make all sorts of excuses."

"I'll tell you about it later," Grayden replied. "Thanks for covering for me. I think we're going to be receiving some new orders."

Beren gave him a questioning look. "Really?"

Grayden nodded.

"There you are!" Ilya slipped her arm through Grayden's and patted it possessively. "You mustn't disappear like that again. I missed you." She gazed up at him with a pout.

"Forgive me, my lady. I received a message from our captain. It looks like Beren and I are going to be reassigned."

"Reassigned? But you just got here!"

Grayden gave an elaborate shrug. "That's the nature of a duty like ours. It can be a cruel master, even to its most faithful."

"I had hoped they would keep you in Doran for a while." She sighed mournfully. "Everyone we socialize with are such bores."

"Perhaps you need to widen your social circle," Grayden suggested.

Ilya's laugh rang out like the tinkling of bells. False bells, Grayden thought, trying not to wince.

"Oh, you are too funny," she purred. "Well, if all else fails, perhaps I will take your advice."

"One last dance, my lady?" Grayden asked as the musicians' break ended and they began a new song.

"Only one?"

"I'm afraid so." Grayden smiled apologetically. "Beren has special permission from our captain to stay out late. Unfortunately, his good humor did not extend to me."

Beren's eyes widened, and he scowled fiercely at Grayden, who pretended not to notice.

"One more dance, before I am deprived of the ability to look upon your lovely face?" Grayden raised her hand to his lips.

Ilya giggled and blushed, then curtsied and allowed him to lead her into a dance. He put every bit of skill he had into the dance, and Ilya's delighted laughter rang out across the room. As the song ended and another began, Grayden whirled her off into the arms of a new partner, where she clung to the man's shoulders, breathless and laughing. Grayden strode over to Beren and patted him on the shoulder.

"Forgive me, but I think I've reached my limit."

"What am I supposed to do? Stay here all night?" Beren asked.

"I'm sure you'll think up a good excuse to leave." Grayden grinned.

"Why couldn't you have said our captain wanted us both back?"

"You? A good friend of the Regeont's and the son of Lord Adelfried? That doesn't sound very likely, now does it?"

"You are enjoying this far too much," Beren accused.

"Maybe a little."

"I hate these parties."

"Find a pretty girl, dance the night away. It'll be good for you."

"I hate you."

"Fair enough." Grayden shot him another grin before making his way to the door.

There was no sign of Miri anywhere inside as he made his way back to the front door, though Grayden did not risk peeking into the study before he left the Manor. As he trotted down the steps, he almost ran into a guard.

"Oh! I beg your pardon," Grayden said.

"Leaving already?" the guard asked.

"I have an important meeting in the morning," Grayden replied smoothly. "I hate to miss the rest of the celebration, but duty calls. You understand."

"Duty." The guard straightened, raising his lantern higher. "I can understand that very well, young master." As the light from the lantern fell on Grayden's face, the guard's demeanor changed. He peered at Grayden quizzically. "Do I know you?" His voice rang in Grayden's memory. It was the guard who had found him "asleep" in the study.

"I don't think so?" Grayden replied.

The guard stared at him for a long, uncomfortable minute, during which Grayden forced himself not to edge away nervously. Then he shook his head. "I'm sorry, that was impolite. Need me to call you a carriage?"

"Thank you, but I can walk to my destination. The night air and a brisk walk will help me sleep better."

"Very good, sir. Be careful. The city guard patrols this area well, but there are pickpockets about. We can't catch them all."

"Thank you for the warning." Grayden sauntered into the night, whistling a merry tune that he had danced to earlier in the evening.

41

Time stood still. The arrow struck before Ioan could move or do anything to stop it. Ioan watched Dalmir's eyes flutter closed. With a shout, he reached out to catch the older man, but the aton got there first. With an uncanny speed and a surprising amount of gentleness, she wrapped Dalmir in her arms, scooping him off the ground before he fell, lifting him like a small child. Frieda turned and stared at the young man who had fired the arrow, fixing him with a stern gaze for a long moment.

Aron wilted beneath her silent reprimand. The bow fell from his hand, landing with a soft thud on the green grass. He dropped to his knees beside it, his shoulders shaking with sobs. Ioan recognized the signs of a man who had never before committed violence and he felt a pang of sympathy for the boy, who had simply been attempting to defend his home and his people from what he perceived to be a threat to their very existence. But he had no time to spare for the lad. He had seen wounds like the one Dalmir had sustained, and he knew there was little time if the older man were to have any chance at surviving. He stepped up beside Frieda and pulled a bundle of cloth out of his pack, pressing it around the wound in a desperate attempt to stanch the bleeding.

Time caught up, and the crowd erupted into a chorus of frightened exclamations and loud shouts directed at the young man, but Ioan blocked them out.

"Can you help him?" he asked Frieda in a low voice.

Frieda gave a jerky nod. "If we can get him out of the tower, beyond the boundary my master erected to keep us safe, his own power should do the rest. But we have little time. As soon as I leave this place, the energy that sustains this settlement will fade and all they have built will be lost. Dalmir gave the correct pass-code, and it has altered my directive: I must now do all that is in my power to aid and protect him, but..." Her pale, impassive face lifted and her gaze swept the settlement. "I have protected these people for so long, I cannot abandon them now."

"You won't have to," Ioan said. Turning to face the elders, Ioan raised his voice. "One of your own has done this terrible thing, raising a hand of violence against the one who was foretold, the Hope Bringer. Even now, his lifeblood drains from him, staining the very ground you have toiled over for so many generations."

He saw a few faces grow pale, and he raised a fist. "Because of this, time is no longer on our side. There is no more time to prepare. We must hasten away from this place, lest the curse of this misdeed falls upon your heads as it has fallen upon your land. But fear not, for hope was promised, and hope has come. Gather what you have brought and follow me, and together we shall leave this place and find you a new home."

A few voices raised in a weak cheer, but for the most part, the expressions on the people's faces were grim. Stoically, they lifted their sacks of food and clothes, mothers and fathers hoisted up their smallest children, and as one they looked to Ioan with expec-tant faces.

Ioan nodded. "Very well. I will show you the way. Drengur?"

The younger man started as though jerked from sleep. He stared at Ioan with wide, frightened eyes. "Ioan?"

"Show them the trapdoor."

Drengur nodded and sprang away, as though relieved to be given a task. Together, they led the people to the trapdoor through which they had come. Frieda followed Ioan, Dalmir in her arms, and behind her came the entire village. Silent and somber, they descended the ladder into Tel's workshop. There were too many of them to fit inside all at once, and soon they were spilling out onto the balcony that overlooked the ancient city.

"What is this?" one woman wailed. "Are we to throw ourselves down?"

A chorus of frightened and angry voices clamored together, but Ioan raised a hand.

"Don't be afraid!" he shouted. "We shall descend in safety." He stepped onto the platform that had brought them up. "In groups of thirty," he continued, "it will take several trips, but I or Drengur will ride with each group to prove that you will come to no harm."

Frieda joined him on the platform, and then a few brave souls shuffled forward and stepped trustingly out onto the lift with them.

"If Frieda goes with us," one old man grumbled in a cranky voice as he joined Ioan, "that's good enough for me." He turned and faced his fellow villagers. "And it ought to be good enough for each of you, too." He jabbed his cane at several of them, his face painted in a deep scowl. "Oughta be ashamed of yerselves! Cowards, the lot of you. Haven't I heard some of you aching for adventure? For freedom to leave our village? Haven't I heard our land called a 'gilded cage' in quiet whispers? Well, here comes someone to unlock the door, and all you can do is peck at his fingers and squawk!"

Several of the villagers shuffled their feet. Then a group of older men stepped out onto the platform. Years of training and discipline helped Ioan school his expression into one of stoic calm, but internally he heaved a sigh of relief as Frieda activated the lift and they descended into the city. Traveling back to the surface with several hundred people in tow would not be a simple task, but at least they were moving. His eyes flicked to Dalmir's still form, held in Frieda's arms. He could see the man's chest rising and falling, but his eyes remained closed. Urgency brimmed to overflowing. They had to get out of this tower.

42

I t had taken far longer than he had anticipated, but at least the prototype engine was complete. Wynn helped Daegan and Keene fit the mechanical marvel they had constructed inside the Trackless, his stomach doing enormous backflips the entire time. When it was affixed with the gears Wynn had designed inserted into the middle and attached to the great treads, they all stood back and admired their creation.

It was not a lovely vehicle. There were no graceful lines or delicate adornment, but Wynn thought it was beautiful, nonetheless. Its outer hull was boxy and made of steel plating that would protect the troops inside from enemy arrows. The great treads would carry them safely over terrain no horse could traverse. The Trackless could carry a complement of a hundred defenders and their gear, and would only use a fraction of the power an airship of the same size would need.

"Which one of you is going to try it out first?" Molly asked.

Wynn and Keene both turned to Daegan.

"No," Daegan protested. "You both put as much effort into this thing as I."

"But you have been working on this for years, my friend," Keene insisted.

"It will carry all of us," Daegan said, an air of finality about his tone.

"Very well," Keene conceded. "But you're driving."

Daegan's expression softened. "If you insist."

They all clambered into the armored transport, and Daegan took hold of the controls. The cynder thrummed to life inside its housing and as Daegan pushed forward on the throttle, the great treads turned. The Trackless lumbered forward. It was not silent. The treads around the gear-like wheels made a whirring, thunking sound, but their speed was already greater than anything Wynn had dared hope for. But the greatest test was still to come. Daegan pushed the right lever forward one notch while pulling the left lever back one notch. Wynn held his breath. The Trackless gave a little shudder, then spun to the left without complaint, its turn radius tight and responsive.

Molly let out a little cheer and threw her arms around Wynn's neck. Wynn embraced her, lifting her off her feet and twirling her around in the spacious compartment that would carry their troops. The Trackless rumbled over an outcropping of rock, causing Wynn to lose his balance. They tumbled to the floor, where Wynn's head cracked painfully against the metal plating, but he held Molly in his arms, protecting her and cushioning her fall as best he could.

"Ooh, did that hurt? Are you okay?" Molly peered into his face, her brows knit in concern.

"The Trackless works," Wynn gasped out, trying to recover his breath from wherever he had lost it. "I'm perfect."

"I meant your head." Molly pushed herself to her knees and helped Wynn sit, her fingers probing the back of his head. "Well, you're not bleeding, anyway," she said at last.

Wynn beamed up at her. "It works!"

Molly chuckled and lightly slapped his shoulder. "Yes, it works. I'm proud of you. We should incorporate some sort of safety harnesses though."

"I have so many more ideas." Wynn pulled himself to his feet. "This could change everything."

She shook her head at him. "Can't you just enjoy this moment?"

But Wynn barely heard her. The Trackless worked, and a dozen new ideas now clamored for attention in his mind. He couldn't wait to get back to the workroom and start sketching out his plans. Using the things they had learned with the Trackless, they could make airships faster, more maneuverable, and more efficient. He wondered if there might be a way to build an airship light enough or with wings like a bird so that cynders would not be required to do all the heavy lifting. What a wonderful accident the explosion of that cynder had been!

Explosion.

A terrible idea penetrated his thoughts, halting the sudden creative onslaught. Emerging from the hole he had buried it in, the snaking tendrils of the idea crept back into his consciousness with a gleeful vengeance. He tried to avert his thoughts, but it was too late, the idea had already taken hold of his mind. A shudder ran through him as he approached the idea cautiously, turning it over in his mind, probing at it for weaknesses. It might work... but he despised himself for thinking of it. As if trying to lift a heavy object, Wynn tried to throw the idea to the side where he could ignore it, but it remained in the center of his thoughts like a rusty bolt that would not come loose no matter how much torque he applied to his wrench.

The terrible thought would not leave him alone. He closed his eyes and shook his head, trying to clear the idea away. Shouts made his eyes fly open. The Trackless ground to a halt and Wynn frowned, wondering what had gone wrong.

He looked about, and then saw to his amazement a crowd of people climbing the path below. They looked dirty and weary, even from this distance, but one of them stood out, striding with an inhuman, fluid motion, carrying another figure in its arms. Wynn squinted. Next to the tall figure, he saw one he recognized.

"Ioan!" he shouted. He hopped out of the Trackless and dashed down the path to greet the new arrivals, a thousand questions burning on his tongue. When he got closer, however, all the questions dissolved into one.

He stared at the tall figure carrying Dalmir in its arms, wonder-struck. Every word he had ever known disappeared from his memory and he merely stood, gaping.

"Wynn!" Ioan approached. "It's good to see you again. We need to get Dalmir inside, and I need to find a place for all these people to rest until we can get them better accommodations. Can you show Frieda inside? I'm worried about Dalmir, and I'm hoping Aunt Nadia can help him."

"Frieda?" Wynn's voice quavered with uncertainty as he looked up into the porcelain face towering above him. It was a face, a beautiful face, though expressionless. The creature turned its head to study him. "What... what is it?" he whispered.

"I can explain everything later," Ioan promised. "But for right now, explanations and questions are going to have to wait."

Wynn nodded, his eyes flicking to Dalmir's limp form. He cleared his throat and looked up at the figure. "Uh... yeah. Frieda, was it? This way."

He led the strange creature to the house, his mind whirling with questions.

Upon seeing Dalmir, Lady Nadia gasped and ushered them inside. Frieda placed Dalmir on a bed and Nadia tended to him with gentle hands. Calling to Cathrine to bring hot water and bandages, she peeled aside his blood-soaked clothes with an astonishing combination of haste and care. As she pulled back the final layers, she paused, her expression furrowing into a puzzled frown.

"What's wrong?" Wynn asked, standing in the doorway. He felt useless. Nobody had given him a task, and the strange, mechanical person stood quietly in the hall. Wynn tried to ignore it, knowing that it was not the time for questions. Could it talk? Would it make decisions on its own, or did it need directions? Who had built it? How was it powered? No... it was not the time for questions, but he could not hold back the floodgates in his mind.

Nadia turned to him and gestured him closer, and Wynn paced into the room to join her. "There is no open wound. I don't understand it; from the amount of blood on his clothes I would have guessed..." She waved her hand over Dalmir's chest. "There is just an ugly mark here, like a recent scar. Did Ioan say what had happened to him?"

"Arrow wound," Ioan replied from the doorway. He gave a weary smile and came over to put an arm around Nadia's shoulders. "About two weeks ago. We've been traveling as fast as we could since then to get here."

"It can't have been at very close range, or very deep," Nadia said.

"Point-blank," Ioan replied. "The arrow almost went right through him. I thought he was going to die before I could get him out of the tower."

Nadia and Wynn stared at him in uncomprehending silence.

Ioan grimaced. "Forgive me, I'm exhausted. There is just so much to tell you." He gestured at Dalmir. "Can you do anything for him? He hasn't woken since it happened. The wound has been healing itself, rather swiftly, as you can see, but he hasn't woken. It worries me, I've managed to force little trickles of water and broth down his throat... but..." He trailed off, shaking his head.

Nadia stood, wiping her hands on her apron briskly. "Broth," she announced with a firm nod of her head. "I'll just go tell Cathrine to get a nice big pot of it started. We'll get him cleaned up and into some clean clothes as well." She fixed Ioan with a stare. "And then you have some explaining to do."

―――――

Ioan's story was incredible. If the aton had not been standing in the corner the entire time he was telling about the adventure, Wynn would have been hard-pressed to believe it had all really happened. But the evidence stood there before his eyes. He determined to talk to the aton as soon as he could, but by the time Ioan had finished telling his story and they had eaten a late supper, Wynn was having a hard time keeping his eyes open. It had been a long, emotional day, so he made his way to his own room, pulled off his boots, and fell into bed.

However, as his head hit the pillow, the terrible idea that had occurred to him earlier that afternoon hammered its way into his thoughts once again. It was a way to create a weapon that would be devastating on the battlefield. Wynn flipped over in bed and pulled his pillow over his head, as if he could hide from the thoughts swirling in his brain, but he could not find a way to turn his brain off. Eventually, he gave up. Getting up, he lit his lantern, pulled out a fresh sheet of paper, and began sketching a diagram for how he could build the terrible weapon.

It was a long night.

43

Shaesta's words rang in Oleck's heart even as he stomped up the stairs to the deck of the sky barge. Of course they couldn't just leave the *Hawk* behind. But how could they take it with them? The damage to the airship was extensive: beyond repair. Anger filled him to the brim and threatened to spill over, as it already had in the hateful torrent of words he had thrown at Shaesta. His conscience twinged at the memory of her expression, all shock and hurt, but he pushed the feeling of remorse aside, clinging to his rage because anything was better than the all-consuming helplessness that threatened to overwhelm him.

Restless, Oleck went to check on Marik. His captain still lay on the pallet, his breathing even, his eyes closed. Oleck sat down next to him, staring at the wall, his mind churning.

"Cap'n?"

Marik's eyelids flickered but did not open.

"Cap'n..." Oleck sighed. "I wish you were awake. I'm no leader, never have been. And now... everyone's looking at me. Mouse is hurt, bad hurt. You're hurt. The *Hawk* is..." He winced. He didn't want to think about the *Hawk*. "And you're not here to tell me what to do. What should I do, Cap'n?"

He sat still, his head bowed, waiting for an answer he knew wasn't coming. Marik did not waken. However, after a few minutes, he heard a rustle at the door and a polite clearing of a throat. Oleck craned his neck to see who had entered the room. Nando and Hrafn stood just inside the doorway, looking awkward.

"May we speak with you?" Nando's question was hesitant.

Oleck stood and joined them in the hall, not wanting to disturb Marik's rest.

"How is he?" Hrafn asked, his hoarse voice sounding subdued.

"The same," Oleck replied.

"Shaesta told us that Mouse needs to get to a doctor," Nando said. "But we were thinking about Mouse and Captain Marik, and of your airship…"

Oleck crossed his arms. "Did Shaesta say something to you?"

"What?" Nando asked. "No… this was something we were talking about amongst ourselves." She gave him a quizzical look.

Oleck waved a hand. "Forgive the interruption. Please, continue."

"There's no use drilling into solid rock," Hrafn said. "We have lost our home, but there is no reason you should lose yours."

"You're talking about taking the *Hawk* with us." It wasn't a question.

The two durven nodded, their expressions serious.

Oleck spread his arms in a helpless gesture. "If you have any ideas on how to do that, I'm open to them. I don't want to leave the *Hawk* behind any more than anyone else does, but she's smashed to pieces. I don't know of any way to fly her out of this forest. Besides, as you said, Mouse needs medical attention, and the way Shaesta talks, I don't think we have a lot of time for experimenting or repairing an airship."

"What if we towed her with the *Oddhaven*?" Nando suggested.

Oleck shook his head. "I thought of that. But this barge is too small to pull the entire weight of another airship."

"What if the *Hawk's* cynders could provide the lift?" Hrafn asked. "And the *Oddhaven* only had to pull her? I know the going would be slower, but I don't think it's an impossible task."

"That might work," Oleck mused. "But we'll have to find out if the *Hawk's* engines are even intact. I didn't think to check when we were there. I don't know how the lack of a trim sail will affect her ability to lift off the ground. If she's too lopsided, the *Oddhaven* won't be able to make much headway, dragging her behind."

"It's worth trying, though, isn't it?" Nando asked.

"Yes," Oleck admitted. "It's certainly worth a try. Shouldn't take too long, either. If this works, I'll need a couple of volunteers to ride on the *Hawk* and try to steer her as much as possible, but if she can lift herself, then towing her behind us should work. Those are a lot of 'ifs,' though." A flicker of hope ignited in his heart, followed by a bucketful of shame. "We'll need Shaesta's help." He stared at his feet. "I'll go talk to her now."

He trudged to the room where Mouse was being tended, knowing it was the most likely place for Shaesta to be. He was right. She was inside, doing what she could to dribble a bit of water into Mouse's mouth. She reached up a hand and brushed at her eyes, and he saw tears glinting on her cheeks. His heart dropped to his feet, and he shuffled them slightly. Her gaze rose at the sound. He saw her lips tighten and her eyes go hard as she turned her attention back to Mouse, stolidly ignoring his presence.

"Shay..." Oleck mumbled. She did not look up. "Look," he tried again. "I'm sorry 'bout what I said. It was uncalled for, I know that. You... you've been a big help these past few sennights, and I know you're trying to... to make it up to us. I was just so angry and frightened and... it all came out at you. And it wasn't fair, cuz it wasn't your fault."

Her shoulders were rigid. She did not turn to look at him.

"I'm no good with words," Oleck continued. "You know that. All I can say is I'm sorry. I am."

"It's fine." Shaesta moved a damp cloth over Mouse's forehead.

"It's not fine," Oleck disagreed. "I know it."

Shaesta shrugged.

Oleck felt his patience thinning, but he forced himself to stay calm. "Look, you don't have to forgive me. I guess I know I probably don't deserve it. But Nando and Hrafn have thought of a way for us to maybe rescue the *Hawk,* and we can't do it without you."

This caught her attention. She glanced up at him, her eyes wide.

"If..." Oleck cleared his throat and raised his eyebrows. "If the *Hawk's* cynder is still intact and if the engine room isn't smashed to pieces, it might provide the ship with enough lift that we can tow her behind us. It won't be easy and we won't be able to go anywhere quickly, but we might manage. Thing is, I'll need someone experienced at the *Hawk's* wheel." He studied her. "It could be dangerous; I'd understand if you don't want to."

She rose to her feet, brushing her skirts out. Her eyes shimmered a little in the dim light coming through the windows, but she managed a small smile.

"I'm willing to try if it means saving the *Hawk,*" she said.

"I thought you might say that." Oleck gave her a tentative grin. "And I am sorry. I had no call to say what I said. It was cruel of me, and you didn't deserve it."

A tear escaped Shaesta's eye and rolled down her cheek. She swiped it away quickly, sniffing. "Yes, I did. That's why it hurt so much."

Oleck lowered his head. "No. Mebbe... mebbe you deserved it a few lunats ago... but you've made your allegiance clear. And at the risk of your family. I shouldn't have said what I said."

"I'd like to be friends again, if you're willing to let me," Shaesta said, her voice small.

"I'd like that, too."

"Good." Shaesta gave him a tiny, tentative smile. "Now, let's go see if we can't salvage an airship."

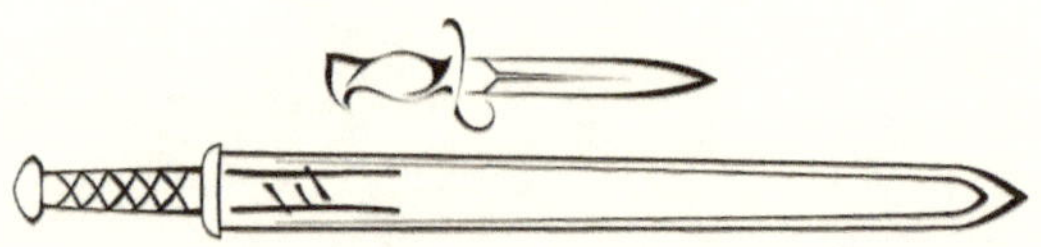

The next morning, they all gathered around as Niveya placed a large leather book on the table. "It looks like Mirianne has lived up to her promise," he said. "This ledger, as well as some other papers she found and recovered for us, appear to be enough to cast a large stain across Lord Elan's name. The numbers in this ledger match up to the ones in Lady Jynna's. There are no incriminating labels, of course, but it might be enough to convince the Council."

"That's not good enough," Beren objected. "Elan told me last night that they are dropping the investigation into the attack on the Academy."

Niveya's eyes narrowed. "Did he say why?"

"Lack of evidence."

"That is not good news." Niveya tapped the ledger on the table. "Headmaster Freidzen was at the prison yesterday. I assume he was there to interrogate the mercenaries again."

"Elan implied as much. He met Uncle Freidzen there before the celebration."

"Three possibilities." Niveya ticked them off. "One, the mercenaries took my advice and Freidzen is keeping the information they gave him to himself. That would be best, since it means

Elan doesn't know that anything in this case points to him. Two, they took my advice, but Freidzen told Elan, and now he's going to work even harder to cover his tracks. The fact that he told Beren that they're dropping the investigation indicates this to be the most likely scenario. Three, they didn't take my advice, which just means they have less sense than I gave them credit for."

"What should we do next?" Grayden asked. "I'm guessing it would be best to proceed as though the worst has happened."

"Yes," Niveya said. "That is my recommendation. Caution can no longer serve us well. We must assume that Elan is panicking, which means we have limited time, and we need solid proof."

"If he told anyone about his plot to have the Regeont assassinated, it was Lady Ilya," Grayden said. "I spent an inordinate amount of time dancing with her last night, and from what she said, it sounds like she is his right hand when it comes to the Regeoncy. If she is his confidant now, it's probably a safe gamble that she was before, as well."

"That's good to know," Miri piped up, sauntering into the room holding a pastry. "But how do you expect to get her to talk?"

"She seemed rather enamored with you." Beren arched an eyebrow at Grayden.

"I'd rather sort apples," Grayden muttered.

Niveya gazed at them, a thoughtful expression on his face. "Her infatuation with Grayden will be helpful. But first, I believe it is time to let the authorities know what we have discovered. If we can get Ilya alone, preferably away from the Manor, I want them present to hear her confession."

Beren stared, his mouth falling slightly open.

"What?" Niveya asked, noticing Beren's amazed expression.

Beren shook his head. "I'm sorry. I never expected to hear you advocate for bringing in the authorities."

"Vengeance is sweet," Niveya replied with a grim smile, "but in this case, the sweeter victory will be to see Roshana's murderer topple from the pedestal to which he has elevated himself. Now, we will have to set this up carefully if we wish to see it succeed."

———

"I WAS SO pleased to receive your note," Lady Ilya cooed at Grayden, her hands clasped tightly around his arm.

Grayden tried not to grimace as they walked down the street, the woman chattering in his ear about every bit of fluff that entered her brain. He regretted agreeing to this part of the plan, but he also knew it was the easiest way. And as Miri was fond of pointing out, simpler plans were the best. At least her brand of irritation was the teenage variety.

"So, where are we going on this mysterious outing you have planned for us?" Ilya asked for perhaps the hundredth time.

Grayden gritted his teeth and pasted as charming a smile as he could onto his face. "It's a surprise."

"I just love surprises," Ilya tittered. "Are you taking me to the patisserie you told me about? Shall we make your young lady jealous? That can be quite an effective way to make someone notice you."

Probably a good way to make sure the desired relationship never happens, too, Grayden thought. He could just imagine all manner of ways such a poorly contrived plan could fail or extract the opposite of the desired results. Thankfully, there was no actual young lady in danger of having jealousy stirred in her heart.

Out loud, Grayden said, "That is an excellent idea. Unfortunately, Miri is not working today. Perhaps another time. Today is just for you. I wanted to thank you for making me feel so welcome at the party the other night. It was so kind of you to dance so often with a simple country boy." He tried not to wince. Possibly he was laying it on just a touch too thick.

"Well." Ilya's cheeks flushed. "It is easy to pay attention to such a charming young man as yourself."

Grayden grinned and ducked his head in a semblance of bashfulness. He stopped in front of Niveya's safe house. "Here we are."

Ilya narrowed her eyes at the unbecoming door. "I do not believe I have been here before. What is this place?"

"It's owned by a man of various talents," Grayden said, opening the door and ushering Ilya inside. "He has many amusing distractions, and I thought a lady of your taste and stature would find them entertaining."

Ilya sashayed inside, exclaiming over the decor. "What exquisitely tasteful designs," she gushed, glancing about the luxurious parlor that stood in such stark contrast to the exterior of the house. Her attention roved to a painting, and she moved to examine it. "This is an impeccable copy of DeTante's *Seven Towers*!" she exclaimed. Her gaze swept to the next painting on the wall and her eyes widened. With quick steps, she moved to study it. Her flirtatious teasing fell away, replaced by the first genuine emotion Grayden had witnessed on her face. Ilya turned and stared at him, all playfulness gone. "How did you know about my passion for art?"

He gave her an honest grin. "I asked Beren," he said truthfully.

"This..." She indicated the painting before her. "This is not possible. If I did not know better, I would say it is a Llewian original."

"The lady has an eye for art." Niveya strode into the room. "Does she know the name of the piece?"

Ilya's face paled slightly. "Betrayal," she whispered.

"Excellent." Niveya beamed. "To know the artist is the mark of the educated, but the true connoisseur knows the individual pieces and can explain the artist's intent."

Ilya's lips curved upward in a shy, tentative smile. "Are you the curator of this amazing collection?"

Niveya took her hand and raised it to his lips. "I am. Do you like it?"

"It is breathtaking."

"Perhaps you would care to see the room where I keep my rarest items?"

Ilya's brows shot up. "Rarer than these?"

Niveya waved a hand. "These are mere trifles in comparison."

"Please!"

Niveya held out his arm, and led Ilya down the hall, Grayden trailing along behind. He ushered them into a small room. Inside the room sat a small table with a chair on either side.

"If my lady would have a seat?" Niveya asked.

Ilya settled herself in a chair, arranging her skirts with great attention to detail. Niveya gestured, and Headmaster Freidzen and the head of the city guard entered the room. Ilya looked up as they entered and ceased her skirt-smoothing, half-rising from her chair.

"What is this?" she demanded.

"We merely wished to have a conversation with you," Freidzen replied. "Please, sit back down, my lady."

Ilya's eyes locked onto Grayden's face and her expression turned stormy. "Did you know about this?"

"I'm afraid so, my lady," Grayden replied, leaning against the wall.

"Do you gentlemen have any idea who I am?" she hissed. "You cannot detain me here in this closet. I demand to speak with my brother."

"That is the problem," Freidzen said. "Your brother is the subject we wish to speak with you about."

Ilya's face drained of color. "Is he well? Did something happen?"

"He is quite healthy," Freidzen assured her. "But we had a conversation with him a few moments ago, as well. You see, some fresh evidence has come to light regarding the attack on the Academy, as well as the assassination of the late Regeont."

Ilya's expression turned quizzical. "The attack on the Academy? My brother said they were dropping the investigation due to a lack of evidence." She traced a tiny pattern on the top of the table. "A shame, too. I cannot believe Lord Adelfried would be involved in such a scandalous thing."

"It turns out he wasn't," the captain of the guard said, his voice dry.

Ilya looked up at him, her fingertip still moving in a slow pattern along the wood-grain of the table. "Oh?"

"That is part of the recent evidence," he replied. "The mercenaries now claim that the money they received for that job came from within the Manor itself."

Ilya's finger froze. "Within the Manor?" she whispered. "Are you saying... treachery?" Her eyes widened. "All this time, I've been living there... who would do such a thing? Why would anyone want to attack the Academy in the first place?"

"The attack was little more than a diversion," Freidzen replied. "To distract us from the Regeont's murder."

"What?" Ilya gasped.

Grayden had to give her credit. If she knew about Elan's scheme, she was doing an excellent job acting like she didn't.

"You sound surprised, Lady Ilya," Niveya said, seating himself across from her in the unoccupied chair.

"I am." Ilya wet her lips. "I am surprised."

"I believe you," Niveya said. "I believe the news that we have figured all of this out has quite startled you."

"What do you mean?" Ilya asked.

"I mean that it's all over. Elan already told us everything."

"He... did?"

"Yes." Niveya nodded, tossing the ledger onto the table next to her. "We've compared the amounts in here to the sums of money paid to the assassins and the mercenaries. When we confronted Elan about it, he realized that we already knew enough to topple him from the Regeoncy and he decided to cooperate. He told us about how you urged him to plot the assassination, and how it was your idea to create a distraction at the Academy and frame Lord Adelfried to throw the city and Council into confusion so that Elan could win the election with ease. He assured us he was the one who insisted that the mercenaries not hurt anyone. You were the one who hired the Motley Tailors to take care of getting Roshana out of the way, and you were the one who took matters into your own hands when the assassins failed."

"What?" Ilya's voice rose in pitch to a screeching level of outrage. "Every word of that is a lie!"

"Is it?" Niveya asked, his tone uninterested.

"Yes! It was all Elan's idea." Ilya leaned across the table, her gaze intense. "I will tell you everything, but only if you promise to keep me safe from him."

Niveya pushed his chair back and stood up. "Gentlemen?"

Freidzen took the chair and sat in it. "We can keep you safe."

Ilya's eyes grew watery. "It was all Elan's idea. He wanted to be Regeont. I told him to wait—Aunt Roshana was old, it was just a matter of time—but he was so impatient. I didn't want to, but he made me..." Ilya pressed her knuckles to her mouth and closed her eyes. "He created this complex plan with the distraction at the Academy and hiring multiple assassins... I tried to warn him that it wouldn't work, that there were too many moving parts... but he insisted that all the smoke and mirrors would keep anyone from ever finding out he was responsible. And then it all just..." Ilya's face drained of color. "The day came. We were in my sitting room. Elan was reading, and I was doing my needlework, when we heard loud noises coming from Aunt Roshana's study. There was a crash, and a loud scream, then we heard her calling for help..." Ilya paused and took a deep breath. "Then silence. Elan was triumphant, exulting in the success of his plan. He just had to go gloat. But when we got to Aunt Roshana's study, the door was open, and the Regeont was still alive. The last assassin stood there, facing her. He attacked, and then Aunt Roshana grabbed something out of the fire and..." Ilya closed her eyes, her face paling. "He screamed so loud. The smell of burning skin. Then he ran right at the window, screaming the whole time. Glass shattered everywhere."

Ilya winced. "Elan yelled at me to run, but I couldn't. I was frozen there. Aunt Roshana got to her feet and started asking Elan questions. At first, she was just making sure we were well, but then... I don't know... her questions kept coming, getting more and more suspicious, and then Elan... he... he had his fist wrapped around the shaft of one of the broken chair legs... I saw his arm go up, and then it crashed down on the back of Aunt Roshana's head. She never saw it coming, never suspected. She crumpled to the ground... sh-she didn't even whimper." Ilya stared about the room, her eyes wild. "I tried to ask him if she was... if she... Elan said he didn't know, and then he knelt down next to her. He lifted his arm again and... I ran. I didn't know where I was going, only that I couldn't stay there. It... it... that awful thudding, over and over again. I couldn't get it out of my head. I still can't!" Ilya's voice rose to a wail as hysterics finally got the best of her.

Niveya looked down at her, his lip curled in disgust, then he glanced up at Freidzen and the captain. "I believe that should be enough evidence?"

"Yes, that is plenty." Freidzen's voice was cold iron. "My brother-in-law will be relieved to hear that his name has been cleared."

Ilya's sobs cut off, her head lifting, her expression alarmed. "What do you mean?"

"They mean, my dear"—Niveya patted her shoulder—"that you have just given us the missing pieces to our puzzle. You have our deepest gratitude."

"But you said..." Ilya stared. She hiccoughed once. "No! But you said..."

"We said a lot of things," Niveya replied smoothly. "None of them were true."

"Except that we will honor our deal with you," the captain said.

"What deal?" Ilya asked.

"Our deal to keep you safe," the captain replied. "We have a lovely cottage all set up for you on Artaulia, where you will live out the rest of your days in peace."

"Artaulia?" Ilya whispered. "That horrible uninhabited island? I... I... you can't!"

"You write down everything you just told us, sign it, and mark it with your seal, and you can spend the rest of your days in peace and safety on Artaulia. Or you can join your brother in prison, awaiting execution," Freidzen replied. "It's your choice, of course."

Ilya lowered her head, her demeanor turning to meekness. "A cottage on Artaulia sounds most generous, thank you."

45

"Wynn?" Molly's voice at the door pierced Wynn's concentration. He hunched his shoulders, trying to turn invisible as he pulled a blank sheet of paper over the one he was currently working on. The door opened and a moment later, he felt a presence at his side; the gentle scent of her wafted around him, a combination of rosemary and mint. He could sense her confusion, confusion he had caused by avoiding her for the past several days, but he could not bring himself to look at her. How could he explain? What could he say? He was a monster.

"Wynn..." Molly paused. "Wynn, can you look at me?"

If only the mountain beneath him could suddenly cave in. If only he had never been born. What would she think of him if she knew? Wynn dipped his pen into the ink reservoir and idly sketched one of his other ideas, a safer idea.

"What is that you're working on?" Molly asked after a moment of silence. Her genuine interest made him feel even guiltier than he already did, but he tried to hide his discomfort.

"The Trackless made me think there might be ways to make our airships more efficient." He drew a few more lines, then began figuring through an equation that had been giving him some difficulty.

Molly craned over his shoulder, careful not to bump him or the table. He appreciated the care she took and turned slightly so she could better see what he was drawing.

"We found so many ways to make the engine more efficient, to get more power out of the smaller cynders. It's just…" Wynn trailed off.

"What's wrong?"

"I'd need a smaller ship to try this on," Wynn explained. "It wouldn't work on the heavy cargo cruisers, or even the lighter transport ships. I'd need something like Captain Marik's *Hawk* or smaller, but ships like that are rare." He waved a hand at the sketch. "Makes this feel like a waste of time."

"I don't think it's a waste of time," Molly said. "What if you built something from scratch?"

"We don't have the resources or time to build an entire airship," Wynn protested. "Daegan would tell me to focus on the things we can do. Now that the Trackless is working, he's sent the designs to the Oreworks teams with instructions to build more of them as quickly as possible. We probably don't have time to complete a whole new armada of airships, too."

"I still think it's at least worth figuring out," Molly argued. "Who knows when it might come in handy? What else are you working on?"

Wynn balked for a moment and Molly's eyes danced as her smile turned teasing. "You're never working on just one project. I know you better than that. Come on, show me."

Wynn hesitated, then shuffled through the papers and pulled another schematic out. Molly's eyes scanned it, her expression serious.

"This is nearly complete," she said, her tone awed.

Wynn nodded.

"You think something like this would actually work?" she asked, her voice incredulous.

"I do. What do you think?"

"Seems risky." Molly's mouth twisted to one side. "There isn't a lot to protect the defender flying it."

"These little skiffs would be faster than anything we've ever seen," Wynn said. "I think they'd be fairly hard to hit. And I've included armor like what we have on the Trackless here in front of the controls to protect the pilot."

Molly nodded. "How many defenders can they carry?"

"Two or three at most."

"What purpose were you thinking? Rescue? Dropping supplies?"

Wynn chewed on his lower lip but didn't answer.

Molly continued to scan the drawing, musing out loud. "They can't be used to attack. With that kind of speed and agility, I don't think even a crossbow would have enough power or accuracy to do much damage, the arrows would get caught in the wind."

Wynn's soul shriveled. He slammed the papers together, harder than he meant to, and dipped his pen. It went too deep into the reservoir and ink flooded up over the brim and spilled. Heaving an exasperated sigh and an incoherent, angry mutter, Wynn dumped a pile of sand over the spill, sopping up the ink before it could ruin his drawing.

"Are you all right?" Molly asked.

"Fine." The word came out with more snap to it than he intended and Wynn instantly wished he could take it back, but it hung between them like a blow. Molly recoiled slightly, and the storm clouds over Wynn's thoughts darkened and sparked lightning.

"What's wrong?" Molly's tone was pleading as she seemed to sense his mood. "You've always seemed to appreciate my questions. I didn't mean to frustrate you. Why... what did I do wrong?"

"Nothing," Wynn snapped. "I just need... I need some air." He gathered up all the papers, careful that she not see the designs he wished to keep hidden, and raced away from the workroom.

He dashed down the hall as though chased by rabid dogs, but he did not hear Molly following him. Wynn threw himself into his own room and stuffed the plans and schematics under his mattress. Then he stood, staring around wildly, his breath coming in swift, uncontrollable gasps. He couldn't breathe. He needed to get outside. Air, he needed air!

Cautiously, he poked his head out into the hallway. Molly did not appear. Careful to keep his footfalls soft and silent, Wynn crept down the hall to the back door. Outside, the sky had turned gray, and turbulent clouds rolled above him, matching his mood. Gusts of wind whipped at him and rustled through the scrubby bushes dotting the mountainside, but he barely noticed the signs of an impending storm. He stumbled down to the little footpath bordering the river. It was their path, his and Molly's. The one they had so often wandered together in the past evenings, seeking refreshment for their minds and clarity for their thoughts. His feet faltered as he reached the riverbank and he fell painfully to his knees on the rocks. The shallow water soaked through his trousers. Even though it was summer, the water this high in the mountains was always cold, and the icy chill bit into him without mercy. He relished the shock of it. It was less punishment than he deserved, but it was easier to embrace the pain than the truth.

He did not know how long he knelt there in the chilly waters of the river, staring numbly at the fish swimming about. Several of them nibbled at his knees, but moved on when they discovered he was not food. Wynn envied them their carefree nature. To be a fish... to have no thought for machines or war or death, to simply swim and eat, seemed far preferable to him than the crushing weight of responsibility he now bore.

"Wynn!"

Molly's voice drifted down to him. He did not move or respond. Perhaps she would not find him. Perhaps she would realize he was not worth searching for.

A moment later, he heard her shoes scraping against the dirt as she clambered down the bank and splashed into the water beside him. The light of her lantern swung about as she shook him, her worried face floating oddly before his eyes.

"Wynn! What are you doing? How long have you been... oh! You're freezing! You'll catch your death of cold!"

Her arms wrapped around his, pulling him up and directing him away from the river in her no-nonsense way. Numbly, he obeyed her directions. It didn't matter, anyway. She would find out soon enough what he was capable of.

"Wynn..." She paused. He could practically hear her pressing her lips together. He waited for the reprimand, the questions, the torrent of accusations and words.

They didn't come.

She snugged herself under his arm and guided him up the path. Curiosity elbowing aside the curtain of his shame, Wynn glanced at Molly out of the corner of his eye; she stood straight and tall as she half carried him away from the river. Her eyes flashed in the near-darkness, her lips pressed into a thin line, but whatever words she wanted to throw at him, she was keeping them tightly constrained.

He let her lead him back inside the forge, where blessed heat rolled over him in waves, bringing him slightly out of his stupor. He put up a mild resistance, then. She relaxed her hold on him and made as if to move away, but he reached out and put his hand over hers. She looked up at him, her eyes brimming with questions and tears. Wynn could not find the words, but he indicated the direction he was going to let her know he wanted her to come, her fingers tightened on his arm and now he was the one leading the way.

At his door, he stopped.

"I need to show you something." The words rasped from his throat.

Molly paled. "You should be in bed," she whispered. "What were you thinking? Sitting in the water like you did... and soup, you need..." She clamped her lips together, as though reading in his face the urgency he felt. "Show me."

He led her through the door and directed her to sit on the chair at his small writing desk. With trembling hands, he pulled the crumpled schematics out from under his mattress and laid them on the desk. Molly stared at him, her eyes wide and wondering. Setting the lantern on the desk, she peered down at the papers, smoothing them gently with her long fingers. She studied the plans in silence for long minutes.

Wynn felt as though snakes had made his entire torso into their nest and were slithering around inside his chest and stomach. His entire body shook with feverish shivers as Molly quietly read his notes. At length, she looked up at him, her expression confused.

"I don't understand," Molly said.

"It's the answer to your question about my skiffs," Wynn replied, hunching his shoulders. "How they can defend themselves, and how we can utilize them in an attack."

Molly made a quiet sound in her throat. He was not sure if it was disgust, frustration, or confusion. "I can read a schematic." She sounded irritated. "What I don't understand is why you didn't show this to me before? Has Daegan seen this? How long have you been working on it? This solves so many problems! Do you think we could make a larger version and affix it to the Trackless?"

Wynn stared at her dumbly. He felt his mouth open, but no sound came out.

Molly narrowed her eyes. "What's wrong?" she asked.

"I thought..." Wynn shook his head. His thoughts felt muddled and foggy. "I..." His nose tingled painfully as potential tears gathered, choking him. "You... you don't hate me?"

"What?" Molly half rose from the chair, concern chasing away her confused expression. "Did you hit your head? Why would I hate you?"

Wynn gestured feebly at the schematic. "For... being capable... of..." He searched frantically for the words to tell her everything he had thought and felt over the past few days, but they flitted about in his mind, refusing to let him grasp them. He began to shiver uncontrollably.

Molly's eyes flicked back and forth from his face to the paper, and he saw understanding dawn in her features. "Oh, Wynn..." Her arms rose toward him, then dropped to her sides. She sat heavily in the chair and put her face in her hands.

He stood there, awkwardly watching her. It was as though he stood on a floor made of glass and any movement would cause it to collapse beneath him.

In a rush, Molly rose and put her arms around him, pulling him close and resting her head on his chest. "Wynn," she whispered. "You are not a monster for being able to think of a weapon like this. You are the smartest, kindest person I have ever met, and I am proud to call you my friend. This weapon you've designed will protect so many of your brothers, so many of our people. Most of the people in Telmondir don't know how close we are to open war. Daegan sits in on the Council meetings, and he knows the truth, what we're up against... the Ar'Mol has been building his army for years. They have more airships, more cynders, and we don't even know what else they've developed to use against us. He's never said so, but I know Daegan is worried. He thinks we can't win. That scares me more than anything else, that someone as smart as Daegan thinks we don't really have a chance." Her arms tightened and Wynn could feel her tears soaking through his shirt. He wrapped his arms around her and held her while she cried. After a few minutes, she pulled away slightly, wiping her eyes. "I've not told anyone about that," she admitted. "I'm not supposed to know, let alone tell anyone. Wynn"—Molly's gaze fell on the schematic—"your idea... I won't make you, I won't even ask you... you can crumple it up and throw it in the fire and forget all about it if it worries you so much. But if you think it could help us in the coming conflict, and it is coming... then you should show it to Daegan."

He nodded slowly and has shivering subsided. "I know. I think I've always known. But it scared me, how easily the idea came. The cynder exploded, and I immediately saw how I could turn it against an enemy. I didn't want to believe I could create something so heinous... that I could be so cruel."

"If you raise your sword to defend the innocent, is it heinous?" Molly asked. "If someone means to do harm to another and you can prevent it, the only cruelty would be turning away."

Wynn turned her words over in his mind. "That is why our soldiers are called defenders." He glanced at the paper again. This time, he did not recoil from it. He remembered Lorcan and the monsters he had created and caused to attack them in the mountains. He remembered the battle on the airship during which he and Beren had been captured. He thought of Molly's words and wondered what other horrors the Ar'Mol had been developing as he built up his army to attack Telmondir. His thoughts turned toward home and the people who lived in his village, the simple people who went about their daily lives with no concept of the threat to their peace that hovered on the other side of the world. Resolve, like bands of iron, wound its way through him. War was coming. It would not be pretty, of that much he was aware with a stark realization. The boy he had been just a year ago would have been eager to face the coming foe, but now he had seen what a battle looked like from the inside. There would be chaos and confusion. There would be struggles and pain and death. If he could do anything, provide anything, that would protect his people, he must do so. With a sorrowful sigh, he gave a single nod.

"You're right. I will show the plans to Daegan in the morning."

46

Miraculously, the *Hawk's* engine room was mostly intact. A few of the connections needed some fine-tuning and repair, but that section of the ship had escaped most of the damage. Oleck, Shaesta, and Nando went together to inspect the wreckage, and found it more encouraging than they had anticipated.

"I think this is going to work," Oleck said. "I'll go back and get the *Oddhaven* and fly her over. We'll lower ropes down to you and Nando. Once you have them fixed to the locations on the *Hawk* that we talked about, you'll need to activate the cynder and see if she'll lift off. We can give you a bit of a boost from above, but the *Hawk* needs to get herself off the ground or this won't work."

Shaesta's stomach did flips, but she kept her voice steady. "All right."

She appreciated his unquestioning acceptance of her words. Oleck didn't even give her a searching look or ask if she was sure. He just gave a nod and began the long trek back to the barge, where the rest of the durven were getting the vessel ready for flight.

The worst part was the waiting. It seemed like hours before

she heard the rush of wind and saw the shadow of the *Oddhaven* approaching. Oleck lowered the barge slowly until it hovered over the prone *Valdeun Hawk* and lowered eight different ropes for Shaesta to anchor to the positions they had determined were still the strongest points on the fallen airship. She and Nando moved as swiftly as they could, clambering across the tilted deck and checking each other's knots. It was difficult to maneuver without slipping, and more than once Shaesta found herself struggling to right herself or clinging to a rope and pulling herself across the deck to the correct anchor point.

At last, the ropes were all secured, and Shaesta and Nando made their way to the helm. They struggled to pull the lever that activated the cynder, but by working together, they managed it. The heart of the airship flared to life with a gentle thrum. Shaesta wiped her forehead with the back of her hand, a sense of relief pulsing through her. Until this moment, she had not believed the *Hawk* would even get past this point.

"Doing well," she commented to Nando. "Now, for the true test."

She grappled with the lift-lever, pushing it down with gentle force. The humming of the airship changed pitch and the body of the vessel shuddered. The hull creaked. The timbers shook and moaned. Sounds of splintering boards filled Shaesta's ears and almost made her shut the whole experiment down. She marveled, thinking about how Marik must have felt as he did everything he could to prevent his airship from crashing into the ground, only to fail. How had he stayed at the wheel? How had he not succumbed to the terror of the moment? Here she was, only inches from the ground, and her entire being was screaming at her to abandon the airship.

Instead, she forced herself to continue pressing down on the lever. The *Valdeun Hawk* trembled and Shaesta imagined it had come to life and she could hear it crying out from the depths of its hull, but she did not stop. With agonizing reluctance, the airship lumbered up from its resting place. Slowly, the *Hawk* righted itself as it rose into the air until it only listed a little to one side. The lines securing it to the barge hung limp and Shaesta wanted to dance. The *Hawk* was rising under her own power!

A durven came to the rail of the *Oddhaven* and called out to let them know Oleck was preparing to move forward. Nando replied that they were ready, and the barge drifted forward until the lines were taut. A moment later, Shaesta felt a gentle breeze on her face and knew that they were moving as well.

Their progress was slow, and Shaesta had to maintain a constant hand on the wheel, correcting their course with vigilance, as the *Hawk* did not like being towed about, and often tried to veer off course. But within a few hours, she had mastered the knack of predicting when trouble spots would arise and could smoothly draw the vessel back into obeisance to the barge and prevent her from causing problems.

It was a full day before they reached Ferndale, which resulted in a flurry of activity and shouted conversation from one ship to the other about the problem of landing. There was no way that the *Hawk* could float with her aft section ripped up the way it was. Eventually, they decided that they would have to bring her down to hover over the water and release most of the anchor lines while they were down, but that she would not land. Several of the durven swung down from the *Oddhaven* onto the *Hawk* so that Shaesta could get a rest and go speak with the physicians.

They settled Mouse and Marik into one of the landing boats and rowed them to the shore where an orderly awaited them. The man smiled at them, his mien exuding patience as they disembarked. His robes, the color of the deep blue water of the lake, fluttered in the breeze.

"Ah, I see you have returned," the orderly greeted them. "Your ship appears to have taken some damage."

"It is the damage to our crewmate and captain we are most concerned about," Oleck replied.

"That is our business," the orderly replied. "A moment."

He disappeared and then reappeared some moments later

with eight other men and women dressed as he was and carrying two stretchers. The orderlies carried Mouse and Marik inside on the canvas beds and then transferred them gently to proper beds with actual mattresses covered in beautiful quilts. Traversing the hall, Shaesta stared into the beautiful rooms; different decorations adorned each chamber, but all were uniquely lovely. There were large paintings and lacy curtains and soft pillows, there were chairs and sofas of all different types, all the rooms had windows and doors that led outside.

The orderlies set Marik and Mouse in rooms near each other, and then set about checking their vitals and asking Shaesta questions about their conditions. She gave her answers through a haze of exhaustion until the questions finally stopped, then she sank down into a chair to wait. Oleck paced to the window and stared through it, keeping an eye on the two airships. Shaesta closed her eyes.

A moment later, someone was shaking her. She opened her eyes, feeling groggy and stiff, and realized she must have fallen asleep.

"The physician is here," Oleck said.

Instantly alert, Shaesta rose from her chair and paced over to Mouse's bed, where a tall woman bent over him. The woman raised one of his eyelids and peered into his eye, passing a small lantern back and forth across his face. The woman straightened and tucked an errant strand of dark hair streaked with gray behind her ear. Her face was pale and her eyes were bright.

"This young man is going to be just fine," she announced. "He's had a nasty bump on his head, but he has been well-tended. Your captain, however, has quite the array of injuries: his left leg is broken in two places, he has three cracked ribs, and a broken collarbone, in addition to a large quantity of cuts and bruises. But I believe both patients will make a full recovery."

"Why haven't they woken?" Shaesta asked.

"Well, that's hard to say," the elderly woman replied. "Come, let's talk out on the veranda. I don't want to disturb this one."

She patted Mouse's hand gently and led them through the door, out onto a stone terrace lined with flowers. "This is better," she said. "I cannot abide being indoors for too long at a time."

"Then why work in a Healing House?" Shaesta wondered.

"It is my passion and my gift," the woman replied. "I love my patients, but I also love this." She spread her arms and turned in a slow circle, indicating the beauty of the trees and flowers and the darkening sky above them. She glanced up at the building. "This was my dream," she said, her voice growing soft. "It took many years to build, but it was worth it. Here, we have created a place of beauty and healing. Now." Her voice turned brusque. "Let us talk about your companions. The boy will be fine. He showed some responsiveness to the light of my lantern, and I believe he will awaken in the next day or two. The other one..." She shook her head. "I am not so sure."

"Marik?" Shaesta asked, confused. "But his injuries were not deep. He even spoke a few words. What is wrong with him?"

The physician squinted. "You are correct in your assessment of his physical condition. Unfortunately, his deepeest wounds do not appear to be physical. Can you tell me more about what happened?"

"What do you mean?" Shaesta asked.

"I do not know him as well as you," the woman replied. "All I know is that I have seen cases similar to this before. Patients suffer a devastating loss of some kind and lose their will to recover."

Shaesta looked at Oleck. "Raisa?" Her soul shattered as she said the name. Raisa had been her best friend for many years. She was like a younger sister to Oleck. Would they ever see her again? "Could it be Raisa?"

Oleck frowned, stroking his beard. "Maybe," he replied. "But it could also be..."

"What?" Shaesta asked.

"Well... the *Hawk*..."

Understanding dawned. "He doesn't know," Shaesta breathed. "He doesn't know... how do we tell him?"

The physician tilted her head and gazed out at the lake. "I'm guessing one of those sorry sights is this *Hawk* you're speaking so cryptically about?" She raised an eyebrow. "Well, whatever it is you think is affecting your friend, perhaps someone should sit with him and just tell him what's happened."

"But he's asleep," Oleck objected.

The doctor smiled. "You'd be surprised how much a person can hear when they're asleep. Now, if you'll excuse me, I have other patients to tend to. I'll make sure that our orderlies know to check in on our new patients at regular intervals."

A moment later, Oleck and Shaesta both stood at Marik's side. Shaesta gnawed gently on the inside of her cheek, wondering what to say. She glanced up at her companion.

"This feels strange," she said.

"Yeah."

"I suppose..." She hesitated. "Well, I might as well just... Hey, Captain... Marik..." Shaesta paused, studying Marik's face, but his eyes remained closed, his face smooth and still. "I know this might seem... agh!" She turned away and put her hands on either side of her neck. "I can't do it, Oleck. This is too weird. He's not... he's not there. And I've had a hard enough time talking to him lately as it is."

"Hey." Oleck put a hand on her shoulder. She looked up at him. "I understand," he said. "Maybe we should try this a bit differently."

"Differently, how?"

"Maybe we're trying too hard. How about I go get us something to eat?" Oleck suggested. "There's a kitchen downstairs, and the orderly said visitors can purchase food there."

"That sounds nice."

"I'll be back soon."

Oleck departed, leaving Shaesta alone. She paced the room a little, her nerves buzzing with pent-up energy. Marik's still form was unnerving, and at first she could hardly bear to look at him, but eventually, the energy dissipated and exhaustion seeped through her. With a start, she realized that it had been over a full day and night since she had last slept. Wearily, she pulled a chair over to Marik's side and sank down into it.

"I thought you died," she whispered. "Twice. When I saw the *Hawk* turn and ram the battleship, and then when you darted between it and the *Oddhaven* and took that blazing bolt... I saw the fire rip apart the back of the..." Shaesta halted, her vocal chords tightening. "I've never felt so hopeless or scared. I know I failed you. When Niveya threatened my parents, I should have come to you; I should have trusted you. I'm sorry. But I want you to know... the *Hawk* isn't gone. Oleck and I, we figured out a way to tow her. I think we can fix her... maybe... it'll take a lot of work... but I couldn't just leave her behind. I know how much she means to you, to all of us, really. She managed to lift herself, just needed help with direction because her masts and sails are... well, maybe this won't help you feel better... but really, I think we can fix her. We didn't leave her in the forest, Captain. And... and it was like she *wanted* to come. You'd have been proud of her, Cap'n." Shaesta sniffled slightly, then leaned forward and grasped Marik's hand, desperation churning in her stomach. "We'll get Raisa back, too. I know we will. She knows it, she knows how h-hard we tried, and she knows we won't ever g-give up. And we won't." Her voice caught on a sob. "Captain, I never meant to hurt you or the crew. I didn't really understand what you all meant to me until I lost my place... I've always l-looked up to you. I promise, if you get better, if you can trust me again, I'll never betray you. I'll die for you, sacrifice anything, if I have to. Just... please... please wake up." The words she still wanted to say tumbled together and jumbled in her throat, lodging there with no way to sort them into anything resembling intelligible speech. Instead, she bowed her head over the hand she still clasped, all her thoughts and sentiments dissolving into quiet sobs. Completely worn out, Shaesta rested her head on the edge of the bed, her fingers still wrapped around Marik's. Her tears spent, she closed her eyes and fell asleep.

47

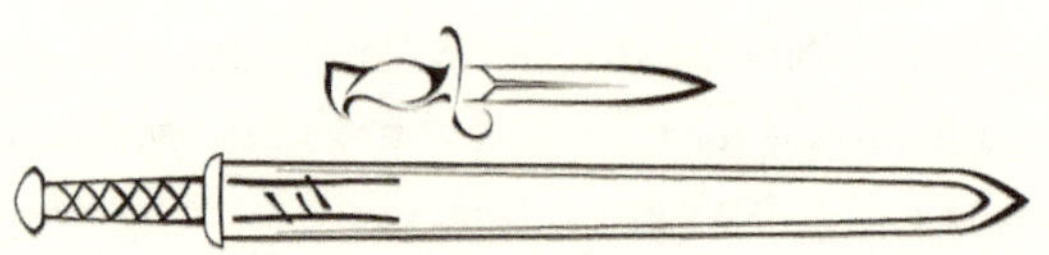

Headmaster Freidzen tapped the folded document on the table and glanced at the captain of the defenders. "This will go a long way with the Council toward taking down Regeont Elan," he said. "You gentleman have done us a great service."

"We were simply doing our job," Beren replied. "I am just grateful you trusted our plan."

"It was a brilliant ploy," the captain said. "I'll be following your careers with great interest, Lieutenants Adelfried and Ormond. I wish you had come here to be part of my command. Perhaps now that this investigation is all but wrapped up, your commanders will give you a more regular assignment here. I could use a couple of intelligent men like you."

"Thank you, sir," Grayden said.

"You have two days of leave to yourselves," Freidzen said. "And then I want you to report to the Academy for your new orders."

"Yes, sir," Beren and Grayden barked together.

The captain and Headmaster Freidzen stood and ushered Lady Ilya into their waiting carriage. Beren and Grayden watched them leave.

"Well," Grayden sighed. "It looks like we're finished here."

Beren nodded. "I wonder what our next orders will include."

Niveya came up and clapped them each on the shoulder. "I'm sure that whatever your father has in store for you next will be an adventure." He grinned, a strange look shadowing his features. "We've had our differences, but this experience has been a good one. I would not mind working on the same side again, someday."

Beren made a noncommittal sound.

Grayden chuckled and stuck out his hand, shaking Niveya's. "As long as we're on the same side, I look forward to seeing you again."

"But I've never been one for prolonged goodbyes," Niveya continued. "You are welcome to use this house during your leave, but I will be packing up tonight."

"What will you do now?" Grayden couldn't help but ask.

Niveya gave an enigmatic smile. "Well, there's a young thief I've been thinking about offering a position to."

"Miri?" Grayden asked.

Niveya nodded. "She can go farther with the Niveyan Syndicate than she ever could staying here on the streets of Doran. And as my son will someday need a wife, she seems like a promising prospect."

"Best of luck with that. Just watch out she doesn't murder you all in your sleep," Beren muttered. Then he grimaced. "Your help was appreciated."

"That almost sounded like gratitude." Niveya smirked. "Don't worry, I won't tell anyone." He rubbed his hands together. "It was an unexpected pleasure, gentlemen. Until we meet again." And with that, he strode away.

A lithe figure slipped down from her perch at the top of a column.

"Miri." Grayden grinned. He had known she was there—and it was probable that Niveya had, as well—though it had taken him a few minutes to notice her presence. "Our thanks for your help in this endeavor. Without you, we might not have gotten so much cooperation from Lady Ilya."

"Without me, you wouldn't have any actual proof at all." Miri tossed her head. "It was definitely a job most people would have to pay dearly for." She grinned impishly. "But it was worth it to get to toss wine in your face and observe that performance you gave."

Beren's brow wrinkled. "What is she talking about, Grayden?"

"Nothing," Grayden said quickly. He had not filled Beren in on all the details he had missed the night before, and he wasn't sure he wanted his friend to know how close they had come to being caught. He changed the subject. "What do you think of Niveya's offer?"

Miri played with the ends of her short hair. "I'll have to speak with Lady Jynna, but it seems like an excellent opportunity. The idea of that house in the country never thrilled me, anyway. I'm more of a mountains girl." Her eyes sparkled.

Beren heaved out a breath. "Well, I wish you every happiness, I suppose. It's not too late to try an honest living, you know."

"What fun would that be?" Miri teased.

"What fun is ending up in a prison cell, or executed?" Beren shot back.

"I think I'll take my chances," Miri mused. "Best of luck with your next assignment." She pecked Grayden on the cheek and skipped off down the hallway, her feet landing lightly, making no sound at all as she disappeared.

"She's going to end up..." Beren shook his head. "I don't know why I care."

"Because you're a decent human being," Grayden replied. "That's why you care. And you're right, you know. People like Niveya and Miri might never be willing to admit it, and they might never get caught or be called to task for their crimes, but that doesn't make them right. And it usually means they end up at the wrong end of the hangman's noose. I think Niveya might actually understand that, in his own way."

"I doubt it," Beren growled. "But either way, I'm happy to be done with this assignment."

"What do you want to do for the next couple of days before we report in at the Academy?" Grayden asked. "Niveya said we could continue to enjoy his hospitality."

Beren grimaced. "If it's all the same to you, I was thinking about grabbing my gear and paying for a room at the Empty Cup. It's an inn down by the docks. It won't be as fancy, but I have no desire to stay here another night."

"I feel the same," Grayden said. "Lead the way, my friend."

48

Sun streamed through the window, pouring into Marik's eyes with uncomfortable brightness. He frowned and turned his face away from the brilliance. A loud rumble came from somewhere nearby—it sounded like Oleck snoring. Cautiously, he opened his eyes. Nothing about his surroundings was familiar; gentle hues of yellow covered the walls, and large pieces of spiraling iron hung in a pleasant sort of aesthetic. The window across the room, now that his eyes had adjusted enough to let him turn his head, was open, and a breeze played with the linen curtains that fluttered on either side. Below the window, sprawled in a chair sound asleep, Oleck was the source of the snoring. A vase filled with bright blue flowers stood on the nightstand next to his bed, filling the room with a subtle fragrance.

His head throbbed, and his whole body ached. He wanted to ask for something to drink, but his lips and throat were so dry he did not think he could form the words. His gaze returned to the little table, where he spotted a glass of water. Marik tried to raise his left arm to reach for it, but it would not move. Frowning, he tried again, and then panic swept through him as memories rushed back: ramming the battleship; the scorching bolt of fire that had ripped apart the *Hawk*; desperately working to keep the *Hawk* in a controlled fall, then... nothing. Had he lost his arm in the crash? He squeezed his eyes shut, his head throbbing and fear shooting darts of cold and pain through his entire body. But he could not hide from reality, no matter how grim; gritting his teeth, Marik opened his eyes, forcing himself to look at his arm.

Blessedly, the arm was still attached to his body. His hand appeared to be fine, as well. A raspy chuckle of pure relief escaped his dry lips as his gaze found the source of his paralysis. Shaesta had fallen asleep with his hand clutched in her own, her head lay on top of his arm, pinning it to the bed. Her mix of dark and gold curls cascaded down the side of the bed like a waterfall of sunshine.

At his dry chuckle, she lifted her head and stretched. Marik's own neck ached sympathetically. Blinking, Shaesta looked up into his face and smiled sleepily, then her eyes widened and she leaped to her feet, dropping his hand.

"Captain!" She threw her arms about his neck, hugging him painfully, then just as quickly backed away, her cheeks darkening. "Oleck! He's awake!" She turned and shook Oleck until his snoring stopped with a surprised grunt.

"Water," Marik croaked.

"Oh, of course!" Shaesta grabbed the glass and handed it to him, helping him tip some of the liquid into his mouth when she realized he was having trouble maneuvering around all the bandages and the sling around his right arm. He drank thirstily, the water pouring down his throat like a healing balm.

By the time the last drops disappeared, Marik felt stronger. With Shaesta's help rearranging his pillows, he propped himself up into a sitting position with a wince.

"Mouse?" he asked tentatively, fearing the worst.

"In the room across the hall," Oleck replied, setting his worst fears at ease. "He got a nasty bump on his head, but other than that, the doc says he'll be fine. She predicts he'll be up and around in the next day or two."

Warm relief flooded Marik's soul, and he sank back onto the pillows and closed his eyes. "That's good to hear."

"You, on the other hand, will take a bit longer." Shaesta's tone was severe.

Marik nodded. Besides the bandages wrapped around his torso and the sling for his right arm, he had already discovered the plaster cast encasing his left leg; but he was alive, and Mouse would be fine. For the moment, that was all that mattered. His stomach complained. "Is there any food in this place?"

"Yes," Shaesta replied. She glanced at Oleck. "I'll go see what I can rustle up. You stay with him." Without waiting for an answer, she all but ran for the door. Marik watched her go, puzzled.

"What's wrong with her?" he asked Oleck.

Oleck scratched at his beard. "I'm not sure. I think she was worried you weren't going to wake up."

"So..." Marik's head started throbbing again. He frowned. "You're telling me she's practically fleeing from my presence because she's happy I'm alive?"

Oleck raised an eyebrow. "I don't understand women. You tell me."

Marik grimaced and changed the subject. "We're at Ferndale, aren't we?"

Oleck nodded.

"Good. I wanted to check in on that girl we brought here with Dalmir. And once Mouse wakes up, I think it's best if we head straight for Telsuma and Adelfried's house."

"Do you know where Adelfried lives?"

"No, but he's one of the Council members. It's probably safe to assume somebody knows where he lives. We can ask around. Showing that seal he gave us will probably clear a lot of obstacles from our path."

"Good point." Oleck rubbed a hand across the back of his neck. "You don't need to hop out of bed just this minute, Cap'n. You were in a pretty bad crash. Walking is going to be a bit difficult for a while."

"We need to tell Lord Adelfried about that weapon," Marik continued, ignoring him. "And if we can manage it, I'd like to find Dalmir. We're going to need his help to rescue Raisa. I don't know how far Adelfried's trust and appreciation will go, but maybe he'd be willing to give us an airship."

"Marik..."

Marik did not meet Oleck's gaze. "You're right... probably better if we ask him to lend us an airship."

"Captain, I think..."

Marik continued, pretending he did not hear Oleck's interruption. "Or, if he's not willing to give us those kinds of resources, maybe we can get the *Oddhaven* fixed up a bit. She's a good, sturdy ship. She surprised me several times with her capabilities. With a little work, she could be a right nimble thing."

"I don't know about that," Oleck objected.

Marik nodded. "You're right, that's probably a bit too optimistic, but I think we could get her into good enough shape that she'd at least be able to perform a few surprises for anyone trying to chase us or shoot us down." He winced. He didn't want to think about being shot down, of tumbling through the sky, of careening into the treetops, the sound of his hull scraping a valley into the forest floor. Spots of light danced in his vision and a high-pitched keening tone rang in his ears. Marik squeezed his eyes shut, trying to drown out the memories in darkness. Thick blankets of gloom piled on top of him, suffocating him beneath their weight.

"Marik!" Oleck had him by the shoulder, shaking him. "Captain, snap out of it!"

Pain lanced through him at the sudden movement and Marik opened his eyes reluctantly and looked up into Oleck's face.

"I'm sorry, Oleck. I just had... a moment... I could see it all happening again. It's fine. I think maybe I just need to lie down for a bit more."

"I think you should try to come out on the veranda, Cap'n. Fresh air would do you a world of good."

Something deep in the pit of Marik's stomach ached. He wanted to curl up under the blankets and go back to sleep. "No, I just need some more rest."

"After." Oleck pulled back the blankets. "Come on. The doc said we needed to get you up and around as soon as possible, seems like now is as good a time as any. Then I'll let you rest some more."

"Tyrant," Marik grumbled.

"Let me just call an orderly to make sure it's all right to move you." Oleck got up and left the room.

Marik laid his head back against the pillows as he waited, a deep sense of grief curling in the pit of his stomach. A moment later, Oleck returned with a short woman in tow. Marik blinked at her, wondering why she looked familiar.

The woman met his eyes and flushed. "Captain," she murmured. "It's good to see you awake."

Marik frowned. That voice. But not that voice. He knew this woman, but why?

"Do I know you?" he asked thickly. His throat felt so dry. "Can I get some more water?"

She hurried to tip the cup to his lips. "We've met once before," she said. "I'm afraid I wasn't very kind to you—but you saved me from the soldiers, anyway."

Marik finished his drink and tilted his head back to get a better look at her. As he did so, his memory jogged and he recalled a sour expression aimed at him. "Criselda? From the tavern in Ondoma?"

She beamed at him. "I made my way here, Captain. And I've done the best I can with the second chance you gave me."

"Do you enjoy working here?" he asked, a touch doubtfully, remembering her less-than-friendly manner. He had a hard time imagining her offering tender care to the sick. Or acting tender toward anyone, for that matter.

She flushed a little and looked down. "I do, Captain. Very much."

He took her hand in his. "Then I'm glad I could help."

She straightened. "Your friend says you need some fresh air. Let's see if we can't help you out onto the veranda."

Marik grumbled a bit, but he did not resist as Oleck and Criselda helped him into a chair that had been outfitted with wheels. A shooting pain stabbed through his wounded leg as they lifted him, and he gasped, grateful for Oleck's steady shoulder under his arm. Once they had him situated, Criselda wheeled him out onto the veranda. Her gentleness and the care in her movements as she made certain not to jostle him quelled his doubts of a moment before.

"You let me know when he's ready to go back to bed," Criselda said to Oleck. "I'll be just down the hall."

The green lawn and the colorful array of flowers were lovely. A soft breeze cooled his face. Marik's gaze swept the gardens, drinking in the vibrant colors while Oleck leaned against the railing. Birds chirped in a nearby tree and quiet sounds of conversation came from within Ferndale. But outside, the two men enjoyed a deep, companionable silence.

Marik leaned his head back, enjoying the warmth of the sun's rays on his face. His eyes fluttered open, and he glimpsed the *Oddhaven* bobbing lopsidedly on the calm waters of the lake. She was a hardy little airship—he had to give her that— but he cringed inside at the sight of her bulky, ungainly form. Then he squinted. What was that thing floating above the barge?

With a startled shout, Marik tried to leap to his feet, all his injuries forgotten. They reminded him of their existence with painful insistence and he fell back into the chair with a shuddering groan.

When the pain had subsided, Marik turned to stare at Oleck accusingly. "What is that?" He pointed, jabbing his finger at the ruined airship hovering above the lake.

Oleck's eyebrows rose. "I would have thought you'd recognize your own airship, Captain."

"But... how?" Marik shook his head. "And why didn't you tell me?"

"Tell you what?"

A grin broke across Marik's face, a grin so wide it hurt. "That you managed to salvage the *Hawk*, you villain!"

"Oh, that... well, you didn't ask." Oleck gave an exaggerated shrug. "We figured you didn't care."

"You!" Marik reached up, heedless of his aches and pains, and grabbed Oleck's arm, pulling him down into a ferocious hug and pounding his back with his good arm. "You... but how did you manage it?"

"It was Shaesta and the durven, really." Oleck fought out of Marik's grasp, pushing him away, his face beaming beneath his beard. "Shaesta wouldn't let me leave until we'd tried to save the *Hawk*, and the durven devised the plan of towing her. Of course, it wouldn't have worked if the engines had taken any more damage. It was a near thing. She's tore up pretty bad. It's going to take a lot to get her fixed up. Might not even be possible."

Marik stared at his airship hovering above the water, his heart near to bursting with emotions he couldn't possibly name. "It doesn't matter," he replied. "She's worth it."

"Aye," Oleck agreed. "That she is."

49

Daegan studied the plans Wynn spread before him with pure amazement etched on his features. "How long did this take you?" he asked.

Wynn scratched his chin and hesitated. "I mean... it took me a while to get it all written down."

"What do you mean?"

"It all kind of came to me at once, the whole idea," Wynn said. "It took longer to draw the schematics than it took for the idea to come together."

"You mean to tell me that this design came to you, fully formed, in a flash of inspiration?"

Wynn's gaze darted to Molly before he answered, hesitantly. "Yes."

"It's brilliant," Daegan said, his quiet praise sending a rush of pride coursing through Wynn. "The idea of miniaturizing the cynders to the point where they can send out blasts of force from something our defenders can hold with one hand is beyond anything I could have ever dreamed. Do you think it will actually work?"

"I don't see why it wouldn't," Wynn replied. "I've gone over it a thousand times. I used a crossbow as the base for my idea, but of course, it's smaller for obvious reasons, and it doesn't need all the extra material since there's no bowstring necessary."

"Molly said you were reluctant to show this to me." Daegan squinted at him. "May I ask why?"

Wynn felt his face grow warm. "I, ah, was worried about what it said about me that I was capable of creating something so deadly."

"Ah." Daegan nodded. "I understand." He paused, placing one hand on the papers before him. "Son, what do you think we will use the Trackless for?"

"Protecting our soldiers," Wynn answered without hesitation.

"Yes, they will be used for that. What will our soldiers be doing?"

"Fighting to protect Telmondir."

Daegan nodded. "And how will they do that?"

"By..." Wynn paused as Daegan's meaning became clear. He continued softly, "Killing the enemy soldiers."

"And if you are assigned to ride in a Trackless you helped build, and it takes you through the enemy lines and deposits you in a tactically strategic location where you find yourself face-to-face with a man about your age bent on killing you? Will you lay down your sword and let him?"

Wynn shook his head. "No, sir."

"I am glad to hear it," Daegan said brusquely. He leaned forward and peered into Wynn's face. "It is good that you understand our enemies are men, like us. But it is also important to remember why we do not simply allow them to walk in and take over. It would certainly be easier to do so, and it would mean less senseless death. But what is easiest is rarely what is right. I am glad you wrestled with yourself over this weapon—it says much about who you are as a man." Daegan turned back to the table. "Now, I have a few adjustments to recommend. Let's get to work."

———

"SOMETHING'S COMING!" Conrad panted as he burst through the door of the workroom. His red face and wild eyes made them all pause. Wynn looked up from the equation he was working on and frowned, concern slicing through him at the obvious distress on Conrad's face. He did not interact with Keene's apprentices much, but Conrad had become a friend since Wynn had arrived. His was a cheerful presence both in the forge and at the table.

"Slow down, lad," Daegan soothed. "What's coming?"

"Something... an airship... huge..." Conrad struggled visibly to produce words.

"Is it one of ours?" The urgent note in Daegan's voice made Wynn put his quill down and rise from his seat.

"Don't know," Conrad replied. "Nobody recognizes it, but it's still pretty far out. Lord Adelfried was outside, told me to come get you."

Without a word, Daegan stood and followed Conrad out of the room. Wynn and Molly trailed behind. Wynn's entire skin prickled as if being poked by thousands of needles as he wondered what awaited them outside. Could the Igyeum be so bold as to send an airship so far into Telmondir's territory? But if the Ar'Mol didn't send it, then who could it be?

They emerged into the late afternoon sunshine. They made a rather sizeable crowd, there on the mountainside: Keene and Gunnar emerged from the forge, and all of Lord Adelfried's family were arrayed, their faces tilted toward the sky. Wynn squinted and put up a hand to shield his eyes.

"Do you think it's an enemy?" Wynn asked nobody in particular.

"I doubt it," Daegan replied.

When Wynn could see reasonably well, he allowed his gaze to travel in the direction Conrad was pointing, his finger jabbing into the air. There, a tiny figure in the distant sky but growing larger with every moment, flew the strangest airship he had ever seen. It almost looked like it had two hulls, one in front of the other. However, as it drew closer, Wynn realized it was not one, but two airships linked together.

"Look!" One of Beren's younger siblings jumped up and down. "Somebody on the ship is waving a white flag!"

Indeed, a white flag was being flapped from the prow of the leading airship with vigor. Suddenly, Wynn recognized the second airship.

"It's the *Hawk*!" Wynn shouted, and he heard an answering rumble of excited voices around him. But as the airship turned slightly, he got his first full glimpse of the familiar vessel and his heart stopped.

The sleek little airship had lost its mast. Its trim sails fluttered in useless tatters. It listed first to one side then the other, bobbing through the air behind the larger airship, the lines between them taut and obviously necessary for more than just towing. But all this, Wynn ignored, his attention captivated and focused on a single detail: the stern of the *Hawk* was gone. The wood of the hull stretched back along her sides and then ended in sharp, jagged splinters. He did not bother questioning what could have done such a thing to the little airship; he knew. As surely as he knew Keene's strikes with a hammer were true, he knew what had happened to the *Hawk*.

They have the weapon, too. The thought rolled through his mind like hoofbeats, drumming a rhythm of ominous dread. His eyes flicked to Molly, and he caught her gaze. Her face was pale beneath her freckles. She had seen it, too, he could tell from her expression, and she understood the implications as well as he. Her lips thinned into a line, her jaw tightening.

Her resolve bolstered his own. There was only one path now. And the *Hawk* would need repairs. Perhaps Marik would be amenable to the idea of a few of Wynn's ideas for upgrading her engine. Despite the evidence of disaster that approached, Wynn could feel excitement brimming in his heart.

EPILOGUE

"And how is our patient this morning?" Doctor Helene asked as she entered the room. Her patient did not reply. She gave no indication that she heard. There was no movement from the chair facing the window. Helene approached the chair. "Rosa?" The girl did not even blink.

A nurse entered the room bearing a tray with the evening meal upon it.

"Ah, Doctor Helene!" Criselda said. "Our Rosa is looking better today, don't you think?"

Helene smiled gently, hiding her weariness. It had been a long, hard day, and Rosa's continued unresponsiveness discouraged her. When prompted, she would open her mouth obediently to eat, but no more. But Helene did not speak of this. She simply asked, "Have you noticed any changes at all?"

The nurse shook her head. "A little more color in her cheeks, perhaps. That is why we call her Rosa, you know. The gentleman who brought her to us did not know her name, and of course she hasn't spoken, but we had to call her something."

"I know," Helene replied.

"Actually..." Criselda hesitated. "I meant to tell you... I can't believe I forgot... that was such a strange day, too... slipped my mind..."

"You forgot to tell me something? About Rosa? Or another patient?" Helene's weariness fell away to curiosity.

"About Rosa," the nurse replied. "About two days ago. That other patient, Captain Marik?"

"Yes?"

"Isn't he the one who brought Rosa to us?" Criselda asked.

Helene tapped a finger to her chin. "I believe so. Him and a few others."

"Well, before they left, he asked about her. I told him she hasn't spoken to anyone, barely even eats... He asked to visit her."

"Did he?"

Criselda nodded. "I brought him up, thought it couldn't do any harm. Well, he walked in here and knelt down next to Rosa— you know how she barely leaves this chair except when one of us puts her to bed? He talked to her for a while, real soft and gentle-like. I couldn't hear what he said, just stayed at the door, didn't want to intrude... but you know... she turned her head and looked at him. Really looked at him. She didn't speak, but it about took my breath away. I've not seen such a response from her before or since."

Helene gave the young girl a thoughtful glance. "Interesting. It seems there may be hope after all."

ACKNOWLEDGMENTS

Thank you for reading! I hope you enjoyed the continuing adventures of Grayden, Wynn, Beren, Dalmir, Marik, and all the rest.

Please take a moment to review on Amazon and/or Goodreads to help your reader friends find this world (and others) of mine. Thank you so much for joining me here in Turrim for a little while.

This is the third book in this five-book series and *Turrim Archive* will continue in book 4: *The Prisoner and the Pirate*, which will release early in 2025. You can keep up with all my publishing news by subscribing to my newsletter, liking my FB author page, or following my Instagram.

J.L.S.